DEATHS
OF
JOCASTA

THE SECOND MICKY KNIGHT MYSTERY

by
J.M. REDMANN

Bella
BOOKS

Ferndale, Michigan
2002

Bella Books, Inc.
P.O. Box 201007
Ferndale, MI 48220

Printed in the United States of America on acid-free paper
First Bella Books Edition.
The first edition of *Deaths of Jocasta* was published by New Victoria Publishers, Inc., in 1992.

Cover designer: Bonnie Liss (Phoenix Graphics)

ISBN 1-931513-10-4

Forward to the Bella Books Edition
of *Deaths of Jocasta*

I originally wrote Deaths of Jocasta in 1989 and it was first published in 1992. The book reflects those times — no cell phones in every pocket or purse, or searching the internet for clues. Time does change, and a book from a fixed point in my past makes clear the distance from then to now. (I can only be glad that the manuscript didn't have a picture attached to it to show the graying of my hair over that decade.)

I've made some changes from that earlier published version, although nothing significant — no new characters, plot lines or . . . sex scenes. I went back to the original manuscript and used that as my guide. I did resist the urge to correct my early novel mistakes — I believe in limits on how much one can rewrite the past, even a fictional past.

There are a number of people I need to thank: You know who you are, yes, I will buy you that coffee/Scotch/whatever the next time we meet. I would like to mention Kelly and Terese of Bella Books for believing in Micky enough to want to bring her back, and for daring to live the bold, adventurous life of book publishers. I also want to thank some people that I may never meet or see, all the readers in the world, especially those who have written me, talked to me, emailed me to let me know that I've written books that are being read.

J.M. Redmann
January 22, 2002

Acknowledgements

A myriad of thanks are due.

First to those daring souls who were willing to have a five hundred page manuscript hefted in their direction: Janet, Brenda, Ruth, Nancy, and Linda from my writer's group. Also Lorena and Ruth who had widely divergent views about the amount of sex in the book (both lawyers).

To Maude and Rock for the nights in New York City and help in title searching.

To Lynn and Maureen for being there in the beginning, and buying all those books. Also to Lynn for answering some outlandish questions about pregnancy and abortion, along the lines of, could you kill someone by . . .? It takes a brave friend to answer those sorts of queries. Any misinterpretation of the facts is the product of my devilish imagination and my fault and mine alone.

To a friend who will remain nameless for the timely manner in which she pointed out legal inconsistencies.

And last, to Joyce Cain, for finally admitting that the computer is mine, and that the useless, not-to-be-thanked cat is hers.

To my friends and co-workers at
NO/AIDS Task Force.

Author's Note

In the Greek myth Jocasta was the mother of Oedipus, who was cast from Thebes, his homeland, and left to die in the wilderness because the oracle at Delphi decreed that he would murder King Laius, his father. Oedipus survived and, as a grown man, met Laius, a stranger to him. They argued and Oedipus killed him. After saving Thebes from the Sphinx, he was made king and married the widow Jocasta.

As time passed, it became clear that something was tainted in Thebes; the gods devastated the city with a plague. Oedipus, the king, had to discover what so displeased the gods.

It was Jocasta who first saw the evil that damned Thebes — that what the oracles foretold had come true. She begged Oedipus to seek no further, but he refused to listen to her and she ran from him, crying, "Alas, alas, miserable! — that word alone can I say to you and no other henceforth forever."

Oedipus, when he realized what he had done — killed his father, and married his mother — rushed to find Jocasta. She was in her chamber, dead. On beholding her, Oedipus could no longer bear to see the world that he created and blinded himself.

Chapter 1

I couldn't find a seat on the streetcar. It was late afternoon and people were going home from work. I ended up standing near the back. More people got on at each stop. A briefcase was poking into the back of my knee. I thought about "accidentally" stepping on his toes when we jostled to a stop, and I heard a distinctly female "umph" from the briefcase carrier. Saved by her sex. She pressed closer to me as more people crowded on. Definitely female. I could feel her breasts through my T-shirt. The man in front of me got off. He was replaced by a well-dressed woman carrying, you guessed it, a briefcase. She was good looking, career woman style. Long dark hair and a discreet amount of makeup. The streetcar started up with a jerk and threw her into me. I was surrounded by breasts. She smiled an apology to me for having to stand so close. I just smiled back.

"Sorry," she said as another jerk smashed her breasts into mine again.

"No problem," I answered.

She smiled at me again. I could feel the warm breath of the woman behind me tickling my neck. Her tits were still firmly planted under my shoulder blades. The woman in front was staring at me with an arch to her brow that I had to be misinterpreting.

I was dressed in a T-shirt and faded jeans, my only accouterment small pink triangle earrings. It doesn't pay to be too blatant in the Crescent City; we're still below the Mason-Dixon line.

"Do you mind if I hold on here?" asked the woman behind me as she reached around me. Her arm was pressing into the hollow just above my hip, but there wasn't much else to hold on to back here.

"No, not at all," I said, "I understand holding on."

"I'll bet you do," she whispered in my ear.

The trolley jerked again, whether stopping or starting, I wasn't sure. Both women were pressing into me, proving to be quite a distraction.

Calm down, Micky. When do you go after ever-so-well-dressed career types? Celibacy does have some drawbacks. Like looking at women who used to be a definite no and thinking maybe . . . I had been celibate for a long time if a briefcase was becoming a maybe.

The car jerked again and the woman behind me lost her grip and was forced to hold on to me. Her hand was on my hip. Then her crotch pushed against my ass. It couldn't be intentional, I told myself. The woman in front of me smiled like she knew what was going on behind me.

This is weird, I thought. However, not weird enough to induce me to stop it. From the feel of it, she had a nice crotch.

Then the woman in front lifted her briefcase, using it to hide the movements of her other hand. I knew what she was doing. Her hand was on my thigh and moving up.

"The next stop. You could get off very easily," she said to me in a husky undertone. Her hidden hand was defining some of the various meanings of "get off."

"I could," I answered.

The trolley rolled to a halt. She led the way off. The woman behind me was still behind me. I glanced at her. A stunning redhead.

2

She winked when she caught me looking. The dark-haired woman led the way to a side street, then motioned us into a hidden courtyard.

It never occurred to me to wonder what I was getting into, probably because, with only two dollars in my wallet, robbery wasn't a big worry. The only other thing these women could want me for was my body. And I had no problem with that.

The redhead closed the gate to the courtyard. Both women dropped their briefcases off to one side. The dark-haired woman got behind me, putting her arms around me to unbuckle my belt. As she was undoing my pants, red hair, now in front, pulled up my T-shirt, exposing my breasts. First her hands, then her tongue and mouth covered them. Dark hair, having unzipped my jeans, was fingering the elastic of my panties, her lips and tongue echoing the movement of her fingers along the back of my neck.

Red hair, still tonguing my breasts, unbuttoned her shirt, then unhooked her bra and pushed it out of the way, showing her pale breasts and very pink nipples. She pushed them very firmly against mine and started kissing me, tongue in cheek, hers in mine.

Dark hair started going beyond the elastic. Red hair was still kissing me, the weight of her breasts a very pleasant warmth on mine. I felt her tongue start to trace my lips, moving slowly to my chin, another kiss, then her cold, wet nose on my cheek . . .

Her cold, wet nose?

Hepplewhite meowed. She was sitting on my chest. Kitty paws on my tits I don't find terribly erotic. I had been asleep and she was trying to wake me up to feed her. She meowed again. I picked her up and deposited her on the floor. I hate cats who assume that their stomachs have priority over my erotic fantasies. I sat up, shaking myself awake.

"Go catch a rat," but as I said it, I was getting up and heading for the kitchen to get her some food. Hep has perfected a fingernails-on-chalkboard meow.

I dumped a can of cat food into her bowl, then stumbled toward the bathroom, her official feeding ground. Needless to say, there was a nearly full bowl of food already there.

The phone rang. I ignored my own reasons for going to the bathroom and went to answer it.

"Well, well," said a familiar voice, "This is the third time you've

3

actually picked up the phone yourself. I almost miss talking to your machine."

"Call back and I'll let you," I replied.

"No, thanks. You're the one I want."

"Be still my beating heart. What can I do for you, besides the obvious?" I flirted. Joanne Ranson was my caller, a woman I'd been too drunk and scared to take as a lover when I'd had the chance a few years ago. Now she was involved with another woman.

"How's your leg?" she asked, her tone serious.

"Getting better all the time. Soon I'll have no excuse for not entering a marathon, except that I hate running. I went back to karate last week," I replied. I had been wounded in the thigh. Joanne felt responsible since it was at her behest that I'd gotten involved to begin with. She was a detective sergeant with the NOPD.

"Good. I'm glad to hear it. Nothing official or even dangerous this time. Idle curiosity really."

"Yes?" I questioned. I wondered what Joanne had to ask me that she couldn't get through her sources.

"An invitation. You have, no doubt, heard of the big bash going on this weekend."

"Right," I interjected.

"I got an invitation."

"So? Most people worry when they don't get one."

"How did my name get on that list? Both Alex and Cordelia swear they had nothing to do with it. They're the only women I know with those connections."

Alex was Alexandra Sayers, Joanne's lover. Cordelia James was . . . well, Cordelia was a long story.

"I'd like to know," Joanne continued, "how my name came to Emma Auerbach's notice. Can you nose around a little for me?"

"Sure. Are you going?"

"Alex didn't give me much choice. Danny and Elly will also be there. I'll save you a piece of cake."

"No need," I was enjoying this. "I'll be there."

"Oh?"

Trying to contain my smugness, I replied, "As a matter of fact, I put your name on the invitation list."

"You?"

"Me."

4

"You know Emma Auerbach?"

"Yep."

"Explain," Joanne said when I didn't elaborate.

"Long story and I have to pee. See you there. Say hi to Alex for me."

"I will."

"By the way, how's Cordelia? I haven't seen her in a while," I said, trying to be casual.

"I thought you had to pee," Joanne countered.

"True," I said, not wanting to appear too insistent. "See you in the country."

"She seems all right. Very caught up in her work. See you," Joanne answered, then hung up.

I went to the bathroom, finally, to pee.

I tried not to think about Cordelia. I had been trying not to think about her for the last few months. Ever since she had walked down my stairs and out of my life, saying she needed time to think. She had called once, leaving a message on my answering machine saying, "I'm sorry, I still don't know. I can't be less than honest with you, and I can't give you a better answer than that. I hope you're doing well."

I answered my phone every time it rang, hoping it would be her. But it never was.

Get on with your life, Micky, I told myself as I always did whenever I thought about her. She's way beyond your reach.

I roused myself, ran a comb through my wild curls, then headed for the grocery store to get enough cat food to satisfy Hepplewhite, at least for a few days.

Every year, on the last weekend in May, Emma Auerbach gives a huge party at her country place. Everybody who is anybody in gay New Orleans is there. Men and women are invited to the Saturday night festivities, but only women get invitations to stay the weekend.

I, however, wasn't invited; I was working, although I strongly suspected that Emma had hired me to do security more as a favor to my bank account than out of any real need for protection. She insisted that I call her Emma, so I did, always feeling like a kid trying to wear her mother's shoes when I said it. She was in her sixties now and would always be Miss Auerbach to me. I would do anything that she asked because, more than anyone, Emma Auerbach had saved my life. Not my life literally, perhaps I should say my soul.

I walked up the stairs carrying a heavily loaded bag of cat food. My office/apartment was on the third floor of a yet-to-be-gentrified building. Yet-to-be-made-livable some of us complained.

My so called office was the large room in the center of my apartment. Off to the left was the kitchen and the bedroom. On the right, a darkroom, the closet, and the bathroom. Not the best arrangement, but it worked for me. In other words, I could afford it.

The door on the landing of the third floor said M. Knight, Private Investigator. I blew some dust off the M. as I locked the door. I was on my way to Emma's.

Chapter 2

The drive across Lake Pontchartrain is hard to describe. Boring might be a good place to start. Twenty-four miles of you, the lake, and a concrete bridge. My dismal Datsun huffed and puffed its way across. I could almost hear it chanting, "I think I can, I think I can." Dry land was welcome. After forty-five minutes more of winding country roads I arrived at Emma's place.

She owned close to two hundred acres. Most of the land was left to itself. Only a few acres had been cut and cleared for the house, an elegant and understated country mansion. It was white clapboard, two stories with ivy twining up all three chimneys. There were several smaller cottages in back for guests.

I parked my car behind the garage, then I went in search of Emma. Via the kitchen, of course. Rachel Parsons, a gourmet chef and Emma's right-hand woman since probably before I was born, was taking one of a series of pecan pies out of the oven. I had spent many hours with Rachel in the kitchen, helping her and making myself useful, until I felt like I really did belong. And Rachel, with her patience and easy smile, became a refuge for the scared kid I was.

She didn't seem much older than when I had first met her, thirteen years ago, only a few traces of gray in her black hair giving a clue to passing time. She was still strong, capable, her back straight and shoulders broad, as I had always known them. Her hair was straightened and pulled back into a practical bun. Few wrinkles lined her face, her perfect skin marred only by a faint scar under her left ear. "White boys didn't see anything wrong with throwing stones at little black girls, like we were plastic ducks at a traveling circus," she had told me late one night, when it was just the two of us in the kitchen. It was the only time she ever mentioned it.

"Made enough for the hired help, I hope," I said as I took a big whiff of the just baked pie.

"Micky, child, do you get taller every time I see you or am I just shrinking?" Rachel exclaimed, putting down the pie and giving me a floury hug.

I squeezed her back. One of the things I always looked forward to was hanging out in the kitchen with Rachel. After Aunt Greta's immaculate kitchen and her tired meals, it was a revelation to be welcomed into a kitchen where people laughed and you could make as big a mess as you liked as long as the food was good. Everyone, including Emma, would pitch in to clean up after one of Rachel's extravaganzas.

"You're the same size you always were, so I must be getting taller," I answered her.

"There's a pecan pie with your name on it. You're getting too skinny."

"I doubt that. But I'll eat the pie, just in case. Where's the lady of the house?"

"There's only one lady in this house and she's standing in front of you," Rachel replied. "Emma is off in that direction. Just go straight and you'll hear her presently."

I followed Rachel's directions until I did indeed hear Emma's voice. She was on the front porch playing with her latest electronic toy, a wireless telephone. Or rather, in her polite but adamant way

8

ensuring that the florist filled her order and made the high school prom make do with daisies, if need be. She finished the conversation, then got up and gave me a hug.

"Michele, dear, you're looking well. And punctual as usual. What would you like?" she asked as we sat down.

Emma Auerbach has high cheekbones, a determined chin, and a pile of gray hair turning gloriously silver. She is equally at home in a library reading a scholarly text, in a bank discussing what she wants done with her money, or hosting a gracious party for a hundred guests. In short, she was a lot of things I admired and wished I could come closer to emulating than I was doing at present.

"The usual Scotch?" she continued, not noticing my hesitation.

"No. No, thanks," I said. "I've been . . . drinking too much." I hated to admit my mistakes to Emma. But I hated even more to lie to her. "I had to get some control over it. I had to . . . have to prove to myself that I can live my life without a shot glass beside me."

"Better to learn that at thirty than at sixty. Or never," was her only comment.

We discussed the details of the party, then the phone rang and she was off on another involved conversation. I excused myself to take a walk around the grounds.

The real responsibility of providing security at a party like this is to make sure that not too many guests fall into the swimming pond. And to make sure that nothing slithers out of the woods to take a refreshing dip with the inebriated guests.

I walked past the pond, glancing at my reflection on its glassy surface. There was a gazebo on the far side, its airy white sides twined with honeysuckle. I climbed up the stairs and perched on the rail to view the expanse of lawn — verdant grass dotted with explosions of colorful flowers, blue irises, pink camellias, some azaleas in full bloom, and still others I couldn't name. The color was balanced by somber live oaks with ponderous charcoal trunks and low-hanging limbs fringed with gray Spanish moss. The lawn was bordered by the surrounding woods. The wind carried the smell of pine overlaid with the sweetness of honeysuckle and magnolia. Although the sun was bright, the temperature was still mild. It promised to be a perfect weekend.

I roused myself and headed back for the house. I needed to unpack. I was staying in my usual room, in the main house, next to

Rachel's and across from Emma's. When I had first come here, Emma had put me there, saying she wanted to discourage any chicken hunting. I was eighteen then, still in high school, and didn't quite get it, though the other women had glanced at me and laughed knowingly.

I spent the early part of the afternoon running errands for Emma and Rachel. Emma let me drive to town in her silver Mercedes. It's amazing how much more polite storekeepers are when they see you drive up in a Mercedes than in a faded lime green Datsun.

Rosie, who was working with me, showed up in the afternoon along with some hand-picked college students (from the lesbian and gay organizations) — the rest of the hired help for the weekend.

The first guests began arriving in the late afternoon. After the requisite politeness, I wandered around the grounds, enjoying the colors of the setting sun and the first cool breeze of evening, the calm of twilight. The stars would shine tonight.

"Micky Knight! And I thought this affair had class," a voice called to me from a newly arrived car.

"Danno," I yelled back. "It did until you showed up." I quickened my pace so that Danny and I wouldn't be shouting across the lawn.

Danielle Clayton and I had both grown up in Bayou St. Jack's, a small town out in bayou country, but we'd never met there. For reasons as simple as black and white. By the time the schools were integrated, I was living in Metairie with Aunt Greta and Uncle Claude. We met in college, two Southern children up in a harsh Northern city. We'd spent long nights drinking bourbon and wishing for warm weather. Danny had come back to go to Tulane Law School. She was now an assistant district attorney.

Her lover, Elly Harrison, was hauling a suitcase from the trunk when I reached them. "Hi, Micky," she said. "It's good to see you running around again."

"Can't keep a good woman down," I bantered, giving Danny a perfect opening.

"Oh, yes you can. The longer the better," she said with a suggestive movement of her eyebrow. Then she gave me a big bear hug and a friendly kiss.

After graduation Danny and I had lived together for a while, first as roommates then lovers. But it hadn't lasted. Danny wanted something serious and I wasn't ready to settle down. She kept telling me that she loved me. Until I finally had to let slip that I was sleeping around to prove to her that she didn't. Danny had no choice but to break it off. I was drinking too much to really care. Or notice how much commitment scared me.

Another woman I'd let slip by me, with regret coming much too late. Danny and Elly were in the process of buying the house they had been renting.

Then Elly hugged me, her slight and slender frame replacing Danny's broad-shouldered sturdiness. I had always felt a little awkward around Elly. Probably because she knows a good deal more about me than I do about her, including possibly, (knowing Danny, quite probably), what I do in bed. At least what I did the summer Danny and I were lovers.

"I'll show you where you're staying," I said, snagging their suitcase.

"How did you manage to get invited out here?" Danny asked as I led them to the their cottage.

"It's a long story, dear Danno," I replied.

"Which you have to get very drunk to tell, I presume," she answered.

"That's the swimming pond over there," I said, playing tour guide. "You can see a bit of the gazebo behind the oak tree beyond it."

"I can't wait to walk around here tomorrow," Elly said. "Do you know how big the place is?"

"Around two hundred acres, total," I answered, "but most of it's forest. There are a number of hiking trails, so you can, if you want, walk your little feet off."

"You've had a busy afternoon," Danny commented.

"Huh?" was my intellectual response.

"Or did you do research before you came up here?"

"Danny, being a D.A.," interjected Elly, "wants information. Like how do you know so much about this place after being here only a few hours?"

"Then, Danny, being an assistant D.A., can ask," I responded.

"Right," Danny said. "How do you know so much, etc.?"

"I've been here before, for one thing. Here's your cottage," I said, making a ninety-degree turn, leading them up a walkway to the porch.

All the cottages were different. This one was pale blue with a broad porch complete with authentically creaking porch swing. Off by itself, nestled closely to the woods, it was my favorite. I turned on the porch light.

"This is great," Elly said.

"I'm impressed," Danny added as she opened the door and led the way in.

There was a comfortably spacious sitting room with a small kitchenette tucked off at one end and a large red brick fireplace at the other end. Off to one side was a hallway that led to three bedrooms. Joanne and Alex would also be out here.

"Looks like we get our choice," Danny said from the hallway where she was poking her head into all the bedrooms.

"How about the one with oak tree outside?" Elly asked. She got their suitcase and put it in the far bedroom.

"Good choice," I noted.

"Okay," Danny said from the room. "Where is that . . . aha!" she muttered to Elly. They came back to the main room, Danny with a bottle of bourbon. "I'm going to make us all drinks and then, dear El Micko, you can enlighten us on how you know so much about this place."

"Good idea," Elly agreed. "This has been a hell of a week. I could use a drink." She went to the kitchenette and started searching for glasses.

"Elly has been having lots of fun with anti-abortionists."

"Right to life," she snorted. "Some of them would kill you if you disagree with them."

"New job?" I asked.

"No, I work part time at the Cordelia's clinic. Cordelia said they've had protesters there all week. We're really just a local clinic in a neighborhood that needs one. You think they'd leave us alone."

"Better a whole community do without health care, than a single innocent life aborted," was Danny's sardonic comment.

Elly took three glasses off a shelf. Danny got an ice tray from the small refrigerator. She cracked it and started putting cubes in the glasses.

"None for me," I said as Danny was about to put ice in the third glass.

"Would you repeat that? I'm sure I heard it wrong," Danny said.

"I'm not drinking," I said. "I'm on duty."

" 'Duty?' " Danny's eyebrows shot up.

"Emma hired me to take care of security for this weekend. Hence, no inebriation while I'm protecting the premises," I circumlocuted. It would do for now.

"Well, that's nice to know. And I must tell you I feel very secure," Danny said sarcastically.

"Glad to know that. I aim to keep the guests comfortable."

"Right. Why do I detect the sound of a bull straining and grunting to drop a big load in the background?" she continued.

"Dan-ny," Elly chided. "How did you get this job?" she asked me.

"Actually," Danny broke in, "I'd feel more secure if you were drinking. I'm not sure how to talk to you sober. Maybe that swamp did some brain damage."

"I have a right not to drink. Particularly your cheap bourbon," I shot back.

"Cheap never stopped you before." Danny had some choice memories of my drinking when I was with her.

"Danny, make two drinks, dear," Elly said.

Sometimes the hardest thing about changing is the people who still expect you to be as you always were. Danny's most potent recollections of me had to be from college and the summer we lived together. I was a heavy drinker then and proud of it. I thought it proved something. I drank because I knew Aunt Greta wouldn't approve. I fancied each drink a victory over her.

"And don't make jokes about that swamp," Elly continued as Danny made their drinks. "Beowulf lost track at one point and we were almost ready to give up and go off in the wrong direction. If we'd done that, we may never have found you."

You'd have found me, I started to say. Just not alive. Then I realized that Elly really was concerned. I had been shot in the thigh and forced to hide in a swamp to avoid the men who had shot me. Danny and Elly, along with their hound dog, Beowulf, had helped find me.

"Yeah, Mick," Danny said, handing Elly her drink, "that swamp was not fun. If you must have gangsters shooting at you, please stay in the city." But there was a hint of conciliation and apology in her voice. I'd hurt Danny when I'd left her. Occasionally a trace of anger would sneak out. Heavy sarcasm, a strident tone to her voice. I never said anything. I tried, like she did, to pretend it was all part of our usual banter. Then there would be a slight change in her tone and the anger would be gone.

"You think it wasn't fun? You should have been in my shoes," I said.

"No, thanks," Danny and Elly said in unison.

"No way," Danny continued. "I don't ever want to see a criminal outside a courtroom."

"I don't want to see any at all," Elly added.

"Look, I agree," I said. "And from now on I'm taking cream puff jobs like guarding secluded parties with selectively invited guests."

"I'll drink to that," Danny toasted, touching her glass to Elly's.

"Can we build a fire?" Elly asked.

"That's what the wood's for," I answered.

"Good. You know what I love to do in front of the fireplace," Danny said as she put an arm around Elly.

"Cook marshmallows?" I asked.

"Of course, that's what I meant," Danny murmured from Elly's neck, which she was now nuzzling.

"Come on, Danny," Elly said laughingly. "We haven't seen Micky for a while."

"Yeah, Mick. What have you been up to lately?" Danny asked, still making progress on Elly's neck, and, I suspected, not much interested in what I had been doing lately.

"Much as I know you'd love for me to stay and talk, I am a working girl and duty is calling, nay, yelling, screaming for me."

"Oh, too bad," Danny muttered, paying no attention to me.

"So long, Micky. We'll talk tomorrow," Elly said, not yet totally consumed by lust.

I waved to her (Danny wasn't looking in my direction) and let myself out. I cut away from the footpath and walked along the border of the woods.

The stars were bright points of ice against the approaching dark of the evening sky. I stood staring at them, a discreet distance from Danny's and Elly's lovemaking. I didn't want to hear Danny's passion nor remember the ways I'd touched her to elicit such cries. I stared instead at the crowded and lonely sky.

I hadn't seen Danny and Elly in about six weeks. I had said I was busy whenever they called asking me over or out. Letting my leg heal and taking it easy, so, no parties or dancing, I elaborated for them. But I knew that Danny and Cordelia were good friends. And that if I saw Danny I would see Cordelia. I didn't want to be idly hanging around in front of her, intruding on her life. Even that was only partly true. I was too afraid of her unconcern, or worse, polite, distant solicitude.

I turned from the night sky and walked back to the house. Perhaps Joanne and Alex were here by now. I could distract myself by trying not to flirt with Joanne. Or Alex. Danny and Elly had reminded me of my past few months of celibacy.

As I stepped onto the porch, Emma called to me, "Micky, dear, you used to tend bar, didn't you?"

I nodded yes.

"Disaster. These college kids can handle beer, but they're not sure what a dry martini is. And there are a few women my age who are members of the martini generation."

"I'll see what I can do," I volunteered

She touched my arm briefly as I passed. I stiffened without thinking, then belatedly smiled. But Emma was hurrying off in the other direction. I headed for the bar.

Aunt Greta's oldest son, Bayard had caught me in the street one day shortly after I'd turned eighteen and moved out of their house and into Emma's. I remembered him standing there blocking my way, a knowing smirk on his face.

"You know what they say about Miss Auerbach?" he said, hitting the Miss with a hard inflection.

I tried to sidestep him.

"You know what she wants from you, don't you?" he continued.

I started to turn around, but he grabbed my arm.

"She wants to fuck you," he said, the 'fuck' a hissing whisper. "That's the only reason she's letting you stay there. Want to put your mouth on her old pussy? Want to fuck an old woman like that?" his voice a close and foul undertone.

"Better her than you," I yelled, jerking my arm away, causing passersby to look. Then I ran from him, not stopping until I was breathless and on a street I didn't remember turning onto.

But he had planted something corrupt and contaminated. It wasn't until after college, after the hold I thought Emma had on me was gone, only after it hadn't happened and hadn't happened over and over again, that I could believe it wouldn't happen. But before time had taught me trust, whenever she put her hand on my arm, as she had just now, I would wonder, is this it?

If Emma had ever had any sexual thoughts about me, she never showed them. I doubted she did. Now. Now I trusted her. Now I knew better. By the time I finally knew she didn't want sex with me, I had pulled back and stiffened too many times whenever she touched me. At times I wanted so much to apologize for my suspicion, but that would mean admitting to it, framing the words to explain how evil I thought she might have been. To take in a scared high school kid with no other place to go only to . . . fuck, Bayard's tainted word.

"An Old-Fashioned?" I heard the barkeep ask. "How about a new-fangled? I'm better at those," he said with disarming ineptness.

"Want a lesson?" I asked, jerking away from memories to the mundane demands of the present.

"Hi . . . Oh . . Yes, ma'am," he answered to my presence.

"Micky. Don't call me 'ma'am'," I told him as I pulled the ingredients for an Old-Fashioned.

I proceeded with my Old-Fashioned lesson. I had to send to the kitchen for sugar. A young college girl brought it to me, making sure her hand touched mine as she handed it to me. She was cute, but she still had a little baby fat left in her cheeks, and not a single, solitary gray hair. I would have to steer Rosie in her direction.

The Old-Fashioned was finally done and passed off to the woman who'd had the temerity to ask for it in the first place. She winked and said she'd enjoyed the show.

"What's your name?" I asked the young cutie.

"Melanie," she replied in a broad accent.

"And I suppose you're Ashley," I said to Inept.

16

"No, ma'am," he said straight-faced. "My name's Rhett, and I don' know nothin' 'bout birthin' no daiquiris."

"What I have done in the kitchen, I have done," Rachel announced, as she arrived to lean on the bar. "It's bourbon time."

Rhett started to fix her a drink, but she waved him off saying, "I want experience to handle my bourbon."

I made her the drink. "Here you go," I said, handing it to her.

"Fix yourself one," Rachel told me, "and come out from behind that bar."

"I'm having a good time here," I replied.

"I'll bet you are," Rachel answered. "I know you, Micky Knight, and I wouldn't even try to budge you from the best cruising spot in the house."

"I don't know, Rach, I'm getting old. Hit the big three-oh a few months ago."

"Honey, you don't know what old is."

" 'Gettin' older, sugar," I kidded her, "I'm not there yet like you are."

Rachel shot me a fierce glance. "Fix her a drink," she told Rhett. "I almost can't recognize Micky without a Scotch in her hand."

It was going to be a long weekend, I could see that. This was not just a party, but a party for people from the party town. Alcohol was a constant.

I decided to cheat. While some brave soul asked Rhett for a drink, I filled a glass with tonic water, adding a slice of lime. No one would tell me to get a drink if I already had one. I edged out from behind the bar, leaving the guests to the tender mercies of Rhett and Melanie. Rachel was getting another bourbon and water.

"Good luck," I said to her, clicking my glass against the just completed bourbon she was eyeing suspiciously.

"I'll need it," she answered, keeping Rhett in suspense.

I left the front room and headed back to the library. Emma was there and in the middle of an argument concerning some obscure area of Baroque music. I didn't know what they were talking about, let alone have any interest in it. Emma gave me a quick nod, then went back to her debate. As I turned to go, I caught her glance at the drink in my hand. Then she was back in the argument, making a point. I left the room.

17

I found myself back in the front room, and Rhett was crooking a finger at me. Rachel and Melanie were out of sight, so I figured it was safe.

"Micky, ma'am?" he said as I approached.

"No ma'am," I admonished.

"Yes, sir," he replied.

"What do you want, little boy?" I could get away with that since he was on the far side of six feet.

"What's a kir?"

"Champagne and creme de kasis," I answered and gave him a kir lesson. Then I scooted around from behind the bar. I didn't want to be there when Melanie came back. Particularly if she'd heard Rachel tell any stories about me.

"Oh, Micky, sir," Rhett called. "For you."

He had refilled my glass and was handing it to me.

"I can make a gin and tonic," he grinned.

"Thanks," I said, taking the glass from him. There wasn't much else to do.

I hurried out to the porch. And right into Joanne Ranson. Joanne didn't get wet, but I was splashed with a significant amount of gin and tonic.

"Micky Knight, in her usual state," was her only comment. Drunk, but she didn't say that.

"Hi, Micky," said Alex, who was coming up the steps behind Joanne. "Oops," she continued, seeing my stained shirt. "And gin, too, one of the more pungent liquors."

"I thought you were a Scotch woman," Joanne said. "When did you start drinking gin?"

"I didn't start . . ." I began.

"Never stopped," Joanne answered. "Go change your shirt, Micky. Gin does reek." She turned her back to me to help Alex with an overnight bag. I was being dismissed.

I stared at her disapproving back for another moment, then turned on my heel and reentered the house, quickly climbing the stairs to my room.

As I took off my shirt, I maliciously hoped that Joanne and Alex would walk in on Danny and Elly by the fireplace. Then I told myself

18

to grow up. Joanne can be a hard-ass, but she's been fair to me, and whatever hurt lingers between Danny and me is basically my fault. And Alex and Elly have done nothing whatsoever to deserve my spite.

I was staring at my less than plentiful selection of shirts, when there was a knock on my door.

I absentmindedly said, "Come in." I was vaguely aware that I had no shirt on, but it had to be another woman entering, probably Rachel or Rosie.

"I'm sorry I sent you to tend bar. It was thoughtless of me," Emma said as she entered. There was a slight hesitation as she noticed my state of dress, then she continued, "given what you told me when you arrived."

"Don't worry about it," I answered, trying to be casual. I couldn't remember Emma ever seeing me like this. I had always been careful in my actions and appearances around her. "I had fun with those college kids."

"I saw you with a drink. I thought maybe I had . . ."

"Tonic water, with a lime. It was the only thing I could come up with to stop people from offering me drinks. What shirt should I wear?" I said, still trying to be nonchalant.

"The burgundy, I think. It sets off your eyes."

"Then Rhett, the college boy bartender, saw my drink was low and made me another one. A real one this time with a generous amount of gin. I was looking for some place to ditch it when I took a wrong turn and ran into someone. Hence the need for a new shirt," I babbled to cover my awkwardness.

"Micky," Emma said. She had picked up the burgundy shirt. "I don't want anything from you that you don't want to give."

"I know," I answered too quickly, cutting her off.

"Why don't you put on your shirt if it will make you more comfortable?"

"It's okay, I'm still drying off," I lied, unwilling to so visibly show my discomfort by hiding my breasts from her.

"What do you think you owe me?" she asked.

"My first born child and any cat that can be guaranteed to hit the litter pan one hundred percent of the time," I answered. She didn't say anything for a while, making me regret my smart answer. What could I say? I owed her nothing and my life.

"Well," she said finally, handing me the shirt, "I hope we get a chance to talk sometime this weekend. Maybe you'll have an answer then."

"I hope we get to talk," I replied.

I reached for my shirt. She was careful not to let our fingers touch.

"Well, Rachel is right," she said as she turned to go. "You do have nice breasts."

I dropped my shirt. Then quickly bent to pick it up so Emma wouldn't catch the look on my face. I would have been less surprised if I'd heard a nun say what she had just said.

"Anything you want," I blurted out, answering her question, not knowing what she could want from me.

"Nothing physical, believe me," she replied, framed for a moment in the doorway, mistaking my answer. Or perhaps not. Perhaps that's what I was offering her.

She was gone, closing the door softly behind her.

I stood holding my shirt.

Damn, damn it, I thought as I pulled it on. I left my room, slowly descending the stairs, wondering what other minefields I might yet step in.

I went back out onto the porch, carefully this time, but no one was there. Then I wandered off onto the star-lit lawn, finally pacing the perimeter where the gray yard faded into the dark woods.

I made a wide arc around the blue cottage, not wanting to come near the warm nimbus of light from it's windows. I caught a glimpse of Joanne and Danny from one lit window, then Alex and Elly half-framed in another, animatedly talking in front of the unneeded warmth of the fire.

For a moment I almost turned to go knock on the door and ask to be invited in, but instead I kept walking. I was out of place tonight, each step jarring on uneven ground. No one had told me that love and friendship would be so hard. But I don't guess anyone can ever tell you.

I halted my pacing, and sat on a low hanging branch of an old oak tree. Rachel said there were bullet holes in it from the Civil War, but I could never find them. I stayed there, a dark figure in the dark, trying to etch the constellations, but instead seeing only the blinking and shuttering of electric lights in the house and the cottages. When the lights in the blue cottage finally went out, I got up and returned to the house. A few hushed voices came from the living room and the kitchen. I avoided them, going instead into the deserted music room. I turned on the stereo, and used headphones to listen to Holst's "The Planets," in honor of my stargazing. When it was over, after the last faint notes had faded, I curled up on the couch and fell asleep. I awoke sometime in the dim morning and stumbled up to my bed, setting the alarm clock for a few hours later.

Chapter 3

I awoke to an insistent buzzing in my ear and slapped off the alarm clock, willing my eyes to open. They weren't very willing.

Saturday sunshine streamed through my window, crisscrossing the bed with its bright paw prints. I swung out of bed, glancing at the now mercifully silent alarm clock: nine-thirty. I heard voices from the yard. Time for me to be up and about. Past time really. My morose mood was gone; I looked forward to the sunshine and bright woods. It would be warm enough in a few hours to make swimming almost obligatory.

I looked out my window, but couldn't see the bodies belonging to the voices, only a few cawing bluejays feeding greedily on bread crumbs.

I dressed hastily—well-patched cut-offs, T-shirt, and old sneakers—and headed for the kitchen. Rachel wasn't there, but evidence of her earlier presence was. I poured myself a cup of coffee, then paused indecisively at the various pastries, muffins, and breads left out to feed the famished. I was reaching for a decadently sugar-laden beignet when Rachel entered.

"Damn cat," was her first remark, followed with, " I'll save it for you," her hint that the beignet would have to wait.

"What now?" I inquired.

"Magnolia tree past the gazebo. She chased a squirrel half way up and now can't get down. Damn cat," she repeated. "She'll wake up every last guest we have, including the ones still in the city, if we don't get her down soon."

"We?" I asked.

"You," she clarified.

"Am I the only butch around here, or what?" I grumbled as I put down my coffee mug.

"Naw, sugar, just the best."

"On my way," I said, exiting the kitchen and heading for the old magnolia tree. Halfway there I could hear distant cat-up-the-tree sounds. The older P.C. got, the stronger her lungs became. P.C. was her name, but what exactly the initials stood for varied: Pussy Cat, Politically Correct, Pushy Chewer, and Proficient Cunnilinguist had all been suggested, the time of day and state of the suggesters obvious by their choices.

Her cries became louder and more insistent as I got closer. I grasped one of the lower branches and hauled myself up. About ten feet off the ground, I looked and saw a twitching tail.

"Come on, P.C., you putrid cunt," I called to her, sure that her limited vocabulary would not catch the insult.

"Talking to yourself?" a voice below me asked.

"Now, why would I lie about my anatomy like that?" I answered, twisting around to see the questioner. Joanne Ranson was looking up through the branches at me.

"And here I thought I'd finally met an honest woman," she replied. "Do you have any reason for being up that tree other than muttering obscenities to yourself?"

"Cat rescue. P.C., the house cat has treed herself."

"Need any help?" Joanne asked.

"Yeah, stay there and catch me if I fall."

"Sure, Micky, no problem," she replied in a tone that told me she would probably be in the kitchen eating my supposedly saved beignet by the time I got to P.C.

I continued climbing, resigned to leftovers for breakfast. I sighted P.C.'s tail again, about five feet above my head. True to form, P.C. saw me, and with rescue assured, started calmly licking herself. The nonchalant cleaning meant that she was ready to allow herself to be draped over my shoulder and ferried, a la Cleopatra on her barge, down the tree.

"Well, I'll be damned. There is a cat up here," said Joanne who, instead of stealing my breakfast, was climbing up the tree behind me.

"Would I lie to you?"

"Yes."

She was catching up. I took a long step, then jumped up, landing several feet higher.

"Careful," she cautioned. "You'll hurt yourself that way."

"Naw, not me," I retorted. And jumped up to another branch. I missed. There were too many branches for me to go more than a few feet. Unfortunately, the branch that stopped me did so by catching a tender part of my anatomy.

"Shit," I said, cursing the branch between my legs.

"That's what you get for showing off," was Joanne's sympathy.

"Thanks, Joanne," I groaned as we were now face to face. "I haven't had any breakfast yet and I've just lost my virginity. Nice of you to be so sympathetic."

"What do you want?" she replied sardonically. "Me to kiss it and make it better?"

I looked at her. She had on dark sunglasses, her eyes unreadable behind the opaque lenses. I couldn't tell if she was actually flirting or just toying with me. I assumed the latter. I grimaced in reply.

"Cat got your tongue?" she prompted.

"No. A magnolia tree's got my maidenhead," I retorted, still sore between the legs. Then I decided what the hell, maybe she was flirting with me. "But I could probably use some first aid later." I tried to look into her eyes, but the sunglasses prevented it.

Joanne has a quiet intensity that most people, myself included, found riveting. She is tall, her dark hair shot through with gray, and, when you could see them, cool gray eyes that never stopped observing and comprehending the world around her. She is older than

I am, somewhere in her late thirties. At times I found myself very attracted to her, but I could never imagine falling in love with her, because I was always much more concerned with impressing her.

"Go save your cat then," she replied.

Definitely toying with me, I decided. Alex was probably sitting in the gazebo listening to the whole thing.

It was time to dislodge myself from the unwelcome bark. I put one foot on a limb and started to heave myself up. The wayward branch rudely yanked me back, having entangled itself in one of the many disreputable patches of my cut-offs. I reached around behind me, trying to become disentangled as gracefully as possible.

"Ants?" Joanne inquired, watching my contortions.

"Tree branch in pants," I answered. "Shit," I muttered under my breath, my shorts entwined with the magnolia.

Joanne was leaning on a branch, a smile playing about her lips. "I had no idea that I would be so well entertained," she said, openly smiling now.

Enough was enough. I stopped fumbling. It was probably just a few expendable fringes that were caught. I planted both feet and pushed up again, intending to tear myself free. Instead, I was greeted with an ominous ripping sound.

"Shit, piss, and corruption," I muttered. P.C. had a lot to answer for. I don't like making a fool of myself, nobody does, but having Joanne witness it made my misadventures excruciating.

"Hold still," Joanne said, still smiling, enjoying her role as onlooker and now rescuer.

She reached around behind me, attempting to find the offending bark. I felt her hand graze the top of my thigh.

"You do know where to get caught, don't you," she commented.

"Thanks, Joanne, you don't know how much I appreciate your being here," I answered.

"Pardon me," she said, as she slid her other hand between my legs.

"Cat-rescuer rescued by intrepid police sergeant," I made up possible headlines to distract myself. I was aware of the light brush of her hands against my thigh.

"There. Got it," she said.

I glanced back at her. Her glasses had slipped down, revealing her eyes. We looked at each other. What passed, in that brief second, was an acknowledgment that we were playing at the edges of desire, unsure of which way to fall. If it had been a warm summer night instead of a bright, open day, perhaps she wouldn't have moved away from me, pushing her glasses back up. And I wouldn't have turned from her, straightened, and climbed away.

I wrapped P.C. around my shoulders. She chain-sawed in my ear as I started to clamber to the ground. Joanne was already there when I dropped the last few feet, P.C. barely acknowledging the landing. I unwound her tail from one ear, then lifted her off my shoulders and deposited her on the ground. Enough of this cat.

Joanne stood, not saying anything, but she never engaged in polite chatter. I didn't know what to say. I couldn't think of any of my usual smart remarks. I turned to the tree, lifted my leg and braced a foot against it, to brush off the bark and dirt that had lodged in the unruly fringes of my shorts.

Joanne put a hand on my raised thigh, firmly this time.

I saw what looked like Alex and Danny across the lawn. Joanne pushed up the fringe of my shorts, her hand higher on my thigh, then she stopped.

"It's a bad scar, isn't it?" she asked, tracing the outlines of the broken flesh with her fingers.

"Bad enough to up my score on the Butch-o-meter a few notches," I replied.

"I'm so sorry," she said, with a somberness and intensity that hit me harder than her desire had. "It should have been me."

"Naw, you've already got one. Don't horde gunshot wounds, Joanne, baby," I answered lightly, backing away from her seriousness.

Alex, Danny, and Elly were crossing the lawn toward us. They were probably close enough to see Joanne's hand on my thigh. Joanne glanced in their direction, deliberately leaving her hand where it was, too gallant to tarnish her apology by jerking it away.

Danny cleared her throat very loudly, thinking perhaps we hadn't seen them.

"Are we interrupting something?" Alex called out jauntily. She probably knew Joanne well enough to know we couldn't be doing what it looked like we were doing. Not to her face.

"Comparing bullet holes," I explained to calm any prurient minds.

"Let me take a look," Danny said as she came closer. "The only time I saw it, it was all bloody."

I pulled up my pants leg, fully exposing the scar. Only then did Joanne drop her hand.

"Gather 'round all ye clowns," I barkered. "Five cents a gander."

"I'm not sure what to make of this, but I now know two women with gunshot scars," Alex said. She put an arm around Joanne and rubbed the spot below her shoulder where her scar was.

"Probably means you hang around with the wrong type of women," I replied, as I rolled my shorts back down.

"In your case," Danny couldn't resist adding.

"Can you show us around?" Elly asked me, changing the subject.

My stomach grumbled. It wanted to show some breakfast around.

"Sure. If we can start at the kitchen," was my reply.

"Haven't you eaten yet?" Danny inquired. She was a morning person and usually up and breakfasted by eight even on weekends.

"No, I've been busy rescuing cats."

"Then we'll catch you later. I want to be outside on a day like today," she said, making the decision for the group.

We waved good-bye. They headed for some of the trails in the woods, each couple arm in arm. I, with my grumbling stomach in hand, went kitchen-ward.

True to her word, Rachel had saved the beignet. I poured myself a large cup of coffee. It was too hot for the now warm day, but I needed the caffeine. Today would be a long day. I couldn't expect to get to bed before three or four in the morning. Somewhere from the far side of the house, I heard the sound of a harpsichord — Emma, from the proficiency of it.

I washed the sugar off my hands and, taking my cup of coffee, went in search of the music. I quietly let myself into the music room.

It was Emma, playing what sounded like Bach, though I couldn't name the piece. I sat down in a far corner, not wanting to disturb her.

She finished the toccata, then, without looking in my direction, said, "I've done it better, don't you think?"

"I didn't mean to disturb you," I said, sorry to have been so noticeable in my entrance.

"No comment on the music?"

"Perhaps you've done it better, but not by much," I answered.

"An admirably diplomatic answer. How do your friends like it out here so far?" she asked, turning to face me.

"So far, they seem quite content. They're out wandering in the woods right now."

"Good," she replied. "You know, this is the first time you've added any names to the guest list."

"I guess." It was. "Is it a problem?"

"No, of course not. I'm glad. You've always seemed so . . . contained. Aloof even."

"Oh," I answered. "Perhaps."

Then a silence until she asked, "Do you have a lover?"

"No." I took a nervous sip of my coffee. "No, I don't. Not at the moment."

"Recently?"

"Uh . . . no, not really," I equivocated.

"Not really?"

"No . . . not really."

Then another silence.

"I've known you since you were . . . what? Seventeen? True, we don't see each other that often anymore. These weekends, Christmas, maybe my birthday. Special occasions. Every time I wonder if you'll be with someone, but you always come alone."

"I don't want distractions at your birthday," I cut in.

"Why?"

"You spoiled me. I have yet to meet a woman who's as good a cook as Rachel."

"I see you're not in a serious mood this morning. But one more impertinent question and you can go back to your coffee. Have you ever been in love?"

I looked into my coffee cup, but no answers were there. "Yes," I finally said.

Emma waited a moment more while I groped for some words to clarify. Yes, I've been in love. I am in love, but I've neither seen nor spoken to her in several months. Is that really love? All these thoughts jumbled through my head. I was too caught in a limbo of indecision—no, Cordelia's decision, all out of my power—to know what to reveal.

Emma turned back to face her harpsichord, letting my answer

satisfy for the moment. "What would you like to hear next?" she inquired.

"Some more Bach would be nice."

She looked through some of her sheet music.

" 'Capriccio in B-flat Major'," Emma announced. Then she turned to me for a moment. "You don't know anyone who can waltz, do you? No, of course not, your generation hardly knows what a waltz is anymore." Emma was talking so as not to dismiss me too quickly with music. "Herbert can, but I am somewhat reluctant to begin this gala evening as part of a male/female couple. It doesn't quite set the right tone. Oh, yes, the capriccio." She arranged herself and started to play.

I thought about volunteering myself. I could waltz. No, not really, I decided. A few years ago, my cousin Torbin had taught me. He was playing Ginger Rogers and needed someone to be his Fred Astair. We had won first place, so I couldn't have been that bad, but I had done little waltzing in the meantime.

Several of Emma's friends joined us. When she finished the last piece, I thanked her for the concert. Then I left, avoiding the bustling kitchen. It was lunch time, but I wasn't hungry yet. I wandered around the lawn, checking the pond for any long, thin denizens, but found only a lone frog. I left him there. A few women were swimming; the pond would be crowded when people finished eating. The sun was warm and direct. I walked into the shade of the woods, the trees muffling the increasing noise from the swimming pond. I ambled through the forest, at times cutting between trails when I got tired of the paths.

Emma was right. In some ways I was an outsider, an observer, now wandering solitary in the woods rather than joining the gay laughter in the water.

I followed the stream that ran out from the pond down a gently sloping hill. There was a trail further away, but I liked the trickle of the brook guiding me. The trees were decked in their rich spring green, the brown pine needles silent underfoot.

After the cloying suburbs where Aunt Greta and Uncle Claude lived, these bright, boundless woods had been a joy to hike in. When I had moved in with Emma, the limits of my life had changed dramatically, from a yard one couldn't even run in, to a forest with no end in sight.

29

I spent the afternoon in the woods, occasionally coming close enough to see the house. Sometimes I stood absolutely still, waiting for a chance animal to come by. I caught sight of a opossum family, and, late in the afternoon, a doe. After I saw her, I turned back to the house.

The sun had dipped into warm rich amber summer tones, the transition time from afternoon to evening.

It was time for me to make myself presentable for the evening. If that was possible. In the upstairs hallway I ran into Emma. She was coming out of her room, dressed for the party. She looked, as she usually did, both striking and erudite, in a black silk outfit, her only jewelry a set of exquisite pearls.

"You look magnificent," I said. "But you always do."

She gave me a slight bow. "As do you," she replied.

"Me?" I looked down at my well worn sneakers. "I'm not even dressed yet."

"You'll look even better when you are. You've always had a . . . sort of animal glow to you. You know that, don't you?"

"Me?" I repeated.

"Yes, you. I had to chase off the women with sticks that first summer you were here. Not always successfully. After that, I gave up." She turned to go.

"Uh . . . Emma?" I called her back.

"Yes, dear?"

Now or never, Micky. "I can waltz."

"You can? But can you lead?" she asked.

"My cousin Torbin, the drag star, taught me. Since he was in high heels, I had to wear the tux."

Emma took a few steps back in my direction, looking me over. Then she started humming The Blue Danube. I bowed. She curtsied. Then I stepped to her, taking her left hand in mine and putting my other arm around her waist. She rested her hand lightly on my shoulder. For a panicked second my mind went blank. Then I remembered the steps, starting slowly, at first not in tempo with her singing, then I caught up. We must have made an incongruous pair, me in torn shorts and sweaty T-shirt, unsteady and awkward, Emma, cool and elegant in her flowing black silk, never missing a step.

For a moment we had it, a flow and sway, then I stumbled, couldn't recover, and broke away with an embarrassed laugh.

"I'll practice. I promise," I said.

"You'll be fine," Emma replied with a smile. A brave smile, I thought.

I went into my room to change. And to practice. What have I gotten myself into, I wondered.

Chapter 4

My outfit for the evening was simple and functional. Black tuxedo pants, with my gray cowboy boots for footwear. They were the dressiest shoes I had. My top was a white dress shirt, left open at the throat. And dangling silver earrings for the androgynous look.

I had gone over and over my half-remembered waltz lessons. I twirled a couple of times with my cowboy boots on to get used to the feeling.

I was interrupted mid-spin by a loud knocking on my door.

"Micky, dear, open up, it's me," a voice called out. "You'd better not be decent, because I'll never forgive you if you revert to decency."

"Just the person I wanted . . ."

But I opened the door and was cut off by the onslaught of Torbin entering with several wig boxes, a makeup kit, and a number of garment bags. Andy was following him at a safe distance, a bemused smile on his face.

"Micky, dearest, darling, dyke cousin of mine," Torbin greeted me as he deposited his load onto my bed. "You are a sight for sore eyes and your bed a boon for sore feet." He flopped down on the one open spot left on my bed.

"Hi, Mick," Andy said, giving me a hug and a kiss on the cheek.

"Good to see you," I said to him.

"Not to be outdone," Torbin said, getting to his feet and giving me a huge bear hug and a sloppy kiss. "I am, as you can see, shanghaiing your room to change in. I couldn't see driving out here in the afternoon heat stifling under a wig."

"Not to mention eight inch falsies," I added.

"Not to mention," Torbin commanded.

"But there's a price, dear cousin Tor."

"Yes? But be warned, I don't know that many good-looking women. Not who are really women, that is."

"I have to waltz tonight."

"Poor girl. You have my condolences."

"Don't sit back down," I caught him as he was about to reposition himself on my bed. "First, a few trips of the light fantastic," I said, pulling him into my arms.

"See, Andy, it's true. Even women, women who are gay, can't keep their hands off me," Torbin bantered.

"One-two-three, one-two-three," I began, ignoring his blather. "And don't worry, I'm a lesbian, I can keep my hands off the places that really matter."

Andy took up the count, allowing us to concentrate on the placement of our feet.

After twenty minutes or so, Torbin announced me fit for a place on his dance card. "Somewhere near the bottom, late at night, you know," he added.

"Thanks, Torbin," I said, feinting a kick to his balls. "You don't need them for what you do, anyway," I added as he jumped back. Then I left him to his makeup and wigs, with Andy's able assistance.

I had never ceased to be amazed at the coupling of Torbin and Andy, a flaming queen (Torbin's self-description) and a computer nerd (Andy's). But they had been together for close to five years now. They still had nominal separate addresses, but that was more as a means to separate Andy's computer equipment from Torbin's makeup. They only lived a block away from each other.

I ambled slowly down the stairs. The evening guests would be arriving around eight or fashionably thereafter. It was about six-thirty now. I was looking forward to the evening, glad that Torbin and Andy were here.

I wandered into the backyard. The sun was still visible, a broken golden circle through the trees, shooting intense amber rays between the branches.

I heard someone call my name and turned to see Danny waving to me. She, Elly, Alex, and Joanne were sitting on a blanket, still in their bathing suits. They had a picnic supper spread out before them.

"Join us," Danny called, making room for me between her and Alex on the blanket.

"Thanks," I said as I edged myself next to their almost naked bodies.

Only Joanne wore a one-piece suit. I looked surreptitiously around at the bathing beauties surrounding me. Of all of us, Danny was the most pulchritudinous. The red top of her suit barely contained her shapely breasts, nipples half-erect.

Uh-oh, I thought, are my hormones raging or what? Not wanting Elly to catch me staring at Danny's tits (never stare at an ex-lover's tits when her current lover is watching), I glanced over at Alex. Danny had her beat in the curve department, but not by much. It was time to start staring at the cheese. All these women were taken.

I glanced around, trying not to look at anything in particular and happened to watch Elly brush a fallen leaf off her shoulder. She was slim, almost boyish, but her long black hair gave her an air of enticing androgyny. She and Alex were chatting, something about a pro-choice rally Alex had been at. Then Elly was talking about having to fight her way through right-to-lifers to get to work, her deep, almost black eyes flashing. No wonder Danny lusted after her, with eyes like that, I bet she was riveting when she . . . I stopped the thought by searching for the right cheese to go with my cracker. (Never try to imagine ex-lovers with their current lovers. Particularly when you've only got your hand for distraction.)

I looked across the blanket at Joanne. She had taken off her glasses and closed her eyes, letting the last rays of the sun warm her face. She seemed relaxed, almost into tiredness, with her perpetually observing eyes stilled for an instant. The sun sketched in the faint lines at the corners of her eyes, the small tracings from nose to lips. Lines of experience, never to go away. Lines of wisdom, I thought, somehow making her more attractive than any full breast or well-muscled thigh ever could. Her shoulders were too broad, her breasts too small for perfection, but I was beginning to realize it wasn't mere flesh that made someone desirable.

I have slept with a lot of women. Some out of boredom, others because I wanted sex or they did. Sometimes just because I could. But only once because of pounding, insistent desire, the kind that distracts and consumes you, pulling at all corners of your life. I wondered if she would be here.

"Want some wine?" Danny interrupted my thoughts. Fortunately.

"No, no thanks. Maybe some club soda," I answered. Alex poured me some.

"Wasn't Cordelia supposed to be here for this picnic?" Danny asked.

"I thought so," Alex answered. "But I haven't spoken to her since earlier in the week."

"She wasn't definite when I talked to her on Thursday," Elly said. "Something about possibly having to sub for someone on call tonight."

"Too bad. Particularly since it had to be her who got us the invite to the thing," Danny commented. "Since it wasn't you," she added with a nod at Alex.

"Nor was it Cordelia," Joanne said. "Have you talked to her lately?" she asked me, her eyes open and watching again.

"No . . . I haven't. Not in a while."

"She probably heard that El Micko was here and didn't want to risk any more Knight adventures," Danny kidded.

But it was probably true, I thought, taking a long sip of the club soda. She had found out I would be here and wasn't about to spend a weekend in the country avoiding messy and awkward meetings with me.

"But if it wasn't Cordelia, then who was it?" Danny inquired. She was an excellent lawyer because she never missed things like that.

"Ask our resident private eye," Joanne answered.

"It's obvious," I stated. "You've become such a well-known and lusted after woman, that there was no choice but to invite you. There were any number of women, and not a few men, who swore on stacks of Sappho's poetry that they wouldn't come this year unless they got a chance to view Danny Clayton in a bright red bikini. As a matter of fact," I continued, "at this very moment there is a hot sun dance going on. Everyone's hoping that it will be so hot tomorrow that you will be forced to take it all off."

"Congratulations," Danny said. "My bullshit meter has never had a higher reading. I happen to know there are very few women who would bother to cross a street to see me, let alone come all the way out here."

"Enough to keep me worried," Elly said loyally.

"Danno? How could you doubt me?" I faked chagrin.

"I know. I've got it figured out," she bantered. "You met and seduced Emma Auerbach in one of your many bar forays. And to keep it quiet, she allows you to invite any riff-raff out here that you want."

I nearly choked on my club soda.

"Oh, dear," Danny said, her tone changed. "Did I accidentally hit the nail on the head?"

"No, I have never slept with Miss Auerbach," I protested.

"Miss Auerbach?" Joanne observed.

"Emma," I corrected. "I've never slept with Emma."

"Don't worry," Alex comforted. "I call her Miss Auerbach, too. She's always struck me as fiercely scholastic."

I saw Rhett loping in my direction. Work was calling, for once, conveniently. "Michele, ma'am," he called, slowing as he arrived. "Emma wants you."

"Emma wants you?" Danny quizzed.

"That's right," Rhett said, ever helpful.

I got up. I would answer Danny's leading questions later.

"Are you going anywhere near a phone?" Joanne asked.

"Probably," I answered.

"Maybe you should call Cordelia and see what's going on with her," she said.

That was the last thing I wanted to do. "Well . . . I might be busy. But I can take you to one, if you want."

"We have to go change," Joanne replied.

"Well . . ." I let it hang, not wanting to argue, but not willing to lie and say I'd call her.

"If you get a chance," Joanne let me off.

"Let's go, Rhett," I said and we started walking across the lawn at a fast clip.

But not fast enough to avoid hearing Danny say, "What the hell has Micky gotten herself involved in now? Not sleeping with her, my ass."

I turned back to them, that quartet in the fading sunlight.

"It's not like that. It's not like that at all," I shouted to Danny. Then I turned away, following Rhett.

The outside lights wouldn't come on. It took me a few minutes of scrounging around in the work shed to find the right fuse, then all was bright. At least where the lights shone.

I took a slow walk around the yard, eyeing the woods for any desperate water moccasins aiming to make a last ditch attempt on the swimming pond. But no, no reptilian terrorists tonight. Even the lone frog had gone home.

The sun was below the horizon, leaving pink mare's tails in the sky. I walked into the gloaming of the trees, their trunks and branches cutting and striping the last tendrils of light across the forest floor. I was on the path closest to the stream, following it down hill, until the shadowed woods engulfed me.

I stood still, watching the shadows lengthen and merge, hoping to catch sight of the first of the nocturnal animals. But all I saw was a squirrel hastening up an oak tree. I looked at my watch. It was a few minutes before eight. The woods were now bereft of all but diffuse gray light, the path only a lighter shadow among the dark patches cast by the trees.

There's a party tonight, Micky, no sense wandering about in the twilight. But I held still for a moment longer, feeling eyes watching me from somewhere in the darkening woods. Not a squirrel or a bird, but I didn't know what it could be. I tried to pierce the deep gray to find the creature, but nothing moved, nothing stirred. I finally let it go.

I turned away from my unseeable creature, following the gray ribbon path back to the bright lights and bustle of the party. From the dim edge of the woods, the house looked shimmering and alive, light and warmth bursting from windows and doors. There's definitely a party tonight, I told myself. I walked back across the lawn.

The dress code for this party was anything you wanted to wear, from tails to outlandish costumes to blue jeans. "Danny," I called, seeing her and Elly. "I don't believe it."

"I couldn't resist," she said.

"And I couldn't talk her out of it," Elly added.

I walked over to them, looking Danny up and down. She had dressed herself as a plantation owner; three piece white suit, black string bow tie, very fake handle bar mustache, and a white straw gambler's hat.

"It is, I must admit, mind-bendingly outrageous," I commented.

"I thought about carrying a whip . . ." she started.

"But that was too much," Elly finished for her. "Considering the likelihood of slave owners in my background," she added.

I looked at Elly, her light beige skin a talisman of her ancestry. Some foremother of hers was raped; it was a horrifying certainty.

How many of us, I suddenly thought, remembering my own mother, pregnant at sixteen. How many of us are here through mischance, an unheard denial, force?

"The mustache was a bitch to put on," Danny was saying, not noticing my distraction. "But so was getting that magnolia behind Elly's ear."

"I've always wanted to be a blues singer," Elly explained. She was wearing an emerald green gown, her hair unadorned save for the magnolia and hanging long and full down below her shoulders. "Have you seen Alex and Joanne yet?" she asked me.

"No," I replied.

"Just wait," Danny said. Then she made a wiping-her-brow motion to indicate that they were hot.

"Come on," Elly said, putting her arm through both mine and Danny's. We strolled toward the house. A young woman, one of Melanie's companions was busy directing arriving cars to the parking area. The back porch was beginning to get crowded. For a moment I panicked, thinking of all the people who might be watching me dance with Emma. Just think of Emma and don't worry about anyone else, I told myself.

Elly saw someone she had gone to high school with. She and Danny headed off in his direction and into a I-didn't-know-you-were conversation. I roamed on, looking to see if Alex and Joanne were as hot as they were rumored to be.

A stunning blond, in an evening gown that left nothing to the imagination and everything to chance, walked up to me. She eyed me boldly, looking first at my tits, then to my crotch.

"Later," she said in a whiskey voice, then walked off.

Now, I thought, as she sauntered away. I wondered who she was. Probably someone I'd slept with a few years back. One of my many one-night stands.

I ambled toward the front porch, waving at Emma as she greeted her multitudes of guests. Men in dresses, women in pants, some in between, we were all here. Someone even came dressed as a priest. Or maybe he was a priest. You can never tell these days.

Out on the porch, I watched the steady stream of arriving headlights. Always the party of the season, this particular one promised to be special. Things were going to happen tonight.

Someone embraced me from behind, entwining her arms around my waist. It wasn't the blond, not tall enough. Two breasts were lodged beneath my shoulder blades.

"I have a question for you," she said, her voice low.

"And I have an answer. Want to see if they fit together as well as we do?" I pressed my ass ever so subtly against her crotch. Tonight was a night for flirting. Outrageous flirting.

"All right," she responded, to my voice and my movement. "I've always wanted to do this," she said, resting her head against my shoulder.

"Do what?" I inquired.

"Flirt with you."

My body felt taut, in need of touch. Eros was afield tonight. First the blond, now this woman. Who was I to circumvent fate?

"Interested in doing more than just flirting?" I asked.

"Not with me standing here," said a voice directly behind my mystery woman. A voice that I did recognize.

I turned around to face the two of them. (Never proposition a woman until you're sure her lover isn't standing behind you).

It was Alex, her arms still lightly around my waist. Behind her was Joanne.

"Should I go get a drink or something while you two arrange an assignation?" Joanne asked equitably enough, considering the scene.

"We'll never know now, will we?" Alex sighed, letting go of me.

"Sorry, I didn't know it was you," I replied, more for Joanne's benefit.

"Who did you think it was?" Alex asked.

"I don't know. Somebody interesting," I mumbled.

"Do you always proposition women you don't know?" Alex inquired, laughing.

I was trying to figure out whether Joanne was upset or not. Her face, as usual, was impossible to read.

"Isn't that the only kind of woman you do proposition?" Joanne said.

"Are you upset?" I countered, deciding the only way to find out was to question her directly.

"No, of course not," Alex answered for her. "Joanne knows that I'm outrageous only when I'm vertical."

"That probably wouldn't stop Micky," Joanne dryly remarked.

"But it will most assuredly slow me down."

Joanne shook her head, then chuckled. She didn't seem upset.

"Besides that," Alex said. "What goes around, comes around." Then she continued hurriedly, to cover up the connotation of that remark, "And I still have a question to ask you," she said to me.

"Ask away," I replied.

"I realize that it's not likely. Cordelia said she would, but she's not here. Joanne claims she can't and most certainly won't."

"Yes?" I asked.

"I have never ever danced a real ballroom dance with another woman. Yerky men, yes. I admit it, I was a debutante. My mother insisted. Cordelia was there, too, she can tell you how much fun it was." Alex rolled her eyes. "As you well know, I've since found better ways to come out."

"Does she usually ask questions like this?" I asked Joanne.

"Sometimes she's worse," she answered.

"Okay, twenty-five words or less: a) Do you, perchance, know how to waltz? and b) Would you consider spinning about the dance floor with me, even though it will probably drive Joanne insane with jealousy?"

"Yes, I know how to waltz. And yes, despite Joanne, I would consider dancing with you."

"Saved," Alex interjected.

"But," I continued, "I'm already spoken for."

"Too bad," Joanne commented.

"Darn," Alex said. "Me, a wallflower. Cordelia will pay for this."

"She probably had to work," Joanne said.

"I hope not," Alex bantered. "If she's going to stand me up, I hope it's because she's having a mad, passionate affair. Not likely, knowing her. But it's the only acceptable excuse."

"Want a quick lesson?" I said to Joanne, not wanting to think about Cordelia having a passionate affair that didn't include me.

"No, thanks," she responded. "I know when I'm well off."

I looked them over. Danny was right, well, not quite. "Danny said you were hot. She didn't say molten," I let out.

They were both wearing low-cut gowns, Alex in black, Joanne a deep red. Each gown had a voluptuous slit, Alex's in front, Joanne's revealing her left leg to mid-thigh. Half seen though the slit were dark textured stockings, held in place with garter belts, purple for Alex, black for Joanne.

"What are you trying to do?" I continued. "Cause a riot?"

Alex laughed, Joanne shook her head self-consciously. "Thanks, Micky, I appreciate it, even if Joanne is too shy to admit she does."

"I am not too shy. I didn't think anyone would mistake me for a bluestocking in this getup," Joanne responded.

"It was tough, deciding what to wear. We thought about one of us in a dress and the other in pants, but could never decide on who in what. Butch and femme present such etiquette problems these days. We thought about both wearing suits, but neither of us have one. So we finally came up with this concept," Alex explained. "High class Lesbians of the town, plying their avocation."

"Too bad I'm poor," I said, then wished I hadn't. Some desires should not be spoken.

Joanne and Alex looked at each other, then at me.

"Gosh, isn't it a nice night? I sure hope the weather holds," I finally said to break the mounting tension.

"Micky," Joanne said slowly, "have you ever slept with more than one woman?"

"Consecutively or concurrently?" I asked, now aware of a pulse faintly beating between my legs. "What do you think?"

"Your reputation would . . ." Joanne began.

"That car looks familiar," Alex broke in.

It did. It was Cordelia's. Alex started down the porch steps, heading toward the car.

"Did we just have that conversation?" I asked, suddenly embarrassed and flustered.

"Probably not," Joanne responded. "Blame it on the country air." She turned and followed Alex.

I hung back, staying on the porch and moving into a shadow. I was discomfited by what had passed, my longings jumbled. I watched Cordelia get out of the car, Alex hugging her after she did. She towered over Alex. Then Joanne embraced her.

Go on, just go on and say hello and get it over with, I told myself. Better to find out in a dark parking lot if she's happy to see me or not, than in a well-lit party. Watching Joanne hug her made me realize how much I wanted to be the one in her arms. I couldn't see her eyes from this distance, but I knew they were hauntingly blue, her hair in the dark appeared black, but I remembered the highlights of burnished umber, the feel of those auburn strands between my fingers.

I closed my eyes and let out a deep breath. Is it really possible to want a woman as much as I want her? We had made love once, no, several times one night. I opened my eyes again, unable to not watch her. I wondered what she would do if I just walked up and put my arms around her. I watched her talking animatedly with Alex and Joanne. Then I saw the passenger door of her car open. Another woman got out, a blond with bright platinum hair, good-looking even at this distance. Cordelia walked around the car to her.

I turned away and slipped into the house.

Maybe it's time to get a drink, I thought. But I wouldn't do that, not in front of Emma. For her sake, if no one else's, I wouldn't drink away Cordelia having taken a lover and not bothering to tell me. Maybe with my reputation, she didn't figure she needed to.

Go find Torbin and make him tell you outrageous and distracting stories. I went in search of him, making sure I got as far as I could from the door where Cordelia and her lover would enter.

Not finding Torbin, I headed for Rachel and the kitchen.

"Micky, honey," she said on spying me. "Emma's looking for you and she said to hold on to you if you passed by."

"Then I'll consider you to be holding me," I said, leaning against a counter.

"Don't you tempt these old bones," Rachel responded.

"Me a temptation?" I played. If I couldn't have Cordelia, I might as well flirt with every other woman at this party. Micky and her reputation. "Now, Rachel, you know damn well, a woman with your experience and knowledge, would just wear out a young thing like me."

"Truer words were never spoken," Rachel answered. "So I'll leave you be. Emma wants to dance with you. Now unhold yourself and go find her."

"Yes, ma'am," I replied.

"Don't you dare 'ma'am' me. Just don't trip," Rachel said as she sent me off.

I went in search of Emma, aware that Alex would be dragging Cordelia to the same place. Suddenly I was glad of the prominence being seen with Emma would give me. Cordelia was from an old New Orleans family, but so was Emma. When Cordelia saw me, I wouldn't be solitary, standing against the wall, but whirling across the floor as the first dancing partner of the host.

I entered the living room, looking for Emma. She was surrounded by a large circle of her friends. She had just finished telling a story and they were laughing heartily. Glancing around, she saw me. "Michele, dear," she said, taking my hand and making an opening for me to stand beside her.

I said hello to those that I knew and Emma introduced me to the others.

"So you're one of Emma's girls?" the elegant woman next to me asked. I nodded yes. "What do you do?" she continued. "Or are you still in school?"

"No, I'm out of school. Way out," I said.

"Do you really think," Emma interjected, "that I would be standing here holding hands with a woman one quarter of my age?

Really, I do have some standards. She's only half my age. And I'm only holding on because Michele is my waltzing partner tonight and I have no intention of letting her escape." The group chuckled appreciatively at Emma's easy banter.

"Time to begin this affair in earnest," Emma said, signaling the string quartet. "Ready for your ordeal by dance floor?" she asked me.

"Only for you," I answered.

The gentle strains of Bach faded out. Conversation lagged with the music. Emma led me to the center of the dance floor.

"Ladies and gentlemen," she said to the quieted crowd, "and all divergences in between, welcome to my annual Gay Gala. And Lesbian, of course. I see some new faces along with many dear old ones. For those of you who don't know what you're getting into, we start this evening the old-fashioned way, with that most elegant of dances," (not with me, I thought), "the waltz.

"Whoever you are and whatever you call yourself, I welcome you," she finished, a grand dame to perfection.

She turned to me with a radiant smile and curtsied.

I bowed to her as the first soft notes of the music began, then her hand was in mine and my arm around her waist.

"You had to pick one with tempo changes," I said to hide my nervousness. Few couples were dancing; most were watching. I didn't see Alex and Cordelia.

"At least you're the right height for this," Emma commented. "I've danced with so few women I could look up to."

"Better worry about my weight," I added, hoping I wouldn't land on her toes.

Somehow, somewhere, I found the steps, the gentle rhythm of the music. Emma was the perfect partner, of course, guiding me, slowing if I got off the tempo.

Torbin is a very good teacher, I thought as my body seemed to know where to go, a whirl that became a pleasant blur, a power and command over my movement, meshing perfectly with the music and my partner.

"You fooled me in the hallway," Emma said. "You really are quite good."

"No, the hallway was the truth," I replied, "this is the illusion."

44

But it was real, a magic moment, repeated smooth steps that shouldn't be, but were.

"Is it premature to ask you to do this again next year?" she inquired.

I laughed, caught happily by her confidence in me and the lift of the music.

"Better wait until this is over. I might trip yet." But I wouldn't. The night was too special for mundane imperfections. Only one focus was possible, holding Emma, dancing with her, making her happy, that concentration gave me an expertise I didn't know I had.

Once, when we were spinning about the room, I allowed myself to glance around, but the faces were a party blur.

The music reached its final diminuendo, softening to violins only. Emma and I slowed with it, dancing closer than we had when the music began.

"I finally feel like you're a friend and not a student," she said.

"Thank you. I hope I will always be a friend," I answered, enjoying the familiarity and comfort of her touch, my stiffness forgotten in the moment.

Was our touching each other sexual? Of course, how could it not be, holding her this close, in this perfect dance? And this, in all probability, would be the extent of our sexual relationship, one voluptuous dance a year.

At eighteen, I had been too scared and fragile to risk touching someone without explicit guidelines and rules. I saw sex as good or evil, abuse or love. But sex has the consequences you allow it to have, I thought.

The music ended.

"That was most enjoyable," Emma said, still in my arms.

"And you," I replied, "said you wanted nothing physical from me."

"Well, I guess this is physical," she answered, then she took my face between her hands and kissed me, for the first time, on the lips.

The crowd cheered, with several cries of, "Go, Emma," and "Let's hear if for older women." I waved to them, as did Emma, both of us enjoying the attention.

As we walked off the dance floor, back to Emma's friends, I glanced about, an idle glance, really. Cordelia was staring at me. Our eyes caught for a moment. She raised her glass to me, with a half-smile on her lips. I nodded briefly in return, then looked away, unsure of what to make of her gesture. Had Danny told her I was having an affair with Emma? Was she sardonically toasting that?

Emma led me into her circle of friends. My back was turned in Cordelia's direction.

A different band now played and the watchers now became the dancers.

"I never could stand rock and roll," Herbert said over me to Emma. "Shall we retire to the relative calm of the library?"

"An excellent idea," Emma and several others assented.

I walked with them, still puzzling about Cordelia's toast.

"So you must have a lover, with dozens more waiting in the wings," said the elegant lady as she fell into step with me.

"Me?"

"No?"

"No," I answered.

"How do you feel about older women?" she flirted.

Cordelia was dancing with her blond. Too short for you, I thought. She started to turn in my direction and I hastily looked away. I linked arms with the elegant lady. Let Cordelia see that.

"I find older women quite intriguing," I flirted back as we left the living room.

Careful, Micky, or you're going to have half the women at this party expecting to sleep with you before the night is over. My loins told me that they, at least, would be happy with the idea. It's dangerous to be around this many women and be this horny.

Elegant woman, Julia, by name, was fun to flirt with, but we quickly established that neither of us was truly serious. We parted company at the library door. I went to the front porch, then onto the lawn. I paused under a tree, looking back at the bright house.

What if she thought I did it for money, crossed my mind. I was still worrying over Cordelia's half-smile. A few months ago her grandfather had died, leaving her a considerable fortune. Was she toasting my supposed success at getting a rich woman for a lover? Likely, I thought, if she had talked to Danny and Danny had passed on her suspicions that I was sleeping with Emma. Danny passing it on was very likely. I had to find Danny and set her straight before the rumors got too out of hand.

46

I started back to the house. Of course, Danny was probably dancing with Cordelia right now. Better than the blond runt.

A figure in white stepped out onto the porch. I stopped, hiding myself in the shadow of a tree. Her height gave her away. It was Cordelia. I backed further into the shadows, not wanting her to catch me staring. She was joined by her blond.

I turned away from them, walking until I was safely out of range of the outdoor lights. Then I turned back toward the house, following the dark edge of the woods around to the back, so that when I finally re-entered the house, it was through the back door. I stayed on the porch, unwilling to be trapped too far inside.

The built blond that I had seen earlier, sashayed over to me. This time I stared at her tits, but she coyly covered her cleavage with a gloved hand.

"Later. But not too much later," she said, then turned and went back into the house.

"Not much," I answered to her retreating curves. She was familiar. I was still trying to place her, when I saw Cordelia enter the dining room. I left the porch, going back out on the lawn. I re-traced my previous circumnavigation and ended up on the front porch again.

Let me find Torbin, see what ludicrous outfit he's concocted, then I'll go hide up P.C.'s favorite magnolia tree, I told myself, feeling foolish at my constant motion.

"Ah-ha, got her." A hand gripped my shoulder. Danny. "Explanation time, dear El Micko," Danny continued. She led me to a corner of the porch. Elly, Joanne, and Alex were there. "Why do we keep hearing you referred to as 'one of Emma's girls'? How did you meet?"

"It's a long story," I answered.

"It's a long night. We've got time," Danny countered.

Someone joined the group, handing out filled champagne glasses over my shoulder. I half-turned to look. Cordelia. "Go on," she said, handing me a glass.

I waved it away. I was unnerved by Cordelia standing so close.

You don't have the right to know everything, Danny, I wanted to say. Some questions I don't have to answer. Some I don't have an answer to.

"Emma keeps a harem, don't you know? I'm number forty-two,

47

available on alternate moonless Sundays, and as the lunch special on Lundi Gras," I replied.

"I'd always wondered how those rumors were started," Emma laughed over my shoulder as she joined us. "Mardi Gras, perhaps, but Lundi Gras? Now," Emma continued. "Why don't you introduce me to your friends? Some of you I know, though Alexandra Sayers, your presence here is a pleasant surprise."

"I guess I'm getting a little too good at straight camouflage. The long, dangling earrings will have to go," Alex answered.

"Does your father know? Or is that a rude question?" Emma inquired.

"He knows, if he wants to know," Alex replied carefully. "Does that make sense?"

"Perfectly," Emma responded.

"Joanne Ranson, Detective Sergeant in the NOPD," I introduced. "Danny Clayton, Assistant District Attorney, Elly Harrison, R.N., and . . ." I faltered on coming to Cordelia.

"Cordelia I know," Emma supplied. "I'm very glad to see you here. I had so hoped you would come, though surely your grandfather is spinning in his grave."

"Perhaps," Cordelia replied, "but I don't live my life to please him, or his memory." She continued, "This is my friend Nina Douglas."

The short blond. As Emma shook her hand, I turned around and got my first good look at her. Definitely too short, probably had to stand on a stool to kiss Cordelia. Boring all-American face, dimples and a nose that could only be described as pert. Pale blond hair and big brown eyes. Disgustingly cute. I turned back around.

"Can I ask pairings? Or is that passé?" Emma inquired.

"Danny and Elly are buying a house," I supplied. "A hard-core married couple."

"Joanne and I," Alex explained, taking Joanne's hand, "but no house yet. Separate apartments still, in fact."

"Micky's our resident tomcat," Danny added.

"Meow," I opined.

"Micky," Alex said, with a grin that should have warned me. "Tell us about your sex life."

"Not tonight, we haven't time," Danny cut in.

48

Thank you Danielle Clayton. In front of both Emma and Cordelia.

"Not much to tell," I answered dryly, hoping to forestall any speculation.

"Oh, yeah?" Danny returned. "What about that time junior year when you and three..."

"No! That was college and it doesn't count," I overrode her. "Danny," I added in an undertone.

"I think I'm too old for this conversation," Emma said, standing up. "Have a delightful evening, girls, women, that is." She breezed off the porch.

"Did I embarrass you?" Danny asked, all innocence.

"How would you like me to recount some of your college escapades to your parents?" I hissed at her.

"She's not your parent."

"Well, still... how about your favorite high school teacher?"

"I guess not," Danny said, suddenly contrite.

"So are you going to tell us?" Alex bantered. "Or do we have to guess what three referred to? Women? Dogs? Cucumbers?"

"Is she always this bad?" I asked Joanne.

"Worse, usually," Joanne replied laconically.

"Pigeons? Fingers? Elephants?"

"I don't remember," I burst out.

"But I do," Danny chimed in. "I had the room next door."

"Three of everything," I said. "Women, men, dogs, cats, aardvarks, three-toed sloths. Every animal, mineral, and vegetable this planet possesses. And a few threes that were quite possibly alien, but it was late in the evening and I don't really remember. And now, you'll have to excuse me," I hurried on, standing up. "I've gotten very thirsty."

"Have some champagne," Alex offered.

"No thanks," I replied. "Water."

"But Micky," Alex said, her hand on my arm. "You haven't answered the burning question of the night."

"I don't think I want to."

"Now, now. Where," she continued, "did you learn to dance like that?"

Finally a safe question. "My cousin Torbin taught me."

49

"The famous cousin Torbin that I've never met?" Alex inquired.

"The very one."

"You've never met Torbin?" Danny asked. "He's here. You've got to meet him." Which started a Torbin hunt. Everybody wanted to meet Torbin. I was hoping Cordelia and her runt blond would disappear, but they followed.

Where was Torbin? I still hadn't seen him since he breezed into my room this afternoon. Finally I spotted Andy.

"Just a second," I said to my followers. "Hi, Andy. So how come you didn't dress up?"

He looked chagrined. Then I burst out laughing. Andy, a computer nerd, had dressed as a computer nerd. He had on black horn rim glasses, held together with fishing wire and tape. And a horribly tasteless yellow, brown, and green checked jacket complete with overly full pen protector in his pocket. Floppy discs poked out of his back pocket.

"Have you seen Torbin? I have an admiring horde panting to meet him."

"He's around somewhere," Andy replied, looking around the room.

Suddenly, the tall curvy blond approached me.

"Now," she demanded. "I must have you now," she said. "Here, on the floor."

The blond, moving quicker than anyone with curves like that had a right to, threw her arms around me and spun me off balance until I was bent precariously backwards, my feet doing little to hold my weight.

"What the . . . ?" I started.

She cut me off with a boisterous kiss. Her hand made a quite blatant and visible assault on my breasts. But now I knew who I was dealing with. Only one person would dare such an outrage.

"Torbin, let go of me," I yelled, elbowing him in his falsies.

"Well, I never," he huffed. Then took me at my word and let go, unceremoniously dumping me on the floor.

"Mussed my lipstick, I declare," he said, hovering over me.

"You'll pay for this," I hissed. Andy was doubled over with laughter. I didn't dare look at anyone else. "Itching powder in your jock strap, pepper in your rouge. I will get you someday, Torbin

50

Robedeaux. Be assured of it," I cursed from my prone position. I had been set up. If I were playing any role but my own, I might even find it funny. But in my present position, I could not.

"Oh, girls, you've left some trash on the floor," Torbin called as he made his grand exit.

"Do you intend to lie there all evening?" Joanne asked, standing very close to my head.

I didn't really mean to, but she was standing over me, with that damned slit halfway up her thigh. From my floor perspective I could see way beyond thigh level. So I looked. And she caught me looking.

"Black lace. Is that the real you?" I commented, trying to discommode her. "Pull me up," I said, extending my hand.

"Someone give me a hand with this body," Joanne said, not at all discommoded.

Cordelia came around to my other side and reached out her hand. I had no choice but to take it. Now I was the discomfited one.

She and Joanne, each holding a hand, pulled me up. I let go of her hand too quickly, disconcerted by her touch. The three of us stood together, confused and awkward for a moment. At least I was, I don't know what they were feeling.

"Well, I hope we've all having a good time here tonight. I know I am," I said sarcastically, trying not to look back at Cordelia. "Now, I really am thirsty. And I really have to get a drink of water." With that I stalked off, more in search of quietude than water. Cordelia had badly thrown me off kilter. How could she just reappear with a cute little blond in tow and pretend that nothing had happened between us? What did she expect me to do? Smile blandly and congratulate her?

I walked quickly past the partying clumps until I was out in a dim corner of the back porch.

What does she think . . . ? Then I knew what she thought, or had a pretty good guess. Micky Tomcat as Danny had said. What could I do? Tell her, 'I know Danny's told you a lot of things about me, and yes, they're all true, but I've changed, really, I have.' Right. Why would Cordelia have an affair with a Cajun bastard who had, and there was no other word for it, a slutty reputation? Particularly when cute little good girl blondes are available?

I left the porch, walking out onto the star-lit lawn. I thought about being supremely childish and climbing the magnolia tree to spend the rest of the evening there. But a couple was entwined at the bottom of it and they didn't sound like they would appreciate being disturbed.

Cordelia has found a new blond twerp. You will survive, Micky, I told myself. And I would. I just didn't want to stand around tonight watching her and her runt.

I roamed among the trees and shadows of the yard. I sighted Rosie and Melanie sneaking off to their cabin. Don't worry, I thought indulgently, I'll cover for you. Hello, young lovers, wherever you are.

I wandered over to the gazebo, wondering who I would find entwined there. Maybe Torbin and Andy, I maliciously hoped. But it was deserted, no deserving couples to intrude on. I entered, walking to the far side, then sat down on the railing, leaning my back against a supporting column. I looked over the lawn to the deepening darkness that led into the forest.

I heard a board creek behind me, someone coming up the steps. I turned to look. A tall woman in white. I almost fell off the railing.

"Are you all right?" Cordelia said, seeing me off balance, trying not to fall into the azalea bushes below.

"Yeah, fine," I answered, grabbing at the column to stop my slide bush-ward. "Not my night for balance," I said, as I fumbled to get my rear end safely re-seated on the railing. "So, how are you?" I winced at the falsely bright tone in my voice, but at least I was sitting upright again.

"Pretty good. How's your leg holding out?"

"It's fine."

She was carrying a bottle of champagne, which she set down. I was desperately trying to think of something to say, or better, some way to leave.

"Is it just coincidence that you always seem to be leaving a room whenever I enter it?"

"Has to be," I mumbled, abashed at having been so clumsy.

"Of course," she said, looking at me, her eyes clear and direct. We both knew I was lying. "How are you?"

"I'm fine," I replied automatically.

"No, really," she countered.

I didn't know what to say, her directness caught me off guard.

52

I sat, holding on to the railing tightly, wanting to go to her and put my arms around her.

"Uh . . . I'm . . ." I didn't know. The silence hung. "I did leave the room. I didn't know what to say to you," I admitted.

"Well, I guess I can understand that," she replied, turning away from me, slumping slightly from the sting my admission had to give.

I stood up, took a step to her, then faltered, unsure of what I wanted, afraid of what she wanted.

"It's okay," she said, her back still to me. "You have every right to avoid me."

"I don't . . . I'm not avoiding . . . things get complicated, don't they?" I finished lamely.

"I had hoped we could be friends."

"We can. If you want."

"I do want." And she turned back to me, the half-smile again on her face.

"Good," I responded.

"Champagne? I brought a bottle out here with me," she offered.

"No, thanks."

"Mind if I do?"

"Of course not. I've heard via Elly that you've had a long week."

"Sometimes they all seem long," she answered, then took a swig straight out of the bottle. "Not the best way to drink champagne."

Another pause. She spoke first.

"I enjoyed watching you dance with Emma."

"Thanks," I replied, then to avoid another silence, "How do you know her? Emma, I mean."

"All the grand old families know one another. Some social requirement or the other. I believe Grandfather Holloway was in the same fraternity as Emma's father. I came out here when I was eighteen and sort of beginning to figure things out. I had always been fascinated by Miss Auerbach. Then Grandfather told me not to be seen with her anymore. No explanation. But I knew."

"And you haven't been out here since then," I said, a statement, not a question.

"How did you know?"

"I've been here every year since I turned eighteen. I would have noticed you."

"You're very kind."

53

"Not kind. Observant."

"Thank you," she said, flustered by my compliment. She took another drink of champagne.

God, you're beautiful, I thought, the soft lights reflecting off the white she was wearing, making her eyes a deep and mysterious blue. But we were only friends and I was afraid to say it.

"What was Danny talking about?" she abruptly asked. "In college."

"Oh, that," I replied, embarrassed. "Youthful indiscretions."

"Why didn't I have a youth like that?" she said, the slight smile playing on her lips. "Good old Cordelia. Always discreet. Doomed to discretion."

"Don't say that," I replied to the disparaging tone in her voice.

"Dance with me," she said suddenly. Then, "Will you?" as if afraid of refusal. "I've always wanted to whirl across the ballroom floor like I saw you doing earlier."

I took a tentative step toward her.

"Didn't you dance with Alex?" I asked to cover the silence.

"Oh, Alex. I've known Alex forever. I think we were born in the same hospital. No, that's probably apocryphal. But definitely grade school. Besides that Alex isn't . . ." and she stopped.

"Isn't?"

"Tall, dark, and . . . handsome," she said, looking at me, then quickly away.

I took another step toward her.

"You're very kind," I said.

"Not kind. Observant," she answered.

She stepped in to me, putting one hand tentatively on my shoulder.

I put my hand on her waist.

"Wait," she said, pulling away. "Let me get rid of this." She put the champagne bottle down a few feet away. Then she came back, putting her hand on my shoulder with the same tentativeness, as if I might break or back away at any moment.

I took her left hand in mine.

"I'll have to hum," I said. "Can you stand it?"

"If you can stand my dancing."

"Fair enough."

54

I started softly singing the only waltz that came to mind. I wasn't even sure what it was.

"I know why I've never spun around a ballroom," she said after our first few awkward steps. "I'm not a very good dancer." She stumbled, as if to prove her point. "Particularly when I've had too much champagne," she added. "I don't think I'm sober." She stopped. "It's okay. I need a few more lessons. Or something." She started to pull away.

No, don't, I wanted to yell. Don't move away from me, don't shatter this slight embrace.

"Don't give up yet," I said, not releasing her, keeping her in our tentative waltz, pulling her a little off balance so she couldn't let go of me. She faltered again, but this time held on to me. We had stopped dancing, but she didn't move away.

"I know I'm clumsy, but I'm not usually this bad," she said, leaning her head against my shoulder. "The champagne."

I heard voices from the lawn.

"People will talk," I said, aware that we were visible, my white shirt, her white outfit, framed by the white columns of the gazebo. "I'm used to it. People always talk about me. But you might not want . . ." I trailed off. Your blond to see us like this. "To be so indiscreet."

"I don't think," she replied, "that I've ever done anything indiscreet in my life. Maybe I want to be the one they talk about tomorrow. I want them to say, wasn't that Cordelia James with that tall, dark woman out in the gazebo?"

"No, it was only Micky Knight," I answered, to keep talking, because if I stopped talking I would . . . I wouldn't stop. Cordelia wasn't sober. What she wanted now, she would regret in the morning. "Anyone can have her," I added, a hint of rue creeping in.

"Don't say that."

"Ask Danny. She'll tell you. Anyone. Don't ruin your reputation with a . . . slut."

"The slut and the wallflower. What a combination." Then she looked at me, lifting her head away from my shoulder, her arms lightened their embrace, ready to pull back. "Don't degrade yourself this way. Just say no. That's all you need to do."

She pulled away, not really moving, but retreating into herself.

Her eyes grayer, less open. I tightened my embrace, wanting to bring her back, but not knowing how to both have her and not take advantage of a warm spring night and good champagne.

"Don't worry," she continued. "I've done this before. Don't take me seriously. I said I was going to get drunk tonight and I've succeeded." This time she did physically pull away.

"I do . . ." I began, but was interrupted. Rudely.

A cry for help somewhere across the lawn. A guest has seen a garter snake, I thought disgustedly.

"Shit," I cursed.

The cry for help was repeated. I toyed with leaving it to Rosie, then remembered that she might be even more entangled than I was. At least I still had my clothes on.

"Duty calls, I gather," Cordelia said.

"Duty annoys," I replied, incensed at duty's timing. But Emma wouldn't appreciate it if someone were really in trouble and I didn't bother to check it out. "I'm sorry," I said. "I'll find you later," I called as I ran down the gazebo steps. "Sorry," I repeated. I was sorry. We had almost . . . I didn't even know.

"It's okay," her voice drifted after me. "Some people are born to be wild, some are born to run, and some of us are born to be discreet."

I started running across the lawn, thinking more about what was behind me than what was in front.

Chapter 5

The cries were coming from somewhere around the main cluster of cottages. Probably just a damn garter snake or a toad on someone's pillow, I snorted. I couldn't imagine anything seriously wrong out here.

I trotted over to the group of people clumped outside the yellow cottage. "What's going on here?" I asked, acting calm and official. After all, I was the only person who knew I was wet between the legs.

"Some animal's in there," the upset woman exclaimed.

"It looked like a porcupine," someone else said. "I got a glimpse of it."

Everyone looked at me, then at the door behind which this vicious creature lurked. How had I gotten into this, I wondered, not particularly wishing to entangle myself with an enraged pin cushion.

With extreme bravery, I marched up to the door. That's as far as bravery got me. I cautiously opened it and poked my head in. Nothing in the living room that I could see. I entered, watching intently for any quivering quills. No movement, nothing. I looked in the kitchenette. Nothing pounced from the cupboards. Taking a broom with me, I started for the bedrooms. At least this cabin only had two.

The first one was animal-less. I even poked the broom handle under the bed to make sure.

"You need help?" Joanne called, entering the cabin.

"You look dressed for a porcupine hunt," I responded.

"Is that what this is?"

"Maybe. Maybe someone's imagination."

I went into the second bedroom. I didn't want Joanne to see a big butch like me hesitating in the doorway, scared of a little porcupine. I couldn't see anything. With the disgusted feeling that I was definitely on a wild porcupine hunt, I knelt down and took a quick look under the bed.

Two animal eyes stared out at me, then winked out. I heard the soft skitter of clawed feet across the wooden floor heading for . . .

I jumped back, of course, crashing into Joanne's legs. Some big butch.

"In a hurry?" she asked, looking down at me.

"There's a porcupine coming after us," I rationalized.

"That's not a porcupine, that's a opossum," she said, looking at the creature that had fled out from the opposite side of the bed. "I don't know who's more scared, it or you."

"Easy for you to say," I answered, getting up. "I was between you and whatever it is."

"Right."

"Stay there, in the door," I replied, regaining my composure. "I'll open the window and chase Ms. Opossum through it."

"What an ingenious plan."

I ignored her and shoved the window open. Then, with my trusty broom at my side, I went on a opossum roundup. Ms. Opossum, evidently unaware of how close at hand freedom was, went back under the bed. I got down on my side and attempted to gently prod her to liberty with the broom handle. She bared her teeth at me.

"Joanne? Can opossums get rabies?" suddenly occurred to me.

"Uh-huh. There's an epidemic going on right now. Also be aware that rabid opossums inevitably go after the tallest person in the area."

I looked back at Ms. Opossum. She didn't look rabid. But then what did rabid look like?

"Good thing I'm on the floor. That makes you the tallest thing in the room," I responded.

"Want me to flush her out?"

I swung the broom a few more times, unwilling to admit defeat. Ms. Opossum moved out of range of the broom handle.

"Be my guest," I finally said, getting up and proffering the broom to Joanne.

As Joanne walked toward me, Ms. Opossum shot out from under the bed and through the now unguarded doorway.

"See," Joanne observed, "just the idea of me coming . . ."

"But she's still in the house," I cut off her gloating.

Ms. Opossum was skittering about the living room. I closed the doors as we went back up the hallway so at least she couldn't get back into any of the bedrooms.

"You can chase her this time," I told Joanne as we surveyed the room.

"In heels?" she responded, not looking like she had any intention of chasing anything.

So I set off, a opossum posse of one. First I propped open the screen door, then I swept Opossum out of the corner she had chosen to cower in. She went to the next corner. I chased her out of that one and she returned to the first corner.

"Making great progress," Joanne observed.

"Eat shit and die," was my only possible response.

This time I herded Opossum directly toward Joanne. Joanne didn't move, merely motioned toward the door. Opossum veered off, and, as luck would have it, went in the direction Joanne pointed. Out the door and into the night.

"It's easy if you know how," she said complacently.

"Luck," I commented and stalked out the door, just to make sure Opossum was really gone and not lurking out on the porch. All clear. Only my bruised ego in sight. The clump of people had probably decided to wait this out in the safety of the house, with food and drink to sustain them through their ordeal.

Joanne came out on the porch behind me.

"Good thing you didn't go into opossum catching as a career," she said.

"Whereas you have obviously missed your calling," I replied.

"Don't be tacky. You're not . . . Shit."

"I'm not? That's nice to know."

One of those impossible-to-catch-opossum-in heels was caught in a gap between the floor boards. Joanne was standing on the porch, looking lopsided, trying to extricate her stuck shoe.

"Want some help?" I asked, laughing at her predicament.

"Knothole. Damn," was her reply. "Would you be useful and pull?" she said, getting exasperated.

"Your wish is my command," I replied with a malicious chuckle. I knelt down, put a hand under her foot and pulled. It didn't budge. "Gosh, Joanne, it's really wedged in. Didn't know you weighed that much. Let me get a better angle."

I moved in front of her, putting one hand under the shoe and the other on her ankle.

"Eat shit and die. Pull first," was her response.

I tried to gently pry up the shoe, not wanting to scuff the heel too much. It didn't want to cooperate. I started to pull a bit harder. My hand on Joanne's ankle slipped, sliding up the slick stocking to her calf. I leaned my shoulder into her thigh to get a better grip.

"Micky," Joanne said.

The heel was starting to become unstuck.

"Micky," she repeated.

Her hand was on my shoulder for support. My shoulder was pressed against her thigh. I realized the slit in her gown was open and my shoulder was pressing into bare flesh.

I stopped and looked up at her. Then I noticed what my head was even with. Her black underwear. Joanne abruptly stepped out of the stuck shoe and moved away from me. I finished pulling her shoe up. I really hadn't been flirting. Well, not as much as she obviously thought I was. I handed her the shoe. She took it and put it on, then walked down the steps. Having nowhere else to go, I followed her.

Joanne turned to face me. "Do you want Alex for a threesome or would you prefer just the two of us?" she asked, looking directly at me.

"What are you talking about?" I replied. Which was an incredibly stupid thing to say.

"Going on an Easter egg hunt," she retorted.

"I'm sorry. Of course I know what you're talking about, I'm just ... I'm ..." I sputtered.

Eros was staging a three-ring circus tonight. I didn't have the vaguest idea how to get out of this, complicated by not wanting to get out of it.

"We've been heading for this. You know that," Joanne said.

"Yes, I know, we have, haven't we?" I mumbled inanely.

"Come on. Let's go." She took my hand and lead me in the direction of the blue cottage.

The idea that Danny and Elly and Cordelia and whatever-her-name-was, (I didn't know for sure that they were staying in the blue cottage, but paranoia made it seem inevitable), would know, perhaps hear, panicked me.

"Not the cottage," I said, stopping. "Danny ..."

"Where?" she asked, as she turned to face me. Then she took my other hand in hers. Her hands were warm and strong; I could feel the slight calluses. She brought one of my hands to her lips, kissing first the back, then turning it over to kiss my palm. I shivered in the warm night air.

"I don't know," I replied, trying frantically to think what my options were. Cordelia had, at best, given me an iffy maybe, the heat of a moment now cooled. Joanne left no doubts about what she wanted. My blood was pounding.

What the hell am I going to do, I thought wildly. I desperately wanted to sleep with both these women. I will probably end up with neither, flashed through my churning brain.

"The woods? It's mild enough," Joanne suggested.

"The woods?" I repeated stupidly.

"You've done it in the woods, haven't you?" she asked.

"No ... Yes ... Of course, I have," I said, trying to remember just what I'd done in my checkered career.

"How drunk are you?" Joanne asked, noticing that I wasn't my usual voluble self.

"Not very," I replied. Not enough.

"Have I misread? Are you not interested?"

"Uh . . . No, I'm interested. I'm . . . I find you a very attractive woman and I want to . . ." I broke off, thinking aloud, always a dangerous thing for me to do. "I'm confused . . ." Boy, was I ever. "What about Alex?" I seized to slow events down.

"She can join us or I won't tell her," Joanne answered.

"Oh." So much for Alex. Where was monogamy when I needed it to make a decision for me?

Then Joanne kissed me. Oh, God, did she kiss me. Hard and penetrating, riveting my whole body to the spot. Thinking, hard before, became impossible. Concentration was spent on the press of her lips against mine, the hard curves of her tongue playing in my mouth.

Then, for the second time of this fickle summer night, someone screamed. It had to be a garter snake, I told myself, cursing inwardly.

The moment broken, our kiss subsided, then stopped. The scream didn't.

"I've always wanted you," I blurted out, too disconcerted by the second interruption to be cautious, to keep desire and need suitably hidden.

"Yeah, me too," Joanne responded to my honesty.

"Got to go," I said, turning from her, trying to locate the exact direction of the scream.

"Behind you," she replied.

For the second time that evening I took off across the yard running. I quickly left Joanne, in her high heels, behind. I raced toward the area of the woods where the sound seemed to come from. Someone must have gone down the path near the stream, I thought as I pounded in that direction.

Suddenly a figure burst from the forest, stumbling in her haste. I ran toward her. It was Cordelia's . . . what was her name? Nina. I caught up with her and grabbed her by the shoulders. She looked terrified.

"What is it?" I demanded.

She just shook her head, her mouth moving but no words came out.

"It's okay," I said, trying to calm her. "What happened?"

"Oh, God," she sobbed, taking a deep breath.

I put my arms around her and held her. Whatever she had seen in the forest, even if it was a garter snake, had badly frightened her. The only thing to do was hold her for a minute, until she could speak. She shuddered against me.

"Oh, my God," she repeated. "She's dead."

"Who?" I demanded.

She shook her head, sobbing.

"Who?" I demanded again.

"In the woods," she gasped out. "I don't know . . . I wanted to see the moon . . ."

"Where?"

"I dropped my flashlight somewhere near . . ." she said, pointing toward the path.

I nodded and let go of her. I could hear other voices across the lawn, coming this way. Nina would be taken care of. I hurried off in the direction she had indicated. I didn't have a flashlight, but there was moonlight and I knew the woods. Whoever was there might be hurt and need help.

I ran into the forest, calling out, hoping whoever it was might hear me. The path was a dim gray ribbon against the charcoal of the wood. Only the common sounds of the night answered my calls. I saw a faint glow down the path. The dropped flashlight from the look of it. I headed for it.

No one was visible in the dull glow of the flashlight. I picked it up, holding still, hoping to hear something, a groan, perhaps the deep breathing of a woman. I heard nothing. Maybe Nina hadn't dropped the flashlight very close to whoever she saw. It was a small one and gave off only a dim amber light. I searched around with the beam. Nothing.

I suddenly wondered if someone had played a sick joke on Nina. Nothing that terrified another person like that could be funny, I thought angrily.

I moved off the path into the woods. The beam of light seemed even more feeble against the dark solid trees. I stepped cautiously through the pine needles and underbrush. I still saw nothing. I walked further into the trees, circling around a thick oak trunk. Only dark shadows and brown leaves appeared in the pencil of light. I turned slowly around, having to stare intently to make out the shapes outlined by the dim light.

Something caught my peripheral vision, at my feet, only a few inches away.

It was a hand, the pale flesh glowing visibly against the dark brown of the pine needle carpet. The arm was flung out as if reaching for my legs. With the light I followed the arm to the torso, then the face.

Her eyes seemed to blink.

Then I felt the bile rise in my throat. No wonder Nina was terrified. Ants were crawling out from under her eyelids. Insects scurried away from my light.

I stepped hurriedly away, out of reach of that grasping hand.

The light, which at first just showed her form, now revealed the ravages of a warm summer night. Some creature had nibbled on her outstretched hand, dainty chunks of flesh were missing from the palm.

I jerked the flashlight off her, then abruptly back, afraid the grasping hand would come closer while I wasn't looking.

A dry heave shook my body. I took a deep breath to drive it away. Then I wondered if I was smelling the damp humus or the faint odor of human decay. I almost retched again.

"Joanne!" I suddenly yelled, to remind myself I wasn't here alone in these grisly woods. "Joanne! I'm over here. Follow my voice!"

"Micky," she answered from somewhere that seemed very far away.

"Yeah. This way. Follow the path until you see my light."

I looked at the unknown woman, left in desolate death. She had to be dead, I thought. Would insects devour living flesh? The idea of touching her, brushing off ants to feel for a pulse nauseated me. She has to be dead, I told myself again.

"Micky, where are you?" Joanne called, closer this time.

"Here. Over here."

I didn't recognize the woman. She wasn't one of the guests, I was sure of that. With a jolt, I realized that I had been at almost this same spot earlier in the evening, when I had walked in the woods. Then I remembered the eyes that I had been sure were watching me.

"Joanne!" I shouted, suddenly afraid to be alone in the dim light with only a corpse for company. "Joanne, can you see my light yet? I'm over here."

"On my way. I see you," she answered, responding to my fear.

I could hear her coming through the leaves. Another light joined mine, then Joanne was beside me.

"Oh, Jesus," she said when she saw the body. She moved quickly and professionally, kneeling next to the woman to feel for a pulse. Then just as quickly she stood up, shaking her head.

"She's dead," I said, not really a question.

"For a while," Joanne answered, standing back beside me.

"I couldn't . . . touch her," I whispered, ashamed of my cowardice, "to find out . . ."

"You didn't need to. If she were alive those animal bites would be bleeding. She's been beyond our help for a while now."

"I guess." I didn't know what else to say.

"Joanne?" I heard Alex's voice off somewhere on the path.

"Alex. Don't come here!" Joanne called to her. "Stay where you are."

"Are you okay?" Alex asked.

"Yeah. Just stay away," she yelled, not anger, but protection in her voice. "The police have to be called," Joanne added to me.

"Of course. I'll go tell Emma."

"You can't cover this up. I know that Emma Auerbach's your friend and that a dead body on her property on this night is going to cause a lot of . . ."

"Joanne," I cut her off, "The police will be called. Emma deserves the courtesy of hearing about it before they are, not after, that's all. We can't do anything for . . . her," I indicated the body.

"Sorry, Micky," she apologized. "Go tell Emma. I'm going to change. I don't want to meet the local boys dressed like this."

She took my arm and turned me away from the body.

"Leave her like this?" I asked, too aware of the corpse in the dark behind us.

"Not much we can do for her now," Joanne replied, leading me back to the path.

We walked together, silently out of the woods and to the lawn.

There were some people milling about, more arriving to see what the excitement was about.

I saw Rosie, signaled to her and gave her a brief version of what had happened. "Stay here. Don't let anyone go into the woods," I told her. "I'll be back soon."

I walked away, leaving Rosie on guard, Melanie faithfully at her side.

"Joanne?" Alex questioned as we reached her.

"Let's go change," Joanne said, putting her arm around Alex.

"You okay, Micky?" Alex asked me, as they started to move away.

"Yeah, I'm fine," I answered grimly. Compared to being dead and eaten by insects, I was great.

I walked toward the house to find Emma. As I got to the back porch, I saw Cordelia. She was holding Nina, who looked small and fragile tucked under Cordelia's arm. Cordelia was saying something to her, smoothing her hair back. She didn't see me. I went into the house.

I found Emma in the library. When she saw my face, she broke away from the group she was with and came over to me.

"Let's go to your study," I said, then let her lead the way.

"I imagine it's serious," she said as she closed the door.

I told her about the body. She listened quietly to my narrative. I was as brief as possible. Emma didn't need the details.

"Do you want me to call the police?" I finished.

"No, I will," she answered. "I know Sheriff Hampton. It would be better if I did." She picked up the phone.

"Emma?" I said, wanting desperately to say Miss Auerbach. "I'm sorry this happened. I should have . . . You hired me to take care of things." I felt somehow this horror was my fault. If I hadn't been running around trying to sleep with half the women here . . .

"Don't be nonsensical," she replied, putting the phone down. "I don't blame you for the simple reason that it's not your fault. What were you supposed to do? Run around telling people not to die on my property?"

"I don't think she just died," I said, voicing the undercurrent that neither Joanne nor I had spoken.

"You think she was murdered? Why?"

"I'm probably way off base," I retreated.

"But why?" Emma asked again.

"She was young. Late teens, early twenties. Too young to die easily. And . . . just a feeling," I finished, remembering the eyes I was sure had been watching.

"I hope you're wrong," Emma said, taking my hand and holding it for a moment, then letting it go to pick up the phone again.

"So do I," I said as I let myself out of the study.

I went back outside to the tool shed. I got several flashlights and a Coleman lantern, which I lit. Scare off the ghosts with a barrage of light, Micky?

Then I went back into the woods, nodding at Rosie and the stalwart Melanie on my way. Carrying both the lit lantern and a bright flashlight, to keep the dark away all around me, I went back to the body.

I had to make sure she was still there. Somehow I couldn't leave this dead woman alone in the dark.

I was torn between being afraid that she was gone, only a nightmare haunting the world I thought to be real, and fearing she would still be there, chewed and convulsed by the rapacity of nature during a warm summer night.

She lay as she had, a pale form against the brown bed of pine needles. Insects scurried away from the burning lantern. I tried not to see them. I placed the lights around her, a haphazard box. Nothing could keep out the darkness of death. But the lights could keep the night at bay, a small bit of the darkness she had been so callously thrown into.

I sat down, a few yards away, next to the lantern, the brightest light. She was young, probably not yet twenty. Maybe even pretty when she was alive. A day, a few hours ago? Her hair was dark brown, her makeup now garish on her immobile face. She was wearing a cheap cloth coat, inappropriate for the weather. Her legs were bare. I couldn't tell if she had any clothes on under the coat. Probably not, a cheap cloth coat thrown on to cover her nakedness.

Raped and left here to die, I thought bitterly. Isn't that what usually happened to young women found in the woods? Left to the scavenger ants. Men who do this should have pictures of decaying corpses put on the walls of their prison cells. This is what you did,

67

you were so clever and hid her body so well, this is what it looked like when we finally found it. This is what her parents identified in the morgue, what a woman stumbled over one summer night, what I sat next to because I couldn't leave her all alone, couldn't leave her deathwatch to insects.

I felt a hand on my shoulder and jumped away in startlement.

"Come on, get out of here," Danny said gently. She was dressed soberly now, looking like an assistant D.A.

"I want to at least keep the insects away," I mumbled.

"One of the things that drove me crazy about you was your insistence on being responsible for the sins of the world . . ."

"It's been a long night," I broke in. "Believe it or not, I'm not in the mood for a laundry list of my many faults."

"It was also one of the things that made me fall in love with you, idiot," Danny replied. "But you still need sleep. It's past four in the morning. Be light soon."

"I hope so. I think this night needs to end."

"Guests have been leaving like the proverbial mice on the sinking ship," Danny said.

"I don't blame them. Not too many gay people like to be in the middle of a police investigation. Isn't Joanne raising hell?"

"Not her jurisdiction. I gather the local sheriff said they could go. Poor Nina gets to stay and give a statement."

"How is she?"

"She'll be okay. She's tougher than she looks. Just not used to tripping over bodies in the moonlight."

"Like the rest of us."

"Yeah," Danny agreed. "Not a good way to end a party."

"You don't have to stay. This is my obsession," I said.

I heard Joanne's voice. It was her professional voice, cool, almost toneless. She was talking to the local police and leading them here.

"A-ha. The cavalry," Danny said.

"Much too late," I answered.

The police arrived, bringing voices and lights everywhere. There was nothing more I could do. I went back to the lawn. Sending Rosie and Melanie to bed, I took up the guard post to keep away the idly curious. Few people came by, most staying away from this part of the yard. A lot of people had left. More were leaving as I stood my watch.

"Mick? They want to talk to you," Joanne said, coming up behind me.

I followed her back into the woods. But this time I didn't go near the body. I could do no more for her. I told them my story (leaving out what Joanne and I had been doing when we first heard Nina's screams). They nodded silently and wrote it down. Then Danny led me away.

"Get some sleep, Mick," she said. "You look like shit."

"Thanks, Danno."

We walked out of the woods together.

"Goodnight," she said, hugging me tightly, then yawning, she turned toward her cottage.

" 'Night, Danny," I answered, glad for a friend like her.

I walked back to the house, tired, but knew I couldn't sleep. The first gray light of dawn was visible, finally fighting the dark night .

I went to the kitchen to see if there was anyone around. But the room was dim and deserted, people gone or gone to bed. There were no voices, no creaking floor boards to indicate anyone about.

I stood in the silent kitchen, wanting to put something between me and the scene in the woods. My hands were trembling. I found a bottle of Scotch. I went back outside, heading in the opposite direction from where the police surrounded the lonely body.

Dawn was still only a gray reflection of the sun. I walked down a trail into the forest to a clearing where I knew the sun would soon shine. The stump of an old oak tree, destroyed by lightning a long time ago was there. I sat down on it, setting the bottle beside me.

The first tendrils of light found their way through the trees. A pale golden dawn. I sat still, listening to the wakening birds calling one another to the morning.

Death hits hard. It always does. She was younger than I.

"Well, you were right about one thing," I said to myself, "You didn't get to sleep with anyone tonight." I was talking out loud to hear the sound of my voice. I sounded cracked and tired, not like the brave sophisticate I wanted to be. I looked at the bottle, but I didn't pick it up. Instead I watched the rising sun as it colored in the glade.

"Drunk enough yet?" Joanne said from behind me. "I saw you cut across the lawn with a bottle."

I turned my head toward her, too benumbed by the night's

69

events to jerk or even be startled at her abrupt appearance. She had taken a shower. Her hair was still wet, her eyes a veiled gray behind her glasses.

"Why don't you put the bottle away and get some sleep?"

"I'd have to be very drunk to sleep. Too drunk to wake from nightmares."

"Shit," Joanne muttered, shaking her head. "You might be a decent person if you weren't a drunken fuck-up," she added angrily.

"Half-right. Yeah, I'm a fuck-up, but at least this time I'm not drunk. I haven't been drunk in a while."

I picked up the bottle and put it between us. Joanne lifted the Scotch and examined the unbroken seal.

"How long?" she finally said.

"Two months."

She didn't say anything, still looking at the bottle as if she didn't believe me.

"I know it's not much," I said. "Not enough to bother mentioning . . ."

"It's a start. I'm sorry for jumping on you."

"It's okay. I'm sure I've done something to deserve it."

"No, you haven't. Not tonight."

"Well . . ." I looked at her. "No need to pin any medals on me yet."

"Two months . . ." Joanne said, then broke off. She walked to the edge of the clearing, then turned back to me. "My father drank himself into his grave. He was fifty-four when he died. My mother . . . I can't remember her sober. I finally gave up hoping that one day she might call me and not be drunk. After twenty years of being disappointed every time I heard her voice, I just had to give up."

"I'm sorry," I said.

"Life goes on," she shrugged, walking back to me. "How do you feel?"

"I feel . . . Oh, God, Joanne," I suddenly blurted out, "I can't sleep because I finally feel things. When I would get hurt or scared before I would drink it away. Now . . ." I stopped and held out my hand, watching it shake. "What does it feel like to die so young? How do you do it? Do you get used to it?"

"No, I've never gotten used to it. I don't think I ever will," Joanne replied. She reached out and took my trembling hand between both of hers, holding it steady. "Tragedies happen every day. It's inevitable that we stumble over them."

"Was it murder or tragedy?"

"What's the difference? Every murdered person is a tragedy in someone's life."

"Was she?" I persisted.

"Yes."

"Raped?"

"Probably."

I shuddered at the common horror of it. "Can you find out?" I wanted to know this women's fate, the final details. Knowing, no matter how brutal, would be better than imagining.

"Yes, I can," Joanne answered.

"Tell me."

"I will."

"Maybe I should try to get some sleep," I said shakily. I was suddenly aware that Joanne looked tired. She hadn't been to bed yet either. I didn't think she would leave me alone in the woods with my Scotch and trembling hands.

"Do you want me to hold you?"

"No, I'm okay," I lied. Joanne, behind her glasses, dressed in the sober clothes of a policewoman, seemed too distant. I wasn't sure just who the woman was who kissed me last night, but she had vanished with the morning light.

"Look at me. Look at me and say that," she caught me.

I couldn't. I glanced across the clearing. Joanne put her hand under my chin and turned my face back to her.

"I'm not okay. How the hell can you be?" she said.

I started crying. Joanne put her arms around me.

"Do you want me to make love to you?" she asked with simple directness.

Of course, I wanted her to make love to me, more now than last night. My desire had gone frighteningly beyond want to need.

"No," I said, afraid to be so vulnerable. Then, "How did you know?" and finally, "Yes . . . yes, I do."

She took off her glasses. Her eyes were unhidden, the flecks of blue in the dense gray brought out by the morning light. Then she kissed me, slowly, no haste or hurry, no sense of obligation on her part, not blatantly sexual.

But desire could not long remain absent. I put my arms around her, pulling her tightly to me, wanting the taunt edge of passion to blunt my thoughts. Joanne responded to my need, her kisses not longer gentle, but heavy, fierce. She pushed me back so that I lay across the stump, feeling its rough ridges as her weight pressed down on me.

She opened my shirt, exposing my breasts to the morning light and the touch of her hands. Leaving my mouth wet and open, she moved her lips to my nipples, tonguing them as her hands undid my pants.

I felt the pressure of her hand cover me, first over the cotton of my underwear, then flesh on flesh, her fingers twining in my hair. Her other hand pulled my pants down, pinning me between the cool roughness of the stump and the warm smoothness of her hand spreading my lips. Her mouth was on my stomach, moving down. Then her tongue went between my lips, her hands pushing on my thighs, spreading my legs open.

I gasped at her probings, the suck and tickle of her lips, the breeze that pulled at the wet spots her movement left open to it. I shuddered, then unbidden, through the relaxation of sensual pleasure, the stark image of the woman eaten and flayed by the creatures of night, struck me, catching and jerking my thoughts away from the present morning to the past night.

I lay still, trying to push the macabre image aside, to immerse myself in the merely physical. But I couldn't. The harder I tried to thrust her memory aside, the more insistent the image became. Until I sat halfway up, to tell Joanne to stop.

"I'm sorry," I said. "I just don't seem able to . . ." I trailed off. Stop thinking of a dead woman.

"Want me to try something different?" she offered.

"No, that's okay."

"Is it something I did?"

"No," I answered quickly, not wanting her to think it was her failure, when it was mine alone. "No, you're great. It's me. I can't help thinking . . . about the scene in the woods."

"I see," she replied. "Try something for me?"

"Sure, if you want. But you really don't need to waste . . ."

"I'm not wasting anything," Joanne cut me off. "Lie back down." I did. "Watch the trees, the light through the branches. Now, the only thing you can think of is what I do between your legs. I want you to concentrate on that. Understand?"

"Yes," I replied.

I felt Joanne's mouth cover me, warming where the breeze had threatened to cool. Then her tongue, a hard spot in the midst of her warmth. I closed my eyes, feeling only what she was doing to me, the pure carnal pleasure of her long strokes moving against me. Up again and away, until all I knew were a few inches of flesh and the rising heat from her friction. Then she touched me, held me, sent a bolt of sensation through me, a feeling that was pleasure, but more than that, release, a powerful relinquishing of tension, holding me until I had to jerk up and roll away from her, having nothing more to let go of.

I lay motionless, gradually becoming aware of the call and cry of morning birds, and Joanne beside me, holding me.

"Thank you," I finally said.

"I like you, Micky," she replied. It was the best thing she could have said. Then she pulled a handkerchief out of one of her pockets and gently wiped me off. She stood up. "Time to head back. The others will be looking for us before they leave."

"What about you?" I asked as I sat up.

"You owe me."

"Of course, I do. But aren't you . . . ?" I asked.

"A bit. Alex and I made love earlier. She knows to expect it whenever I have to go look at dead people."

"Oh," I said, nonplused at her admission. "I feel like I took advantage of you," I finally said.

"Hardly. Remember I offered."

"That doesn't mean I didn't."

"Micky, needs and emotions are such a tangle, particularly sex, at times, it's impossible to say who's right or wrong. Do you feel used?"

"No, I don't. I feel a hell of a lot better than I did an hour ago."

"So do I. Why don't we leave it at that?"

"Okay," I said. "Thank you."

"I think Danny's going to hang around for a while. But I know

Alex and Nina want to get out of here as soon as they can," she said as we started walking back to the house.

"Poor Nina," I said, remembering the abject terror on her face as she stumbled from the woods. "Nothing like walking into the scene of a horror movie."

We were back on the lawn. I could see Danny and Elly over near their car. Then Cordelia, Alex, and Nina appeared from around the house carrying suitcases. We walked up to the cars, Joanne's parked next to Danny's, Cordelia's several yards away.

Danny eyed the bottle of Scotch that I was carrying back with me. I put it in her trunk.

"Here, you look like you need this more than I do," I said.

She picked up the bottle, examined it, then shrugged her shoulders and put it back in the trunk.

"Have you had any sleep at all?" Cordelia asked, coming up behind me.

"No. I couldn't sleep. It's okay. I'm used to these kinds of hours," I joked to hide my discomfort at her presence, sure it was obvious I just had sex with Joanne.

"You look tired," she said.

"So do you," I replied, glancing at her. Her hair was wet and brushed back from a recent shower, but her eyes were bloodshot and circled.

"I am. I thought I would catch up on my sleep this weekend."

"Go home and take a nap," I advised. I didn't like to see her so tired, no glint in her blue eyes.

"You heading back?"

"No, I'm going to stay out here and help Emma. Clean up and stuff."

"Come on, C.J., time to blow this joint," Alex called to her.

"Take care, Micky," she said.

"You, too," I answered, then half-turned, pretending it was perfectly okay for Cordelia to leave, that our good-bye wasn't important. Too late, I saw her start to lift her arms to hug me, then quickly drop back, when I moved away. She went back to her car.

"Get home safely," Elly said as she got in. Nina joined her in the back seat.

Alex hugged Joanne good-bye. Then, with an indecipherable

glance at me, she said, "See you back in town, Micky. Don't get into any trouble. So long, Danny." Then she got into Cordelia's car.

It doesn't count, Alex, I silently said to the disappearing car. This morning doesn't count. It wasn't a rough act of passion, adultery, if you will. It was the only way to stop my hands from shaking.

Joanne, Danny, and I looked at each other. A cop, a lawyer, and a P. I. We could be a TV series. Except none of us looked plastic enough.

"Get to bed, Mick," Danny said. "No one wants to see your face around here."

"Good morning to you, too, dear Danno," I answered.

"Anything going on?" Joanne asked, with a nod of her head in the direction of the thicket were the dead woman lay.

"They carted her away almost an hour ago," Danny said. "The police are combing the woods. Looks like some mother's going to know for sure what happened to her daughter."

Joanne nodded somberly.

"Not much really for us to do. Emma Auerbach can handle these guys," Danny continued.

Joanne and Danny didn't need to stay. I knew they were doing it out of friendship.

"Let's see if we can find some coffee," I said, leading the way to the kitchen. I left Joanne and Danny there while I went to change my clothes. That would make it less obvious that I had been up all night. After scrubbing my face and brushing my teeth, I headed back to the kitchen. More people were there, some of the policemen, most of the college kids. Rachel was fixing coffee.

Conversation was tired and inconsequential. No one wanted to talk about why we were gathered in the kitchen. The guests that hadn't left last night were going now.

The aftermath of death can be so banal. Coffee, food, getting home, the weather. Or perhaps it is death that makes the details that follow seem so minor.

Most of the police left sometime late in the morning. Joanne and Danny soon followed them. I spent the day working with the college kids, cleaning up the remains of the aborted party. None of us went near the woods.

At around five, Rachel told me to go see Emma in her study. When I got there, she was tearing a check out of her checkbook and handing it to one of the college students. She motioned for me to sit while she finished paying the last two of them.

I suddenly realized how tired I was as I sat waiting for her. I looked around the room, attempting to keep myself from nodding too obviously. Then I noticed a check on Emma's desk with a signature I recognized. Cordelia James, it said. The check was made out to the pro-choice group that Emma worked with. According to Rachel, Emma's mother had known Margaret Sanger. Working for reproduction rights was a family tradition. Of course Cordelia would be donating to pro-choice with her clinic picketed as it was. She could afford it.

Rhett startled me by saying good-bye. I shook his hand and mumbled some appropriate farewell (I hope).

The students left, leaving me with Emma. Her head was bent over her checkbook, writing what I presumed to be my check.

She looked up, tearing out and handing the check to me in one swift motion. I put it away without looking at it.

"Did you get any sleep last night?" she asked.

"A little," I hedged.

"Do you want a ride back? Rachel and I decided that we would leave today. No one feels like staying here. I could get one of the students to drive your car back."

"No, that's okay. I'm fine," I lied. I didn't want Emma to know how tired I was. I stood up to go, before my nodding head betrayed me.

"Micky," she called as I started to leave. "Thank you for all you've done."

"It wasn't much."

"Still . . . I do wish we had gotten a chance to talk."

"Yes, so do I," I said. "I'll see you in the city, sometime," I added as my farewell.

"I'd like that," Emma's voice trailed me into the hallway.

I went to my room, moving quickly to keep my weariness at bay. I threw my clothes into a suitcase and without even a final glance around, I went out, stopping only for a hasty good-bye to Rachel.

Then I was in my car and heading back to the city. I don't know how I managed to stay awake driving over the Causeway. The only thing I distinctly recall was driving on Elysian Fields and being struck with the incongruity of the name, with a dead body so close in my memory. Was there a paradise waiting for her? And how had she ended up so close to where I had stood only a few hours before? What had I almost seen?

I was too tired to think about it.

Chapter 6

The image of the dead woman continued to haunt me. I had stayed with her too long on that night to let go of her easily. I needed something to distract me. Bars and casual sex came to mind, but I talked myself out of it, wanting to be sober when Joanne called to tell me what had happened to the young woman.

On Thursday I got my distraction. A phone call from Cordelia. Rather a message on my machine, asking me to call her. Her work number, I assumed, since I didn't recognize it. I had stared at her home number, unable to call, so many times that I had it memorized. Even though it was evening, I called the number she had left. I let it ring ten times before giving up.

I wasted a considerable amount of time trying to decide whether or not to call her at home. I finally, after chastising myself for being an indecisive wimp, convinced myself to wait until tomorrow and call her at the number she had left.

I called the next morning, at what I hoped was early enough to be professional, but not so early as to seem anxious.

Dr. James was with a patient. I left my name and number. Then I debated as to whether I should stay around my apartment or deliberately not be there for her call. If this was love, maybe I was fortunate to have avoided it for so long.

The phone rang. I started to grab it, then stopped and let it ring three full rings before I picked it up.

"M. Knight, P.I.," I answered, trying to sound cool and business-like.

"Hi, Micky. Cordelia."

"Hi, how are you?"

"I'm . . ." then she broke off, talking to someone in the back-ground. It sounded like a discussion about medication.

"Busy, I gather," I said when I heard her back on the line.

"Yes." Then there was an awkward pause. She continued, "I need a private investigator."

I almost said, "And you're hiring me?" What I did say was, "Why?"

"Can we meet? I'd prefer not to discuss some things over the phone."

"All right. When and where?" I was hoping she would say tonight, my place.

"How about Monday? Here at the clinic?"

"Is that what this is about?"

"More or less," she answered. "I'll fill you in on Monday. Is that okay?"

"Sure," I replied. There was nothing else to say. We set a time for Monday and she gave me directions. And that was that.

I stared at the receiver and wondered what Cordelia wanted me for and how to pass the time until I found out. Monday. I put the receiver down.

If I didn't figure out some way to keep occupied, I knew I would convolute myself into a knot trying to guess what she wanted. And by Monday afternoon have landed on every possibility, but the right one.

I could do bills and other boring detective stuff, but that's never been my ideal way to spend the day. I did manage to get part of the expense report for my last job completed. But something more distracting than routine paper work was required.

Books. I made the long, arduous trek to the library, trusting in divine faith that my card wasn't expired. I picked up an assortment of Dorothy Sayers. Some of her Lord Peter Wimsey books, not so much for detective ideas, but for dating tips. How did Lord Peter get Harriet Vane to marry him? Also, to the amazement of the librarian, the Sayers translation of Dante's Divine Comedy. Hell, the fun one. I wanted to keep all parts of my mind occupied.

By late afternoon, I had ascertained via Lord Peter, that the method for making a woman fall in love with an offbeat detective was to save her from the gallows by proving her innocent. Somehow that didn't seem to have much bearing on Cordelia and myself.

I gave up on reading, not feeling much wiser.

The phone rang. I grabbed it.

"I'm coming over in around twenty minutes. I have information for you," the voice on the other end said. It took me a second or two to recognize it over the traffic noises in the background. Joanne. And her information could only be about the woman in the woods.

"I'll be here," I replied.

"Good," was her only response.

Thirty minutes later, the phone rang again.

"I'm held up," Joanne said, again not waiting for my greeting. "I don't know when I'll get away."

"I'll be here. Come over if you're not too tired." I didn't think I could stand waiting for too many more things. Even bad news about dead people.

"Don't wait up." She hung up.

When 9:30 arrived and Joanne still hadn't shown up, I gave up on her. I called her number, just to check, but there was no answer. Probably still working.

It was my bath time. Mornings I take showers, in the evening, I allow myself the luxury of stretching out in the bathtub when I have the time. Which I certainly had now. I have one of those old Victorian models, complete with paws, large enough for me to stretch out in.

I undressed and ambled into the bathroom, running water to fill the tub. I used to, on long nights like this one, sit in the tub for perhaps an hour, sipping Scotch.

Maybe now that I'm not drinking, I can afford to run the air conditioner more often, I thought brightly as I stepped into the tub. The water felt good, as it coolly soaked away the day's sweat and grime. Everyone deserves a bathtub they can stretch out their legs in.

I finally stopped my soaping and splashing, letting my body sink and relax in the water.

In the silence, I heard the sound of footsteps. Inside my apartment. I've always wondered if it would be difficult to kick a burglar while clutching a towel around your body. But it was not something I had particularly wanted to put to the test.

"Who the fuck is it?" I yelled, hoping the ominous tone of my voice would scare away any burglars. That and the fact that there was nothing to steal.

"There you are," my burglar answered. Joanne. I breathed a sigh of relief. She did have a key for occasional cat feedings.

"You scared the shit out of me," I retorted.

She opened the door and looked at me.

"Funny, the water doesn't look brown," she said, but her voice still had the tight quality I had heard earlier. "Do you know how that girl died?" she continued.

"No, but I guess you're going to tell me." She came into the bathroom, pacing back and forth, in and out of my sightline. "I don't gather it was very pleasant," I said. She seemed oblivious to my sitting naked in the bathtub.

"A botched abortion," she said, abruptly ceasing her pacing, but still not appearing to be really aware of me.

"What?" I questioned. Botched abortions were a thing of the past, I thought, now that they are legal.

"If she had been taken to a hospital, instead of dumped in the woods, she would still be alive," Joanne said, the tightness slipping, the anger coming through.

"Why?" I was still trying to comprehend how someone died from botched abortions in this day and age.

"Any number of reasons. No ID of the doctor, no malpractice, no license check, none of them worth shit."

She started pacing again.

"Joanne . . ." I said, but she was out of my sight. I stopped, trying to form questions.

"Victoria Edith Williams. Vicky. Eighteen," Joanne said, her voice still angry. "Graduated from high school last week. The youngest of four children." She was back in my view again. "Wanted to be an airline stewardess, so she could see the world," Joanne continued, still walking. "Maybe not the loftiest ambition, but, damn, it was hers. Besides, we'd all be in trouble if we were judged on our ambitions at eighteen."

"Joanne," I repeated, trying again to slow her down. "Why are you so angry?" I blurted out.

"Because," she said, and she stopped to look right at me, "she doesn't get any second chances. Some incompetent quack takes a few belts or hits or whatever and his hand slips. He dumps her in the woods to die, rather than risk her telling someone in some ER that he smelled like gin or something. Fucking bastard." Her voice was loud and harsh, a cold fury lurking beneath the words. She started her pacing again, trying to relieve the anger with motion, it seemed.

"Joanne . . . I'm sorry." It was all I could think to say, because I was thinking about other things. My walk in the woods just before the party. Why didn't I go back and look?

"No, I'm sorry," Joanne replied. "Barging in like this, foul tempered." Her pacing slowed, but didn't stop.

"I . . . Something was there," I said. "I was there, in the woods around eight."

"What?" Joanne stopped to look at me.

"I . . . I'm not sure. I felt I was being watched."

"Did you see something? Anything at all?"

"No . . . nothing." I picked at my memory, trying to see what it was, a shape, a color, but nothing showed. "I don't know. Maybe a sound, something at the edge of perception."

"Really just a feeling?" she questioned.

"Yeah . . . I guess. I should have gone back to check it out."

"Don't you start," Joanne said brusquely.

"Start what?" I retorted.

"If only—why didn't I—the standard crap."

"If I'd followed my instincts, maybe Vicky Williams would be alive today," I shouted at her, stung by her harshness. "If . . ."

"Not likely," she cut me off. "Pardon my interrupting with reality. She was from Marrero. Probably had the abortion done in the city. That fucking shithead managed to hit the uterine artery. She probably went into shock within a few minutes. If she was lucky. And she probably died in the trunk of a car somewhere on the Lake Pontchartrain Causeway."

"Then what the hell was in the woods?" I was still shouting. Joanne, was in all likelihood, right. My anger was now at my help-lessness. That this young woman had died needlessly and that there was nothing I could have done to prevent it.

"Probably a squirrel," Joanne answered and resumed her pacing.

"Too big," I retorted.

"Yeah, right," she said from out of my vision. "You planning to turn into a pickled P.I., or are you going to get out of that tub any-time soon?" She was still out of sight.

"I didn't have a chance to finish scrubbing when you barged in."

"Should I wait outside while you finish?"

"No," I replied. "Here, be useful. Scrub my back." I tossed a washrag in the direction of her voice.

"Bend forward," she said.

I obeyed.

"Wash, not flay. I need that layer of skin."

"Sorry. Just trying to get the dirt off."

But her washing was gentler when she resumed. I became aware of her touch, how close she was. Where her breath hit the damp spots on the back of my neck. The abrupt appearance of desire shook me.

I had lied to Alex. No, to myself. The first time, in the woods, had been for comfort, friendship. Not now, not this time. This time counted. Desire flared. I became acutely aware of my nakedness, the water lapping at my nipples, making them hard. Joanne had to notice.

I felt the washrag slide into the tub behind me, but the pressure of her hand remained on my back. I wondered vaguely what I would say to Alex the next time I saw her. But here, with the insistent press of Joanne's hand on my back, it didn't seem important.

Her hand moved to my shoulder.

I turned to face her.

There was nothing to say. Her arms went around me, holding me roughly, and we kissed. I didn't know if I should hold her, get her wet with my damp arms, but her kisses demanded more response than I could give with only my tongue and mouth.

Then abruptly, and it was all beginning to feel too abrupt, too rapid for my emotions to ride, she broke away, standing up and stepping back, partly out of my sight.

As there had been no words for the start, there were none now. I wondered what I had done, then wondered if it had anything to do with me, as angry and upset as Joanne had been a few minutes ago.

"Let the water out," she said.

I twisted around to look at her. She had taken off her shirt. I kicked out the stopper with my foot, not wanting to turn from her. She moved back toward me, closer, inviting me to watch her. She kicked off her shoes with a rough impatience, then slowly unzipped her pants. Coming even closer, so I could touch if I wanted, she took them off.

"Don't forget your watch," I said.

As she started to undo the band, I leaned forward, keeping my hands on the rim of the bathtub. I kissed her on the V of her underwear, pressing against the mound hidden by white cotton. I left a wet mark.

Joanne quickly pulled off her underwear. She stepped into the tub, first one foot, then the other, placing them both between my legs. She stood over me for a moment, letting the tension build.

I looked at her above me. She still wore her glasses, keeping me uncertain about what was in her eyes.

Bracing her hands on the tub, she lowered herself, slowly, making me watch her. Her strong shoulders, her small breasts, erect and firm. Her knees pressed on the inside of my thighs, opening my legs.

The water was dangerously close to the rim of the tub, prompting a thought about my irregular schedule of drain cleaning. Then Joanne put a hand on my breast and drains became monumentally unimportant.

Her palm pressed into my flesh, then both hands pushed my breasts together. I gasped. She pushed harder.

This would be no gentle, lacy love-making. I'd hardly expected that of Joanne. And I realized, as I thrust my breasts back at her pressing hands, I wanted the coarseness, the full physical brunt of sex. A few bruises in the morning wouldn't be out of place.

I put my hands on her hips, pulling her toward me, not even bothering to wonder if the tub would overflow. She let her weight tip and be carried on the hands pressing into my breasts. Just when the pressure was almost too much, when I would have had to pull away, she released me, letting her body lay across mine. Only now did she remove her glasses. We kissed again, making every part of our bodies touch. I ran my hand down her back, feeling the scar under her shoulder. My hands moved, until I was cupping her ass with both my hands. Then I started to slide one hand between her cheeks, exploring, searching for the opening to her vagina. But she shook her head no, not letting me in, giving me no control.

She took her mouth away from mine, moving it to my breasts, sucking hard on one nipple, twisting the other between her fingers. Then her hand moved to my thighs, forcing my legs to spread. Water still covered my bush. I expected her fingers to enter me, but she didn't. She took a breath and her tongue was suddenly between my legs, insistently prying me to even greater openness. Several long strokes left me gasping, then she came up for air. A quick breath, then she was between my legs again.

The water drained slowly. She had to lift her head for a breath again. The insistent warmth of her tongue was on me again, forcing me to thrash in the ebbing water. Her arms wrapped around my thighs, holding me in place. The water finally drained out, all but a few puddles sucking wetly beneath me as I moved. I could watch Joanne now, her mouth covering me, her hair undone, fanning out over my thighs. Her tongue, her lips, either or both, I was no longer sure, pressed into me, sucking and stroking, until I couldn't know whether to pull away or push to her. No matter, her arms held me where I was, stronger than the spasms that shook my body. She had my legs spread as wide as they could be in the confines of the bathtub.

I heard myself let out a long moan and I knew I had no control. I'm usually aware of how my body responds, the noise I make, but not tonight. This was too intense for me to do anything but gasp and jerk and wonder for a brief second how much more I could take.

"Joanne," I cried, oblivious to anything but her touch.

Then wave after wave of sensation rocked through my body. My orgasm blotted out sight and sound. Joanne had been between my legs, eating me, then she was next to me, holding me, gently kissing my cheek, my forehead, my mouth. I couldn't recall her moving.

For a moment, I was afraid, unsure of what I had said and done in that brief oblivion. Then afraid of anything that had that much power. As if drinking and fucking around the way you used to was any better, I told myself. There were times when I had lost track of hours, even days, not brief moments. But they hadn't mattered.

My breath lengthened, returned to normal.

"You survive?" Joanne asked.

"Ask me in the morning," I answered, then I tightened my arms around her, aware of her body.

She slowly moved from beside me to on top of me. Her hands were on my shoulders, gently pushing me down. She lifted herself while I slid between her legs until my head was poised beneath her, ready to suck the glistening drops of water that clung to her. God, did I want to do this, I realized, as I spread her lips, pausing for a moment to gaze at the inviting flesh. I put my mouth to her, my tongue gently licking.

I wanted to please Joanne, to make all the right moves. It wasn't something I had worried about before. I strained, listening for her to make noise, her heavy breathing, but it was hard with her thighs covering my ears.

"Is this all right?" I finally asked.

"Just keep going."

"Anything you want me to do differently?"

"No."

I started again. I felt her hand touch my face, a reassuring gesture, brushing hair off my forehead. Then her fingers stiffened and she gasped, then gasped again. She lowered herself slightly, opening to me. Now I could hear her breathing, ragged and harsh. Then I heard an intake of breath, a silence, her body taunt and still, then her breath rushed out as she shuddered.

I knew that was it. Even in sex, Joanne was quiet and controlled. At least with me. I gently kissed her a few more times, letting her be the one to move away.

She did, lying next to me for a few minutes, then standing up. She extended a hand to me, to pull me up.

"Let's dry off," she said as she stepped out of the tub.

"Good idea," I answered.

She threw me a towel. We dried ourselves, saying little.

"Should I go, or do you want me to stay?" she finally asked.

"Stay. If you want," I replied, not sure which scared me more. She nodded what I guessed was agreement.

"You hungry?" I asked, trying to be a decent host.

"No. Tired. Are you?"

"No, just trying to be polite."

"Don't. Polite isn't your natural state," Joanne answered. "And I'm too worn out for it tonight."

"Okay. Do you want to borrow something to sleep in?"

"No. Unless you have some objection."

"Me? No," I replied. Joanne was right, polite hosting was not one of my strong points.

"Can I borrow your toothbrush?"

"Help yourself."

I left her in the bathroom and made a quick check of my bed, not wanting to find any of Hepplewhite's clever little surprises. She was innocently asleep at the foot of the bed. The sheets were in company condition.

Joanne came into the room. She hadn't dressed, instead she had wrapped a towel around herself and draped her clothes over one arm. Those she neatly laid over the back of the one chair in the room.

"Are you sure you want me to stay?" she asked. "Sometimes I can be . . ." And she faltered. Joanne Ranson didn't say a lot, but I'd never seen her at a loss for words.

"An aggressive, overbearing bitch?" I supplied, unable to leave Joanne groping for words. If it wasn't a night for me to be polite, neither was it a night for her to be unsure.

"Something like that," she replied.

"Those rumors are exaggerated. Stay. I'd like your company." Disconcerted as I was by the probing of her gray eyes, I preferred them to dismissal. I wanted Joanne to like me well enough to stay the night.

She nodded, not saying anything, but she pulled back the covers and got into my bed.

I went into the bathroom to quickly brush my teeth. I also left some food for Hep, so she wouldn't be too meddlesome in the morning. After turning out the lights and making sure my door was locked, I went back into my bedroom and got into bed beside Joanne.

She put her arms around me and hugged me very tightly. I returned her embrace, then wanting more, kissed her. She broke off.

"I'm sorry. I really am very tired," she apologized. "I wasn't too rough earlier, was I? I did come storming in here."

"Naw, I'm used to a few bruises," I answered, brushing it off, trying to be casual about her refusal.

"You that kind of girl?" she asked, giving me a questioning look.

"No, not often," I answered.

"Anything you haven't done?" Joanne asked, still appraising me.

"No elephants, I swear," I joked to turn aside her queries. I doubted that Joanne would approve of my sexual history. I wasn't sure that I did. "At least none that I can remember," I added, still joking to fill the silence.

"It's okay," she replied, then touched me, briefly, on the cheek. "See you in the morning." She rolled over to fall asleep.

She was tired. It took only a minute or two before I heard her steady breathing.

I lay awake, wondering for one panicked minute what I was doing sleeping with Joanne. Imagining Danny's disapproval, Alex's anger, and Cordelia . . . I backed away. Joanne was here. It was too late to escape the consequences of it.

I looked at her, sleep doing little to relieve the tiredness and strain etched on her face. And I realized that there was no way I could have said no to her. Not if she wanted me.

We made love again in the morning, sex that rapidly turned hot and sweaty, no less intense than that of the night before. For both of us, though in different way, I suspected, it was an escape, a release from the everyday. Even a lover, after a certain time together, becomes everyday. Perhaps Joanne needed the passion of the illicit, that tug of desire from areas off-limits. I wanted to ask, "What about Alex? What will she think? Does she know? Will she know? Are you tired of her?" But I couldn't. Something in Joanne said not to ask, not to intrude between our sweaty and gasping bodies.

Later we went out for brunch, being sure, (at my suggestion, I must admit), to avoid a place where we might run into Danny. But still we talked of nothing substantial. I asked no questions and Joanne ventured no answers.

She drove me back to my place, stopping next to a parked car.

"Well, it was fun," I said, with a forced jauntiness. "Thanks for brunch." She had paid. I started to get out, not wanting any messy lingering.

"Micky," she stopped me. "Thank you. I don't know what else to say."

"I owed you. Remember?"

She shrugged off my answer.

I got out.

"Can I call you?" she asked through the car window.

"Yes. Call me. I would like that," I replied, knowing what she meant.

" 'Bye, Mick. I'll let you know if I find out anything more about Vicky Williams."

"Good-bye, Joanne."

She pulled away. I watched her drive off. We hadn't mentioned the dead woman's name since that first conversation last night. For a few brief hours we had forgotten about her.

Joanne was probably going to her office. I was left to spend the rest of the weekend remembering Vicky Williams.

Dante wasn't much of a distraction. Not that I had thought he would be.

Chapter 7

Monday inched by, morning creeping into afternoon. My appointment with Cordelia was at five-thirty. After office hours, I presumed.

Around four-thirty I decided that motion was required. I got in my car and headed for the clinic. I took the long way there, using side streets. Then I drove around the neighborhood for awhile, checking it out. In its better days, it may have been middle class, but those days were long gone. All that remained was a shabby gentility on some of the older buildings. They alternated with empty lots, already crumbling new buildings and ramshackle clapboard, built with no intention of permanency. The clinic itself was on the corner of a busy avenue. It had been built, perhaps as a school, in the red brick style of an earlier age. Attempts had been made to make it look taken care of—a new sign out front, already graffitied, some recently planted shrubs, but I didn't think the trash around their roots was meant as fertilizer.

I pulled into the potholed parking lot at five-o-five. I sat in my car for a few minutes, reluctant to be so early. Instead I told myself it would be useful to watch the people who went in and out of the building.

I didn't see any anti-abortion protesters about. Probably too late in the day for them. People that self-righteous had to be early risers.

The door opened. A nun came out. A nun? Out of a building that was a hot target for right-to-lifers? There was a Catholic church a block away, but this still didn't strike me as a nun hangout.

Time to find out what was going on. I got out of my car, made sure it was locked (didn't want those nuns stealing any of the lesbian porn that I always kept on my back seat), and headed for the building.

The first few rooms I passed were filled with secondhand toys and battered children's books. A few kids were still here waiting for their parents, some contentedly, others less so. Farther down the hall were some classrooms that had been divided into offices. Several of them on the left side of the hall had crosses in them. Curiouser and curiouser.

The clinic occupied the last part of the building, but only the right side.

A harried-looking, young receptionist took my name, telling me that Dr. James was with a patient and would I please wait.

I sat down. Few people were here. A sign promised late hours Tuesday and Thursday evenings. The receptionist was filling out assorted paperwork, making a slight dent in the pile on her desk. Every once in a while a nurse came out of one of the examining rooms. I remembered that Elly had said she worked here evenings and some afternoons, but I didn't see her.

I glanced at my watch. It was almost six o'clock. I got up and paced around, going out to the main hall.

One of the office doors opened. Another nun. What was going on here, I wondered. She locked the door. Evidently she belonged here. Then I realized that she looked familiar. A face from my years with Aunt Greta and all those masses I was forced to attend. Sister?

I probed my memory. Something with an A. She turned and walked out.

I heard voices back in the clinic. The last patient was emerging from one of the rooms. She was followed by the nurse I had seen earlier. Cordelia came slowly out of the examining room, writing something on a chart. She didn't notice me.

I headed in her direction. "Doctor, insanity runs in my family. It seems to have run into me. Can I be cured?" I asked loudly, getting her attention. Being nervous can bring out the worst of my flippancy.

"Oh, hi, Micky," Cordelia said, looking up. She looked tired, but my antics did bring a hint of a smile to her lips.

"Or will I always be like this, hopelessly inane?" I continued.

"It's okay, Betty, I know this character," Cordelia said to the nurse. "Yes, you're hopeless. My office," and she pointed me into a room at the end of the hall. "I'll be with you in a minute."

I went into her office while she conferred with Nurse Betty. Probably to assure her that I was harmless. Her desk, like the receptionist's was covered with paperwork waiting to be done. Cordelia hadn't spent much time decorating—an Impressionist calendar, a few prints on the wall, Van Gogh sunflowers, that was it. And on her desk a picture of a marmalade kitten.

She entered.

"Have a seat," she said as she walked to her desk and sat down.

"So . . ." I said, not sure what question to ask first.

"Here, look at these," she said, rummaging in one of her drawers for a few seconds. She handed me several sheets of paper. "Chronological order," she added.

I looked at the papers. My first glance told me they had been done on a cheap dot-matrix printer. Then I started reading.

My dear Dr. James,
So your grandpa left you money. How convenient. Money buys a lot of things. You're too tall and ugly for anyone to want to fuck. The money will help your sex life. That cunt of yours must have really been itching while you waited for him to kick the bucket. But you took such good care of him he died two years sooner than anyone would have thought possible.

"This is crap," I said, looking up at her, not bothering to finish.

"I know."

"Are they all like this?"

"Pretty much. That was one of the first ones. One of the first I knew about."

I looked at the other ones. They were addressed to other staff members. I came across a second one to Cordelia. This one wasn't just nasty, but threatening, ending with, "We'll take pity on you and fuck you. We'll just have to cut a foot or so off to make you short enough."

"Obviously some man who's threatened by tall women," I commented. "Has anything happened?"

"Phone calls started about a week ago."

"The same sort of thing? How about a trace?" I asked.

"Pay phone. He—it's a male voice—just says things like, 'You're next,' and hangs up."

"Has anyone been first?"

"No, not yet. So far it's only letters and phone calls. But . . ."

"But you're not sure it'll stop there."

"Exactly," she answered. "Between the protesters and this stuff, a lot of people here are getting spooked. I don't blame them."

"I gather you want me to look into it?"

"Yes, do what you can. Hopefully, just the idea that someone is investigating will help settle things down a bit."

"What else can you tell me?"

"Not much. The letters and the phone calls. And the protests. Any chance they're linked?"

"Possibly. Nuts abound. Who's gotten letters?"

"I'm not sure. I haven't asked everyone. People have come to me with these."

"Phone calls. The same voice?"

"Again, I'm not much help. I've gotten one call. So far."

"Is it all right if I ask around?"

"That's what you're here for."

"What about the anti-abortion fanatics? How often are they here?"

"Usually once or twice a week. You wouldn't think we'd be worth it."

"Why?" I asked.

"We don't really perform abortions. A few very early ones, essentially sub rosa. Menstrual extraction, so to speak. Most we refer."

"So why picket this clinic?" I asked, puzzled.

"I don't know. I'm sorry, I haven't given you much to go on," she finished.

"It's a start. Hopefully, it's just a crank who'll disappear. This hasn't been a clinic very long, has it?"

"No, we started about six months ago. This building used to be a parochial school. But it's been empty for the last few years. So I . . . an anonymous benefactor bought it and converted it."

"I see. Why are there nuns here, if you . . . if the building is privately owned?"

"Community service. They operate a soup kitchen and the daycare."

"How do they feel about sharing a building with a clinic that dispenses birth control and abortion information?"

"Not happy, as you can imagine. The word abortion has never been said out loud. But it was share with us or be out in the street. There aren't a lot of suitable buildings in this neighborhood, particularly for a poor parish. We lease the space to them for a nominal fee."

"Strange bedfellows," I commented.

"It works out. They stay on their side of the building and we stay on ours."

"Have they gotten any funny letters or strange phone calls?"

"That I don't know," she replied with a shake of her head.

"Can I ask?"

"You probably should. Sorry."

"It's my job." Sister What's-Her-Name, I decided, would be very unlikely to recognize me. "Any chance they're behind the anti-abortion protest?"

"No, they're not."

"How can you be so sure?"

"I asked. Confronted, actually," Cordelia answered with a rueful half-smile. "I cornered Sister Ann, she's in charge, and started to read her the riot act. She told me that when one gets in bed with the devil one has no business complaining about hot bedsheets. In other words, they don't like the birth control, but they'll tolerate our work."

"You think she was telling the truth?"

"Yes. She's gotten a few bottles heaved through her window, too."

I nodded. Nuns lied, I was sure, but only if they thought they were doing it for God.

"Anything else you want to know?" Cordelia asked.

A lot of things. Few of them pertinent to this case.

"Why me?"

She sat up straight, perhaps taken aback at my question. I couldn't be sure.

"Why hire me for this job?" I persisted.

"Well . . . Joanne . . . I talked to both Joanne and Danny. They said you were good. Also . . . I felt a woman nosing around would be better than a man. Those letters . . . the women might not discuss them with a man. A stranger." She coughed. "And . . . I trust you," she finished, turning her head, so she wasn't looking directly at me. "Enough reasons?"

"Enough," I replied. "When do I start?"

"Tomorrow. If you want."

We looked at each other across her desk. I wanted.

There was a knock on the door.

"Dr. James?" It was Nurse Whatever-Her-Name-Was.

"Come in, Betty," Cordelia answered.

"Everything's finished and I'm taking off now," Betty said, standing in the door.

"Great. Thanks a lot," Cordelia answered. "Betty, this is Michele Knight, a private investigator who's been hired to look into those letters and phone calls."

I stood up and extended a hand.

"Betty Peterson," Nurse Betty supplied, shaking my hand somewhat hesitantly. She wasn't accustomed to shaking hands with women, it seemed. "How do you do?" she politely added.

"I'm going to be around tomorrow. Can we talk sometime, at your convenience?" I asked, getting down to business. She looked tired.

"Ah, yes, I think I can," she replied. "I'll see you then. Goodnight, Cordelia. See you tomorrow."

Betty Peterson left. Cordelia had gotten up and was getting ready to leave, too.

"Oh, here," she said, taking something out of her purse. She handed me a check. "A retainer."

"You didn't ask my fee."

"I know what you're worth," she answered, ushering me out of her office. She turned off the light, then locked the door. "I'm meeting Alex for dinner. I'm sure she wouldn't mind if you joined us," Cordelia said as we walked out into the main hallway.

I wasn't so sure. I couldn't even be sure that Joanne hadn't told Alex about our sleeping together. But I could be sure that I didn't want to spend the evening being polite and uncomfortable with Alex. Even though it meant giving up dinner with Cordelia.

"I can't tonight," I lied, as we walked down the hall. "But maybe . . ." then I stopped. Sister Ann was reentering the building, but it wasn't her presence that silenced me. It was the woman with her. My Aunt Greta. Here. And no way to avoid her.

"Working late as usual, Dr. James?" Sister Ann called to Cordelia, as she unlocked her office door.

It was not possible that Aunt Greta would not recognize me. She still looked the same, the same dry and humorless expression carved on her face, lips ever-so-slightly turned down, as if continually prepared for a frown. Her hair was a dusty brown, rid of all the gray I remembered from the years I had lived with her.

"Of course," I heard Cordelia answer. "People don't get sick on a nine-to-five schedule."

Aunt Greta's lips curled downward into a full frown and her eyes narrowed disgustedly. She had seen me.

"Sister Ann," Cordelia was continuing. "I'd like you to meet Michele Knight. She's a private investigator who's going to be looking into some threatening letters we've received."

"How do you do?" Sister Ann said politely to me. She reached out her hand to shake mine.

Aunt Greta looked like she had just discovered a three-day-old tampon dropped over the Christmas turkey. She broke in, "Michele, how odd to find you here."

"You know each other?" Cordelia asked.

"My Aunt Greta," I answered tersely.

"I'm not really an aunt," she replied. "You see, we are not

96

actually related. Michele was born, well . . . without the benefit of marriage. Claude's brother LeMoyne took her in. He was a very kind man. Of course, after he died, we took over the care of her," Aunt Greta explained.

"I am not illegitimate," I irrationally defended. It wasn't so much a reply to Aunt Greta as an explanation to Cordelia and Sister Ann.

Aunt Greta didn't change her expression, her smile still rigidly in place. "A mark of LeMoyne's kindness that he did marry your mother. Of course, that fooled no one. He wasn't your real father," Aunt Greta patiently explained then turned her head ever so slightly, indicating that this conversation was over.

"He was my real father," I answered. "He cared for me and loved me. That's more real to me than just blood."

"Now is not the time to get into our family history," Aunt Greta responded primly.

"You should have thought of that before you called me illegitimate," I answered churlishly.

"Some things demand an explanation," Aunt Greta told me.

I didn't answer. My father, the man I considered my father, had always let people assume that I was his child. Once, when someone had pointedly commented on how different we looked, he had replied, 'Yeah, I'm real lucky. I don't know how a freckled, pasty-faced, balding guy like me got a beautiful brown-eyed, curly headed kid like Micky. Particularly with all those Sundays I spent fishing.' To me he simply said, 'I love you. I consider you my child.' I began asking questions as I got older, prompted by Bayard taunting me, telling me, 'We could get married, we're not real cousins.'

Aunt Greta made sure I knew the truth about my background. At first I thought she did it to hurt me, shame me. Only later did I realize that she had to let people know I was not really related because she didn't want anyone to think that someone 'as dark' as I was shared her heritage. Aunt Greta never said it, but Bayard had more than once called me "half-a-nigger".

"You know, Michele," Aunt Greta continued, "I heard you spent Christmas with Charles and Lottie. I don't know why you didn't come by our house. You know you're always welcome."

"I spent last Christmas with Torbin. We only dropped by his parents briefly," I explained, then wondered why I bothered answering her. Perhaps because she had done a good job of training me to answer her.

"Oh, yes, Torbin. How is Torbin?" We don't see much of him these days," Aunt Greta inquired.

"Torbin's fine." Torbin had saved me from being the family scandal. He made it a point to send out flyers to his shows to the entire family. As he said, 'I've flunked demure and discrete. But magna cum laude in outrageous is mine.'

"Fine? Or still the same?" Aunt Greta got her barb in, then continued, "My nephew Torbin is rather flashy. He's an actor," she explained to Cordelia and Sister Ann.

"He's a drag star in the French Quarter," I elaborated.

"Michele," Aunt Greta chided me.

"Well, he is." Torbin wouldn't appreciate Aunt Greta stuffing him in the closet.

"I've met Torbin," Cordelia said.

Aunt Greta gave her a quick look, then said to me, "Well, I'm glad Torbin's fine, but I don't think we need to flaunt his odd behavior."

"Why? Because you really are related to him?" I retorted, suddenly tired of the polite dance we were engaged in.

Cordelia put her hand gently on my shoulder to restrain me. But I was beyond restraint.

"Michele! That was uncalled for," Aunt Greta reprimanded me.

"Pardon me, I'm just the bastard cousin. Don't got no manners," I retorted. I briefly wondered what Cordelia and Sister Ann thought as they witnessed us, the hard, bitter intimacy that years of living together had ground in.

"Sister," Aunt Greta said, turning away from me, "Raising this child was a trial." She was using the tone of voice that I'd learned to despise, sweet, rational, lowered so she could talk about me and pretend I couldn't hear it. As if I weren't there at all.

I knew I had to get away from her, from her unctuously insinuating voice. I muttered a goodbye as I spun away and stalked out of the building as quickly as I could. I felt like running, but I wasn't going to give Aunt Greta the satisfaction.

What did you think, I wondered as I walked across the parking lot to my car, that she was going to apologize and admit she'd been unkind to you? She's beaten you just now, by causing you to lose your temper, to act like the kind of person she said you were.

"Micky. Are you okay?" Cordelia called from behind me.

"Sorry," I mumbled as she caught up.

"No, I'm sorry. I had no idea . . ."

"I shouldn't have let her get to me."

"You weren't prepared to see her here," Cordelia said.

"Still . . . after all this time, they shouldn't matter."

"It doesn't work that way," she gently replied.

"It should. Some day you should be able to stop dragging all your past around with you."

"I know. I wish . . . I'm sorry this happened. And I'm even sorrier that . . . about the things that happened to you."

"Not much, if you believe Aunt Greta's version," I remarked bitterly, knowing that most people would believe her. Pillar of the church versus promiscuous lesbian.

"I believe you," Cordelia said firmly. She put her hand on my shoulder.

"Better be careful. They're probably watching." The parking lot was on Sister Ann's side of the building.

"So?" Cordelia didn't move her hand.

"Thanks."

"Sure you don't want dinner?"

"Lost my appetite," I answered. "But thanks anyway. Maybe some other time."

"Will you be okay?"

"I lived eight years with her. Ten minutes more hardly matters."

"That doesn't answer my question."

"Yes, I'll be okay. I'll see you tomorrow," I replied. "Enjoy dinner." I unlocked my car door.

She leaned forward and brushed her lips against my cheek. Then she turned and walked across the lot to where her car was parked.

I got in my car. I wondered if Aunt Greta and Sister Ann had been watching. I hoped Cordelia wouldn't end up regretting standing by me.

I pulled out, not wanting them to think I was waiting for her. But I stayed at the exit until I saw Cordelia get safely into her car and start it. I waved, unsure if she would see it, then drove away.

Chapter 8

I arrived at the clinic around 8:30, hoping to get there before it
got too busy. But the waiting room was already packed. I decided
that, until told otherwise, I had been given carte blanche to
investigate this however I saw fit. I started by wandering around
the building.

The building did indeed appear to be split down the middle according to use — Catholics on the west side, godless Commies on the
east, with the hallway as DMZ or purgatory, depending on your
outlook.

There were stairs at either end of the building. I climbed the
nearest one. There had been little renovation up here, the classrooms were still definitely classrooms, complete with original
graffiti. Some of the rooms had chairs left in an empty circle or

scribbling on the blackboards, attesting to fairly recent use. I walked through all the rooms, only one had had any work done on it, the paint scraped, the other rooms remained peeled and blistered, institution green curling back to reveal a duller shade of institutional green.

I looked out one of the windows. This was the clinic side. It overlooked a scruffy lawn that was bordered with a wrought iron fence, then a broad, but cracked and broken sidewalk and the street. The wrought iron, a ragged army of spears, some missing their points, was imbedded in a low stone wall, making the whole fence about eight feet tall. When it had been in its prime, freshly painted and scrubbed, the fence had probably been effective at keeping the world out of this school. Or the students in. But now it ended abruptly in the middle of the block. Whatever had completed it, either going farther down the street, or turning ninety degrees to enclose, was gone. The street beyond the fence was a slow side street, leading into the busier avenue that the front door opened onto.

I crossed the building to the window opposite. This side overlooked the parking lot. The white lines that used to order the cars were worn into illegibility. Beyond the lot, a few trees, one a stately oak, proud and defiant next to the shopworn asphalt, then a vacant lot.

"Can I help you?"

I turned to look. Sister Ann.

"No, as I'm sure my Aunt Greta has told you, I'm beyond help."

"No one is beyond help. I heard footsteps over my head and came up to see who was here," she explained.

"Have you gotten any strange letters?" I asked. I didn't want to argue my state of helplessness.

"Me? No," she replied. "What are you doing up here?"

"Me? Looking." One terse answer deserved another. "Anyone on your staff? Any threatening phone calls?" I persisted.

She looked at me for a moment, as if making a decision.

"I'm not sure," she finally said.

"Not sure?" I pushed.

"Nothing's been said. Not that Sister Fatima would. But . . . I think it was last week. I saw her open a letter, her face turned white and she hastily threw it into a trash can. Could that be one of your letters?"

"Where is Sister Fatima now? Will she talk to me?"

"I doubt it. She didn't talk to me. Sister Fatima is in her seventies and, bless her, lives in a more genteel age."

I nodded my head, remembering some of the older nuns I had met. I wondered why Sister Ann had decided to answer my questions.

"Anyone else?" I asked.

"Not that I know of," she replied. "But . . . I did get a strange phone call a few days ago."

"Strange? How?"

"It wasn't threatening, at least, I didn't feel threatened. But it was someone who knew my name, because he used it. Then he asked, 'Why did you become a nun?' and hung up."

"That's all?"

"Yes," she answered.

"Why are you answering my questions?" I couldn't imagine her wanting to be in the same room with me. Not after Aunt Greta's spiel.

"I disapprove of poison-pen letters. I hope you can do something about them." She turned to go.

"Thank you, Sister."

She smiled at me, then walked out of the room. Probably pleasantly surprised that I knew how to say thank you, after hearing the Greta Robedeaux version of my life.

I went back downstairs. The daycare center was now full and squalling. People were spilling out of the clinic waiting room into the hallway. No way to see Cordelia now.

I went out the back door. There was a walkway that led only to a fringe of weeds and wild shrubs demarcating the property line. The lawn of the clinic, though not likely to win any garden awards, at least showed signs of having been mowed in recent memory. Unlike the lot behind it. Anything could be concealed in the dense greenery of that back lot.

Then I noticed windows at ground level. A basement? The first floor was high enough that the building might have been able to fit a basement between it and the barely below ground water table. I hadn't seen any entrance on the first floor. I circled the building looking for a way in. No entrance appeared. It would have been very easy to break in through just about any of the windows. Several of them had broken panes and most had frames that looked warped and rotten. But I decided to try the legitimate approach first.

I re-entered the back door. And, since I was looking for it, found a door tucked under the back staircase. With a lock on it. Being bolder about breaking and entering while under an ill-lit staircase than out in a yard in daylight, I pulled on the lock to see how secure it was or if the hasp was as ready to fall out as it looked. Whoever was in charge of locking locks had settled for verisimilitude. The lock wasn't really closed. I pocketed it to make sure no one would decide for a more realistic effect while I was in the basement.

It took a little fumbling to find the light switch. One bulb for the stairs, a few more scattered through the basement. As basements go, it bordered on the dismal — a dirt floor and that pervasive damp feeling being below ground always has when you're this close to sea level. The ceiling was low, only a few inches above my head and covered with spider webs. Some of the beams and pipes were low enough to give me a headache if I wasn't careful. Squat brick columns were placed about every fifteen feet. I wandered around for a bit, careful to stay near the sporadic light that came through the dirt-caked windows or from the few electric bulbs. If I were a rat, I'd want to live in just this sort of basement. It was too damp for storage. Perhaps a mushroom grower's dream. That was about all.

I headed back upstairs, putting the lock back on and carefully not locking it. There wasn't anything to steal down there.

"Micky Knight. What are you doing here?"

I turned to look at a white uniformed figure. Millie Donnalto. She lived with Hutch Mackenzie, Joanne's partner.

"Millie. Would you believe that Hutch hired me to check up on you?"

"Absolutely not," she replied, as she gave me a big hug.

"How about that I've become hopelessly smitten with you and follow you everywhere?"

"Less likely," she laughed and gave me an extra squeeze to prove she wasn't worried about any lascivious behavior on my part.

I liked Millie. Because, even though she's totally straight, she was fearless about hugging a notorious lesbian like me in a public hallway. Even one which nuns and the like walked about in.

"Working," I replied, as she released me. "Gotten any nasty letters lately?"

"Oh, that," she said. "My first, two days ago. Ugly things."

"Can I see it?"

"Sorry, I threw it in the trash," she answered.

"Too bad. Are you willing to tell me what it said?"

"Sure. But not here. Follow me."

Millie led me down the hall into the storage room for the clinic. She shut the door behind us.

"Little ears from daycare," she explained.

"Graphic, I take it."

"Obscene, in that dirty sense. Anyway," she continued, "it went on, at length, about my . . . uh . . . preference for men with large genitals."

"So whoever sent it has laid eyes on Hutch," I commented. Hutch was at least six-foot-six and linebacker-sized.

"I guess. It's not a thought I like. I know Bernie, our administrative assistant, got one, because I saw her burn it."

"Did she say anything about it? Was it poor dot-matrix?"

"Yes and yes. She lives with her mother. She's nineteen and saving for school. Her comment was something like, 'How could someone think my mother and I . . . ' then it burned down and she had to drop it."

I nodded. I would ask Bernie about it.

"Nasty stuff," she commented. "It leaves a cold feeling, like someone is watching us." She shook her head. "It means it's not just random, doesn't it?"

"Probably. It wouldn't hurt to play it safe for a while. Don't go anywhere alone around here, leave in groups. You know the drill," I said.

"Yes, unfortunately. This has me nervous, I don't mind telling you. And I'm glad you're around."

"Thanks," I smiled.

The door swung open. Nurse Betty entered. She looked from me to Millie, then down to the floor, a slight blush spreading over her cheeks. I wondered how my reputation had spread so quickly.

"Uh . . . I'm sorry . . . I have to get . . . there they are," Betty stammered, heading for a box of rubber gloves stacked on one of the shelves.

"Thanks, Millie," I said. "Be sure to say hi to Hutch for me. Perhaps you can answer a few questions," I turned to Nurse Betty.

Millie gave me a wink behind blushing Nurse Betty's back and, taking the gloves for her, went out the door. To complete her discomfort, I shut the door.

"Have you gotten any obscene letters?"

"I'm sorry, I'm busy now," she said, flustered at the closed door.

"You could have answered me in the time it took to tell me you're busy."

She looked at the door and then at me standing next to it.

"Yes, I have," she finally said, probably unwilling to get close enough to me to get through the door.

"Do you still have it?"

"I gave it to Cor . . . Dr. James," she answered, going the formal route.

I remembered the letter from the ones Cordelia had shown me. It was to Peterson, R.N., and commented on her insatiable sexual appetite, accusing her of sleeping with a different man every night.

"Any truth to it?" I asked.

"No, of course not."

"No?" I questioned.

"No," she responded angrily. "It's bad enough having that . . . that sort of trash. I don't need your ugly accusations now."

"Not accusing, just asking," I laconically replied. I noticed a small cross around her neck.

"No, I do not sleep around. And I'm sure you'll find this hard to believe, but I believe in the sanctity of marriage and I'm . . ." then she ran out of indignation and blushed again.

"A virgin?" I supplied.

"I'm sure you find it amusing," she retorted defensively.

"No. I think the important thing is for people to choose what's right for themselves," I said. "Without ridicule or intolerance from those who disagree."

"Oh," she replied. "I'm sorry. I guess I'm just upset. Those accusations . . ." and she trailed off.

"Are pretty nasty. Have you gotten any phone calls?"

"No, only the one letter."

I opened the door.

"Thank you," I said as she walked through it.

"You're welcome," she replied, polite enough to really be a virgin.

I caught Bernice, the administrative assistant, between patients and paperwork. She confirmed Millie's story and added another letter, which she had also burned. She also confirmed that the letter was right about her living with her mother. And like Cordelia, she'd gotten a phone call. Her name, then 'Motherfucker,' was all he had said before hanging up. She explained the phones to me. Each of the doctors, Cordelia and two others who were part time, had a phone in their offices with a private line. There was another phone on her desk and one in the back. Only the main phone number was listed. Cordelia and Dr. Bowen had both gotten calls on their private lines.

Dr. Bowen wasn't in, but I had seen the letter to her among those Cordelia had shown me. It suggested that her husband was divorcing her because he'd caught her fondling her son while giving him a bath.

Bernice told me that Dr. Bowen was indeed going through a nasty divorce. And she added that the idea of Jane Bowen being a child molester was absurd.

I thanked Bernie, as she insisted I call her, and let her get back to her work.

The waiting room was starting to empty since it was lunch time. I had seen Cordelia once crossing between examining rooms, but she hadn't seen me. I wandered back out into the main hallway, planning to hang around and chat for a moment with her. At least let her see me hard at work.

I walked down the hall, glancing in all the doors, trying to get a feeling for who belonged where. As I passed by Sister Ann's, she motioned me in.

"I thought you'd like to know," she said as I entered. "I got one today." She handed me a letter printed with a poor dot-matrix printer.

"Thank you," I said as I sat down opposite her and started to read.

My Oh-So-Dear Sister Ann,
You weren't always such a good nun, were you? We know the things you liked to do before you put on that convenient habit. We know you still do them. We know what goes on underneath that skirt of yours.

The letter continued with some specific descriptions of what she was doing under her skirt.

It ended with a threat. "Be careful or we'll help God get you for your sins."

I handed it back to her.

"Should I call the police?" she asked.

"If you want. They might be able to do things I can't. But I doubt obscene letters are at the top of their priority list."

"True," she nodded.

"Any . . . you're not going to like this question," I qualified, "truth to the letter?"

"No, I don't think so," she answered. "Why do you ask?"

I told her about the other letters.

She nodded and glanced again at the letter, throwing it down quickly.

"Perhaps," she said. "I didn't become a nun until my twenties. I was even engaged for a brief time."

"To a man?" I stumbled out. Nun sexuality was not something I was well versed in.

"Yes, to a man," Sister Ann replied.

"Oh. What happened?"

"Things changed. No, I guess I changed. What I wanted changed," Sister Ann slowly replied.

"What happened to him?"

"Randall? I haven't thought of him in . . . a long time. After I took my vows, I broke all contact with him. I don't know what became of him."

"Did you . . ." then I stammered, realizing the question I was about at ask. All my training concerning nuns kicked in. One certainly couldn't ask them about pre-vocational sex. "Never mind," I finished.

"The letter exaggerates greatly, as they all do. But I can't say I've never been kissed. Somehow the letter writer found out about my indecision about being a nun. And twisted it badly," she answered the question I hadn't asked.

"Sorry," I apologized, to let her know I only asked nuns questions like that in the line of duty.

"Perfectly all right," she replied. "It does point out the pattern in these letters. The writer learns something about the person, includes it in the letter and then dumps sexual innuendo on top."

"A bit more than innuendo," I added.

"A bit," Sister Ann echoed.

"Can I make a copy of this?"

"Certainly, if you like."

"Thanks."

I picked up the letter and went back to the clinic. The waiting room was empty now. There was a copy machine back in the office. Since the anonymous benefactor who had hired me had also, I suspected, bought the copier, I felt I had the right to use it without asking permission. No one was around to ask anyway. I went past Bernie's desk into the office.

Then I saw Nurse Peterson kneeling down behind one of the file cabinets. She jumped when she saw me. Once again she was caught alone in a room with a lesbian.

"Sorry to have startled you," I said, as I turned on the copy machine.

"I didn't hear you come in," she replied.

"Sneakers."

"Oh . . . of course," she replied, as she straightened up, then walked by me to leave.

"Is Cordelia around?" I asked.

"She left about ten minutes ago."

"Lunch?" I inquired.

"No, to the hospital to see her patients there. She should be back for her two-thirty appointment."

Nurse Peterson continued walking away. I made my copy, disappointed at not having seen Cordelia.

Well, it's obvious why Cordelia hired me, I thought as I walked back to Sister Ann's office. Because I was a woman, and not for any other reason. The women, and so far it seemed to be only women, who had gotten those letters probably wouldn't talk to a strange man about what was in them.

I handed the letter back to Sister Ann and thanked her. Then I went to my car, trying to decide what to do next. Cordelia wouldn't be around for several hours. I wanted to call Andy and ask him about printers, I also wanted to talk to Elly, but she wouldn't be here until later in the day. It was time to go back to my office. I'd catch Cordelia tomorrow, I decided.

I drove around the neighborhood, just on the off chance of spotting someone leering at the clinic with a laptop computer and a portable dot-matrix printer. No such luck.

I drove back home.

I left messages for both Andy and Elly, not getting either of them. For a brief minute I enjoyed the idea of Danny wondering why I was calling Elly, then I remembered that Cordelia had certainly told Danny I was investigating the letters.

After that I did exciting things like fix lunch, feed the cat, and sort bills into piles. The must-be-paid-immediately-or-risk-losing-life-and-limb pile on one side and the no-mention-of-visits-from-ex-Saint-linebackers-yet pile.

The phone rang. It was Joanne.

"Can I come over?" she asked.

"Sure. When?" was my answer.

"Six or seven. Is that okay?"

"That's fine."

"See you then. Thanks."

She hung up. I had wondered if she would really call me. Or if I had just been . . . handy. I still wasn't sure. I also wondered why she thanked me.

I went to take a shower. I wasn't going to worry about it.

Chapter 9

Joanne arrived a little after six. She didn't say much, but neither did I. We made love, half-spread between the couch and my living room floor. Then we moved to my bedroom and its air conditioner. We made love again, still getting hot and sweaty even in the cool of the bedroom.

"Are you hungry?" she asked, turning to me when we had finished.

"Somewhat."

"Let's go," Joanne said, sitting up.

"No, wait, . . . I'd like to lie here a bit longer," I replied, not wanting to abruptly jump up after our lovemaking, as if it were merely a physical need now sated.

I felt her stretch back beside me.

"I'm sorry," she said. "Sometimes I get so caught up in getting things done, that I forget there are moments when that's not the point."

She put her arms around me. I curled into her embrace, letting her hold me, my head nestled against her shoulder. We lay still for a moment, just holding each other.

"Dinner time," I said, breaking away.

"Thank you," Joanne said.

"For what? Finally letting you eat?" I joked.

"For letting me hold you."

"I . . ." I started to make another joke, something like I got off, too, but that wasn't what she meant. "I . . . thank you. Sometimes it's nice to be held."

"Yes, it is," Joanne answered. "Let's get out of here. Some place with air conditioning in more than one room."

"Inexpensive," I stipulated.

"Of course," Joanne said. She knew I wouldn't let her buy my food twice in a row.

After dinner, we lingered over coffee. I told Joanne about the letters. She agreed with me in not liking the accuracy of some elements of them. She offered to check around to see if there was any record of a poison-pen that preferred a word processor for his missives.

Then there was a pause. Into which I inserted the question that had been nagging me.

"What about Alex?"

Joanne looked at me. "I need this," she said. "I . . . Either she'll understand or she won't." She shrugged, closing the subject.

We paid the check and left.

"Show me the clinic," Joanne said as we got in her car.

I gave her directions, glad that she was interested.

The neighborhood had changed with darkness. The buildings, shabby by day, took on a reclusive, ominous look at night. Locked and shuttered, little light escaped. No one was visible on the dim streets. The street light at the corner wasn't working. Shattered by vandalism or left unlit by the neglect of the city, I couldn't tell. We drove slowly by the front of the building, then turned down the side street that bordered it.

111

"Should there be lights on?" Joanne asked.

"I don't know. There are late hours tonight, but surely not this late." It was past ten now.

"Let's look," Joanne said, parking her car. "Just remember, no heroics," she admonished me as we got out.

"No, ma'am, sergeant, sir."

She gave me a stern look, but said nothing. We walked around the fence into the yard. It appeared that the inside hall light was on. Shards of light appeared through several door frames. Joanne motioned me along the street side as she headed for the side next to the empty lot. I noticed she had pulled her gun.

I crept slowly beside the building, listening for any sound that might indicate this was something other than a night light. Sight, not sound, confirmed our suspicions.

A foot was silently slipping out of a window, not five feet in front of me.

Unless someone on the staff had cat burglar fantasies, that foot belonged to a someone who didn't belong in the building.

Joanne had said no heroics. Since the person was about to step on my head, I figured the most cowardly thing I could do was apprehend him before he caught sight of me.

I grabbed the dangling foot and pulled. I vaguely hoped that the foot didn't have a hand holding a gun attached, but I figured if I were going to get shot, it would be just as easy to get me in the back as I ran to find Joanne.

The foot belonged to a very strong leg. It kicked and jerked out of my grasp, disappearing back into the window.

I jumped, grabbing the window sill and hauled myself up. I glimpsed the body attached to the foot in silhouette as it went through the door into the lit hallway. I clambered through the window and went in pursuit.

Just as I got to the door, the lights in the hallway went out. I couldn't see a thing. I can't stand here waiting for my eyes to adjust, I thought, whoever it was had to have seen me. I started to edge back into the room. Then I heard a noise to my right, maybe twenty feet down the hall. If you can't see them, they can't see you. I ran toward it, hoping I would crash into something soft and human.

There was a slight shuffle at the sound of my approach, giving me the exact location of my target. The leading edge of my elbow caught someone's stomach. He went into the wall with a grunt. Then I felt a knee in my groin. This body was fairly tall and knows how to fight, I thought as I bent over. I spun out of his reach. For a moment I thought about calling Joanne, but didn't because that would only reveal where I was. Besides, Joanne had to have heard the scuffle and my yelling wouldn't bring her any quicker.

Then I was tackled, my assailant doing to me what I had hoped to do to him. We were on the floor, him on top. He tried to grab my arms, but I jerked them free. Then with my left hand I caught his shoulder, pushing him away. And, more importantly, giving me a pretty accurate picture of where to punch him in the nose. My right hand swung back, ready to strike.

The lights blazed on.

"Stop! Police!" Joanne's official voice filled the hall.

I looked at my assailant, fully intending to stop after I punched him, not before.

I caught myself just in time, barely grazing her jaw instead of breaking her nose.

"Micky!" Cordelia said, as surprised to be sitting on top of me as I was at being under her.

"Oh, shit! Are you all right?" I exclaimed, wondering how much damage my pulled punch had done.

"I'm fine. I'm sorry," she said as she got off me. "Here let me help you. Are you okay?" She extended a hand and helped me get up.

"Only my pride," I mumbled. "Were you climbing out a window just now?" I asked, remembering my dangling foot.

Joanne joined us.

"What happened?" she contributed.

"You saw someone climbing out a window?" Cordelia questioned.

I nodded. We exchanged stories. Cordelia had been seeing patients until after nine, then stayed to finish paperwork. She had seen the main hallway light come on and heard noises. She wasn't too worried, she explained as there were often people here this late. She'd come out to look, the lights went out, and I'd rushed her.

Joanne, hearing the noise, had come in the front door, finding it unlocked.

I was the only one who had seen another person. Cordelia pointed out that the front door shouldn't have been left unlocked. The intruder had probably run out that way.

"Whoever it was, they're gone now," Joanne commented. "Let's see if they took anything. Cordelia, check the clinic. Micky, the rest of this floor. I'll do the upstairs," she ordered. Giving us no time to dissent, she headed up the stairs, still holding, I noticed, her gun. Just in case he was hiding out up there.

Cordelia gave me a quick smile, then a shrug and went into the clinic. I headed down the hall, checking doors to see if any locks had been tampered with or if anything looked out of place. Nothing. I turned and headed to the back of the building, rechecking to see if I had missed anything. Still nothing.

I walked to the back door and looked out at the overgrown lot behind the clinic. Someone could hide for days in that and not be found.

Then I noticed that the door to the basement was open. The lock was lying on the floor. The door that I had so carefully closed and semi-locked this morning. I turned on the light and went down the stairs. The basement, ill-lit in daylight, was now worthy of a Vincent Price movie.

"Nothing down here but a vicious gang of killer rats," I said out loud, noting silently that Joanne was certainly right, whoever I had seen was long gone.

I ventured from the stairs to the first pool of light. The basement appeared as barren as it had this morning. Dampness and dirt, a pervasive moldy smell. Hardly threatening. I walked on to the next pool of light.

The only person foolish enough to go into this basement is you, I told myself, seeing only more dirt and undisturbed spider webs. Then why was the door open? Any number of reasons came to mind. The killer rats may have decided to move into a better neighborhood, for example. Maybe my foot person opened it looking for a way out. Maybe even hightailed it out one of those rotten windows. But he (or perhaps she, I couldn't be sure) certainly hadn't left a plethora of clues in this dismal basement.

It was not likely that whoever broke in had anything to do with the letters. Probably someone trying to steal drugs from the clinic.

There were even fewer lights in this part of the basement. The next one was a good thirty feet away.

Then I noticed some loose soil lying on the hard packed dirt floor. Odd, I thought, freshly turned from the feel of it. Perhaps the killer rats were digging their way out.

I continued to the next light.

As I got to it, something beyond it caught my eye. A lighter shape against the dark dirt. A piece of paper, perhaps?

I headed toward it, leaving the light behind, losing the object several times in my shadow. The damp and the darkness seemed to be enshrouding me the further I get from the light. This basement badly needs to be aired out, I thought, as the fetid smell of the dampness assaulted my nose.

Then I recognized what I was walking toward. And realized that what I was smelling wasn't the moist air of a basement.

I stopped, the hand pale against the dark earth, outstretched and grasping for me. Just as the other one had been.

Only the arm from the elbow down was visible, the rest of the body hidden by one of the thick brick supports. It was covered in dirt as if some hasty attempt at burial had been made. The hand seemed to be reaching out of its hurried grave.

I turned my head away, took a quick gasp of air, and forced myself to go closer, circling around to see what lay behind the column.

She was splattered with dirt, shoved in a trough that was impossibly shallow for her. Her eyes were open and staring, mercifully oblivious to the inadequacy of the earth at covering her nakedness. For she had no clothes, nor jewelry, nothing to mark who she was and how she had come to be left here.

I felt my lungs burn, begging for a breath. I was reluctant to take in the decayed air.

She wasn't here this morning, I suddenly thought. I would have seen her. She hasn't been here rotting for days and days.

I let my breath out. And was assaulted with the smell of putrefaction. The dank air of the cellar seemed to amplify the stench of her decomposition. I gagged. Then I ran, to get away from the reach of her hand and the long grasp of decay. The pools of light seemed distant, hidden by shadows and their horrifying secrets.

Finally reaching the stairs, I bolted up them, taking two at a time, stumbling into the clear air of the hallway. For a moment, I just leaned against the nearest wall, purging my lungs of the foul air. Then I shook myself, abashed at my panic.

Cordelia came out of the clinic.

"Micky, what's wrong?" she said when she saw me.

"Where's Joanne?" I answered.

"I don't know," she replied, coming over to me. "What's wrong?" she repeated, putting a hand on my shoulder.

"We're going to need to call the police," I said, trying to think what to do. Joanne will know, I thought.

"Why? What's missing?" Cordelia asked.

"Nothing . . . there's another one," I finished, so softly she had to lean in to hear.

"Another . . . oh, my God!" She shook her head as if in disbelief, then pulled me to her, holding me.

"Am I interrupting something?" Joanne said, descending the stairs.

"I wish to hell you were," I replied. We broke our embrace.

Cordelia turned to Joanne, still keeping an arm around my shoulder.

"There's a body in the basement," I stated matter-of-factly, steadied by Cordelia's arm.

"What?" Joanne exclaimed. "Are you sure?"

I nodded.

"Can you show me?" she continued.

"Yeah. You might want a flash light," I answered. And a hand-kerchief soaked with something potent.

"I'll get one," Cordelia volunteered. She dropped her arm and went to get the light.

"How did a body get in the basement?" Joanne asked angrily.

"I don't know."

"It doesn't matter. We need to call the police, the local precinct."

Cordelia returned with the flashlight.

We went back down into the basement. I led the way, my steps slowing as we left the last pool of light behind. I covered my nose with my hand, even before we were close enough to smell the stench.

"There," I said, pointing to the ghostly arm, still reaching into nothingness.

Joanne and Cordelia both went past me. I reluctantly followed them, unwilling to hang back in the dim shadows.

"Goddamn it!" Joanne's voice rang angrily as she saw the naked young woman where death had carelessly flung her.

"She can't be twenty," Cordelia said, her voice soft after Joanne's rage. Cordelia knelt beside the young woman, uselessly feeling for a pulse. She stood up, backing away and shaking her head. She almost ran into me, jumping when I put my hand on her back to stop her. She stayed next to me; I left my hand gently resting on her back. Cordelia continued, "She's been dead for at least a day or two. Putrefaction is already beginning, you can tell by the green staining in the flanks and . . ." My hand jerked as Cordelia spoke; these were things I didn't want to know. "But I'm not a pathologist," she finished, "I'll leave her to the experts."

"Shit," Joanne said, her expression tight and angry. "Out of here," she added, turning away from the body.

No one spoke as we left the basement.

"Where's a phone?" Joanne said as we got to the top of the stairs.

"This way," Cordelia replied, heading for the clinic.

I didn't move, as if motion were useless, but Joanne grabbed my hand and led me into the clinic. Still holding my hand, she picked up the receiver, and punched in a number she obviously knew. She was brief and to the point. The police would be here in a few minutes.

"Anyone want coffee?" Cordelia asked when Joanne hung up.

"Yeah," she replied, letting go of my hand, then adding, "I'll get yours," to me.

I sat down on the couch in the waiting room. Cordelia lowered herself into a chair opposite me. She took a sip of her coffee, then burst out, "How does a dead body get in our basement?"

"I don't know," I replied again.

Joanne handed me my coffee, then sat down beside me.

"This isn't going to be fun," she said. "Particularly for you," she added, looking at Cordelia.

Cordelia nodded.

"Anyone here with you?" Joanne asked her.

"Well . . . I sent Betty home when we were finished with the last patient. I guess around nine."

"So you've been here alone here since then?"

"Joanne, what are you implying?" I cut in.

"I didn't kill her," Cordelia said.

Joanne looked at her.

"I know that," Joanne said, her tone softening. "I do. But you're going to be asked these questions and a lot more. You might want to call your lawyer."

"I didn't kill her," Cordelia repeated.

There was a loud banging on the front door. Joanne got up.

"I'm sorry," she said, still looking at Cordelia. "I'll do what I can." Then she went to open the door.

I looked at Cordelia. She was staring fixedly at the floor. Then she looked up at me.

"I know you didn't . . . I'll do everything I can," I said.

"They can't hang you if you're innocent," she replied and smiled weakly.

We heard the heavy tramp of footsteps coming up the hallway. A policeman entered the waiting room. He started taking down basic information, names, addresses, etc. The rest of the footsteps went down into the basement.

We sat silently after the policeman finished his questions, unable to talk because of his presence. After about half an hour or so, Joanne joined us. She just shrugged her shoulders, then went and sat down at the far end of the room.

I got up and paced, making the policeman watch me. I finally got tired of his staring eyes and sat back down. Joanne sat still, tension evident only in the constant motion of her fingers. Cordelia couldn't seem to get comfortable, changing position every few minutes.

Finally, a middle-aged man in a rumpled brown suit came in. He was followed by two other men, one in uniform, one not. He looked at us, then calmly fixed himself a cup of coffee.

"So, O'Connor, what's the story?" Joanne asked, breaking the tension.

"I'm sorry," the man said, turning to her. "I've forgotten your name. Joanne . . . uh . . . ?"

"Detective Sergeant Joanne Ranson," Joanne supplied evenly. She handed him her identification. He grunted and barely glanced at it, tossing it back to her. He was making clear whose territory it was.

He turned to me. "Michele Anti-gone Knight," he read off the policeman's notes.

"Antigone," I corrected.

"Antigone," he repeated. "Now, what kind of name is that?"

"Greek."

"Greek, huh? So your daddy was Greek?" He was toying with me.

"No," I answered. "My mother was Greek. My daddy read Sophocles."

He grunted in reply.

"Now, Miss Greek Knight, what were you doing here?"

"I saw a light on. I investigated."

"Just like that? You just wandered by and saw a light on?" he asked sarcastically.

"I'm a private investigator."

"Now, why would a pretty little girl like you do work like that?" he goaded me.

I started to make an angry retort, but I realized that that was what he was trying to get me to do. I calmed myself down enough to tell him, in a terse monotone, what I was doing here. I mentioned the letters and the phone calls, hoping he would connect them to the dead woman, or at least see the possibility of a connection.

His now familiar grunt was the only response when I finished. He went and refilled his coffee cup.

"You and Detective Sergeant Ranson just happened to show up here at the same time, huh?" he said, looking at both of us to let us know how likely he believed that to be.

"Ms. Knight and I know each other socially," Joanne supplied, her voice cool and professional. "We had dinner and Michele told me about this case. I expressed interest and we drove by. You know the rest."

"But that's the problem. I don't. I don't know how a dead woman got in the basement." He was pacing the room now, putting on a show, I suspected. "I don't know why that dead woman was there. There's a lot I don't know." Then he stopped directly in front of Cordelia. "Perhaps you can tell me, Dr. James."

"I don't know," Cordelia answered.

"You don't know? The name Beverly Sue Morris doesn't ring a bell with you?"

"No, it doesn't."

"Oh, I see. You have a lot of patients, here. Day in, day out. I guess it's hard to remember just one."

"I'm good at remembering my patients. I don't remember her," Cordelia replied.

"We found her purse buried in a corner, Dr. James. In that purse we found one of those little cards. A doctor's appointment card. An appointment for last Friday at three p.m. With a Dr. C. James. That you?"

"Yes, but . . . she wasn't here on Friday."

"You're sure?" O'Connor demanded.

"Yes."

"Positive?"

"Yes. Positive."

"If you didn't perform an abortion on Miss Beverly Sue Morris, on Friday at three, then why was there a receipt and a filled out and signed, by you, insurance form in her purse? Now why do you suppose that poor Miss Beverly Sue Morris paid for an abortion she never had?"

Cordelia looked stunned.

"There's got to be a mistake . . ." she finally said.

"No mistake," O'Connor retorted.

"But . . . that's not right," she said, shaking her head. "I didn't . . . on Friday . . ."

"Don't say anything else," I suddenly broke in. "Call your lawyer."

"Quiet, you," O'Connor snapped at me. "Now, Dr. James, why don't you tell me what you did on Friday?"

"He's only trying to trap you. They'll twist whatever you say . . ."

"Sergeant Ranson, your friend in interfering with police work," O'Connor interrupted.

"Michele," Joanne said, a warning tone in her voice. But if Joanne had really meant for me to be quiet, she would have said so.

"No," I shot at her, so O'Connor would believe I was defying her. "Cordelia. Don't answer any more questions. Call your lawyer."

"But, Micky . . . I'm innocent," she said, still trying to make sense of what was happening. But she didn't say anything else, only shaking her head at O'Connor's further questions.

"Search the files," he finally said, seeing she would answer no more questions.

"No, you can't," Cordelia burst out, standing up. "Those are confidential."

"Beverly Sue Morris is dead," O'Connor shot back. "I don't think she much cares about confidentiality now. I think she might be more interested in us catching her murderer."

"They are confidential," Cordelia repeated.

"Or perhaps you don't want us to see what's in those files," he taunted.

"Get a search warrant," she defied him.

He nodded to one of his men, ignoring Cordelia.

"She is right, you know," Joanne spoke up. O'Connor turned to glare at her. "Detective O'Connor," she continued, "I'm sure Dr. James is only interested in protecting the rights of her patients. It will be more useful, in terms of your investigation, if you don't obtain evidence illegally."

O'Connor continued glaring at her. Joanne coolly returned his gaze. It turned into a staring contest. O'Connor abruptly turned on his heel.

"We'll get a search warrant, Dr. James. And we'll tear this place apart. We'll search the whole building. We'll spend days doing it," he stated angrily. He paused to let that sink in. "But all I want is the file for Beverly Sue Morris. Do you object to my 'disturbing' your patients' rights? Or do you object to my seeing that file?"

"There is no file because she wasn't a patient here," Cordelia answered.

"So you say."

"Joanne . . ." I said.

"By the book, Sergeant Ranson. I'm doing it by the book," O'Connor responded. "Merely inquiring if Dr. James wants to do her civic duty and help us catch a murderer."

"I want to talk to my lawyer," Cordelia said.

"Fine. You do that. And I'll work on getting the search warrant. And if I get it first . . ." he trailed off.

"Can he do . . . ?" Cordelia said, looking from me to Joanne.

"One way or another, I'll see those files," O'Connor interjected.

Joanne nodded her head slowly.

"All right," Cordelia said tightly. She stalked to the filing cabinets. I watched her angrily flip through files. Then she tensed, the angry motion still. For a moment, nothing moved, then O'Connor stepped in and took the file that she was holding in her hand.

"Beverly Sue Morris," he read triumphantly.

"But that's not . . ." Cordelia said dazedly. "Let me look at that," she said as she took the file back from O'Connor. She rapidly flipped through it. "She was one of Jane's patients. Jane Bowen, our part-time gynecologist/obstetrician. This doesn't make sense," she added, half to herself.

"What doesn't make sense, Dr. James?" O'Connor asked.

"Jane's only here Mondays and Thursdays. Not Fridays," Cordelia answered.

"If Jane Bowen couldn't see a patient, would you take over for her?"

"Yes, at times," Cordelia replied, but seeing where his questioning was leading, continued, "But I didn't perform an abortion on her on Friday. I don't perform abortions here."

"Where do you perform abortions?"

"We do them at a gynecological clinic that Jane is affiliated with," Cordelia answered carefully.

"Do you perform abortions, Dr. James?" O'Connor questioned.

Cordelia met his gaze for a moment before answering, "I have. I can. I don't usually. It's not my specialty."

"Care to come down to the station and answer a few more questions now, Dr. James?" O'Connor dug at her.

"Not until she's talked to her lawyer," I answered for her. And I talked to Danny, I thought.

"How did poor Beverly Sue get in the basement?" he asked, ignoring me.

Cordelia's head jerked up.

"I don't know," she replied angrily at him.

"Or don't remember?"

"Are you pressing charges?" Joanne asked. "By the way, how was Beverly Morris murdered, if she was?" she continued.

O'Connor glared at her again.

"What about the intruder who 'just happened' to show up right before we found the body?" I questioned.

O'Connor turned his glare to me.

"For all we know that body's been there since Friday afternoon," he replied.

"It wasn't there this morning," I reminded him.

"Who, besides you," he broke in impatiently, "didn't see the body and did see the intruder?" he demanded. "Did you see this mysterious burglar, Sergeant Ranson?"

"No, I didn't," she finally replied. "But if Michele says . . ."

"Michele," O'Connor cut in, "who just happens to be working for Dr. James's clinic. How convenient. Not good enough, Ranson, you know that," he finished, then started to turn away, but shifted back to her and said casually, "How come you never married? Smart lady like you should be able to get a man."

I wanted to get up and hit him. He was good. But only if you were on his side.

"I've been married," Joanne replied tersely.

"Yeah?" he said, still seemingly casual. "What happened? I never heard that."

"We're divorced," she responded neutrally.

"Yeah, well, I'm Catholic. We don't believe in divorce."

"Just practical things, like transubstantiation and the infallibility of the Popes," I commented.

"You got a Catholic problem?" he shot at me.

"Oh, no, I think the Inquisition was one of the most benign periods in history," I retorted, deliberately baiting him.

He turned his back to me. He probably didn't know what the Inquisition was.

Cordelia came back into the waiting room. She looked drained. She sat staring at her hands, as if they had somehow deceived her.

"It's late, O'Connor. Is there any real need for us to be here?" Joanne asked, after he continued to ignore us for about twenty minutes.

"Naw, you can go," he said, not even turning around.

I stood up. Joanne walked over to Cordelia and put her hand on Cordelia's shoulder.

"Let's go," she said gently. "We'll take you home."

Cordelia nodded assent, shakily standing up.

"Not Dr. James," O'Connor said.

"Then we'll stay," I said, sitting back down. "I'll stay," I amended.

"Are you charging me with something?" Cordelia asked him.

"Well, it is late," he said. "I'll be nice, Dr. James. This here patrolman," he nodded at on of the uniformed officers, "will take you home. And he'll hang around just so you don't decide to take any sudden trips. We want to know where we can find you."

"Home. Then here taking care of my patients," she retorted.

"You do that. Just be careful." He motioned the patrolman and Cordelia out. "Take good care of your patients," his voice floated after us.

"Damn him," Cordelia said under her breath.

Joanne and I walked with her to her car, the patrolman following behind. He got in the driver's seat.

"Call your lawyer," Joanne said as Cordelia got in. She nodded tiredly, shutting the door.

"Cordelia . . ." I said, leaning in the window. But there was nothing to say. I put my hand on her shoulder. "I'll be here tomorrow."

She turned to look at me, then covered my hand with one of hers.

The patrolman started the car. I moved away as he backed out.

Joanne and I walked around the building to her car. It was almost four in the morning. We got in and she started the car.

"Bastards," I said to the policemen in the building, adding to Joanne, "There's got to be a way to prove she didn't do it."

"If she didn't," Joanne said, as she pulled away.

"If? What do you mean if?" I demanded angrily.

"People make mistakes."

"Let me out," I said, suddenly furious. "Just fucking let me out of the car." I opened the door even though we were still going.

Joanne jammed on the brakes. She grabbed my arm. I tried to pull away. She reached with her other hand and got the back of my neck, pulling me roughly back in the car.

"You idiot," she said harshly. "You damned idiot. What good are you going to do anyone by running off half-cocked like that?"

"How can you think she did it?" I spat back.

"I don't. At this point I don't know anything was done." She shook me harshly and pulled me closer. "I haven't seen an autopsy report and I don't know how that girl died." I felt her fingers pressing into the back of my neck, tightly, angrily. "It may have nothing to do with Cordelia," she finished.

"What if she died of a botched abortion?"

"I don't know. Take things one step at a time."

"She didn't kill that woman," I stated.

"People make mistakes," Joanne replied tersely.

I grabbed Joanne by the shirt.

"No, not Cordelia. You can't say that."

"Can you promise me she's perfect? That her hand can't slip? You've seen how tired she is," Joanne retorted.

"Maybe not that. But I can promise you that if she did make a mistake, she wouldn't let the woman die, then dump her in some dirty basement to cover it up. Not Cordelia."

Joanne didn't say anything. But her grip slowly loosened, finally turning into an embrace, her hand gently rubbing the back of my neck.

"No, not Cordelia," she finally said.

I let go of her shirt, resting my hands along the ridge of her collarbone.

"Will you help?" I asked. "Can you?"

"Yes, of course."

"Thanks."

"Don't thank me. Alex and Cordelia have been friends since junior high. I could never explain — not to mention Danny."

"Danny'll help."

"Yeah, if she can."

"She'd better," I replied.

I looked at Joanne. I felt pressure from her hand on the back of my neck pulling me closer. We kissed, the anger becoming passion.

"My place?" she whispered in my ear. "I think I'd better change clothes before I show up for work tomorrow."

"Yes," I assented, breathless from our kissing.

Joanne drove us to her apartment.

"Shower?" she asked as she let us in.

"Yeah," I agreed, wanting very much to get the grime of this day washed off. "You first," I offered.

"Together?" she amended.

We did, making love under the streaming water, then collapsing into bed and a goodnight kiss. Then a kiss that wasn't goodnight, sex taking us past exhaustion, so when we finally rolled away from each other, we had no choice but to sleep.

I was awakened a few bare hours later by the phone ringing. Joanne answered it.

"I know ... Yes, I was there," she confirmed to someone. "Uh-huh ... she was with me. We'd gone out to dinner together." Then a pause. "I'll let you know as soon as I know something ... Alex, she's my friend, too ... Sorry, I'm tired ... That's okay, I needed to get up ... Yeah ... I'll call you. As soon as I know something. 'Bye."

She hung up.

"Bad news travels quickly," I said propping myself up on one elbow.

"I guess," she replied, lying back down. "God, I'm tired."

Her alarm clock went off.

"Sorry. No rest for the weary," I said.

Joanne got out of bed.

"I've got to keep moving or I'll never be awake by the time I get to work."

I slowly swung my legs out of bed.

"Me, too," I mumbled, still sleepy.

"You can sleep in," she offered.

"I want to go to the clinic. Tell Cordelia to shut up if she starts trying to be too nice a Southern girl and helping those poor hard-working policemen."

"Good idea," Joanne agreed as she headed off to the bathroom.

I forced myself to do some stretches. Anything to keep my body

126

moving. I finally woke up, not from the exercises but from remembering what had happened last night.

I was dressed when Joanne came out of the bathroom.

At my request, she dropped me off at a bus stop. I wanted to go back to my place and get my car. And change my clothes. I didn't want Cordelia seeing me in the same things I had worn yesterday. Joanne had offered to drive me to my apartment, but I wanted her to find out what was going on as soon as possible. She didn't need much persuading. We both wanted to know what was in the autopsy report.

Chapter 10

I arrived at the clinic around nine-thirty. The building was crowded and hectic, but voices were lowered, hushed whispers hissing down the hallways.

The police had sealed the door to the basement, the yellow tape glaring against the dull green walls.

The waiting room was quiet, subdued. Fewer patients were here than yesterday. I wondered if it was just standard fluctuation or if word had gotten out. Would you want to see a doctor in a building where they'd just found a dead body?

"You want to change your appointment?" I heard Bernie saying into the phone.

O'Connor would be interviewing anyone who might have seen Beverly Sue Morris here on Friday. And, of course, they would talk to their friends.

"Hi, Micky," Millie said, as she came out to put something on Bernie's desk. "You look like death warmed over. Late night?"

"Fairly. How's Cordelia?"

"She looks like death, period," Millie shook her head. "Do you know what's going on here? I've called Hutch, but he hasn't gotten back to me yet."

I nodded, then looked at the patients in the waiting room. "Store room?"

"Twenty minutes," she replied.

I nodded.

She headed back toward the examining rooms.

Cordelia stepped out of one of them. She looked up and saw me, giving me a wan smile. Millie was right, she looked exhausted, dark circles under her eyes, her skin a sallow shade. She glanced at something Millie was showing her, then back at me, a nod, an acknowledgment and then she reentered the examining room.

I went back into the hallway, glad that O'Connor and his boys weren't present, although I had no illusions that he wouldn't show up later. I had hoped to snag Bernie's telephone, but she obviously was going to be on it for a while. I went in search of a pay phone.

"Good morning, Michele," Sister Ann called to me from her office as I walked by.

"Morning," I replied.

She beckoned me in.

"The tape on the basement door. Do you know why it's there?" she asked.

"I do. And I'll even tell you if you'll let me borrow your phone to make a quick call. Local."

"Fair enough." She got up. "I'll run and get some coffee. How do you like yours?"

"A rumor of milk. Thanks."

She headed down the hallway.

I dialed Danny's office. She wasn't in, so I left my name and Cordelia's clinic number.

Sister Ann returned, handing me a mug of coffee. She looked expectantly at me. I took a sip of coffee, then closed her door. I sat back down.

"There was a body in the basement," I stated flatly.

"Oh, dear. Deceased, I presume."

I nodded.

"How . . . ? Who found it?"

"I did."

"I'm so sorry. Are you all right?"

I shrugged a fake nonchalance.

"One of the old men of the neighborhood?" she inquired.

"No," I shook my head. And I told Sister Ann about the young woman I had found. I didn't leave out the part about her being a patient of Cordelia's. Sister Ann would find that out soon enough anyway. Better from me.

She said nothing, listening intently to my story. When I finished, she said, "What do you think happened?"

"I know what didn't happen," I answered. "I know Cordelia didn't mess up an abortion and then cover her mistake by dumping the body in the basement."

"That young woman had an abortion?" Sister Ann asked. I'd forgotten I was talking to a nun.

"I don't know. Not for sure. I haven't heard the autopsy report yet," I answered, tensing for the lecture.

"What you say is true . . . Don't worry, I'm not going to proselytize," she said, seeing the tight look on my face. "I'm sure you and I disagree and I don't care to waste my time in a useless argument. Dr. James is, at least according to her moral code, not a murderer. Nor is she one of those weak-willed people who fall into this sort of abyss, because 'things got out of hand.' "

"No, she's not."

"But still, a young woman died and ended up in our basement. That disturbs me."

"And me," I added.

"What . . . ?" she began, but was interrupted by a knocking on her door. It opened and Aunt Greta stepped in.

"Here are the reports that Father Flynn . . ." Aunt Greta stopped when she saw me. "What are you doing here, Michele?"

"Indulging my latest perversion, Aunt Greta. Nuns."

"Don't be offensive," she reprimanded me.

"It's a state of being for me," I retorted.

"I'll be with you in a minute, Mrs. Robedeaux," Sister Ann broke in. Aunt Greta stood her ground. "If you'll just wait in the hall," Sister Ann prompted.

Aunt Greta backed out, leaving the door open. I got up and shut it.

"The police will surely question you," I said. "They're out to get Cordelia."

"I can only tell them the truth," Sister Ann answered.

"Do that. Just make sure you tell them the whole truth and not just the truth they want to hear."

She nodded.

I stood up.

"If there's anything I can do . . ." she said.

"I'll let you know," I finished.

I went back into the hall, pointedly ignoring Aunt Greta. I saw Millie duck out of the clinic and make for the store room. I went to join her.

"Is it okay if Bernie listens in?" she asked me as I slipped through the door.

"Sure," I said, leaving the door ajar.

"Hi," Bernie said as she came in. "Anything to get away from that phone."

I told them the story, including all the details, just as I had with Sister Ann. I emphasized that we didn't know how the young woman died.

"The paperwork doesn't prove anything," Bernie interjected. "Hell, people are probably stealing tons of receipts and insurance forms right now. Speaking of which, I'm sure the phone is ringing. Keep me up-to-date," she added as she headed back to her phone.

"Do they think the woman was murdered?" Millie asked.

"So far. Their theory seems to be that Cordelia butchered her on Friday and left her to die."

Millie made an angry, hissing sound, then shook her head. "Who's on the case?" she asked.

"Some bull by the name of O'Connor. He was pissed to hell that Joanne was here."

"Joanne's a hard-ass," Millie said. "Well, she is," she added in response to my look.

"I thought Joanne and Hutch got along," I replied.

"Oh, they do. Hutch says Joanne's the best cop he's ever worked with. She doesn't make mistakes. And if you work with her, you don't either."

"You try not to."

"I'll ask Hutch about O'Connor. But if I were doing an investigation, I wouldn't like Joanne looking over my shoulder."

"I'm doing one and she is," I answered.

"How bad is it for Cordelia?" Millie asked, her tone serious.

"I don't know yet. Soon."

She nodded somberly. "I need to get back. Thanks for filling me in."

I followed Millie back to the clinic. Aunt Greta was making the halls too dangerous to be out and about in. O'Connor, I was guessing, was due to show up anytime now.

I had just sat down and procured a magazine replete with promises on ways to improve my love life, when Bernie called me.

"Phone call," she said. "Take it in Dr. James's office." She pointed the way.

It was Joanne.

"Micky," she said, then uncharacteristically, paused.

I waited.

"It's not good," she said.

"How not good?"

"Bad. A perforated uterus. She died of shock and blood loss sometime on Friday afternoon. An incompetent abortion, in the medical examiner's opinion."

"Shit," I breathed.

"Yeah."

After a pause Joanne continued. "There's more. Another woman. She was found early this morning around the Industrial Canal. And . . ."

"A botched abortion," I finished, hoping Joanne would contradict me. But she didn't. "How . . . ?" I started, but I wasn't sure of my question and Joanne had no answers.

"You going to stay at the clinic?" she asked.

"I think so."

"If I learn anything else, I'll call you."

"Okay, thanks. Joanne . . ." I started to ask if I would see her, but backed away.

"I'll try to come by the clinic after work. If you'll still be there?"

"I will."

"Right." She hung up.

132

I sat for a moment, still cradling the receiver, then I put it down and started back for the waiting room. I was trying to decide when and what to tell Cordelia.

"Another phone call, Micky," Bernie called to me.

I turned back to Cordelia's office.

It was Danny.

"How'd you get your nose stuck in this?" was her greeting.

"You know me, Danno, can't take me anywhere. I keep stumbling over dead bodies."

"A bad habit, Mick."

But there was no sense of fun in our banter. Just a way to ease into the serious part.

"I know. What's the story?" I asked.

"So far as I know, the case is circumstantial. Nothing directly proving that Cordelia performed an abortion on this woman, and, even if she did, that that was what killed her. O'Connor might arrest her, but he probably won't. He needs a few more pieces of this puzzle."

"That's it?" I said. "A few more pieces of the puzzle? What are we supposed to do? Hope he doesn't find them?"

"Look," Danny cut me off. "I've talked to Hastings Johnson and Karen Shapiro. They're on this one. I told them it stinks. And that I'd be on the stand as a character witness for Cordelia James, because if there was ever a person who wouldn't commit murder, then she is that person. Okay?"

"Sorry, Danny," I apologized.

"You've heard the latest?" she asked.

"Perforated uterus and another body."

"My, you're quick. Dare I ask who your source is?"

"Joanne. But only because she called first."

"Good. She'll keep O'Connor honest. Find out what you can."

"I'm doing that." I heard O'Connor's voice in the outer office. "Speaking of which. Guess who just arrived."

"Call me if you have any complaints of police brutality."

"I will."

"I'll be here. Seriously, call me if anything happens." If he arrested Cordelia.

Danny and I said good-bye.

"You can't barge in here," I heard Millie exclaim.

"I can't, huh?" O'Connor replied. "You are obstructing a policeman in the performance of his duty. I need to see your esteemed Dr. James. Now, if not sooner."

I stuck my head out to observe, but didn't move to interfere. Millie could probably handle him better than I could. Another figure in white came up behind him.

"If you go in there," Elly said, " you might have to drop your pants and get a shot in the rear."

"Dr. James's office is three doors down, on the left. Why don't you wait there?" Millie suggested.

O'Connor grunted. I ducked back inside and made myself comfortable. I could hear his lumbering steps coming down the hallway. I wanted to be here when he interviewed Cordelia.

He grunted noisily when he entered and saw me ensconced behind Cordelia's desk. I'm sure he would have liked to have had Cordelia looking across her own desk at him sitting behind it.

"Good morning," I said cheerily. "Or is it afternoon yet, Detective . . . O'Connor." I left a pause just long enough for sergeant to fit in.

"What are you doing here?" he growled.

"My nails," I replied, as I nonchalantly examined my left hand.

"Well, little Miss Private Investigator. Do you know how Beverly Sue Morris died?"

"Perforated uterus. Very likely a botched abortion. As did the woman whose body was found near the Industrial Canal early this morning."

He grunted his displeasure. "Who told you that?" he barked.

"You mean I was right? It was really just a wild guess."

"Bullshit! Who told you? Ranson?"

"No," I prevaricated. "An old college buddy." I let it hang.

"Who?" he demanded. Then without waiting for an answer. "This is bullshit. It was Ranson."

"Danielle Clayton. I'm sure you know her."

"Uh," he grunted a vague negative.

"The Sherard murder case? The Rampart Street rapist? I thought you cops kept up with the D.A.s with the best conviction records."

He merely grunted again. But he knew who Danny was. And he got my message. By the book.

"Are you here to arrest me?" Cordelia stood in the doorway.

"Come in, Dr. James. Sorry your chair's taken," O'Connor said with a glance at me.

I got up, motioning Cordelia to her chair. I perched on a window sill behind her, looking protectively over her shoulder. She needed to be sitting for what O'Connor was going to tell her.

"Nice to see you didn't run away. Surprising considering what we've found." And he paused. A cheap dramatic effect.

"Which is?" Cordelia cut into his silence.

"Poor Beverly Sue Morris. She bled to death. Her uterus was perforated."

"Oh, no," Cordelia said, her jaw clenching.

"At least Beverly's got company," he continued relentlessly. "Alice Janice Tresoe, age thirty-two, three kids, by the way. She didn't like dying, it seems. Someone bound her at her wrists and ankles while she struggled. They pulled her out of the Industrial Canal this morning. Someone perforated her uterus, too. She was a patient of yours, too, wasn't she?"

"Oh, my God," Cordelia exhaled, turning her face from him as if she'd been hit. "She was here just last week."

"Why don't you tell me about them, Dr. James? It'll make it easier on all of us," his voice was gentle, almost kind. "Just get it over with."

He didn't say anything more, just let the silence invite a response.

Cordelia bent her head. She was crying. Then she straightened herself, not bothering to wipe the tears.

"The only thing I can tell you," she said clearly and distinctly, not letting her voice break, "is that I did not kill those women. You can question me as long as you like, but that's the only answer I can give you." She met his gaze, not wavering as he stared at her.

"You can bet on that, Dr. James. I will be questioning you for a long time."

"Until someone catches the real killer," I nettled him. "And by the way, where's the search warrant for that file?"

O'Connor pulled a piece of paper from his jacket pocket and handed it to Cordelia. He ignored me. "Maybe with a little sleep, your memory got jogged and now you remember something about that insurance form, huh?" he prodded.

135

"No, I don't," Cordelia answered, as she glanced at the search warrant.

"Too bad. How'd you get to be a doctor with a memory like that?"

Cordelia didn't answer him, merely handed back the search warrant.

"Perhaps you should do a little research, Detective O'Connor," I put in. "If you did, like I've already done, you'd find out that Dr. James sees between twenty to forty patients a day. Average, say twenty-two a day. Times five and a half is one hundred and twenty-one people a week. All with insurance forms and receipts, not to mention prescriptions and notes for school, employers and the like. That's a lot of name signing."

"So?" he grunted.

"Now, I'm sure you don't think Dr. James fills out all that paperwork. If she's lucky, she has time to glance at it. The patients do a lot of it. The nurses, Millie Donnalto, Betty Peterson, Elly Harrison, some and Bernice LaRoue most of the rest of it."

"Yeah, right. None of this is news to me," he said.

"If you'd been around here as often as I have," I continued, "you'd notice that, at times, it can be very busy here. A lot of people about. And that the reception desk is easily accessible from the waiting room. And . . . well," I stood up and reached into my back pocket, "I had no problem lifting two receipts and an insurance form. No one saw me." I walked around the desk holding out my purloined goodies for O'Connor to see.

"Doesn't prove anything," he remarked.

"And neither does the evidence you have," I returned.

"You could have stolen them last night."

"Give me ten minutes and I'll do it again."

"We'll see," O'Connor said, standing up. "Just don't go anywhere, Dr. James," he said as he went through the door. "And take very good care of your patients," he added.

"Asshole," I said loudly.

"What was that?" O'Connor asked from out in the hallway.

"Hemorrhoids. I'm taking advantage of Dr. James and getting some free medical advice," I called after him.

He grunted and continued down the hall.

"Now, about this asshole I'm having a problem with . . ." I continued, watching the door to see if O'Connor would storm back. He didn't.

I turned to face Cordelia. For a moment I thought she was crying again, but she wasn't. She was laughing, covering her mouth so she wouldn't do it out loud.

"Thanks, Micky," she finally said. "God, it's good to have people like you around at a time like this."

"Wish I could do more," I replied. I wanted to walk over to her and put my arms around her. Knowing O'Connor was lurking around the corner stopped me. Also not knowing if Cordelia would want me to hold her.

"Hey, Micky, I thought I heard your voice," Elly said, as she came in. "Oh, honey," she continued, seeing Cordelia's tear streaked face. She went over to Cordelia and put her arms around her. "It's been rough, hasn't it?" She stroked Cordelia's hair gently.

I wondered why I hadn't had the courage to do that.

"I'm okay," Cordelia said. "What are you doing here this early?"

"Reinforcements," Elly answered, letting go of Cordelia and perching beside her on the arm of her chair. "I was finished with my visits early, Danny reached me and said you might like some company."

"What does Danny think I am?" I interjected. "Chopped crawfish?"

"No, of course not," Elly replied. "She just expects you to have this thing solved by quitting time and she figured you might have to run around a bit to do that."

"No problem," I bantered back.

"I'm okay," Cordelia said, standing up. "I have patients waiting."

"Millie's doing prelim," Elly said. "Go wash your face."

"Thanks," Cordelia said. "Both of you." She headed for the bathroom at the far end of the hall.

"Are you going to the meeting?" Elly asked me.

"What meeting?"

"For the building. In about forty-five minutes. Evidently the police presence has upset some people."

"You'd think it would have been the body in the basement," I replied.

Elly grimaced. "I think that's what 'police' is a euphemism for."

"Yeah, I'll be there."

"Good, I need the moral support. Nuns always intimidate me. Back to work," she said.

I let her lead me down the hallway. Elly branched off to one of the rooms and I continued out to the waiting room It was almost empty, whether because of lunch or the ominous police presence, I wasn't sure.

"Micky, did you really steal some forms off my desk?" Bernie asked.

"Guilty as charged."

"Could I have them back? Those things disappear so quickly I was always sure someone was taking them," Bernie continued.

I handed the forms back to her, somewhat the worse for being in my pocket. I glanced at O'Connor to see if he had heard Bernie complain about the missing forms. He was too close to have missed it, but he was ignoring me.

I sat back down, unable to find my magazine of hot sex tips. I settled for one that promised to tell me how to eat chocolate and lose weight.

O'Connor finished questioning the staff, using the storeroom to, I presume, prevent me from overhearing him ask about the things I had told him earlier.

After that he and the other officers went down into the basement. I had heard noises and knew there were a couple of other cops down there.

Emma Auerbach walked into the clinic. She looked as surprised to see me as I was to see her.

"What are you . . . ?" I asked.

"I'm on the board of directors for the clinic. I thought Cordelia could use some support," she explained.

"She probably could," I agreed, thinking that Emma was excellent support. Then I told her what I was doing lurking about.

"I'm glad to see you," she said when I finished.

The last patient came out and after the requisite paperwork at Bernie's desk, left. Elly and Millie joined us. I made introductions. Then Cordelia emerged. She and Emma hugged.

"Meeting time," Millie said.

Bernie agreed to stay and guard the fort, as it were. The rest of us headed up the stairs to one of the larger classrooms where we would be meeting.

People were already there, Sister Ann and two other nuns, some civilians. They were arranging tables in a square. We helped them finish up, then sat down on the window side. Most of the church people sat on the opposite side. Sister Ann compromised and sat at one of the middle tables.

A priest that I'd never seen before entered. Followed by Aunt Greta. She sat down next to him, arranging a notebook and some papers in front of him.

He started the meeting by introducing himself as Father Flynn from blah, blah, blah parish, I didn't catch it. He evidently considered himself in charge of the meeting, ably assisted, of course, by Aunt Greta.

"This is, needless to say, a trying time," he intoned. "We are all upset by events of the past few days. Are you planning to close the clinic or keep it going part time?" he ended by asking, looking vaguely at our side of the table.

"It will continue full time," Cordelia answered.

"But how will you manage, with only two part-time doctors?" Father Flynn asked.

"One full-time and two part-time," Cordelia replied shortly.

"But I understand that," and he looked at a piece of paper that Aunt Greta was holding under his nose, "that your full-time doctor . . . a Dr. James was responsible for that poor young girl's death. Surely you don't plan to keep him on?" He looked at us as if it were a settled question.

Cordelia and Emma exchanged glances. I could almost see them counting to ten before they spoke. I kept myself under no such restraints.

"Your information is wrong," I stated. "Dr. James has not been proven responsible. Nor will she be."

"But the police . . ." he started.

"The police have chosen convenience over truth," I cut him off. "What evidence they have is highly circumstantial and very easily faked."

"Who are you?" Father Flynn asked, not very thrilled with my rebuttal of his prepared argument.

"Michele Knight. I'm a private investigator," I said. "I've been looking into the threatening letters and phone calls to the clinic and I'm the one who found the body."

"But the police . . ." he repeated.

"Not the police I've talked to. O'Connor's is by no means the only opinion on the matter. I've discussed the case with a Detective Sergeant and an assistant D. A. and they both think it stinks." He had his police and I had mine. At least whatever he said now, the police wouldn't be a monolith coming down against Cordelia.

"This is ridiculous. This girl doesn't know what she's talking about." Aunt Greta wouldn't be quiet very long. "You must do what you know to be right."

"Yes, thank you," Father Flynn said.

"The clinic is not under your control, Father," Cordelia spoke up. "Any decision concerning its operations is ours and ours alone to make."

"But surely you cannot allow a doctor under suspicion of murder to continue treating patients. Unless and until he is proven innocent . . ."

"That is our decision, not yours," Emma interjected.

"It cannot be solely an isolated decision," he retorted. "The reputation of your clinic affects us and our actions. It is insupportable that we be seen to support and condone a murderer."

Both Emma and Cordelia started to talk, but Father Flynn, hitting his full moral vigor, overrode them.

"Because I know from the police, and this is a fact, not an opinion," he thundered, "that what killed that unfortunate young woman was an incompetent abortion. One way or another a murder was committed. A child and a young woman have both died. We cannot be perceived as supporting that."

"I made a commitment to provide medical care for this community and I will not be hounded out by rumor and innuendo," Cordelia angrily shot back. "I don't know what happened to the young woman in the basement. I do know that I did not perform an abortion on her and I most certainly did not kill her."

"You're Dr. James, I take it," Father Flynn brilliantly deduced.

"Yes, I am."

"It would be best for all concerned if you quietly stepped aside until the police clean this thing up," he told her.

140

"If they do," I added.

"That's not possible," Cordelia quietly stated.

He shook his head sadly, as if faced with a recalcitrant child. Aunt Greta tsked dryly. A weighted silence fell, people shifting uneasily.

"But, Dr. James," I jumped in, "a reputation is an important thing. So what if a few hundred people are suddenly left without access to a doctor? A few cancers not caught early enough, blood pressure unmonitored, some undernourished babies. Hey, we all die sometime, but a bad reputation is forever."

"You don't care about reputation because you don't have one," Aunt Greta hissed at me.

"Sure I do. A bad one. It took a lot of work, but it was worth it."

Aunt Greta was getting her white, splotchy look. For a moment, I thought of backing down, apologizing, anything to protect myself, but then I realized — there's nothing she can do to me anymore. I stared defiantly at her.

"You were a difficult child from the start." Fury started creeping into her voice. "I gave you a righteous and Godly path to walk on," (and clichés into her speech), "but the minute you left my house, you deviated from it. I have only controlled myself for your dear, departed father's sake . . ."

"Hypocrite!" I lashed out at her.

"For his sake! You tramp!" she exploded, as if she'd been waiting years to call me that. "Thief! No shame. Sleeping with women, you lost your reputation the minute you left my house."

"Not true," I retorted defiantly. "It was before I left your house. It was so much easier to fuck strangers than be with my 'family' . . ."

"How dare you!" Aunt Greta screeched back. "Using such . . ."

"Pharisee. You self-righteous bitch," I shouted at her. Other voices were raised and shouting. Never say "fuck" in front of a bunch of nuns unless you want to create a commotion. Aunt Greta was calling me every name her prissy vocabulary would allow. And I was screaming back at her.

Suddenly there was a very loud bang and the cacophony ceased. Sister Ann had taken a large book and dropped it on the table.

"This is getting us nowhere," she said into the sudden silence.

141

"The purpose of this meeting is to constructively deal with the murder of a young woman and its consequences. Not solve family disputes."

"This is hardly . . ." Aunt Greta fumed.

"Silence, please," Sister Ann cut her off. "Cordelia is right. This community needs medical care and unless we can find a full-time replacement for her and a method of paying that person, she cannot just stand aside."

Father Flynn started to speak, but Sister Ann continued before he got past his first "but".

"At the same time," she said, "rightfully or wrongfully, people are afraid and rumors are spreading." She turned to Cordelia. "Would you agree to some compromise? Perhaps to have a nurse or other attendant always with you? I know your staff is overworked and I would certainly volunteer a few hours of my time, if that would help."

"If any patient requests it. Usually one of the nurses is there," Cordelia replied.

"And I think we should, jointly, come up with some public statement that will calm things down a bit and allow us to continue our work here. Any objections to that?" She looked around the table.

"I would have to review any statement that concerns this parish," Father Flynn stipulated.

"It will, of course, have to be acceptable to all concerned," Sister Ann replied. "I suggest we meet again to hammer out the main points. Perhaps the same time Friday?" She again looked around the table. Heads nodded, some readily, others reluctantly. "Now, is there anything else, before we adjourn?"

"Yes," Aunt Greta spoke up.

I turned my back and looked out the window.

"I demand an apology," she said. "I will not leave this room without one."

I started to say, "then rot here, bitch," but stopped myself. It would accomplish nothing, only make me sound childish. I was already feeling abashed at my earlier behavior, like I was a kid in a room full of grown-ups, out of place and unsure of the rules. My only consolation was that Aunt Greta had behaved as badly as I had. I kept my back resolutely turned.

"Apologize, child. You'll feel better," Father Flynn said.

"No," I replied, not turning. "I will never apologize."

"I should have called the police when you snuck out of my house," Aunt Greta said.

"I was of age," I answered.

"For the money you stole," she replied.

I turned to look at her. The self-righteous smirk was in place. "I didn't steal any money."

"Yes, you did. Over a thousand dollars. That's why you have to sneak out in the middle of the night."

"I didn't steal any money," I repeated, not for Aunt Greta, but for the others listening. Probably Bayard had taken advantage of my sudden departure.

She continued her litany. I turned my back to her, refusing to listen. I had thought that screaming at her, calling her all the names I had always wanted to say, would cleanse me, release some of the stored fury, but it hadn't. There would be no cathartic shrugging off of the years spent with her.

"Come on, Greta, let's go. 'Charity suffereth long and is kind,' " Father Flynn cut into her tirade. I heard them leave. Only distance silenced her.

I finally turned from the window when all the footsteps had ceased echoing in the hallway.

Emma was still there.

"I didn't steal the money," I repeated.

"Michele, dear, I know that. I was there, remember? I saw what you brought out of that ugly house. One battered suitcase and a small box of books. And I watched you unpack everything. I didn't see a thousand dollars. And even if I hadn't been an eyewitness to your not stealing the money, I'd hardly take the word of that termagant over yours."

"Thanks, Emma," I said, smiling at her choice of words. I surprised both of us by hugging her tightly. As I should have done a long time ago, except for Aunt Greta teaching me to expect people to use me. And Bayard giving me a reason to think Emma was using me.

"Thank you," she said as I released her.

I shrugged it off, but couldn't help smiling at Emma. In a way

143

that Aunt Greta would never know, or understand even if she did, I had won a victory over her today.

"No, thank you. Ten, no, a thousand Aunt Gretas and their accusations couldn't equal your belief in me."

"Sensible woman," Emma responded. "I must be off. Watch over Cordelia for me, will you?"

I agreed, then walked Emma to her car. After waving good-bye to her, I went back to the waiting room. And waited, ostensibly, watching over Cordelia for Emma, but really, just watching, hoping for something to fall into place.

Joanne arrived around five-thirty.

Hutch showed up a minute later, followed a few minutes later by Danny.

Hutch and Millie, taking advantage of heterosexual privilege, kissed hello. Danny and Elly discreetly hugged. Joanne and I just nodded. Danny also hugged Cordelia when she emerged from her last patient. We moved, en masse, toward the parking lot. I elbowed Danny in the side when I caught sight of O'Connor. Danny was in the process of inviting everyone over for dinner. And on the verge of holding Elly's hand. She straightened up at my hint.

O'Connor grunted at the sight of us.

"Well, well, what do we have here?" he asked.

"A group of people," I answered.

"Detective Ranson," he said, "you just happen to be here a lot, don't you?" He clearly didn't like her hovering over his investigation.

"It happens," Joanne shrugged. "Do you know my partner, Hutch Mackenzie?"

Hutch shook O'Connor's hand, towering over him as he did.

"Yeah, well, I can see why they paired the two of you," was O'Connor's comment.

Joanne stiffened.

"We work together real well because the crooks always think what you're thinking," Hutch said in his best man-to-man tone. "I first met Joanne on the judo mat. I figured, hey, no problem, I'll have her down in no time. Then I was looking at the ceiling, wondering what had happened." Hutch put his arms around O'Connor's shoulders buddy fashion, which only emphasized how much bigger Hutch was. "Then I said to myself, all right, bitch. And I got up and I got serious. And there was the ceiling again. And again. She threw me four times. Then I gave up. We make a great team, Joanne beats the crooks up and I sit on them."

"I meant no offense," O'Connor said, looking up at Hutch.

"None taken, Detective O'Connor," Joanne replied coolly.

"Well, Dr. James," O'Connor said, slipping away from Hutch. "Did you assemble your troops for my benefit?"

"No," Cordelia shook her head.

"Two police officers, a district attorney," he nodded at Danny. "Miss Private Investigator, your staff. I'm impressed. But not impressed enough to let you get away with murder." With that, he got in his car and drove away.

"Asshole," I commented.

"Just doing his job," Hutch shrugged.

"Abrasively," I answered.

With O'Connor gone, Danny repeated her invitation to dinner.

"Why don't I call Alex and have her meet us there?" Cordelia volunteered. "She's called twice today and I haven't gotten back to her yet."

"I'll do it," Joanne said. "I need to call her anyway." She declined Cordelia's offer of keys to get back into the clinic and went instead to the pay phone on the corner.

I suddenly felt tired, letting myself lean against my car, enervated by the day. I didn't feel up to parading around Danny's house with Alex there, pretending I wasn't sleeping with Joanne.

"Wake up, Mick, you haven't had dinner, yet," Danny chided my nodding head. "By the way," she continued, "where were you last night?"

"Here, most of it."

"After that?" she queried.

"In bed asleep," I replied, giving her a it's-none-of-your-business glare.

"Whose? I called you this morning around seven," she said.

"In the shower."

". . . and again around eight."

Danny, after our affair, always enjoyed being tacky about my random sex life. It used to be a game we played, but I didn't appreciate it now.

"She'll meet us there," Joanne said, as she crossed the parking lot.

"Good, the more the merrier," Danny said. "That makes eight of us."

"Sorry, seven," I said. "I'm exhausted. I'm going to go home and collapse."

"Sure, Micky. I'm used to you turning down a free meal and booze to go home by yourself," Danny jibed.

"You do look tired," Elly backed me up.

"Goodnight, girls," I said and headed for my car. I was on the verge of yelling at Danny, telling her to leave me the fuck alone, but my anger wasn't really toward her, rather the events of the past few days. I was vaguely aware of Danny, Elly, and Cordelia saying goodnight to me.

I got in my car. Joanne appeared at my window, leaning on the door.

"You okay?" she asked.

"Yeah, I'm fine. Tired."

"Is that really all?"

"Yeah. Really. Say hi to Alex for me," I replied. But I wasn't able to keep my voice as neutral as I would have liked.

"I'm sorry," she said.

"I'm okay. Just tired," I covered.

"I'm sorry," she repeated. "I thought we could be casual. I never meant to hurt you."

"We are casual. I've fucked a lot of women," I said harshly, barricading myself. "Don't think . . . that you matter more than any of the rest of them," I added callously.

"All right," Joanne replied shortly.

"Do say hi to Alex for me."

Joanne straightened up. I took her hand, preventing her from leaving. I watched Danny's car pull out into the street, followed by Cordelia's. I turned back to Joanne. I pulled her to me and kissed her. At first she was stiff, unresponsive, then her mouth opened slightly, letting my tongue in. She put her arms around me and returned my kiss roughly.

146

"Shit," she said, breaking off. "We can't do this here."

"I suppose not." I started my car. "You know where I live. And you have a key."

Joanne backed away from my car.

"Goodnight, Micky," she said, deliberately not giving me an answer.

"So long," I said and started to pull away. Out of my rearview mirror, I watched Joanne stalk over to her car. Then I drove away.

She came over after she left Danny and Elly's place.

Chapter 11

Joanne woke me at an obscene hour in the morning. "I have to go back to my place and change," she explained.

"Have fun," I sleepily replied.

"Roll over," she told me, her hand pressing on my shoulder, forcing me onto my back.

"It's too early in the morning," I demurred.

"You wanted me here," she countered, running her hand across my breasts, then down between my legs.

"Joanne . . ." I said, but her hand was starting to wake me up. Sleep could wait. I grabbed her, intending to throw her on her back and get on top, but she wrestled me down. Joanne is stronger than she looks, I thought, as I lay under her. She was on top of me, holding my wrists in her hands, pinning my arms against the bed.

"Spread your legs," she ordered.

We were fighting, I realized. Or continuing our sparring from last night. I had won that round by driving away and making her come over here. Now she was paying me back. I kept my legs together, trying to decide how much resistance my pride demanded.

We stared at each other, a battle of wills ensuing. Her weight shifted, pressing between my legs. I stubbornly resisted, even though I wanted her. Slowly her pressure pried my thighs apart.

I jerked up, taking advantage of the lightened pressure on my hands. But I didn't get free. We grappled for a minute, but I was unable to get her off balance. Her leg was between mine now, pressing into me.

"Spread your legs," she demanded again.

"Put your finger up me, all the way," I countered.

"You like that?" she retorted. But her finger was probing into the folds of my flesh, until she found my opening. I gasped as her finger shot into me.

Somehow anger had seeped into our having sex. No, I'd invited it by what I'd said last night.

"Two?" she asked, not waiting for an answer before putting the second finger up me. She pushed hard, deeply into me.

"No," I grunted at the heavy pressure. I caught her wrist before she could thrust into me again. "No, don't. I didn't mean it," I said.

She pulled her fingers out, but didn't say anything.

"Last night . . . in the parking lot . . . I didn't mean it," I clarified.

Joanne took both my hands and held them. We lay like that for a moment, then she softly touched her lips to mine.

"I'm sorry," I said.

"Micky Knight, you are the only person I know who has more defenses than I do," Joanne replied.

"A record, I suppose."

"Likely," she agreed.

"I don't know what made me say that."

"I probably scared the shit out of you by suggesting we had gotten more than casual."

"Yeah, you did," I said.

"Don't worry. That makes two of us."

"What do we do now?"

"I don't know," Joanne answered. And there was nothing else to say. We lay quietly, holding one another.

"I do have to go to work," Joanne finally said. She sat up and swung her legs out of bed.

"When will I see you again," I asked

"Soon."

"Tonight?"

"If you want," she answered, after a fleeting hesitation.

"If it's okay," I backed off, remembering she had other obligations. Another lover. "Maybe some other time would be better."

"Tonight," she answered. "But it'll be late, probably after ten."

"That's all right." I wondered if she was working late or seeing Alex. I didn't ask.

Joanne hurriedly dressed, kissing me good-bye. Then she left.

I fell back asleep.

When I woke up again, it was past ten o'clock. I took a long shower, waking myself thoroughly. I called the clinic and chatted briefly with Bernie. She told me that things were basically calm, considering. Then I called Andy to ask him about printers. We talked briefly, but he couldn't give me much information that would help me catch the letter writer. Computer printers can't be traced the way typewriters can. I thanked him and told him to remind Torbin that my vengeance awaited him.

Perhaps, in light of the murders, the letters were unimportant, but I had been hired to look into them. Besides, I wasn't convinced that the two weren't linked.

I began the laborious task of trying to hunt down a possible printer. I took an expurgated excerpt from one of the letters to different computer stores. They were all willing to show me a printer, but none of them could identify the exact printer it came from. I thanked them and promised that if I ever entered the computer age, I would let them know.

When I got back to my place around four, a message from my favorite policeman was waiting on the answering machine. O'Connor wanted me to come down to the station and "talk." I called to make an appointment for our "chat." Right now would be fine he said. I grunted in imitation of him and agreed.

So I spent the rest of the afternoon and early evening repeating over and over again my chase of the intruder and finding the body. O'Connor kept looking for flaws in my story. Particularly the part about the body not having been there in the morning. I got tired of it before he did, but my unvarying answers finally wore him out. He gave me a statement to sign and grunted me on my way.

I headed for the clinic. Since it was Thursday they had evening hours. Cordelia should still be there, I told myself as I turned into the parking lot.

Lights were on, but there was no one in the hallway when I entered. Nurse Peterson was the only person in the waiting room. She started when she saw me.

"Sorry, didn't mean to scare you," I said.

"That's all right. It's just with everything..." she trailed off and finished putting some files away.

"Understandable. Did you work Friday? Last Friday?"

She nervously slammed the file drawer closed. I seemed to have an unsettling effect of her.

"Friday?" she asked. "Uh...yes...I think so."

"Oh, it's you," Cordelia said, coming out of her office and seeing me in the waiting room. "You still here, Betty?" she asked, as she came down the hall and caught sight of Nurse Peterson.

"Just finishing a few things. I'm leaving now." To prove her point, she picked up her bag and left. Probably didn't want to get stuck with a notorious lesbian and a...I wondered what she thought Cordelia was.

"You look tired," I told her.

"Only because I am tired. Want to look at the latest mail?"

I grimaced, but nodded. She led the way back to her office.

I glanced over the letters. One to Elly, one to Millie, and one to Cordelia. The same pattern of nasty sexual innuendo with additional comments about how good they were at taking care of patients, particularly young women wanting abortions.

"Doesn't like animals, does he?" I said. He had mentioned Elly's and Danny's dog and Cordelia's kitten.

"How does he know my cat's name?" she asked. "Does he spy on us?"

I looked again at the letter. He did mention Rook, which I gathered was the name of Cordelia's kitten.

"I don't know." I looked again at the letters. "But he doesn't know everything. You and Elly. The letter to her calls her a frigid half-breed. And you're still too ugly to get a man."

"So? That's just filth."

"These letters haven't caught on to your sexuality."

"Interesting. But what does that prove?"

"Idle chatter. It's possible to stand in a grocery store line and mention your cat's name."

"But not being a lesbian."

"So the letter writer doesn't know you very well. Maybe someone who works here, or is around a fair bit."

"A large number of people."

"But if I hang around here enough, maybe I can flush him out," I said.

"Or scare him off. I'd settle for that."

"So you'll be seeing a lot of me in the future. Think you can survive?"

"It'll be hard, but I'll manage," she said. "Seriously, it's been . . . difficult the last few days. It's good to have my friends around."

She looked across her desk at me, a gentle smile on her face. I suddenly felt shy, at a loss for words. I glanced down at my feet, then quickly back at her, but her gaze had shifted. Oh, God, I'm sleeping with Joanne, slammed through my head.

"Let me pack up and we can get out of here," Cordelia said.

"Good idea."

She started arranging the papers on her desk, putting a number of them in her briefcase.

"Do you know what's going on with Joanne and Alex?" she asked abruptly.

"Uh . . . no . . . Is something . . . ?" I groped.

"They seemed . . . at odds last night. And they didn't leave together."

"Maybe they met later." I didn't like lying, but there didn't seem much way around it.

"No, they didn't. Alex came back to my place for tea and sympathy. She said Joanne was going somewhere else last night."

Cordelia was still packing things into her briefcase. I went over to the window, looking out, keeping my back to her. I was getting an unpleasant feeling in the pit of my stomach.

"Joanne's hard to understand," I commented.

"Sometimes," Cordelia replied. Then, "Alex thinks she's having an affair. Is she?"

"No, I don't think so," I quickly lied, hoping to end this conversation.

I felt Cordelia's stillness behind me.

"You're lying," she caught me. "She is, isn't she?"

I didn't say anything.

"Is it serious?" she probed.

I shrugged my shoulders. I didn't know.

"Come on, Micky," Cordelia said, standing beside me. "You see Joanne all the time. If anyone would know, you would. If . . ."

Then Cordelia stopped and looked at me. Just looked.

"It's you, isn't it?" she finally said. She abruptly turned from me and went back to her desk, slamming her briefcase shut. "It's none of my business," she said tightly. "I'm really tired. I need to go home and get some sleep."

"It's not like that," I spun to face her.

"Then what is it like?" she demanded, confronting me. "Are you sleeping with Joanne?"

"Well . . . yes . . . but . . ." I stumbled.

"Don't tell me," she silenced me. She picked up her briefcase and started for the door. "Alex is one of my closest friends. I can't be objective . . . don't tell me anything you don't want me to know."

She stood at the door, her hand on the light switch, waiting for me to precede her down the hallway.

"Will you tell Alex?" I asked as I passed her.

She turned off the light, and followed me into the waiting room. She didn't say anything until she had finished locking the clinic and we were in the hallway.

"I don't know. I honestly don't know. I need time to think," she said as we walked out of the building. "I wish I didn't know this." She turned her back to me and locked the main door.

"So do I," I answered.

"Danny was right," she said as she went past me to the parking lot.

"Right about what?" I demanded, following her.

"How . . . reckless you are. Inconsiderate."

"Goddamn Danny!" I burst out, angry, using her as a target.

Cordelia turned back, facing me.

"Don't say that. Not in front of me. Danny's my friend. I held Alex last night while she cried. But I don't suppose you give a damn," she spoke angrily. "While you and Joanne were . . ."

"Of course, it's all my fault," I retorted. "I threw Joanne down and said, 'come on, babe, let's fuck.' I'm sure Danny's told you that's how I seduced her."

She started to say something, then stopped and spun away.

"Goodnight, Micky," she said as she unlocked her car, not even bothering to look at me.

"You lied to me," I yelled at her. "You said you would tell me what you decided . . . when you walked out of my life last March."

"When I know," she overrode me.

"When's that going to be? When Hell freezes over?" I demanded.

"No. Tonight. Good-bye, Micky." Still not looking at me, she got in her car and started it. She drove past me and pulled out into the street without even looking back.

I hit my car, pounding the hood with my fists, then just leaned against the metal, sobbing.

I finally got in and drove back to my place. Joanne was there waiting for me.

"What happened?" she asked when she saw me.

I told her.

"I don't want Cordelia to tell Alex," she said when I finished. "I'll do it. Please ask her not to tell Alex until I get a chance to."

"Cordelia's not speaking to me. You'll have to do it."

"All right," Joanne replied shortly. "Give me your phone."

I picked up my phone and started to hand it to her, then stopped. This was my fault. I dialed Cordelia's number.

"Hello?" she answered.

"Don't tell Alex," I said. I figured she'd know who it was. "Joanne wants to talk to her first."

"Is she there?"

"Yes," I answered.

"Staying?"

"I don't know."

154

"I won't tell Alex. I'd rather not."

"Thanks."

"Don't thank me," she replied. A pause, then she finally said, "Goodnight, Micky." She hung up.

I put the receiver down.

"She won't tell Alex."

"Thanks," Joanne said, pacing the room.

"Don't . . ." but I didn't want to repeat Cordelia's words. "I'm sorry, Joanne."

"Can't you lie any better than that?" she asked.

"I tried. Don't worry, everyone will know it's my fault. What chance did you have against the all-time dyke slut champion of the Southeast?"

She sat down next to me.

"It's not that black and white."

"Sure it is. Ask Danny. Or Cordelia," I said.

"Come on," she said, taking my hand. "Let's get some sleep."

"Hadn't you better leave?"

"Do you want me to?"

"No, but I'm a slut."

"Stop it," she said angrily. "You're not a slut."

"Sure I am. Ask Danny. Ask Cordelia. Ask Alex. Ask any number of women whose names I can't remember," I answered bitterly. "Go back to Alex."

Joanne got up. "Come to bed when you stop feeling sorry for yourself," she said, then went into my bedroom.

"Joanne . . ." I started, following her. I remained in the doorway, watching as she calmly undressed and got into my bed. "Joanne," I said. "I'm not worth it. Go home to Alex. Please."

"Lie beside me. Talk to me," she replied.

I sat down on the edge of the bed, keeping my clothes on.

"I've made a mess, haven't I?" I finally said.

"Doesn't everybody? Get undressed and come to bed," Joanne answered.

"Joanne. What about Alex? Is it worth losing her over me?"

"Micky, I know some rule book somewhere says we're not supposed to do this, but real life isn't played by the rules. My life certainly hasn't been."

"Cordelia told me that Alex was over at her place last night."

155

"So? They make a good couple," Joanne said.

"Not like that. Tea and sympathy. Alex was crying, Cordelia said," I explained, hoping to elicit some guilt from Joanne.

"Good. She can use something to cry over."

"Joanne? How can you be so . . . ?"

"Cruel? Callous? Look, honestly, I don't like making Alex cry, but my sleeping with you is hardly the end of the world. If she and Cordelia want to run around and pretend that it is, that's their problem, not mine," Joanne answered.

"How about me? I don't like making Alex cry." Or Cordelia despise me.

"You're not, don't think that you are. Her most poignant childhood memory is of some cat being run over. That's it. My father used to throw cats against the side of the garage when he was drunk. And if he was drunk enough, us kids, too," she added bitterly.

"That's not Alex's fault."

"No, it's not. But it's not my fault that she lives in a safe, little blue-blooded world."

"That makes it okay to cheat on her?" I demanded.

"I've made no promises. We're not Danny and Elly, with joint accounts and house-buying plans. I've never said forever, and I've never said I wouldn't sleep with somebody else. Maybe she expected it. I guess that's the way they do things. If you sleep together for over six months, then it's permanent and indelible. If she's crying, it's only because she has expectations I can't meet."

Joanne put her arms around me and pulled me on top of her.

But I had one more question.

"Do you love her?"

"Yes," she finally said. "But love isn't always enough."

She kissed me. We made love without saying anything more.

"Joanne?" I said when we were finished and I lay next to her in her arms. "Why isn't love enough?"

"Shit, Micky, sometimes you ask the oddest questions."

"Philosophy major. Bent me all out of shape."

"Then you should have a better answer than I do. If I had any real answers, I could stay with Alex. Not be mucking around," Joanne replied.

"Don't worry about me. Great sex, good company. I'll be fine."

"But I do worry about you," she said, brushing her hand against my cheek.

"You're not doing anything to me. At least nothing that I don't want done."

"Not yet. Give me time. Where do we go now?"

"Whenever we get temperamental, in opposite directions," I said half-seriously.

"We're both so angry. Too angry, I suspect. But I wanted someone who knows what it was like to be hit as a kid."

"No one ever hit me," I said.

"What about your aunt and uncle?" she questioned. "They never hit you?"

"No, not really. I was spanked a lot. My cousins sometimes hit me, but they were kids."

"Older or younger?"

"Bayard was five years older. Still is, I guess. Mary Theresa three years and I was a little older than Gus," I answered.

"Which one hit you?"

"Well . . . Bayard, mostly."

"Anything else?"

"Why do you ask?"

"Why do you think?"

"Were you abused?" I asked her.

She didn't reply at first.

"Yes," she finally said. "But I don't want to talk about that now."

"Neither do I."

We lay still, holding each other tightly. When we woke the next morning we were still next to each other, Joanne's arm around my waist.

Chapter 12

We made love again, before Joanne left for work. She had brought a change of clothes this time. After she left, I took a quick shower and got dressed, planning to go on to the clinic. I didn't dawdle, but I didn't hurry either. I was reluctant to run into Cordelia.

It was going to be a hot day, I noticed as I got into my car. That didn't put me in a more cheerful frame of mind. Nor did the line of protesters in front of the clinic. The parking lot was jammed. Park and Protest, I gathered. I finally parked by blocking Cordelia's car.

I got out and glowered at the rag-tag line of protesters.

"Are you here to have an abortion?" one of them accosted me, a young man with perfectly combed brown hair.

"No," I answered. "I'm here to have all the cars that don't have legitimate business in this building towed. Starting with yours," I added.

"You can't . . ." he started.

"Private property, buddy. I'm going to get a list of license plates that belong here. Any not on that list is gone. Got that?"

I turned away from him and marched into the building. Then ran up the stairs to a room overlooking the parking lot. The right-to-ifers were doing their best exodus imitation. I guess they weren't willing to get towed for the cause. I had no idea whether I could really get their cars towed, but I saw no point in telling them that. I went downstairs to the clinic.

"Hi, Micky," Bernie greeted me. She, at least, seemed happy to have me here.

"Hello, Miss Knight," Nurse Peterson said.

"How'd you find a place to park?" Bernie asked. "I ended up a block away."

"The power of suggestion," I replied. "I suggested that if their cars didn't belong in the lot, they would be towed."

Bernie burst out laughing. Nurse Peterson looked like the idea of such deviousness was unthinkable. But virginity will do that to you.

"Plenty of parking places now," I added.

"Maybe if those weirdos are gone by lunch time, I'll move my car," Bernie said.

"Do you trust me?" I asked, sitting on her desk.

"Absolutely," she replied.

"Give me your car keys."

"Brave woman," she said as she fished them out of her purse.

"No, you are. Letting me drive your car."

"Bernie, what happened to my nine-thirty?" Cordelia asked as she came down the hallway to Bernie's desk. She stopped abruptly when she saw me perched on it, with Bernie handing me her car keys. "Hi, Micky," she said stiffly.

" 'Morning, Dr. James," I replied.

"Can't we do anything about those damn protesters?" Cordelia said shortly.

"We've cleared the parking lot. Or Micky has," Bernie answered.

"How?" Cordelia asked, then, "Never mind," when she noticed it was me she was asking.

"I told them I was a card-carrying deviant and that I would spit on their cars, thereby ensuring that all their kids would turn out queer," I retorted, irked at her shortness.

Cordelia gave me a furious don't-you-dare-mention-gay look.

"Fine. Whatever works," she finally said, not in a pleasant tone of voice. "Call Mrs. Jenkins and get her to reschedule. The earlier the better," she added to Bernie. Then she went back down the hall to her office.

I borrowed a note pad from Bernie, on which I made up a list of probable license plate numbers.

"Good luck getting through the line," Bernie added after she gave me directions to where her car was.

After snarling my way through the protesters, I found Bernie's car and drove it back to one of the many vacant parking spaces. Then I wandered around the lot, pretending to check tag numbers, every once in a while scowling at the protesters. After re-parking my car, I sat on its hood, the guardian of the lot. Every car that pulled in, I asked what their business was. Politely, of course. I didn't want to scare away any more of the patients than already had been. Any of those that wanted or seemed to need it, I escorted into the building. I sent a few right-to-life reinforcements out into the cold, cruel world of parking in the street.

By late morning, the sun was beating down, making the sunny side of the street a toasty place to be. I was perched on the hood of Cordelia's car, which was parked in a comfortably shady corner of the parking lot. The right-to-lifers, not an attractive crew to start with, were looking boiled and bedraggled. God makes the sun shine, I thought merrily.

A car drove into the lot, pulling along side Cordelia's.

"Hi, Micky," Alex said as she got out.

"Oh. Hi, Alex," I replied.

"What's going on here?" she asked.

"The anti-choice forces are clustered . . ."

"Not them. They're old hat. What are you doing hanging out in the parking lot?"

"Guarding the forces of light against the evil of bigotry," I answered.

"Uh-huh, that's about what I figured," Alex replied.

"What are you doing here?"

"I heard you were here," she bantered.

"Right."

She leaned against the hood.

"I'm trying to find out what everyone seems to not want to tell me. C.J. called me last night and arranged a lunch date, with her there's-something-you-need-to-know voice. Then Joanne called this morning just after I got to work, also wanting to meet me for lunch and asked me to put Cordelia off. So I called C.J. and she said it was a good idea for me to see Joanne first. Then she suggested dinner tonight. Anyway, Joanne just called saying she couldn't make lunch, how about dinner, in her serious, we-must-talk voice. So you want to go to lunch and tell me what's going on?" Alex asked. "I could even get sandwiches and we could have a picnic in the parking lot," she added.

"Uh . . . thanks, Alex, but us guardians of justice must never relax our vigilance."

"Not even for an oyster po-boy?"

"Besides," I said in a more serious tone, "You should probably talk to either Joanne or Cordelia first."

"Oh, no, not you, too," Alex moaned. "But you know what's going on?" she queried.

"Well . . . yeah."

"Actually, you'd probably be the best person. C.J. and Joanne are both likely to be too serious about the whole thing. You and I could probably put it in the proper perspective."

"Oh, Alex," I shook my head.

"Don't worry. I'm not carrying a small pearl-handled revolver in my purse. I'm not even carrying a purse. You're the 'other woman', aren't you?"

"Oh, shit, is it that obvious?"

"No, but given Joanne's schedule, the list of possibilities wasn't very long. Besides, I was kind of hoping it would be you."

"Hoping?" I looked at her incredulously.

"Well, yeah. Let's be adults. I always figured the two of you would have to sleep together or start throwing punches. I'm glad it's the former and not the latter."

"I don't know what to say, Alex."

"Then let me talk. I'm good at it. Can I ask a question? How is she?"

"Joanne? Okay, I think. It's hard to tell. Angry. At times."

"Yeah, something's gotten to her. But she won't talk to me. I care about her . . ." her voice trailed off.

"I'm sorry, Alex. I never meant . . . I'm the fuck-up here," I finished.

Alex put her hand on my shoulder.

"Remember, we're supposed to be adults," she said. "Besides, I sleep with Joanne Ranson. I know better than to fall for that Micky Knight is an evil Donna Juana shit. You're not the villain, I'm not the villain, and Joanne's not the villain. If there is a villain, well, I think we'd have to go a long way back to find him."

"Meaning?" I asked.

"I'm not sure. It's one of those things Joanne doesn't talk about. But . . . one day my mother was over. My mother knows all about me and is happy that I'm with a respectable officer of the law."

"Yeah, you could be with a scruffy semi-employed P. I.," I couldn't resist adding.

"In which case my mother would be happy that I was with someone who is independent enough to follow her own path. My mother is that type of person. Anyway, she was over visiting us, being my mother. I think she and Joanne ended up talking about why we don't live together. What impact being found out could have on our careers, particularly Joanne's. My mother was her usual, wonderful, sympathetic self. After she left, we went to Joanne's."

"Late, after eleven, the phone rang. I picked it up. I thought it was the wrong number, a slurred, drunken voice. Until she demanded to speak to Joanne."

"Her mother." I could see where this story was going.

"Uh-huh. They talked for about fifteen minutes, Joanne's expression getting angrier with every minute that passed, her replies terse monosyllables. Until she said, 'I don't want to talk about it,' and slammed down the phone. Then yanked the plug out of the wall. I made some offhand comment about don't forget to re-plug it in the morning. Joanne started yelling that she'd plug her phone in whenever she felt like it and didn't need me to tell her how to run her life, and so on. I did realize that she wasn't really angry at me; I just happened to be there."

"Lucky you," I broke in.

"Usually she flares for a minute or two, then gets control. But this time she didn't. She continued, finally going at me for my pampered existence. No drunken moms in my family."

"That's not fair to you."

"Those little hurt girls never go away, do they?"

"No, I don't guess we do," I answered, remembering my yelling match just a few days ago with Aunt Greta.

"Joanne started drinking. One after the other. Sometimes she'll have a drink or two, but she's strict about it. She was getting drunk. I ended up leaving. I hated leaving her in that state but . . . I'm not very good at dealing with that kind of anger. Joanne was right, my family never fought like that. That's why I'm glad she's with you."

"Alex, that's a non sequitur," I commented.

"I think right now she needs someone who understands the anger. I don't gather your mother is likely to take you and Joanne out to dinner on her birthday, like mine did."

"No, not likely. Not at all likely. Hell, she won't even get drunk and call me up."

"Would it be prying too much to ask what happened?"

"She left. When I was five. Found something better to do than hang out in the bayous raising a kid."

"I'm sorry, Micky." Alex put her hand on my shoulder, then she rubbed the back of my neck.

"Hey, life goes on," I shrugged it off. Alex continued to rub my neck.

"So they say," she answered.

"What now? Do we meet at dawn to duel?"

"Sounds good to me. Witty repartee at ten feet?"

"Barbed comments at five?"

"What do we do?" she said quietly.

"What do you want?" I asked.

"I would like Joanne back. But I don't know if that's up to you or me or even her. In the meantime, take good care of her."

"That's it? Aren't you . . . ?"

"Jealous? A bit. I've always wanted to have an affair with a really tall, dark, good-looking woman. But no, I get tea and conversation with Cordelia James. Joanne does have a lot to answer for."

"But, Alex, Cordelia's tall and good-looking."

"C.J.?" Alex paused to think about it. "I suppose, but by tall I didn't mean giraffe."

"She's not that much taller than I am."

"No, but you're a lot cuter."

Alex let her arm drop so that it was around my waist.

"Alex," I kidded her back. "Don't flirt with me. You know I'll sleep with anything that has a vagina."

"Anything?"

"A few minor exceptions."

"Good. Glad to know you have some standards. On the serious side. I love Joanne. Enough to let her go if need be. I just want you to know that. And enough to want to be friends with the people who care about her. Okay?"

I draped my arm across her shoulders. "Alex, if Joanne is insane enough to throw you over for me, then she's too crazy for me to want to be with."

"See, I told you that we were the best people to discuss the matter. Cordelia has this adultery thing. I don't guess she ever got over her dad sleeping around."

"Tell me about it," I said, with a nod of my head in the direction of the clinic.

"Uh-oh, C.J. been moralizing at you?"

"A bit." To put it mildly.

"I'll talk to her." She stood up, went to her car, reached in and picked up some books that were on the seat. "Just give her these books and tell her we had a lovely chat in the parking lot. And that you and she can have dinner tonight."

"Not likely."

"Like everyone else, Cordelia has her little overreactions. But she's remarkably tractable when shown the error of her ways. Tell her I said hi and that I will talk to her; she doesn't need to talk to me."

"Okay, I will. Thanks, Alex."

"No problem. I'd talk to her at some point anyway."

"Not just for that. For . . . I don't know . . . not coming after me with a .22."

"I can't shoot straight. Take off my glasses and I can't even see the side of a barn."

She set the books down next to me, then put her arms around me and hugged me, resting her head against my chest. "So I don't have much choice but to be reasonable and mature."

"Sure you do. You have lots of choices. I don't know that I could make the one you've made. You can't tell me this doesn't hurt."

"Hugging you? No, it's lots of fun."

"You know what I mean. It would be very easy for you to hate me. It's a lot harder to put your arms around me, knowing that . . ." I started to say that I'd been holding Joanne only a few hours ago, but I backed away from so blunt a contrast.

"That Joanne was sleeping with you last night?"

"Yes."

"Hell, Micky," she said, "sometimes we have to choose to forgive or to hate. I honestly believe I'd much rather forgive Joanne than hate her. You, too."

"Some things are unforgivable."

"That hasn't happened yet. Not to me. You and Joanne live with it. But I don't. It's unforgivable to beat a child."

"No one beat me. A few spankings. I survived."

"Micky, sometimes the worst violence isn't physical," she said softly.

Alex tightened her arms around me. I rested my chin on the top of her head.

"Now," she continued after a moment, "I hadn't intended to get so serious. I thought we could stick to discussing sex."

"We probably should have."

We were rudely interrupted by a protester yelling at us. "Would you stop that pornographic display?" the offended man shouted. "There are women and children here."

Alex and I, needless to say, continued hugging.

"Micky, even if it gets you in trouble with Cordelia, can I ask a favor?"

"Anything."

"I would really like to offend those people," she said.

"And?"

"Kiss me, you fool—I've always wanted to say that—if we can reach, that is."

"I'll slump."

So Alex and I kissed in the parking lot with about fifteen hard-core conservative bigots watching us. And probably a few nuns.

"Good," Alex said when we broke off. "Now tonight when Joanne is sitting there, trying to figure out how to tell me about the two of you, I can say, oh, by the way, honey, if you hear any stories about Micky and me kissing on the parking lot of Cordelia's clinic, well, I just want you to know it's true. And, yes, I know that the two of you are doing 'it' but I didn't let that stop me from carrying out my obligation to offend numerous bigots at every opportunity."

"Alex, you are fucking incredible," I laughed.

"And vice versa," she parried. "Bye, Mick. Maybe you should just give the books to C.J. and smile knowingly. You know how to smile knowingly."

Alex got into her car.

"So long, Alex. It's been fun."

"Yeah, it has. Let's be friends."

"I'd like that." I waved as she pulled out. Joanne would be an idiot to give her up.

All that remained of the protesters were the few stalwart enough to have survived watching two women kiss. I guess they were afraid if enough people saw how much fun we were having, they'd all convert to being queer. Well, it seemed like a good way to prevent abortions to me.

Emma's silver Mercedes pulled into the lot. For a second I wondered what she was doing here, then I remembered that today was the day for the rescheduled meeting that Aunt Greta and I had so unceremoniously ended before.

We said hello and I explained my presence in the parking lot. She nodded approval at the much diminished protest line. Between Alex, myself, and the shining sun, they were down to about five diehards.

"Come, let's go to the meeting," Emma suggested.

"No, not me," I answered, shaking my head.

"But you have to be there. You defend Cordelia so much better than she can ever do. Come along," Emma said, decisively taking my arm and leading me into the building.

"But what if Aunt Greta is there?"

"I would welcome it," she stated, but didn't elaborate.

We walked together up the stairs to the room where the meeting was to be held. The tables hadn't been moved from Wednesday. Most of the same people were already there, sitting on the same sides as before.

Only Nurse Peterson was missing from the clinic side. Millie,

Elly, and Bernie said hi to me. Cordelia greeted Emma. There was only one chair left on our side. I let Emma take it and ensconced myself on a window ledge to survey the action. I put Cordelia's books on the next window sill. I would give them to her later.

Father Flynn, with, of course, Aunt Greta, breezed in. She looked around the room, saw me and set her lips in a hard line.

Father Flynn opened the meeting with a brief welcome. Then Sister Ann read the prepared statement. It was fairly bland and non-committal. Perfect for the situation. Events were distressing, blah, blah, every effort to help the police, blah, services not to be inter-rupted, and so forth.

Father Flynn wanted a stronger statement about the heinous-ness of the crime and hope that the criminal would soon be appre-hended. Emma countered with a suggestion that we express confidence in all the staff and volunteers of the various groups in the building. Sister Ann compromised and added both. She read the statement again and both sides seemed vaguely content with it.

"Is there anything else?" Sister Ann asked.

No one said anything. Sister Ann gave a brief nod and the meeting was over. I quickly looked out the window, wanting to avoid any last parting glances with Aunt Greta. A chorus of chairs scraping back told me that people were leaving. I heard Emma's low voice discussing the next board meeting with Cordelia.

The soft brush of a shoe made me look.

"Michele." Aunt Greta. She was standing only a few feet from me. "You know you are welcome anytime you care to visit. I'm sure Claude would like to see you."

Had she changed? Were there pieces and places to her I had never seen? "No," I answered warily, "I didn't know that. I never felt very welcome."

"Well," she said. "I'm sorry you feel that way. Of course you resented us because Claude and I weren't LeMoyne and our house wasn't a large shipyard out in the bayous. I thought you'd outgrow that."

I studied her, but she wasn't really looking at me, her eyes focused somewhere behind me. "I guess some little girls never grow up."

"So I gather. I was only trying to help you," was her reply.

I'd heard her say that too many times. "Were you? When you

hit me with Uncle Claude's belt until I was black and blue from my shoulders to my knees? Was that supposed to help me?" I retorted bitterly.

"You could have stopped that any time you chose. All you needed to do was apologize. It's really your own fault for being so stubborn. You needed discipline."

No, nothing had changed. For one brief moment, when she had come over to me, I had hoped that Aunt Greta had wanted to connect, after all these years, welcome me. That I felt a flash of disappointment surprised me. The eight years I had spent with her seemed such a blur of disappointments. After that I didn't think she could ever disappoint me again. As we always had, we would only talk at each other, never connect.

"And you had no choice but to beat a child black and blue until she apologized for something she hadn't done," I returned, the disappointment eroding into bitterness.

"So you say, Michele. I never hit you that hard."

"So you say," I answered tersely, feeling a familiar enervation and disillusionment seeping over me. Leave, just leave, I silently told her. For once leave me alone.

"I did want you to know that I forgive you. For stealing the money when you left," she added at my uncomprehending look.

"I didn't steal any money."

"Of course you did. You needn't bother denying it."

"I never stole any money from you," I repeated.

"Nonetheless, I forgive you."

"How kind of you to forgive me for something I didn't do."

Aunt Greta ignored my sarcasm. She would have her say. "And there is another thing, Michele. I feel it is my duty to tell you this, even though I know it will be painful for you." She stepped in closer and lowered her voice to a harsh whisper. "That doctor," a jerk of her head in Cordelia's direction, "do you know who she is?"

"Yes," I answered.

"No, I don't think you do. I'm sorry to tell you this, but it was her father who caused the accident that killed LeMoyne. I guess trouble runs in her family."

"I know who she is. And I know what her father did," I answered.

"You do? How do you know that?" Aunt Greta demanded, taken aback that her announcement didn't have the impact she had anticipated.

I shrugged. I didn't care to tell Aunt Greta anything about Cordelia.

"How can you have anything to do with her?" Aunt Greta hissed at me.

"She's not her father," I retorted.

A knowing look crossed her face. "Is she . . . like you?

"She's a decent, caring person," was the only reply I made.

"Oh. And well-to-do. That family has lots of money. I see how you can associate with her."

"You've given me your news, Aunt Greta. Please go." I wanted to yell at her, just scream, "You don't understand. You don't. You never did." But she wouldn't understand.

"I don't really blame you, Michele, for how you turned out. I know you were influenced, corrupted by that woman." Aunt Greta was referring to Emma.

"That's not what happened," I retorted, turning away from her. I wanted to get away, to leave Aunt Greta in the past. Not to ever give her the power to disappoint me again. I noticed that Emma and Cordelia were watching us. As close as they were, they could probably hear every word. Aunt Greta had never met Emma.

"What business did that woman have taking a young girl into her house?" Aunt Greta insinuated. "What did she want with you anyway?"

"I was leaving your house on my eighteenth birthday. Whether I had a place to go or not," I shot back. We wouldn't connect, but we couldn't back away either. We would argue, the same rage rattling around in its empty cage. "Emma didn't want anything of me." I would be defiant, Aunt Greta would try to break my defiance.

"No one believes that," Aunt Greta retorted.

Emma stood up. "I'm Emma Auerbach," she said with a controlled quietness I'd never seen in her before.

"Well," Aunt Greta huffed, giving Emma an appraising look.

"What are you accusing me of, Mrs. Robedeaux?" Emma asked softly.

Cordelia got up, standing beside Emma. I noticed that Father

Flynn and Sister Ann were still in the room. I hadn't seen Elly or Millie leave. They were both still probably behind me. Aunt Greta, too, noticed our audience.

"My adopted niece," she said, "when she was living with me, went to Mass twice a week, got As in school, was required to do housework everyday and was always in her bed by ten p.m. But something happened once she left my house. She was . . . seduced into a corrupt lifestyle. I couldn't stop it. She was eighteen by then."

"I don't seduce children, Mrs. Robedeaux," Emma said. "What choices Michele made were her own."

Aunt Greta, from the safe vantage point of moral superiority, stood looking at Emma. I recognized the turn of her mouth. She had looked at me that way so many times.

We're going to play this game again, I thought. Aunt Greta, the self-sacrificing martyr battling against evil and corruption. It was her favorite role and I was her favorite battlefield because I wasn't enough of her child that she could be blamed for my fall from grace. I was infuriated at her dragging in Emma and Cordelia with her ugly insinuations.

"The wrong choices," Aunt Greta spat back. "Under your watchful influence."

Fine, let's play this out. It was time for me to be a defiant, disobedient child.

"You're wrong," I told Aunt Greta.

"Don't bother protecting her," she jabbed a finger in Emma's direction.

"I'm not. If you don't believe anything else I say, believe this—I was sleeping with women long before I met Emma. In bed by ten o'clock, out again by ten-thirty. Too bad you weren't astute enough to notice all the mornings I came to breakfast hungover. Or high. If I went to Mass, did the dishes, and got decent grades, you didn't give a shit what I really did."

"Michele, I've told you, I don't blame you. You don't need to behave like this," Aunt Greta said. "And watch you language," she added, more for Father Flynn's sake than mine, I suspected.

"You don't blame me? I blame you. I blame you for being a self-righteous hypocrite who couldn't be bothered seeing anything you didn't want to see. I . . ."

"Michele! That's enough," she berated me.

No, not this time. It won't work anymore. I'm thirty now, not thirteen and Aunt Greta doesn't have Uncle Claude's belt to back up her demands. A rage welled up from that little girl who didn't grow up. Suddenly, the only thing I wanted was to fight back. "You ought to be thankful that I slept with women. At least I wasn't pregnant by the time I was seventeen. Now, wouldn't that have been embarrassing for you, if both Mary Theresa and I . . ."

"Michele! I don't know what I've done to deserve this from you," Aunt Greta cut in.

"Nothing. You've done nothing. You've been a blameless, put-upon woman your entire life," I yelled at her. My hands were trembling with rage, some monster had been let loose. "Hey, do you remember Mrs. Linden, a Godly and righteous woman you told me? When she canceled that prayer breakfast with you? She wasn't too busy. She just didn't feel like facing you after having had sex with me the night before."

"That's an outrageous lie," Aunt Greta bellowed.

"She had a mole on her upper thigh and her pubic hair was blond, so you were wrong about her dying her . . . "

That was punctuated with another, "Michele!" from Aunt Greta.

But she couldn't stop me, couldn't shut me up, couldn't punish me later. Power. She no longer had any over me. Revenge offered itself to me. I took it with no remorse and no care. "The first time I smoked dope was when Bayard gave me some. I was twelve at the time. He thought it would be funny—"

"That's an evil lie —"

"— Be funny to see his little cousin, excuse me, adopted cousin, get shit-faced. He was dealing in college, you know."

"She is not a well child," Aunt Greta said starting to walk away, but Emma and Cordelia were in her way. "See what you've done," she sputtered at Emma, turning her humiliation into accusations.

"Just wash your hands, you goddamned little Pilate," I yelled at her. "Not your problem, not your fault, you didn't see, you didn't know. You didn't see . . . anything, did you?" But I couldn't say that. I spun away from her, striding to the corner of the room, until the wall confronted me. I hit it with my hand.

"Shh, don't do that," Elly said, standing beside me. She took my hand in both of hers, preventing me from hitting the wall again.

"I don't know what you're talking about," Aunt Greta replied.

She backed away, pushing between Emma and Cordelia. "You're disgusting," she said to Emma as she brushed past her.

"Mrs. Robedeaux," Emma called after her, "I don't suggest you repeat your insinuations unless you have proof to back them up."

"I won't be threatened by a woman like you," Aunt Greta retorted.

"No, Mrs. Robedeaux," Emma softly answered, "I won't be threatened by a woman like you. When Michele came to live with me, I gave you several thousand dollars, as a supposed payment for expenses. I had no legal obligation to do so, my lawyer advised against it, but I felt it would . . . ease things for us all."

Aunt Greta stood staring at Emma, tightly clutching her purse. She made no reply.

"Let's be blunt, Mrs. Robedeaux," Emma continued, "I bought you off. I can only wonder, if you indeed have the reservations you claim, why your complicity was purchased for a few thousand dollars. What does that make you look like, Mrs. Robedeaux?"

"It's late, I must be going," Aunt Greta said, her lips pressed in a hard white line.

"How much money did you make off of her?" Cordelia suddenly demanded angrily, marching toward Aunt Greta until she was only a few feet away. "Don't you remember the money my grandfather sent you? To make up for what my father had done? Five hundred dollars a month until she turned twenty-one. But you just acknowledged that Michele left your house when she was eighteen. What happened to that money, Mrs. Robedeaux?"

"I don't know what you're talking about," Aunt Greta replied.

"The lawyers for my grandfather's estate will know," Cordelia retorted.

"It was for . . . expenses," Aunt Greta sputtered. "You wouldn't understand," she finished up hastily.

"No, I don't guess I would," Cordelia replied.

Then we all stood and stared at each other for one long, awkward moment.

"Come along, Greta," Father Flynn said. "Remember, 'ye without sin can cast the first stone.' " He sighed, then started to hustle Aunt Greta out.

"You know, Michele," she said, briefly looking in my direction, "your Uncle Claude would really like it if you would visit sometime.

It's not nice of you not to come out and see him." And then she was gone.

"Surely there must be better secretaries than that woman," Emma commented.

"But not cheaper ones," Sister Ann replied.

"Are you sending your lawyer after her?" Emma asked Cordelia.

"It's tempting," Cordelia replied.

"Yes, it is," Emma added.

"No, let her be," I surprised myself by saying. Cordelia and Emma both turned to look at me. "She's . . . I want her out of my life. Don't go after her on my account," I finished.

"I may go after her on my account," Emma answered. "That was an ugly accusation. Perhaps a letter from my lawyer will teach her to control her tongue better, if not her thinking."

I wondered why Cordelia, as upset as she was with me, had chosen to tangle with my Aunt Greta.

"You okay?" Elly asked.

"Me? Oh, I'm fine," I answered.

"Rough for you."

"Naw, it was fun to see Aunt Greta finally get a few potshots in her direction."

"Was it? I've found that justice often comes only long after it's needed," Elly said softly.

My only reply was a bare nod.

"You okay?" Millie asked, joining us.

"No, I'm imminently suicidal," I replied.

"Wrong question or wrong time?" Millie inquired.

"Same question. Twice," Elly explained.

"Well, in that case, can I have your belt and any sharp objects?" Millie bantered. "Other than your tongue."

"Yeah, keep away from that, Hutch would object."

Millie shook her head, then in a less frivolous tone said, "I didn't know you and Cordelia went back so far."

"We don't. We only met a few months ago," I clarified.

"But you had to know before today about her father," Millie said. "She wouldn't have sprung that on you."

"I've known for a long time," I replied, sharper than I'd intended.

Emma put her hand on my shoulder.

173

"Good-bye, Michele," she said, hugging me.

I caught sight of Cordelia over Emma's shoulder. She'd obviously heard the last part of our conversation. Her face was somber.

"Thanks for being in my corner," I said to Emma.

"You're most welcome, dear. I must run. I'm late, but it was worth it."

Emma left, then Cordelia said, "Sorry, ladies, time to get back to work."

She quickly packed up her briefcase as Elly, Millie, and Bernie went out the door. I hung back. Cordelia started to follow them. I took a few hasty steps and caught her in the hall.

"Thanks," I said.

"Don't thank me." She kept walking.

"Don't say that. You certainly didn't need to tangle with Aunt Greta . . . not the way you feel about . . ."

She shrugged and started down the stairs.

"Fifteen years too late is better than never, after all," I added, stung at her nonchalance.

She spun back to face me. "What is that supposed to mean?" she demanded. Then, not waiting for an answer, she turned away. "You are so damned infuriating," she threw back at me as she continued down the stairs.

Grow up, Micky, I suddenly thought. You're not the only one with problems here. "I'm sorry. I shouldn't have . . . sometimes I am capable of speaking without bothering to think first."

"It's okay," she replied, giving me a wan smile. "And I'm sorry. I lost my temper at that woman . . . for the way she treated you."

"Thank you," I said, taking a tentative step to her.

"I'm sorry it came too late to do much good."

"It did me a lot of good."

"Even so . . ." She didn't move as I took another step.

"Friends?" I asked.

"Of course."

I put my arms around her and hugged her tightly. We held each other for a moment, then she stiffened and pulled away. Probably remembering that I was sleeping with Joanne.

"I have to get back to work," she said. "They're waiting for me." She hastily turned away, grabbed her briefcase, and headed down the stairs.

I remembered the books Alex gave me. I went back to retrieve them from their window sill, taking time to see what the forces of evil were up to. Sun stroke, it looked like. The few remaining protesters were sitting on the curb, placards at half-mast. I spent a few minutes watching them sweat. Then I headed for the cool of the clinic.

"Bern, baby, Bern," I said, plopping myself down on the least papered edge of her desk. I dangled her car keys in front of her.

"Hey, thanks, Micky," she said as she took them.

"Snuggled up next to a lime green Datsun," I bantered.

"Lime green. Yucko."

"That's my car you're insulting."

"Oh. Sorry," Bernie repented.

"But not my color choice. Feel no remorse."

"None felt."

She had to answer the phone. I looked at the books Alex was returning. Modern stuff, including several that I recognized as coming from lesbian publishing houses.

"Is that any good?" Bernie asked, her phone call finished.

"I don't know. I've never read it. I'm merely a go-between. Besides, do I look like the kind of girl who would read this trash?"

"Most definitely. Say, Micky, what did . . . well . . ." Bernie seemed a bit embarrassed. "Do you really . . . ? It's none of my business."

I was disappointed in Bernie. I didn't think she'd chicken out.

"But can I ask anyway?" she restored my faith.

"Ask away," I said, leaning in toward her.

"Are you . . . have you really slept with a woman?" she whispered conspiratorially.

"Oh, sure. Hasn't everyone?" I replied nonchalantly. My answer flustered Bernie.

"Uh . . . well . . . no," she responded.

"You're young. Don't worry about it."

"You're joking, aren't you?"

"No."

"But, Micky, you don't look like . . . ?"

"Be wary of stereotypes, Bernie, baby," I chided.

"But . . . what do two . . ." she leaned toward me and lowered her voice even more, "women do with each other?"

I stifled my first reaction, which was to burst out laughing. You, too, were once naive, I told myself. A very long time ago. Instead I looked at Bernie, watching the blush that slowly started in my silence. When her cheeks were a pleasing rose shade, I finally replied, "Have a hell of a lot of fun. That's what two women do when they sleep together. If you want to find out, I could . . ."

A throat cleared loudly behind me.

"Bernie," Cordelia said, "I want Mrs. Ludlow's file."

"Right away," Bernie replied, jumping up to get it.

Sister Ann appeared on my other side.

"Cordelia," she said, "Here is the final statement. I thought you might like to give it a last look before I release it."

Cordelia took the piece of paper from Sister Ann and started reading it.

"Quite a display out in the parking lot, Ms. Knight," Sister Ann remarked dryly to me while Cordelia read. "I did manage to convince Sister Fatima that one of you was male. Don't ask me which one."

"Here. Thanks. It's fine," Cordelia said, handing the statement back to Sister Ann. She busied herself with a file she picked off of Bernie's desk. As soon as Sister Ann was out of earshot, she said in an undertone, "My office. Wait in there." Then she spun away, taking the file out of Bernie's hand without a word, and strode back down the hallway.

"To the principal's office," I muttered. I picked up the books Alex had given me.

Elly gave me a quizzical look as I passed her in the hallway.

"Pick up the pieces," I acerbically commented as I let myself in Cordelia's office. I did not like her assumption that she had a right to order me around. Even if she was paying me.

Cordelia kept me waiting half an hour.

After shutting the door, she sat down heavily, then said, " 'Scene in the parking lot?' I'd like an explanation."

"We were putting the fear of the devil into those self-righteous bigots."

"How?" she demanded.

"Nothing Sister Ann wouldn't let two sixteen year olds do at the prom."

"Depending on their sex," Cordelia corrected. "So you and Joanne were in the parking lot making out."

"Not Joanne," I replied. "She has better sense than that." Particularly with O'Connor lurking about.

"Who?"

"Alex," I answered.

"Alex? That's not funny," she retorted icily.

"It's not meant to be. Here, she asked me to return these books to you." I put them on Cordelia's desk.

She looked at the books, then at me, then back at the books.

"Was it really Alex?" she finally asked.

I nodded.

"So you're sleeping with Joanne behind Alex's back and Alex behind Joanne's? Dammit, can't you keep your pants zipped?"

I looked down at my zipper.

"It seems possible," I retorted. I was getting annoyed at Cordelia. Whatever our relationship was, she had overstepped the bounds of it as far as I was concerned. She had no business telling me who I could or couldn't sleep with. With the exception of herself.

We glared at each other across her desk. "Besides," I continued, "I'm not sleeping with Alex and she knows about me and Joanne."

"She hasn't seen Joanne yet."

"We talked," I explained.

"You . . . I thought Joanne was going to. Couldn't you keep your mouth shut?"

"Of course not. Mouth and pants open all the time. I saw Alex in the parking lot and I just had to yell, 'Hey, you know I'm fucking Joanne, don't you?' "

Cordelia's jaw tensed. I would not win any diplomatic awards today.

"Keep your voice down," she said in a harsh whisper. "And another thing," she continued angrily, "keep your hands off my nineteen-year-old secretary."

"What?"

"I heard you proposition her . . ."

"I was not propositioning her," I interrupted.

"Then what were you doing?"

"Answering her questions."

"Oh, please, how naive do you think I am?"

"I don't think you're naive. I think you're being an overbearing moralist. If you weren't a dyke, you'd be out on the picket line where you belong."

Cordelia almost jerked out of her chair, her eyes changing to a chill blue. She sat still for a moment, before replying, biting off her words, "I prefer to consider what I'm doing and think about the consequences before I act. If that makes me an overbearing moralist, so be it. Rather that, than following my vagina wherever it leads."

"Better than leaving it behind. Not by your standards, perhaps, but I am an adult, Joanne and Alex are adults, and we can run our lives without your interference. And I can most certainly keep my hands off nineteen-year-old virgins. I don't need your lectures about standards. If I want to fuck Alex, and Joanne, and Bernie, and a dozen other women, it's none of your business."

"Haven't you already? Certainly Joanne, Alex, and the dozen other women. Probably in the last month."

"No, the last week. Two a night. Sundays off. That was how Alex found out. She bumped into Joanne coming out of my bedroom."

"Does anything stop you? Don't you have any standards."

I tensed, furious at her arrogance. "Not a single one. There's nothing I won't do. Want a list?" I shot back acidly.

"I don't care to know."

I stood up and leaned across her desk. "Not sanitary enough for you? Below your standards? Keep your sex in cheap novels?"

"Please leave," she said, not looking at me.

I strode around the desk, grabbed the arms of her chair, and spun her around to face me.

"Sex with women, sex with men, sometimes, I was too drunk to tell. I can't remember half the people I've slept with. Hell, by the time I was nineteen, I'd probably fucked more women than you ever will. Sex for the hell of it, sex for money, you name it. Ever been tied up, Dr. James?" I shook her chair, making her look at me.

"Get out, Micky. I mean it." She glared at me this time.

It was a command that she expected to be obeyed. She sat in her chair, staring at me, challenging me to back down. Magnificently powerful, I thought, looking into her blazing blue eyes. I resented her for it. No one had ever told her she couldn't be strong. Or proved indelibly how shifting control and strength were. Like Bayard had for me.

Cordelia sat before me, in her assumed omnipotence.

I knelt down in front of her, then ran my hand under her skirt.

"Come on, Dr. James. You can fuck me. You hired me. Isn't that what you really wanted?"

I started to push her skirt up with my other hand, bending my face toward her lap.

She grabbed my hair and jerked my head back.

"Stop it! I don't buy sex."

For a moment, we hung there, my hands on her thighs, her fingers in my hair, staring at each other across some vast distance. Then her fingers loosened in my hair, and she took my face between her hands. She pulled me to her and kissed me. It lasted only a moment, then she wrenched herself away, pushing me back and turning her chair aside. I had to catch myself with my palms to keep from falling back.

"Please leave, Micky," she said, no longer commanding. For one brief second, she hadn't been in control. "Please," she repeated.

I stood, brushed off my knees, and without saying anything, let myself out of her office.

Mercifully, Bernie was on the phone, so I didn't have to banter with her. I left the clinic, walking out the rear door. I sat on the back steps, staring at the lush summer green of the overgrown back lot. The buzzing of bees carried through the still, sultry air.

Why had I done that I wondered? Flaunted my . . . past in front of a woman who could only feel contempt for what I was. I had guaranteed her disapproval, perhaps disgust.

That makes it safe, doesn't it, I suddenly thought. It makes it impossible for her to love me. Like I had made it impossible for Danny to love me. I had gotten what I'd really wanted. I didn't like the thought. Maybe I'm just protecting myself by not imagining possibilities that will never come true. We'd been together one night. For a lot of reasons, none of which had anything to do with her wanting to spend the rest of her life with me.

I heard the door open behind me.

"Where do you want the pieces?" Elly said, sitting beside me on the stairs.

"Oh, hi, Elly. I'm okay. You can go eat your sandwich where it's cool."

"Want a bite?"

"No, thanks. I'm fine."

"What happened? I don't think I've ever seen Cordelia so flustered."

"We discussed my moral standards. Or lack of them. That would probably fluster anyone."

"What business is it of hers?"

"She thought I was propositioning Bernie." I conveniently left out Joanne.

"Were you?"

"No, of course not. Well, maybe mild flirting. She was asking me about being a lesbian. And I was answering her questions. In my usual style."

"That's what got Cordelia so upset?"

"I guess," I hedged. "Maybe it was the manner in which I answered some of her questions. Besides, it's hard to believe I'm an innocent once you've heard the Danny Clayton version of my life story. Sorry, Elly," I caught myself.

"It's okay," she replied equitably.

"I guess you've heard the Danny Clayton version, too," I said sheepishly.

"At length."

"Oh . . . well," I shrugged my shoulders.

"I've always wondered what the Micky Knight version is," she said. "There are usually two sides to any story."

"Only one true."

"Which?"

I looked at Elly, wondering what she wanted from me.

"I suppose Danny's told you I gratuitously slept around on her, making a point of rubbing her face in it? That if she tried to talk to me I was a sarcastic bitch?"

"Not quite those words."

"If that's what Danny told you, she was being polite. I made sure she regretted ever thinking she was in love with me. I gave new meaning to the word 'despicable'."

"Why? Not that I'm not grateful, mind you."

"Grateful?" I asked.

"If you had stayed with Danny I wouldn't be with her now."

"Danny and I would have broken up at any rate. I just made sure we did it at my convenience. Don't be grateful to me."

"Why?" she asked again.

"Why not?" I countered. Then immediately, " I don't know. I really don't." Because Danny had said she loved me and I knew that couldn't be true.

"If you don't want to tell me, I won't press."

"What are you going to tell Danny?"

"Nothing. This conversation is between us."

"I don't know," I still hedged. "I . . . can't explain." I couldn't.

Elly glanced at her watch. "Well, back to the zoo." She got up.

"Sorry, Elly," I said.

"For what?"

"Just . . . I don't know." Then, to change the mood. "I left Danny because I knew someone like you would show up someday and I didn't think she'd have enough sense to dump me when the right woman arrived. Now, get back to work before Cordelia thinks I'm propositioning you."

"I doubt that," Elly replied. She put her hand on my shoulder and gave it a friendly squeeze.

"Elly," I called her back. "Do you remember any of the women — the murdered women? Beverly Sue Morris? Alice Janice Tresoe?" Then I added, "Vicky Williams?"

Elly looked at me. "The woman in the woods? Why do you think she's connected?"

"A botched abortion and she gets dumped at a party Cordelia's going to. It's hard not to connect it."

"True." Then Elly was silent.

"Do you remember any of the women?" I asked again.

"Yeah, I do," Elly said slowly. "Alice. I remember her looking at me and saying, 'I can't be pregnant again, can I?' She had three kids already."

"Was she pregnant?"

"Yes. She decided to have an abortion."

"When?" I asked.

"On the day she died," Elly answered.

"Thanks, Elly," I said softly.

She nodded and then went back into the building.

I sat where I was for several minutes, then finally noticed that I was hungry. I walked across the yard, around the truncated wrought iron fence and headed for a grocery I had seen on the avenue.

I brought back my lunch and sat on the steps eating it, trying to figure out what to do next. No satisfactory answer came to mind.

After I finished eating, I walked around the building. The protesters were gone, the parking lot was uneventful. Few people were out on either the avenue or the side street. The mid-afternoon sun made me sweat even at the leisurely pace of my walk. I ended back where I was, but, not wanting to sit like some gargoyle on the stairs, I strolled over to the edge of the overgrown back lot. The tall weeds and small trees were motionless, shimmering green in the bright sunshine. Nothing stirred in the still air; even the humming bees seemed to have gone home. I could smell the faint tang of leaves, a slight honeysuckle scent mixed with it. I picked one of the near flowers and sucked the nectar out of it.

"Well, Miss Knight, ever on duty," O'Connor approached me across the yard.

"Someone has to prevent you from arresting the wrong person," I replied.

"Is that what Dr. James is paying you for?"

"No. My sense of honor demands it."

"Of course. Honor. A rare commodity these days."

"What are you doing here?"

"Visiting the scene of the crime. Who knows what might happen. Perhaps Dr. James' memory will miraculously improve."

"She didn't do it."

He ignored that. "Perhaps the one question I don't know the answer to will resolve itself."

I didn't reply, knowing that he wanted me to ask.

"Don't you want to know what that question is?"

"You want to tell me, so go ahead."

"Are you in it with her or has she got you duped?"

"Make up your mind, so you can find evidence for whatever you want to believe."

"Did you put the body in the basement for her?"

"No, but I did slit the throats of thirty-six orphans at her request. She paid me a buck a head."

"Ever sarcastic. I rather like your sense of humor. I hope you're not involved."

"How kind of you," I answered coolly.

"Do you smoke?" he asked, reaching into his jacket pocket for a pack of cigarettes.

"No, I don't."

"Good. It's a bad habit."

A breeze sprang up, lifting the hair off my forehead. The cooling air was welcome.

"Don't light that," I suddenly said, catching an odor on the fresh breeze.

"Why? Are you one of those?"

"No," I answered. I paused, trying to separate the myriad smells of a hot city day, hoping I was only imagining one of them. "Do you smell anything?"

"No. Twenty years of smoking's ruined my nose."

I stood still, taut, sampling the air.

"Oh, Jesus," I let out as I was hit with a draft of fetid air, an odor that didn't belong in this warm summer afternoon. I glanced at O'Connor. His face held a somber look of concentration, the cigarette unlit.

"What is it?" he asked, no playful banter in his voice.

"A dead . . . animal. A dog, maybe," I said.

"I hope so," he replied.

"Oh, Jesus," I repeated, softly, hugging myself as I shivered, despite the heat of the sun.

"Shall we check it out?" he asked, looking intently at me.

"No, I don't . . . I don't like seeing dead dogs."

O'Connor turned around and strode purposely for the parking lot, calling out several names as he went. He immediately returned with a number of his men. They plunged grimly into the overgrowth. I watched as they slowly and methodically searched through the tangled brush. The minutes ticked by, punctuated only by the steady snap and swish of their movements in the weeds.

I stayed where I was, unable to move, still testing the air, hoping that somehow I could prove myself wrong. I wanted desperately to call out to those men, "I'm sorry, I made a mistake. You won't find anything."

Then one of them shouted, "Here. Over here." And nothing more.

I sat on the grass, unable to get away from the smell now that it had been confirmed. It seemed to be everywhere. I kept breathing the decay to be sure that this was real, that this summer day had really veered so hauntingly awry.

O'Connor finally emerged from the brush, his face red and sweating, crushed tags of green clinging to his pants. He headed straight toward me. I noticed he was holding a handkerchief in one hand. I guess he had smelled the decay once he got close enough. He didn't say anything, but showed me what was in his other hand, a plastic evidence bag containing an insurance form. Signed by Dr. C. James.

"We found her clothes and purse about ten yards away. This was in it," he said, after I'd read it.

"How do you know it's hers?"

"Not definite yet. But my instinct says so and it's not often wrong. You want to help me?"

"No, I don't," I replied.

"Then why did you point out that body?" he asked. "A few more days in this heat and the medical examiner might have a hard time telling whether she was eighteen or eighty. Let alone what she died from."

"My goddamn sense of honor," I retorted.

"I getting a search warrant. And then I'm going into the clinic. If I find," he flipped the insurance form to read it, "a file for Faye Zimmer, I'm going to arrest Dr. James."

"Why tell me? You want my permission?" I replied sarcastically. "How long will it take you?"

"Not long. I've already put in the call. One of my guys is on his way to pick it up right now," he answered, then continued, "You still going to side with someone who's made a fool of you?"

"She didn't do it."

"I got evidence that says she did."

"You've got evidence that somebody is setting her up. Find

184

someone who hates Cordelia, or even Emma Auerbach, and you might find your murderer."

"So, who would hate her like that? You're stretching, Miss Knight."

"Someone from Cordelia's past, who's found this a perfect opportunity for vengeance. Or Emma's past. Cordelia just opened this clinic in the last few months. Emma's been very noticeable is the pro-choice movement recently. Somebody's noticed. Do a little more footwork before you take the easy way out."

"Give me some names. Make a few suggestions. You know both Dr. James and Miss Auerbach. Who would hate either of them enough to kill a few innocent women to get back at them?"

I sat, trying to think of any possible names. O'Connor was right, murdering women just to make it look like Cordelia was botching abortions was an improbable sort of revenge.

"Well," he demanded.

"I working on it," I replied.

One of his men was walking across the lawn to us. He held out a piece of paper as he approached. O'Connor took it.

"Thanks, Rob," he said. Then, "You want to come with us?" he asked me, as he turn toward the clinic.

I jumped up, angrily walking in front of him. He kept pace behind me into the clinic.

I nodded at Bernie, but didn't say anything. O'Connor and I walked to the file cabinets. Then I put out my hand for the search warrant. We would do this by the book. He handed it to me, waiting patiently as I read it over. I handed it back and stood looking at him, but he motioned me to go ahead. I opened the drawer and started flipping through the Zs. It was in back, not in perfect alphabetical order, but Faye Zimmer's file was there.

"Shit," I muttered, looking at the accusing paperwork in my hand. O'Connor took it from me. He said nothing, just watched me.

"Five minutes," I said. "Give me five minutes to talk to her."

"I'll be waiting," he replied. "My men will be outside. If she's really innocent, it's not a good idea to run away." He turned and went back out to the waiting room. But he didn't stop watching me.

Nurse Peterson came out one of the rooms.

"Where's Cordelia?" I asked as I walked down the hall toward her. "I have to talk to her. Now."

Nurse Peterson looked unsure.

"It's important," I said. "I'll wait in her office."

"All right," she agreed and went back into the room she had just left.

I entered Cordelia's office, aware of O'Connor's eyes on my back. I paced as I waited for her, unable to be still. About a minute later, she entered.

"This had better be good," she said, standing in the doorway with her arms crossed.

Not good, not good at all, I wanted to say. Instead, I motioned her in, shutting the door behind her.

"Sit down," I said, trying to think how to break it to her.

"I'm in a hurry."

"Please."

She sat, her arms still crossed. I sat opposite her.

"Two things," I started. "First . . . I was way out of line earlier. I'm very sorry. I . . . I'm sorry."

"Okay. I accept your apology. But I have patients waiting."

"And second . . . you're not going to like this."

"Why? Are you sleeping with Alex?" she cut in.

"Oh, God, no," I said, shaking my head. "I don't guess there is any easy way to tell you this." I plunged on, "They found another body, apparently a patient here. You're about to be arrested for murder. O'Connor is outside waiting for you now."

She didn't say anything for a minute, didn't move.

"I . . . guess my patients will have to wait, then, won't they?" she said slowly. She looked at her desk, in stunned bewilderment, as if she had no idea what to do now. I don't guess they teach you how to be arrested for murder. "Who was it?" she suddenly asked.

"Faye Zimmer," I replied. "Her file was . . ."

"Oh, my God, no. I just saw her on Wednesday . . ."

"Call your lawyer. Call now," I said as she looked at me, to get her to take action in the few moments we had.

"Yes . . . yes, you're right," she replied, sitting forward. She started looking for the number.

"I'll get a hold of Danny and . . . Joanne."

She didn't even notice my stumbling over Joanne's name. "And we'll get . . ."

There was a knocking on her door. Then it opened and O'Connor appeared.

"I know why you're here," Cordelia said to him.

He stepped into her office. I got up and closed the door. No sense putting on a show.

"Miss Knight has explained the situation?" O'Connor asked.

"Yes, Micky has."

"I'm placing you under arrest, Dr. James. You have the right to remain silent . . ." O'Connor recited the list for her.

Cordelia sat motionless, listening to him, staring straight ahead until he finished. Then for a brief second in the silence, she looked at me, her eyes a wide, troubled blue. She stood. As she did she moved her Rolodex around so I could see it, almost as if straightening her desk. It was open to one particular card. Cordelia took off her white jacket, hanging it up as if she were only going home for the day.

"I don't guess . . . ask Alex to feed Rook, would you?" she said to me. "Alex has keys and tell Bernie . . ."

"Don't worry. I'll take care of it," I answered. Then I added, "Do you have to do that?" as O'Connor pulled out a pair of handcuffs.

"Standard procedure," he replied.

"She's not going anywhere," I told him.

"I'll wait until we're in the parking lot," he said, putting the cuffs back in his pocket. "For you, Miss Knight. Shall we, Dr. James?"

I walked out first, followed by Cordelia, then O'Connor. I wanted to protect her, at least deflect the staring gazes.

Bernie shot me a glance as we went by, but I returned a curt nod to her questioning look. Several other men seated in the waiting room got up and went with us. O'Connor's reinforcements.

When we got out of the building, O'Connor stopped and pulled out the handcuffs.

Cordelia looked again at me.

"Don't worry. I'll take care of . . . what I can," I said to her. "Ask to see your lawyer. Get your legal protection in place."

"Thanks, Micky," she replied.

O'Connor put the cuffs on her. She still looked at me, her only friend in this crowd. They led her away. I didn't follow. I could do more good by going back in the building and getting on the phone. I spun around and reentered, not waiting to watch them load her into the police car.

"Micky?" Bernie questioned as I strode back into the office.

"Cancel the rest of Cordelia's patients," I told her.

"What will I tell them?" she asked, her voice unsteady.

"That . . . that Dr. James had been unexpectedly called away."

"Okay," Bernie nodded.

I headed for Cordelia's office. The first number I called was the one from the Rolodex, Elana Dreyfuss, Esquire. The police had to let her call a lawyer, but they didn't have to do it immediately.

I told Ms. Dreyfuss who I was and why I was calling.

Her response, in a very professional and erudite voice, was, "Shit." Then she asked where they had taken Cordelia and listened intently as I gave her the details. She told me she was on her way and hung up. Cordelia had a good lawyer.

Then I dialed Danny's number.

"D. A.'s office, Danielle Clayton speaking," she answered.

"They've arrested Cordelia," I stated without preamble.

"What?" she exclaimed. Then added the obligatory, "Shit."

I filled her in on the details, the discovery of the latest body. Danny told me she'd make some phone calls and let me know what she found out. We hung up without bothering to say good-bye. It didn't seem important.

Elly knocked and entered, followed by Bernie and a woman introduced as Jane Bowen, one of the two part-time doctors at the clinic.

"What's going on?" Elly asked.

I told them. "Someone needs to say, 'shit'," I finished.

"This is shit," Bowen supplied. "I'll take any you can't cancel," she said to Bernie. "Who's on for tomorrow morning? Aaron or Cordelia? I'd prefer not to take it, but I will, if he can't," she added.

"God, my mind's gone blank," Bernie fumbled.

"I think it's Dr. Goldstein," Elly said. "Someone should call him in any event."

"I'll call," Bernie recovered.

"Transfer him to me when you're done. We'll work out something," Bowen instructed. "Boy, do I want a cigarette. Too bad I gave up smoking," she said as she exited.

"To the telephone," Bernie followed her down the hallway.

"I've called Danny," I told Elly.

"Good," she nodded.

"And Cordelia's lawyer."

"Better."

"And I'm about to call Joanne."

She nodded, then said, "This is troubling. Someone killed all these women."

"Not Cordelia," I interjected.

"I know. But whoever did it has gone to a lot of trouble to make it look like she did. Tell me if Danny or Joanne find out anything," she added as she slipped out the door.

I called Joanne. She didn't say "shit."

"Oh, fuck," was her expletive of choice. Then, "I'll get back to you."

"Joanne . . ." I stopped her. "I ran into Alex."

"I know. She called earlier."

"Oh."

"I'll talk to you later. Okay?"

I heard voices and a general hubbub in the background. Joanne sounded busy.

"Okay. Bye." We hung up.

Then I sat. And waited. And hated it.

Nurse Peterson shyly stuck her head into the doorway.

"Miss Knight?" she said.

"Yes?" I motioned her in.

"Has Dr. James really been arrested?"

"Yes, she has."

"So, she did kill those poor young women," she said in a soft undertone.

"No, she didn't," I countered. "Being arrested and being guilty aren't the same thing."

"Oh." Nurse Peterson blushed at my outburst. Then she said, "Do you think God is punishing those women for having abortions?"

I looked at her, trying to guess if her question was on the level. And what level that might be. "I think those women were murdered. By another person. Not God."

"But do you think," she said, troubled, "that abortion is wrong?"

"I think abortion is very complicated. Too complex for me to make the decision for anyone other than myself."

"Have you ever . . . aborted a child?"

"Me?" I said, taken aback at the question. "No, of course not," I replied.

"So you personally disagree?" she asked, seeking, it seemed, validation.

"It's never come up. That's one of the advantages of being a lesbian."

"You're . . . oh," she said, blushing again.

Evidently my sexuality was news to her. I suddenly wondered what had made her so nervous when I first questioned her, if it wasn't my lesbianism.

"But," I continued, "if I were raped and impregnated, I would probably have an abortion." I would most emphatically have an abortion, but I didn't see the need to rub her face in it.

"I'm trying to sort out some things for myself," she said. "I . . . Do you think it was God's intention that those women were to die? A punishment they deserved?"

"Why would He bother?"

"What do you mean?"

"Those who sin spend an eternity in hell, right?" She nodded. "How long is eternity?" I asked.

"How . . . one can't know that," she replied. "Forever."

"And the average human life span? Seventy or so years?"

"About that, yes."

"With an eternity in which to punish us, why does God need to bother with the few years we have here? Since death is inevitable, how much of a punishment can it be? If confession and repentance are really possible, why take that away to give a punishment that is inevitable? To send the guilty to hell fifty years early? What's fifty years to eternity?"

Nurse Peterson didn't immediately reply. She sat slowly down.

"That is something to think about," she finally replied. "It is sad that they died, then, is it not?"

"Yes, it's sad. And nothing, no matter what their supposed sin, that they could have deserved."

"Thank you," she said. "I've always been taught that abortion is wrong. Murder. How do you justify it? For yourself?"

Again I got the feeling that she really wanted to know, that she was searching for an answer. "There are many kinds of murder. Dreams and hopes can be killed, too. To lose the chance to live the life you want is, to me, a walking murder. Which can you live with? I can't choose for another person."

"I'm sorry, I'm taking up a lot of your time," she said. "You must have better things to do than answer my questions."

"No, I'm just sitting here waiting for the phone to ring. Besides, I don't think I'm answering your questions. I'm only giving you my answers."

"Yes, you're right." Then she paused. I thought she was going to get up and leave, but she didn't. She looked at me, took a deep breath and said, "My sister, my younger sister . . . had an abortion. She asked me to go with her . . . I refused." She stopped and fumbled with a Kleenex.

I was hearing a confession, I realized.

"I told her if she did that I never wanted to speak to her again. I was very angry at her. I got what I wanted. I never spoke to her again."

"She died?"

"Yes, two weeks later. A car accident . . . I wonder which of us is the worse sinner."

"I'm sorry," I said. "You would have spoken to her if you'd had time."

"I hope you're right. She was . . . so young, only eighteen. I can't bear to think of her going to hell for . . ." she trailed off, unable to finish.

"She didn't go to hell, " I stated. I pulled a few tissues out of a box on the desk and handed them to her.

"Thank you . . . thank you for saying that," she said.

"A truly omnipotent God could not be so cruel," I added.

"Do you believe in God?"

"I don't know," I replied. "I don't mean that lightly. I don't know. I can't know, really know, until I die. I leave it at that."

"You have . . . thank you for talking to me. Most people, like you, who believe as you do, don't talk to me about this."

"The reverse is also true. I'm very surprised you wanted to hear what I had to say. And that you trusted me enough to tell me about your sister."

"Sometimes a stranger is best," she replied, standing up to go. "I wanted to hear someone who would not automatically condemn her for what she did."

She slipped out of the door and walked softly down the hallway.

I sat, trying to read Dante, and waited for the phone to ring.

After a while Elly poked her head in the door. "Patients are all gone," she said.

"Danny hasn't called."

"I know. I'm going home. You should, too. Cordelia has a very good lawyer."

"Yeah, you're right," I answered tiredly, putting Dante away.

"I'll see you sometime soon," she said.

"Bye, Elly," I answered.

She waved and disappeared down the hallway.

Joanne or Danny could call me at home as well as here. I turned out the light, wondering if there was anything else I needed to do to close Cordelia's office.

Only Bernie was still out front. She was shuffling paper around in a desultory manner. Her eyes were red-rimmed and blood shot.

"Micky?" she asked, but no question followed.

"Time to go home, Bern," I told her.

"But . . . what'll happen to Cordelia?"

"She's innocent," I replied.

"But innocent people have gone to jail before. And the chair."

"Not rich, white, well-connected people like Cordelia," I reassured her, hoping I was telling the truth.

"Yeah . . . I guess," she answered.

"Come on, time to get out of here. Cordelia will be okay."

"All right. You're right," she said.

I waited while Bernie turned off the lights and locked up. It was after six.

Bernie and I walked out to the parking lot, leaving the clinic silent and deserted. The rest of the building was busy—a senior citizen group, a youth group, some indeterminate group.

"Goodnight, Micky," Bernie said. Then she very shyly and awkwardly hugged me. She quickly turned and got into her car, but I still caught the hint of a blush.

" 'Night, Bern," I called as she fumbled with her keys, then I headed for my car.

All I need is for Bernie to get a crush on me, I thought. But I caught myself smiling in the rear view mirror. She was cute. And I was flattered.

God, what a day, I thought as I pulled out onto the street. And it's not over yet.

Chapter 13

I had hoped to arrive home and find my answering machine lit and blinking like the Fourth of July. But, no, it stared silently at me. I was even glad of Hepplewhite's meows, anything to break the expectant silence of my apartment. I turned on the air conditioner, hoping it would cool my room by bedtime.

I thought about reading, but knew I didn't have the concentration for it. Then I remembered a phone call I'd promised Cordelia I'd make. I dialed Alex's number.

"Hello?" she answered.

"Hi, Alex, this is Micky. Cordelia asked me to ask you to feed her cat."

"Why can't C.J. feed her own cat?"

"Oops," ran through my head. I had assumed that Joanne had already talked to Alex. "You don't know?" I asked, rather stupidly.

"Know what?" Alex replied, a worried note creeping into her voice.

"Shit, I was sure you would have talked to Joanne by now," I said.

"Micky, what happened? Who's hurt?"

"No one. Cordelia's been arrested," I said flatly.

"Oh," was all Alex said. Then a silence.

"Alex? Are you there?"

"Oh . . . yeah. Yeah. This is . . . not what I expected," Alex finished hesitantly. "I'll feed her cat. That's no problem . . . God, I don't know what to say."

"Say 'shit', Alex, everyone else has. Except Joanne. She said 'fuck'. Take your pick."

"Shit, piss, and corruption. Fuck me. There, now I feel better. Oh, shit . . . poor Cordelia."

"Yeah, I know."

"Well, look at the bright side. Maybe she'll meet some nice girl in jail."

"Alex," I threatened.

"Not very bright, admittedly," Alex replied, then in a more serious vein, "Is there anything I can do? Other than cat duty?"

"Not that I know of. I've been trying for hours to think of something."

"Okay," she said. "Oh . . . Micky? You haven't heard from Joanne, have you? I mean, I know, we're supposed to be insanely jealous of each other, but I've never let insanity stop me before. We were going to meet for dinner, but she called it off."

I told Alex about my phone call to Joanne.

"Yeah, she just left an odd message on my machine," Alex said when I finished. "Here, listen to it and tell me what you think."

I heard Alex rewind her answering machine, then a click and Joanne's voice saying, "I can't make dinner. I just can't. I'll talk to you . . . sometime." That was it.

"I don't know," I told her when the message finished playing. Joanne had sounded angry, distant perhaps, but it was hard to tell from a tape over the phone.

"I don't either, but if you should hear from her . . ."

"I'll let you know."

"And Micky? If she comes over? It's okay. Just let me know she's all right."

"I will."

"Thanks."

I wondered what the hell Joanne and Danny were doing. And why they weren't calling me.

Around ten-thirty the phone finally rang. Danny.

"Involuntary manslaughter. She made bail and is now asleep in our extra bedroom. And I'm exhausted. If you have any questions, read tomorrow's papers."

"I will. Goodnight, Danno."

"Okay. One question. But that's all."

"Is she okay?"

"Okay?" Danny said, her voice rising. "Okay? Ignatious 'Law and Order' Holloway's granddaughter is arrested for manslaughter. The news media is having a field day with it. She's exhausted. Even if she's found innocent . . ."

" 'Even if?' " I interjected.

"When she is found innocent, she will still have this thing hanging over her. Her reputation as a doctor is probably shot to hell. 'Okay'? Yeah, as much as one can be under the circumstances," Danny said, her voice becoming raspy and hoarse as she finished.

"No more questions, Danno. Get some rest. If there's anything I can do . . ."

"Yeah, I'll let you know. I'll tell Cordelia you asked about her. She needs her friends now. 'Night, Mick."

"Goodnight. Say hi to Elly for me."

I heard her click off. I gently replaced the receiver.

I waited another hour, hoping Joanne would call, but she didn't. I hoped she was with Alex. I should have asked Alex to call me, too. But the "other woman" doesn't have such privileges, I supposed. Stop, I told myself. Alex would call you. Joanne might have tried to call me while I was on the phone with Danny, given up, and gone home to bed. I went to take a shower. I needed one after today, maybe it would relax me enough to fall asleep. I let myself take a long, cooling shower.

When I went back into my big room, Joanne was there, sitting at my desk, drinking bourbon.

"Joanne?" I said, not sure if I was surprised more by her late appearance or her drinking. Both were disconcerting.

"Hi, Mick. Do you know what burned flesh smells like?"

"Uh . . . not really."

"Some punks lit an old wino on fire. He lived for a couple of hours afterward. That's what I spent my day doing. Can you think of a better way to spend a day?"

"Joanne, Alex is worried about you," I said.

"Oh, she is? So? I'm fine, just fine."

"She asked me to call her."

"It's late. She's probably asleep. She sleeps regular hours."

"She sounded pretty worried."

Joanne shrugged, but didn't reply. Instead she reached over and picked up my phone, then dialed a number. Alex's, I assumed.

"Alex? Joanne. I'm with Micky. I'm fine, so don't worry about me. I was going to have dinner with you tonight to tell you Micky and I are fucking, but I guess you know that by now."

"Joanne!" I cut in.

"You did test negative, didn't you, Micky? Alex wants to know, but she's too polite to ask," she said, not bothering to cover the receiver.

"Goddamn it, Joanne!" I burst out angrily. Then I grabbed for the receiver, but she kept it away from me.

"Well, did you?" Joanne taunted me.

"Yes. I did," I answered, realizing that she was deliberately provoking me. I stood back, letting her have the phone. "Don't worry, she's drunk, Alex," I said loudly.

"And getting drunker," Joanne said. "But you've fucked drunks before, haven't you? I'm just another one."

"Joanne."

She held the receiver out to me.

"Come on, you and Alex can compare notes."

Warily, I took a step toward her to the phone. She calmly handed it to me.

"Alex?"

"Micky? Are you all right?"

"Yeah, I'm . . ."

Joanne pulled the towel off me and started sucking one of my nipples.

" . . . I'm okay," I finished, trying to push her away, but she put her arms around me and held on tightly. Fine, I decided, having my tits sucked had never done me any harm.

"Is she really drinking?"

"Yes," I replied. "It's okay, I can handle it," I added with more assurance than I felt.

"Call me in the morning," Alex responded.

Joanne put her hand between my legs, causing me to grunt. I needed both hands and I needed to get off the phone.

"I have to go, Alex. She'll be okay," I said.

"Micky? Tell Joanne that I love her."

"I will."

Alex hung up. I tossed the receiver in the direction of the phone, then grasped Joanne by her shoulders and pushed her away from me.

"Hey, Mick, shouldn't have given me your key if you didn't want it," she shrugged, but didn't fight. She sat back down and took another swig out of the bourbon bottle.

"Alex says she loves you."

"Who gives a fuck!" Joanne exploded, slamming down the bottle. "She doesn't know what love is." She took another angry swallow of bourbon.

"Neither do you, it seems," I shot back at her.

"Maybe not. Maybe I don't," she said softly. She stared fixedly at her hands for a moment. "We'll never catch them. They poured a bottle of rotgut over him and then threw a match. Random violence. Too random to catch. Unless we get real lucky. Random luck to catch random violence."

She paused and took another swallow. I was letting her drink, hoping she would pass out, or at least get drunk enough to be quietly led off to bed.

After a few minutes of silence, I said, "Come on, Joanne, let's get some sleep. We both need it."

She shook her head slowly. "Can't sleep," she replied. "I'll dream of burned old men and bleeding young women. Did you see her?"

"Who?" I asked, confused.

"From the empty lot. The young . . . can you call a fifteen-year-old a woman? Can you call someone who slowly bled to death from a botched abortion a girl?"

"No, I didn't see her."

"Good. Good for you. Keep her face out of your dreams. The young and the old. That's who we kill these days. Old men while they sleep and young girls who are desperate. It's a world gone mad. Fucking mad," she added savagely.

"It seems that way," I commented uselessly.

" 'Seems'? They're dead, aren't they? I saw their bodies at the morgue. They didn't 'seem' dead to me," she shouted angrily.

"I'm sorry. I don't know what to say." I could think of nothing that would diffuse Joanne's fury.

"Don't say anything," she retorted. "That's not what I came here for. If I wanted to talk, I'd be with Alex."

"Then why are you here? Just to yell at me?"

"To fuck you," Joanne said bluntly. "To get drunk, have sex, and forget what I saw at the morgue today. Do you want to fuck?"

"Joanne . . ."

"Do you want me to leave?"

"No, you can stay," I answered.

She got up and came to me, then kissed me, a heavy, wet kiss. I could taste the sharp bite of bourbon on her tongue and lips.

Why not? I suddenly thought. Why not get drunk every once in a while? When bodies, or memories, piled up and needed to be pushed aside for a few hours?

I savored the forbidden bourbon I found in her mouth, thrusting my tongue deeply inside to find the hard taste of it.

Her hand ran down the length of my body, going directly between my legs. I gasped as a finger entered me. She had to work it in, since I wasn't very wet. I shifted slightly to open my legs more to ease her way in.

"I didn't think you would say no," Joanne muttered in my ear.

"It's cooler in the bedroom," I said, trying to ignore the harshness in her tone.

"By all means, let's be comfortable," she answered, sarcastically, pulling her finger out. She led the way to my bedroom.

Joanne took off her jacket, throwing it carelessly across a chair, then hastily finished undressing, throwing the rest of her clothes on the chair with her jacket.

"Lie down," she ordered.

I got in bed. She stood, watching me, then swung a leg over me, sitting astride my stomach.

"I haven't taken a shower. I probably stink. I hope you don't mind," she said, looking down at me.

"What the fuck is your problem?" I demanded, suddenly angry. "Do you want to do this or not?"

"My problem? A fifteen-year-old girl was drugged and spent yesterday slowly bleeding to death. Why should that be a problem?" she yelled savagely.

"What's that got to do with us?" I yelled back.

"Nothing. You're right. Not a fucking thing. Do you want to do this? Yes or no?"

She moved down on me until her crotch was over mine, then she pushed into me. She bent over and kissed a nipple, still slowly rubbing her groin into mine.

"Yes or no?" she repeated, blowing on the wet spot her mouth had left, making my nipple almost painfully erect.

"Yes," I said finally.

She straightened up and stopped moving.

"Typical Micky Knight. Rub her cunt a little bit and she'll do anything," Joanne said callously.

"Goddamn it, Joanne!" I exploded, furious at her. I tried to sit up, but she easily pushed me back down. Then I abruptly twisted, trying to roll over and get her off me. But she went with me, letting me get all the way over until I was on my stomach, then she put her weight back down, pinning me under her.

"What did I do to deserve this from you?"

"Nothing. What does anyone do to deserve what they end up with? What did that wino do to deserve to be made into a human torch? What did that girl do to deserve to have her uterus shredded?"

"That doesn't give you the right . . ."

"You said yes, didn't you?" she cut me off. "You wanted to be fucked, didn't you?" Her knee forced itself between my thighs. "Don't say yes if you don't mean it."

"No wonder Alex is afraid of you," I taunted her. "What's the matter, can't you get it any other way? Don't think you're some tough butch, you don't hold a candle to some of the women I've slept with." I was angry, trying to hurt her, to get her back.

"It's hard to compete with the number of women you've slept with. They sell road maps of your cunt, so many women have been there."

"Goddamn it, bitch, you want to fight . . ." I shouted, thrusting up, trying to dislodge her. She grabbed one of my arms from under me, and shoved her weight against my shoulders, roughly forcing me back down. Still holding my arm, she twisted it behind my back.

"We'll fight," she finished.

I was clearly defeated, but I wasn't about to admit it. I strained with the arm she had pinned, trying, with brute strength, to get it free. I struggled under her, bucking and twisting. But I didn't have the leverage or the power. She slowly pushed my arm toward my head.

"Joanne, you're hurting me," I said, finally forced to stop fighting.

"Bitch, huh?" she said. "Come on, Mick, let's be friends. Spread your legs."

"No," I retorted.

She had already forced one knee between my legs, now the other one pressed on the inside of my thigh, catching the muscle, until I had to move it away to escape the pain. She had my legs open. A finger went up me, another one started stroking my clit.

Somehow the pleasure made me struggle more than the pain. I didn't want the two linked. I finally stopped, realizing that my fighting only made her fight back. She had forced my arm almost to my neck and it hurt. She released a bit of the pressure when I stopped struggling.

I lay still, rigid, as her fingers moved in me, trying to feel as little as possible. I knew that somewhere there was a Joanne who would be appalled at what she was doing.

"Joanne, please stop," I stated calmly, matter of factly. "You're hurting me."

"Don't fight," she answered, "and I won't hurt you."

"I don't mean physically. I don't care about that. I'd prefer you break my arm than for you to use me like this." I tensed my twisted arm, straining against her. "Go ahead, break it. Just don't rape me."

Suddenly my arm was free. Joanne rolled off me to the far side of the bed. She had curled up, her back to me. I reached for her, putting a hand on her shoulder. She jerked away from my touch.

"Joanne?"

She abruptly sat up, her back still to me.

"I'm sorry, Micky . . . I've got to go." She stood up, reaching for her clothes.

"Joanne, don't go." She was crying.

"No . . . I don't know what . . . " She was fumbling with her clothes, trying to ignore the tears.

I rolled over to her side of the bed, then sat up. I reached out my hand to her.

"Joanne, I'm okay. Please don't go," I said. I never thought I'd see Joanne Ranson break like this.

She looked at me, at my outstretched hand. For a moment, she didn't move, almost as if giving me time to reconsider, to reclaim my hand. I held it stretched out to her. Tentatively she reached out and grasped my hand.

"Don't go," I repeated.

She nodded, then slowly sat down on the bed, still keeping a distance between us. She sat still, silently staring ahead, occasionally wiping tears away with her free hand.

"I'm sorry," she finally spoke. "I didn't mean what I said. I didn't mean any of it."

"I know," I replied.

"Do you?" She looked at me. "I hope to hell you do." She moved next to me and put her arms around me. "I hope to hell you do," she repeated, then laid her head against my shoulder. I felt her tears drip down my breast and fall onto my thigh. I held her, letting her cry.

"Oh, God, Micky, I'm so sorry," she sobbed.

"It's okay. I'm okay. I'm sorry for what I said."

"I know you're okay. I know that," she said. "I don't want to hurt you. I wish to hell I hadn't." She kissed me, her lips wet and salty from her tears. "I do care about you."

"I love you," I suddenly said. And if she hadn't been holding me, I probably would have jumped up and ran. "I mean," I qualified. "I care about you. I guess I love you, but... well, like a friend. I mean... oh, hell, I don't know what I mean. I guess I mean what I said," I finally finished, disconcerted and flustered.

"It's okay, Micky. I love you, too," Joanne stated simply. "Will you be all right?"

"Yes, I will," I replied. Then, "Joanne? What happened?"

She tensed in my arms, then slowly lifted her head off my shoulders and looked at me. "Your cousin molested you, didn't he?" she asked.

I had to look away from her before I could answer. "Yes. Yes, he did."

She reached for me, turning my face until our eyes met. "What happened? Can you talk about it? Have you ever?"

"No," I said slowly, answering the last question. "I never have."

"Why not?"

"Not that important," I shrugged.

"Just important enough to have never mentioned to anyone."

"Yeah, I guess," I replied, hearing my voice shake. "It wasn't that bad."

"No?"

"No. He just put a gun to my head and made me give him a blow job. I didn't think he'd really pull the trigger, but..." My voice broke. "It wasn't really that bad," I got out. "Only a couple of times..." I started crying.

"Goddamn him!" Joanne spat out. "How'd he get a gun?"

"Uncle Claude kept it around in case of burglars. But their house was never broken into. I guess because of that gun," I said caustically.

"Don't say it wasn't bad. Don't do that to yourself. Don't shrug it off like it didn't happen. Because if it didn't happen to you, then it didn't happen to me and it's not happening now."

I remembered the leer on Bayard's face when he said, "Let's go to my room. I want to show you something." I pounded the mattress. I think I hit Joanne in the thigh, but she didn't say anything, just held me closer.

"I'm so sorry," she murmured to me. My fury subsided into uncontrollable crying.

I finally lifted my head, wiped my tears with my forearm, then used a corner of the sheet.

Joanne said, "Lie next to me." She kissed me on the forehead as I curled against her.

She sighed and I felt the tension in her body as she said, "It was my father." Her voice was soft, low. "Dad worked on the oil rigs out of Morgan City. He kept a small apartment there. My mother would meet him, to go drinking or whatever. They had a rocky marriage. She would leave him and us kids would stay with him."

"How many kids?"

"Me. Tim and Tom, the twins. And Susie, my younger sister."

"You the oldest?"

"Yeah. When I was ten, he started being nice to me, letting me do things the other kids couldn't, stay up late, get a Coke. He wanted to be my friend, he said." Her voice didn't betray it, but her hand jerked, only slowly releasing as she continued talking. "He let me stay in his apartment with him, while the other kids were left in the room over the garage. One night . . . one night, he came into my room and told me that friends did things for each other. Sometimes they hurt, but real friends didn't mind."

"Oh, shit," I said.

"Yeah. Shit. He raped me."

"Joanne. I'm so sorry."

"I don't know that you could call it rape. I didn't say no. I didn't say anything. I wanted to be his friend. I didn't do anything to stop him."

"How could you?" I burst out. "How the fuck could you? Joanne, how could you even know what was happening? What the hell did you know about sex at that age?"

"Not much. Not enough to keep from getting pregnant."

"What?" I burst out again.

"Fourteen and pregnant by my father." Her hand tightened again.

"When I told him . . . that I thought I was pregnant, he denied it," she said bitterly. "He said he knew what kind of slut I was. He'd seen the way I went after men. But he offered, since he was a friend," she spat the word out, "to help me take care of it. If I didn't tell anyone, he would take care of it."

"Abortion wasn't legal then, was it?" I asked, doing some quick arithmetic.

"No. It wasn't. He called a week later, giving me an address and a time to be there. Since it wasn't his, he wasn't going to go with me. I had to learn to be a big girl and clean up my own messes . . ."

"Oh, Joanne . . ." I said.

"It was a back street. A dingy, ugly building on a back street. I remember getting on the table and feeling something wet under me, like they hadn't cleaned it very well from the last person. Last woman. We were all women. There was one big, bright light that he focused between my legs. I remember that light . . . and the pain. God, it hurt. Then a curt dismissal, telling me to wear a sanitary napkin and to expect some blood. All those women with lowered eyes, cowering. The abortionist was a criminal. But we were criminals and sluts, too.

"I bled. And bled. I got home and snuck up the stairs to my room, hoping I would stop bleeding before my sister noticed. We shared the room.

"I guess I fell asleep. Or passed out. I woke to the sound of my sister screaming. I was lying in a pool of my own blood. My parents weren't there. Bars, somewhere.

"One of the neighborhood women came over. I don't remember whether Susie got her or she heard the screams. But I do remember some doctor in the emergency room saying an hour or two more and I would have bled to death."

I instinctively tightened my arms about her, holding her close.

"For a long time afterward, I wished I had died."

"No," I said.

"Not now. Not anymore. But then . . . I couldn't deny I'd had an abortion. There was no hiding that. My mother stormed into the hospital room, demanding to know who had done it. Gotten me pregnant. She never believed me. 'No, of course it wasn't your father. Now, tell us the truth.' Over and over again. A few weeks ago, when she called, she asked me again. 'You can tell me after all these years,' she said. 'It was Dad.' 'That old story again,' she replied. Still not believing me."

"I'm so sorry, Joanne."

"Yeah, well . . . six months later, he tried again, like nothing had happened."

"He raped you after . . ." I exploded.

"No. He put his hand up my dress, and I started screaming hysterically. I couldn't have stopped myself if I'd had to. Of course, people came into the room. He just sadly shook his head, saying he didn't know why I screamed. He'd been sitting reading."

We lay still, holding each other.

"Joanne . . . I . . . thank you."

"For what?" she replied, puzzled.

"For . . . telling me. And listening to me. It's . . . consoling to know that . . . it happened to other people. Maybe I didn't deserve it."

"Goddamn it! Of course you didn't. Don't ever, ever think that," she said fiercely.

"If someone I admire as much as you, someone as strong as you are . . . " I trailed off.

"It doesn't matter, does it? Alex and maybe Cordelia and Danny, I'm not sure, got away, because the people who cared for them were decent. You and I got caught because we didn't have decent people around us. A fucking crap shoot."

"And, if it's not our fault, it's not Alex's fault that she got away."

"Yeah, you're right. I shouldn't be angry at her because she didn't have the shit beat out of her as a kid. I should be glad that someone got away."

"Do you love her?" I asked.

"Yes," Joanne replied. "Yes, I do. She's put up with a lot of crap from me. I don't know why she sticks around."

"I do."

"Did she really say she loves me?"

"Yes, she did. Go back to Alex."

"You that anxious to get rid of me? Not that I blame you."

"Hell, if it was just me . . . you could stay for a long time. But . . ."

"But?"

"But you and Alex have been together for a while . . . when I've seen the two of you together, you seem at ease and comfortable with each other. My edges aren't just rough, they're sharp. And . . ." I fumbled. She loves you. After everything, still loves you. I didn't know if I could be so loyal. "And besides, Cordelia would never forgive me if I stole you from Alex."

"What does Cordelia's forgiveness matter?" Joanne asked incisively.

"Oh, not much," I hedged. Just the world.

"Uh-huh," Joanne answered. Then in a serious tone, "Honesty's not fun, is it? You're not someone to get involved with lightly. I wasn't watching where I was going. I'm sorry for the ways I've hurt you."

"Yeah. Now, no more honesty. I can't stomach anymore." Then I added, "What a novelty."

"What?"

"You're the first woman who's ever left me before I left her," I replied.

"Some accomplishment."

"How about some sleep?"

"I guess it is rather late to head back contritely to Alex."

"Yep. Goodnight, Joanne." I turned out the light.

" 'Night, Mick," she said tiredly. "Mick?"

"Uh?"

"I meant it. You are special. And, in some crazy way, I love you."

"I love you, too, Joanne."

When I woke, bright sunlight was streaming into the room. And a not very bright cat was clawing at the door and meowing dissonantly.

I jumped up to silence Hepplewhite and let Joanne sleep, but she stirred and sat up. Then she got up, hugged me as she went by and stumbled to the bathroom. I heard the shower as I dumped some food in Hepplewhite's direction. I sliced an apple and peeled an orange to provide something resembling breakfast.

I sat on my bed, nibbling a few slices of apple, waiting for Joanne to get out of the shower, trying to think of some clever and worldly way to say good-bye.

"Breakfast," I said, pointing to the fruit as she entered the bedroom.

"Thanks," she replied, taking an orange slice. "I used your toothbrush."

"You're allowed."

She started to pick up her clothes.

"Joanne," I said, suddenly not caring to be clever and worldly. "Do you think Alex would mind . . . ?"

She turned to look at me. Fear of refusal made me falter.

"If?" Joanne prompted.

"If we . . . made love one more time?"

"No, I don't think so. And even if she did, I still would."

"Thank you."

We made love very gently and slowly, a fitting farewell.

Then she got up and got dressed. One last lingering kiss and she was gone.

I took a shower, not because I needed to, but because it felt good. Then I put on some Bach and got dressed.

I knew I should feel noble and virtuous for bravely sending Joanne back to Alex, but I didn't. I felt adrift, at loose ends. What had happened was what had to happen. I was okay. Sort of. Perhaps . . . bereft. But, other than that, okay. Right.

I wondered what was happening with Cordelia. I debated getting the paper to read all about it, but I wasn't sure I wanted the local news version of her arrest. I was hoping that Danny would call and at least plug a few more of the basic holes. It wasn't like her to not call.

There is nothing more aggravating that waiting for the phone to ring. I finally gave up and went out and got a paper. Front page stuff. I was right, I didn't want to read the news version of it.

I finally decided, enough was enough. If Danny wasn't going to call me, I would call her. I dialed her number.

"Hello?" Cordelia answered.

"Uh, hi, this is Micky," I said, too nonplused to hang up. "How are you?"

"Okay."

"Where are Danny and Elly?"

"They went out. Groceries and such, I believe. I just got up a little while ago."

"Oh."

"Alex called here last night looking for Joanne."

"Oh," I said again. "She called me, too."

"Joanne wasn't with you?"

"Well, yeah, at some point," I admitted.

"Oh," she replied. "Do you want to leave a message for Danny?" she asked shortly.

I almost said tell Elly the usual time and the usual place, but I didn't think Cordelia would appreciate the humor.

"No, that's okay. I was calling to find out how you were."

"I'm fine."

"So I gather. I did call Alex about feeding your cat," I said, trying to put a good foot forward. Unfortunately it ended up in my mouth.

"I was just going to call her. Does she know Joanne's okay yet?" Cordelia replied frostily.

"By this point, I should think so."

"I'll call her, anyway."

"Don't. I mean, Joanne's there. She's probably busy."

"How do you know?" Then immediately, "Never mind. It's none of my business."

"Sure it is. You know all the other details. Why not this one, too," I said sarcastically. "Joanne has regained her sanity and dumped me in favor of Alex."

"Oh," she said. "How are you?"

"I'm fine."

"Fine?"

"I'm fine. You're fine. Let's leave it at that."

"If you want. It was decent of you to end the affair."

"How kind of you to notice," I remarked caustically.

"I didn't mean that. I meant . . . Alex loves Joanne and . . ."

"And Joanne loves Alex, so you think Micky Knight should keep her fucking hands to herself," I burst out.

"Don't tell me what I think," she retorted angrily.

Count to ten, I caught myself. This woman's just been arrested for murder.

"I'm sorry," I said after a pause. "I didn't get much sleep last night. I was . . ."

"Don't tell me about your sex life," she cut me off.

What was her problem? I thought. "I didn't have sex last night, goddamn it," I shot back.

"Of course not," she replied coolly. "Good-bye, Micky."

"I'm sorry," I said, regretting my outburst.

"I know. Good-bye."

"I am."

There was a long pause before she replied. "I know. I'm just . . . not at my best. I need to end this conversation."

"Okay. I . . . I'll talk to you . . . some time."

"Yes, you will. Good-bye, Micky."

"Good-bye, Cordelia."

I hung up, feeling more alone than I had when Joanne left. At least Hepplewhite liked me. Or liked being fed.

It was going to be a long, hot weekend.

Chapter 14

Monday I went to the clinic, but Cordelia wasn't there. Part of her bail arrangement was agreeing not to see patients. Bernie was busy canceling and rescheduling. Bowen and Goldstein would cover as best they could.

Better air conditioning than mine, I told myself when I wondered what the hell I was doing here. I roamed about for a while, upstairs, downstairs. I avoided the back door and sight of the overgrown lot, until I realized I was evading it and made myself walk out to it to at least at within a few feet (okay, yards) of the tangled and now trampled edge.

"Smelling the roses again, Miss Knight?" The ever-vigilant O'Connor.

"Wishing for a horrible head cold," I retorted.

"I have some bad news for you. From your point of view."

"Then don't tell me."

"Autopsy report on Faye Zimmer. Fifteen years old."

"I know."

"Sergeant Ranson?"

I nodded and he continued.

"She didn't need an abortion. She wasn't pregnant."

"What?" I exclaimed.

"Faye Zimmer was murdered. Someone put something sharp up her and killed her."

"Jocasta," I said, my brain making one of those dazed connections.

"What?" he asked.

"Nothing," I mumbled.

"Jocasta?" he repeated.

"Oedipus Rex. Sophocles wrote the most well know version. Oedipus unknowingly killed his father and married his mother. When he discovered what he'd done, he blinded himself. But his mother, Jocasta, commits suicide. In one version, a later Roman one, she kills herself by forcing a knife into her womb," I finished disconcertedly, wondering what O'Connor thought of my jumbled thought patterns.

He grunted, then said, "I thought you might want to know."

"Why?" I demanded.

"It's like this, Miss Knight," he told me. "I make piles. First pile is evidence, what'll go in court. Next is what I'm sure of, but can't prove yet. Last pile is what people tell me, she says, he says. Question marks. For a while you were a real big question mark. But you wouldn't have pointed out that body if you were in it with her. That I'm sure of."

"Cordelia didn't kill anyone."

"You're so sure of that. Why?"

"She wouldn't do it."

"So you say."

"Look, you've questioned her. She's not stupid enough to dump a body a hundred yards from her back door while being the prime suspect of another murder."

"Not stupid. Maybe arrogant."

"No," I said firmly.

"I don't like fumble-fingered doctors who leave people dead, but anyone who would kill a fifteen-year-old girl that way makes me sick," he said harshly.

"Then find the person who really did it," I retorted.

"Look, this is what we know. All the victims have been patients at this clinic. Even Millie Donnalto and Elly Harrison had to admit that Dr. James treated some of these women. For Alice Tresoe, I have two witnesses that said she was six weeks pregnant and on her way here. And that was the last time anyone saw her alive. We got paperwork on all the rest proving they were here. Give me another suspect besides Dr. James."

"Someone's setting her up."

"And who might that be?" he asked sarcastically.

"I don't know. But as soon as I find out, you'll be one of the first to know."

"You do that. Just don't be selective in what you find out." He turned on his heel and headed back across the lawn.

"I won't if you won't," I called after him.

He grunted in reply. I waited until he was out of sight, then I went back into the cool of the building.

Sister Ann beckoned to me as I stood indecisively in the main hallway. "I got another letter. I thought you might like to see it," she said as I approached.

I nodded and she led the way back to her office.

"Coffee, or is it too warm?" she asked as she handed me the letter.

"Yes, please," I replied. Caffeine might help. I looked at the letter. Same printing, same ugly speculations.

Sister Ann came back and put a mug of coffee in front of me, then sat down with her own cup.

"Who's Beatrice Jackson?" I asked.

"Me. A long time ago. Before I entered the convent."

I nodded, glancing again at the section of the letter that detailed Beatrice Jackson's lascivious behavior.

"Who would know that?" I asked.

"Oh, dear, let me think . . . that name is a rather distant memory."

"Who around here?"

"No one, I should think. Perhaps Sister Fatima. I guess the people who would know I used to be Beatrice Jackson would be the ones who knew Beatrice Jackson."

"Did you show this to the police?" I asked.

"Yes. They're rather busy these days." Then there was a pause. Sister Ann continued, "I gather Dr. James is having a rough time of it."

"Yes, she is," I replied, wanting to say she didn't do it, but beginning to feel like a broken record. "I hope they catch the real criminal some time soon," I had to add.

"Indeed," Sister Ann offered noncommittally. Then out of the blue, "Is she your lover?"

"Who?" I asked inanely.

"Cordelia."

"No, of course not," I quickly replied. "Not my type."

"Oh?"

"Too rich, too white for me," I answered. "Bayou trash and high society don't mix."

Sister Ann looked oddly at me. Then replied, "That sounds like something your aunt might say."

"Goddamn her," I burst out. Then remembered where I was. "I'm sorry. I'm . . . profoundly embarrassed. I forgot you were a nun."

"I hope I've gotten beyond the stage where I'm offended by mere words."

It was my turn to look at Sister Ann oddly. "Besides," I continued, "I doubt Cordelia prefers the company of women." I didn't think she would like me coming out for her, particularly to a nun.

"I was under the impression she did."

"What gave you that impression?"

"She did."

"Oh . . . well, we're not lovers."

"I don't mean to pry. I just noticed a connection between the two of you and assumed that that was it."

"No," I shook my head. "You don't approve of that kind of stuff anyway."

"What kind of stuff?"

"Perversion. Deviant sexual behavior. Don't we go to hell for that?"

"I've always believed," she replied, "that if God is going to be strict about anything, that He will be strict about the rules concerning hate, not love. And if two people love each other that has to be better than two people hating each other. Beyond that, it's for God to sort out. I'm too frail to be such a judge."

I had always viewed religion as a monolith bent on crushing all who deviated from its doctrine. And I had been quite a deviant.

"That's it?" I questioned, not sure if her tolerance were to be believed, thinking it perhaps the ephemera of a hot afternoon, or worse, a trick to catch my trust.

"That's it," she calmly replied.

"Well, maybe I'll have to re-think religion," I finally answered.

"Please do."

"It'll take a while."

"I imagine. Don't worry. I'll not make it my personal task to convert you to Catholicism. I doubt I could undo the damage your aunt has done."

I shrugged noncommittally, wondering if anything could undo what Aunt Greta had done.

"But do feel free," Sister Ann continued, "to come by and see me even after this is over. You needn't be worried that I will be frightened off by unsavory language."

"I might do that," I replied. "Visit, not try to frighten you with my vocabulary."

I took our coffee mugs back to the kitchen and washed them out. Sister Fatima was there. She told me I looked familiar and asked if I had a brother. I told her I was from a large family and that we all looked alike.

I headed back to the clinic, but, without Cordelia, it was both busy and disorganized. I left Bernie my phone number and told her to call if anything happened. She nodded, but she was on the phone again so we didn't talk.

Not that there was much to say. I went home and had a late lunch.

I spent the next day doing a title search for another client. Boring, but safe and profitable. I also tracked down a possible word processing poison pen perpetrator. He was in prison in Angola and wouldn't be back on line for a long time. I drove by the clinic in the evening, but no lights were on. I kept driving.

I continued title-pursuing in the morning and waiting for the phone to ring in the afternoon. I couldn't call Danny and risk talking to Cordelia again. I wouldn't call Joanne until she called me. She was probably busy with Alex, not to mention the rest of her life.

They didn't call. O'Connor did.

"More bad news, Miss Knight," he greeted me.

"You're moving to my neighborhood?"

"We got a look at your precious Dr. James' files."

"Legally?" I interjected.

"By the book."

"Coloring?" He ignored me.

"We found a file for Vicky Edith Williams. You remember her?"

I did. The woman in the woods at Emma's.

"Seems she was a patient of Dr. James'," O'Connor continued. "You think it's just coincidence her body got dumped in the woods and Dr. James shows up there at the same time?"

"Not coincidence."

"You want to tell me what you know?"

"I know Cordelia didn't leave that body in the woods."

"You know a lot of things your girlfriend didn't do," he baited me.

"She's not my girlfriend," I retorted.

"I thought you were friends," he countered.

"I thought you meant, like a boyfriend," I stumbled, wondering if I had given O'Connor something he hadn't suspected before.

"No, no such thought," he commented.

"I think she's getting married," I lied.

"She was engaged, but she broke it off a few months ago." O'Connor certainly did his homework.

"So what do you want? Me to congratulate you on your agile detection? You've looked through those files before. How come you never noticed it?"

"It was misfiled, under V, not W. Or else it wasn't there when we looked the first time," he added almost as an afterthought.

"So either it wasn't there or you guys are incompetent assholes and missed it the first time," I countered.

"Interesting possibility, isn't it?" he said, ignoring my taunt.

"Why are you mentioning this to me?"

"It makes me curious, that's all. I have to look at all the angles."

"About time."

"I thought I was tracking a fumble-fingered doctor. But Faye Zimmer told me different. I want who murdered that kid."

"So do I."

"I hope you mean that," he said, then hung up.

I sat for a while going over in my head what I knew, what was possible. Someone was setting up Cordelia. And doing a very good job of it.

I got in my car and drove to the clinic, really just to be doing something. It was a few minutes after five when I arrived.

"No one's here," Bernie told the ringing phone as she breezed out the door, intent on making her escape. She plowed into me, then jumped back in embarrassment and confusion at the physical contact.

"Hi, Bern," I said, thinking to myself, definitely a baby dykling. "Anything going on?"

"Oh, the usual. Well, the unusual, but nothing terribly exciting."

"I see."

"I have to go baby-sit," she said, explaining her hurry. "Betty's locking up."

"Hurry on. I'll see you later."

She waved and headed for the door. I entered the office. Nurse Peterson was there.

"Oh, hello, Miss Knight," she said when she saw me.

"Hello," I replied. "Noble of you to close up as often as you do."

"I don't mind. Bernie does so many extra things for the rest of us."

"Yeah, she's a good kid. Can I ask you a few questions?"

"Of course. I've certainly asked you enough."

"The women Cordelia's accused of killing. Do you remember any of them?"

"I only started here recently, about two months ago. I know that one of the women was a patient here. The one you found . . . in the basement."

"Beverly Sue Morris?"

"Yes, her. I think she was one of Jane's patients."

"Did Cordelia ever see her?"

"She might have. I don't really know."

"Was she here Friday afternoon?"

217

"I honestly don't remember."

"What about Faye Zimmer? Alice Janice Tresoe? Vicky Edith Williams?"

"Who?" she asked. "Could you repeat those names?"

"Faye Zimmer, Alice Janice Tresoe, Vicky Edith Williams."

"I think . . . I remember Faye Zimmer. She seemed awfully young . . . she came in here for birth control pills. I guess now that she's . . . gone, privacy doesn't matter much."

"It's lost once you're dead. For murder victims, it's stripped away," I told her in a quiet voice. "Do you remember any of the other women?"

"No, I'm afraid I don't. I usually work with the kids. My specialty is pediatric nursing."

"Do you like working here?" I asked, gently probing.

"Oh, yes," she smiled, her face becoming animated.

"Even with your views about abortion?"

"This isn't an abortion clinic. Most of what we do here has nothing to do with abortion. I'm here because I've always wanted to do this kind of medicine. I can get to know my patients, not just hand them a pill. I can make a difference. When I worked in a hospital, at times I felt like I was just another white uniform. Cordelia said the only rule here is to be a kind, compassionate, responsible adult."

"How about the people? Do you get along with the rest of the staff?"

"Yes, everyone is nice. Kind. Even though we disagree about things, I feel like, well, I'm in a family here. It makes me . . . I don't know."

"Makes you what?"

"Sometimes I wonder about things. I mean, Millie lives with a man. They're not married. And she's made it clear that . . ."

"That they have sex." Millie would, I thought.

"Yes. I was taught that that was wrong. But I can't look at Millie and see a sinner, or some evil harlot. That's what my father calls women like her. And Cordelia . . ."

"And Cordelia?" I prompted.

"She's very smart. Very dedicated and hardworking. One day we were talking and—I'm twenty-three now. I've had the same boyfriend for two years and everyone expects me to marry him. I'm not even sure that I like him. Cordelia told me that she had almost married someone to please her family. She didn't say it like that. She said, 'to meet expectations that had been handed down from generation to generation, to the point that I imposed them on myself. But then I realized that their expectations didn't equal my happiness, wouldn't make up for love that wasn't really there.' Then she told me . . ." Betty abruptly halted.

"Told you about her personal life?" I suggested.

"Yes, I guess you would know," Betty said with a rueful smile. "I was taken aback. And I think I said something stupid like I thought she was pretty enough to get a man.

"She replied that what mattered was that she was finally strong enough to know who she was and what she wanted. That the hardest thing she'd ever done was to give herself the right to her own life."

I nodded, suddenly wondering what it had been like for Cordelia to struggle against what everyone thought she should be, those generations of expectations.

"I asked her why she told me," Betty continued, "She replied that she was tired of lying. That even silence can become a lie. Like Millie, I can't put her into the category I've always been told to put people like her into."

"No," I answered. "Cordelia's a hard woman to categorize."

"Can I ask you a question?" Betty asked, her voice changing. I nodded. "What if, well, there is something you believe in, but, to achieve it, you do things you don't like?"

"The end justifies the means?"

"Yes, I guess that's a better way to put it."

"If you use means that are repugnant to you, what kind of person do you become by the time you gain your end?"

"What about bombing abortion clinics to prevent abortions? If you believe abortion is wrong."

"Kill people to protest killing?"

"No. You make sure the buildings are empty. Civil disobedience, I believe you call it."

"I'd call it blowing up a building. Even at two in the morning, you can't guarantee a passerby won't get hurt or killed in the explosion. Civil disobedience is a nonviolent form of protest in which the protester risks the consequences."

"Is it wrong to destroy a building to prevent murder?"

"At the risk of committing murder?" I asked.

"But to save a life . . ."

"We'd ban guns and cars if existence were the only standard. We, as a society, have chosen to sacrifice lives for certain freedoms, such as driving a car at highway speeds," I noted sardonically. "An unwanted pregnancy that a woman is forced to carry to term is, in my opinion, nothing less than involuntary servitude. Nine months of slavery, if you will. That is why she must have the choice. Why we must be willing to accept the loss of lives—if that is what you believe a fetus is—for this basic freedom."

"I guess it is not an easy question," she replied, probably wanting to avoid another lecture on my part.

"No. I don't think we'll solve it tonight."

"No. But thank you for talking to me, Miss Knight." She turned off the lights.

"Call me Micky. It's what I answer to best."

"I must go. It's late."

"Yeah, I just came by out of habit," I said, following her into the hall.

"Please call me Betty," she said as we walked to the door. "Is Micky short for something?"

"Michele."

"That's a pretty name."

"Oh, I guess. I never thought about it."

We reached the parking lot.

"Goodnight, Micky," she said as she got in her car.

"Goodnight, Betty," I answered. I watched her as she started her car and drove away. Betty Peterson was asking a lot of questions, as if desperately seeking answers. But to what? I wondered if her questions were as theoretical as she wanted them to seem. My recital of the murdered women's names had jarred Betty. I was sure of that. But why? What questions could I ask that would get her to tell me? I got in my car and drove home.

I'd supped and showered and was sitting reading when the phone rang. About time, I thought, wondering which of my long absent friends had finally remembered by existence.

"Hello?" I answered.

"Hi, Micky, this is Alex."

Alex? "Hi, what's up?"

"An invitation and a party. The invitation is for you and the party is for us. A good-bye old apartment, hello, two bedrooms. Joanne and I are moving in together."

"Oh. Congratulations."

"I'm not calling you to brag. Well, not much. Joanne's going to invite you, too. But I wanted to call and do my Melanie Wilks imitation. Now, Scarlet, (or should it be Lavender?) ah don' care what you were doin' with my woman, but y'all come to my party. There, how's that?"

"Next, please."

"Ah, well, I was never destined to be a Southern belle. It's this Saturday. Will you come?"

"Uh . . . sure, Alex. If you can stand to have me there, no one else should object."

"Good. It'll be the scandal of the summer," she bantered. Then her tone changed, "Micky? Joanne told me everything."

"Oh," I said, then repeated, "Oh." There didn't seem much else to say.

"Joanne said she finally went too far. And it wasn't pretty."

"I had something to do with that. Me and my smart mouth."

"Sticks and stones . . ."

"Sometimes I think words do the most damage."

"No, Micky, not words. Apathy and hatred do the most damage. Words just convey the message."

"Yeah, maybe you're right. So what do I wear to this party? Can I bring anything?"

"I think something red and outrageous would be appropriate, don't you? Just bring yourself. We'll supply the rest. We can afford to throw a real party with the money we'll be saving on rent."

"Red and outrageous. Just for you, Alex."

She gave me directions to her place and we got off the phone.

I called Torbin and left a message on his machine. "Red and outrageous. Saturday night." He would know what to do with it.

Then I went to bed.

Joanne called the next day, seconding Alex's invitation. Torbin left, "Scarlet and blasphemous. But you'll have to bring your own shoes, dear." Those were the messages on my machine when I got home.

I called him back, insisting on merely red and outrageous. We haggled for a bit. He finally lured me to his way of thinking by promising to provide two more-than-decent bottles of champagne for me to take to the party. It was, he said, the traditional other woman gift.

Having exhausted my title searching, I went to the clinic in the morning. Keeps me off the streets, I thought as I entered the building.

"Hi, Bernie," I said as I sauntered across the waiting room.

"Hey, Micky," she grinned at me. "The gang's all here."

I started to ask what gang, then I saw what she meant. Cordelia was coming down the hallway.

"Bernie," she said, "when you're scheduling, leave a little extra time between patients, I have to tell them . . ." then she saw me and broke off. "Micky. Hi." She smiled at me, as if she were really glad to see me.

"Hi." I couldn't help smiling in return. "How are you?"

"Okay. Considering," she replied, with a shrug. Then she awkwardly put her arm around my shoulder and leaned in to kiss me. Our lips brushed. I don't know if it was intentional or not, I had been turning my head toward her. She might have been aiming for my cheek. But she didn't remove her arm from my shoulder, even when I put my arm around her waist. I did notice that none of this was lost on Bernie. Oh, well, she had to learn somewhere. Just what, I wasn't sure.

"What are you doing here?" Cordelia asked.

"I was about to inquire the same of you," I replied.

"Good lawyer. I can see patients provided I inform them of the charges pending against me and that I have someone with me at all times. Also, that I perform no abortions."

"I'm being a detective. That's why I'm here."

"How do you feel about being a witness? Betty called in sick today. Or are you shy about being in an examining room? Elly said she can be here around lunch time, so it's only until then."

"Sure," I agreed, not adding that there wasn't much I felt shy about. Cordelia found a white lab coat for me to add a patina of respectability to my presence.

So I spent the morning ensuring that Cordelia did inform the patients about her arrest and that she didn't perform any abortions.

I even made myself useful by noting some of the basics, like name and address. I could handle that. I found myself increasingly impressed by Cordelia's compassion and gentleness with her patients. This, in spite of the difficulty of having to tell every one of them that she was out on bail for manslaughter. A few people refused treatment, but I noticed the patients who had been with her for a while shrugged off her arrest as some bizarre miscarriage of justice. It was reassuring to have their reactions confirm my own.

Elly relieved me at lunch time. I willingly left her to the world of urine samples and shots and got back in the detective business. I returned to my place and made phone calls. Neither Joanne nor Danny could do more than confirm what Cordelia had told me. No new news of the murders. I went down my list and called Jane Bowen.

"So who's side are you on?" was her response after I identified myself and told her what I wanted.

"Cordelia's. I'd like to find out the truth," I answered.

"What if the truth never comes shining through? If all you get is a muddled and dirty version?" she said, then added, "That incriminates Cordelia?"

"I'm not the police. I won't be content with the muddled and dirty version."

"All right," she said, making a decision. "I performed an abortion on Beverly Morris on Friday morning, the day she died, at the other clinic I work for out in Metairie. Everything went well, no complications. She was fine when she left."

"So what happened?"

"Nothing should have happened. What the police want to hear—and I can't tell them this didn't happen—is that Beverly developed complications, couldn't reach me because I was gone by then, and went to see Cordelia on Friday afternoon. And that Cordelia let whatever complication Beverly developed kill her."

"But Cordelia didn't perform the abortion?"

"No."

"Why would Beverly Morris' paperwork say she did?"

"Got me. Maybe it was coded wrong. Complications from an abortion could turn into an abortion."

"If Beverly Morris was hemorrhaging from the uterus, could Cordelia have treated her at the clinic?"

223

"It's unlikely. Any competent doctor would have sent her to a hospital. And Cordelia is a competent doctor. But—this is where truth gets dirty—Cordelia was the last person there on Friday. I called around a quarter to six and she was still here. That's not unusual, her staying after everyone else is gone. Usual enough that I could call that late and hope to get her."

"Just unfortunate in these circumstances."

"Yes. Very," Jane agreed.

"What about Alice Tresoe and Faye Zimmer?" I asked.

"I delivered two of Alice's kids. I'll ... miss Alice," Jane said simply, then continued in her brisk, professional voice, "Cordelia and I performed an abortion on Alice late Saturday morning, after all the other patients had gone. It was just the two of us. I left shortly after we were finished. Cordelia stayed with her."

"No one else was there?"

"No," Jane replied, "Just the two of us."

"Why did you do her abortion at Cordelia's clinic and not at yours?"

"It was very early in Alice's pregnancy, making it a simple procedure." Then Jane was silent.

"Why Saturday morning with just the two of you?" I questioned, wondering what Jane wasn't saying.

She gave a harsh laugh. "The police didn't ask that."

"They should have," I answered.

"Alice was HIV-positive. Do you know how many places perform abortions on HIV-positive women?" She wasn't seeking an answer, so I didn't give her one. She continued, "That's why Cordelia and I were doing it by ourselves, after regular hours. All you need is one person seeing a doctor come out of a 'simple procedure' gowned, masked, gloved, with eye protection, the whole nine yards, to start rumors."

"Who else, besides you and Cordelia, might know?"

"We don't put HIV in a patient's chart. We keep that separate."

"Abortion?"

"The same. And it's coded. A private code that only a few of us know."

"Who?" I asked.

"Cordelia, myself, Aaron—but he can never remember, so he's always asking one of us—Millie, Elly, and Betty."

"That's all? How about Bernie?"

"No. We only give out that information on a need-to-know basis."

"So only you and Cordelia would have known about Alice Tresoe's abortion?"

"Probably. We have what we call the shredded file, notes and comments on patients. Like Tuesday afternoon at three is HIV-positive or uses injection drugs, so don't leave syringes lying around. Things a health care provider would like to know. But it's in code and Cordelia keeps it in her office under lock and key. It gets shredded every week."

"Who has access to that file?"

"Only those of us who directly treat the patients. Cordelia, myself, Aaron, Betty, Elly, and Millie. I think Betty or Millie scans it in the morning so we can know what to expect."

"Could anyone else get access to it?" I asked.

"It's possible. But they would have to know the code for it to mean anything. And Cordelia keeps the only copy in her safe deposit box."

I scribbled a few notes. It would be hard for an outsider to find out which patients were having abortions. And it was even harder to believe an insider would be party to the murder of these women. Betty might be against abortion, but she wasn't this kind of murderer.

"What about Faye Zimmer?" I asked.

"I don't remember her. But according to a note in her chart, Cordelia consulted with me about problems she was having with her period. As far as I know she didn't have an abortion."

"Victoria Williams?"

"That name means nothing to me."

"Thanks for your help," I said. I had run out of questions.

"I don't think I was much help," Jane replied. "The truth still looks pretty muddy to me."

It did to me, too.

Chapter 15

I went to the clinic again in the morning. Millie was there. "Good to see a friendly face," she told me.

"Good to be a friendly face," I replied.

"It's going to be a zoo today," she said, speaking to both me and Bernie. "Have you been able to get hold of Elly?"

"No, she's probably making rounds," Bernie shook her head.

"Betty's out sick again today," Millie explained for me. "I hope she's okay. She's got to be real sick to take off two days."

Cordelia came down the hallway carrying a kid. She smiled, walking past us to the waiting room. "Here you go, Mrs. Hill. She didn't even cry when I gave her a shot," she said to the child's mother.

Dr. Bowen came out of the same examining room Cordelia had been in and joined us. "Morning, ladies. Note I didn't say 'good',"

Bowen greeted. "This is a real hassle having to baby-sit you," she said to Cordelia as she came back to where we were.

"I know, I know. Sorry, Jane," Cordelia replied. "I hope it doesn't last much longer. This has to be cleared up soon."

"But better to have you here, than not," Bowen added.

"We all agree on that," Millie seconded.

"Thanks. I appreciate it," Cordelia said, looking at each of us in turn. "Well, girls, back to work," she added with a shrug.

"Women, please," Millie corrected lightly.

"Here, Micky, you can have these," Bernie said as they headed for the examining rooms, Millie and Cordelia in one and Bowen in another.

Bernie handed me some letters. Same dot matrix printer, same obscene style. One to Elly, one to Cordelia and, oh, be still my beating heart, one of my very own. Nice to know I rated. The letters, in explicit style accused the three of us of killing pregnant women because we were jealous of their having men when we were unable to get any.

I found the premise of the letters amusing. I almost said something to Bernie, but discretion did rear it's ugly head. It's one thing for me to waltz around wearing a lavender L, another thing for me to put one on other people. Cordelia and Elly could tell Bernie if they wanted her to know. Things were volatile enough without "dyke" being whispered in the hallways.

Unfortunately these letters gave no better clue to their origins than had the previous ones. They all had been postmarked in the city and mailed a day or two ago. Not much help.

"Hi, how are you?" I heard Bernie answer the phone, a pause, then, "Oh, yeah, she's actually sitting right here. Micky, the phone." She handed the receiver to me with a quizzical expression.

"Hello?" I said.

"I'm afraid there's been a mistake," a voice I didn't recognize said.

"Who is this?" I asked.

"I need to talk to you. I can't go to the police . . . it's all a mistake . . . I'm sorry, you have the wrong number." She abruptly hung up.

"Who was that?" I demanded of Bernie.

"Betty. Betty Peterson," she answered.

"Do you have her address?" I asked.

Bernie quickly flipped through her Rolodex. I wrote down the address and phone number.

"See you later, Bern," I said, heading out the door.

"But, Micky, what's is it?" she called after me.

"I'll let you know," I replied, halfway to the building door. Something very odd was going on. Who had walked in on Betty Peterson?

She lived on the Westbank in an area I was unfamiliar with. The drive out there took a while and finding her address ate up more time. Some nonexistent street signs slowed my progress. I finally arrived at the address I had gotten from Bernie. I was confronted with a cluster of cottages, jammed together on one lot. The kind of place you lived when you were just starting out. Or where you ended up when life hadn't been kind.

I scanned the mailboxes to figure out which cottage Betty was in, but none of them had Peterson on them. Several were nameless, though.

A woman in one of the closer cottages was sweeping her porch.

"I'm looking for a Betty Peterson. Do you know which one is hers?" I asked her.

"No," she answered, not really bothering to look at me.

"I'm looking for a woman in her early twenties, about five-four, brown hair, brown eyes. A nurse. I'm a friend of hers," I said.

"Well, now," she said, finally looking at me. "We got a nurse here. Back over in eleven, end of the lot."

I thanked her and headed for number eleven.

It was better kept than most of them, the tiny lawn neat and orderly, flowers planted and blooming. If Betty Peterson did live out here, it was in that cottage.

I knocked on the door.

She immediately opened it, as if she had been watching me, but only a few inches, enough to look out at me. Or prevent me from seeing inside.

"Are you all right?" I asked.

"Please go away," she replied with a furtive glance over her shoulder.

"If you're okay, I'll go," I said.

"You can't be seen here. Go," she whispered. "I'm all right," she added. I wondered if it was true.

"Sure?"

"Yes. I must talk to you, but it's not safe now."

"Are you being held?"

"No. It's not safe for you," she said. "I'll contact you soon."

"Call me. Three in the morning if need be."

Suddenly the door jerked open. Betty gasped. The man who stood in the door was as tall as the frame, with deep, sunken eyes. His face was gaunt, planes and knobs, jutting brows. He had been one of the anti-choice protesters hovering in back of the rag-tag line. He was too tall to miss.

"You," he spoke. "You're from the clinic." He sounded decidedly unhappy to see me.

"Yeah, we were worried about Betty," I answered. "I was in the area . . ."

"Murderer," he cut me off.

His hand shot out and he pushed me back down the stairs. Betty's cry was cut off by the slamming of the door.

I stumbled backward, trying to regain my balance, not succeeding, and I ended up sitting at the bottom of the stairs. Good thing the flowers were there to break my fall. I picked myself up. I wasn't hurt, maybe a few minor bruises. Even if Betty didn't want the police, I did. That was assault in my book. Nor was I very confident that she was going to be all right. Her assurances sounded more like wishful thinking to me. He had pushed me down the stairs like I was nothing. I'm five-ten and hit the scales between one-fifty and one-sixty. Not an easy hunk of meat to push around.

I headed back to the street. There was a convenience store down the block with a pay phone in the corner of its parking lot. I made for it.

"I think you'd better pick up Betty Peterson as a material witness and I think you'd better do it now because she may be in danger," I said, following O'Connor's grunt of greeting.

"Whoa," he said. "Now why do you think that?"

A car started in the back part of the lot the cottages were on.

"Because she wants to talk to me and some guy just threw me down the stairs to prevent her from doing so."

"Could it have been something you said?"

"No, it wasn't. He . . ."

A car pulled out of the cottages' driveway.

"Shit," I continued. "They're getting away." Betty and the man were in the car. "Old blue Chevy. License plate EVN7 . . . damn," I said as he turned the corner, preventing me from reading the rest of the number. "I'm going after them." Without pausing I gave O'Connor the address, then I slammed the phone down on his questions and ran to my car.

I pulled a U-turn and sped after them. But they weren't in sight as I turned the corner. I drove on, carefully checking side streets. No blue Chevy. I drove until the road ended, forcing me to turn either left or right. I turned right and worked my way back to Betty's street, hoping to get lucky. I didn't. They could be anywhere by now.

I got back on the pay phone. "You've got to find her. I don't think she's safe," I told O'Connor.

"So what do you want me to do?" he inquired wearily.

"Find her."

"I called the local precinct and gave them the description."

"Local, hell, they're probably way beyond local," I retorted.

"What if she went with him of her own free will? What am I supposed to hold them on?"

"Listen, the guy looks like Frankenstein without makeup. Coercion comes easy for men like that. Besides, I want to press charges for assault," I said.

"Okay, Miss Knight. You want me to find Betty Peterson, I'll do what I can. Then we'll see." He left it at that.

I went back to Betty's cottage and nosed around. It was locked up tight, but I looked in all the windows. An ordinary, even mundane appearance. A few nursing books, the Bible, some common magazines. A cross on the wall over a small TV set. Everything was neat and orderly, the bed made, dishes done. I could see no clues, not to the case, not even to who Betty Peterson really was. Something had caused this conservative, religious woman to doubt, but her home gave no indication of what it might have been.

I stayed there until almost one in the morning, hoping they might return, but they didn't. I called O'Connor every few hours, but he had nothing to report.

Weariness finally forced me home. That and the hope she might try to call me. But all that met me when I got home was a hungry cat. No phone messages. I picked up my phone and brought it into my bedroom, setting it beside my bed.

I set my alarm clock for early in the morning and collapsed onto my bed, turning away from the green three-sixteen staring at me from the clock face.

Just as I was starting to doze, the phone rang. I grabbed it before the first ring had finished.

"Micky, I'm sorry to call you so late." It was Betty.

"Where are you? Are you okay?"

"Yes, I'm fine. I wanted to make sure you weren't hurt. Bill shouldn't have pushed you like he did. He's . . ." she paused.

"He's what?"

"He feels that the slaughter must be stopped," she continued, her voice quieter, as if she were afraid someone might hear her. "And that justifies anything."

"Abortion? Is that the slaughter?"

"Yes. They, those children, are beings, with every hope and dream we've grown to know, waiting for them. Killed for a woman's ease and convenience."

"It's not that simple. Sometimes it is every hope and dream a woman's ever had that gets taken from her."

"Women have choice. These children don't. They die because she won't pay for her mistakes."

"What a perfect world you live in." Suddenly I felt an anger I couldn't stop. Betty had answered her questions with clichés of black and white, no room for the relentlessly gray world I found myself caught in. "Choice, huh? Do you know what the word rape means, Betty?"

"Yes, I do. Most pregnant women didn't get that way from rape. Most women said 'yes'."

"I don't know most women. And I don't know what they said. To be honest, I don't remember what I said. It wouldn't have made a goddamned bit of difference. I was thirteen and he was eighteen. My cousin. Baby-sitting me. Choice?" I spat the word. "I didn't get pregnant only because he preferred sticking his dick in my mouth instead of my cunt."

"Dear God," Betty whispered, shaken by my blunt fury. "I'm sorry, I didn't know . . ."

231

"No, of course not. Doesn't fit into your precious little scheme of selfish women having abortions just to avoid some slight inconvenience. What do you think of suicide? Against your religion, too? Because, if that piece of shit had gotten me pregnant, I would have killed myself."

"You say that . . ."

"I would have killed myself," I repeated. "It would have been my only choice."

"I don't know what to say," Betty softly replied.

"Don't say anything. I don't want to hear anymore of your goddamned clichés."

She was silent for a moment. I half-expected her to just hang up on me. "Miss Knight . . . Micky, I haven't just . . . I know the answers aren't simple and easy. I can look at my life and know what an unintended pregnancy and child would mean. I'm not a man who asks a sacrifice I can't make."

"Your sister. Did you offer to raise her child?"

"I . . . oh, God." She was silent for a moment, searching for an answer, it seemed. "No . . . no, I didn't think she would go through with it. I didn't think . . . to offer," she was fumbling for words. "It wasn't my place. I . . . have known desire. But I have resisted. I didn't put myself in that situation."

"Her kid, her problem, right?"

"You bear the consequences of your actions. It isn't fair to force them on others."

"An unwanted child is a punishment to be born, not a life to be saved? You didn't believe in the sanctity of life enough to make the sacrifice you demanded of her?"

"Oh, dear God, forgive me," she said, starting to cry, deep sobs that let me know I had hit an irreparable hurt.

I just let her cry. As she had no words for my pain, I found none for hers.

"Micky," she finally said, her voice cracked and broken.

"I'm here."

"It has to stop. You must help me."

"Help you how?"

She caught a breath, steadying her voice. "I'm not God to judge. Dear Lord, forgive me for what I might have done."

"What have you done?" I asked gently.

"Cordelia performs abortions. I know that."

"She didn't perform the abortions that killed those women."

"I wasn't sure. I . . . thought perhaps she had, perhaps she had . . . made a mistake. But when you told me their names, I knew Victoria Williams wasn't a patient at the clinic. I remember reading about her murder in the paper. Cordelia couldn't have been responsible for her death."

"Did you leave her file for the police to find?"

"No. I got Cordelia to sign a few blank forms. And . . . I wasn't always careful where my keys to the clinic were. And I didn't ask the right questions. I won't let that happen again. I will take whatever consequences come my way. But I can't allow . . ."

"What can I do to help you?"

"I wanted to believe that it was God's will that those women died. 'An eye for an eye.' For killing their children."

"Fay Zimmer, the last woman, a fifteen-year-old girl, wasn't pregnant," I told her.

For a moment Betty didn't say anything, then very softly, "Are you sure?"

"Yes."

"The thought is horrible. It wasn't God who killed them," she said very slowly.

"Who did kill them?" I asked.

Betty hesitated before replying. "I don't know. Not for sure. And I must be sure before I do anything else. I could be making another horrible mistake."

"What are you going to do?"

"Pray. Pray that this will soon be over. When I know for certain, then I will need your help. Will you help me?"

"Of course, I will. But, Betty, I don't like this. Could the man who pushed me down the stairs, be the murderer?"

"It's . . . not a thought I like."

"Nor I. Are you with him now?"

She didn't say anything for a moment, then a quiet, "Yes."

"You're in danger. Call the police."

"I can't call the police. Not yet."

"I'll come and get you. If he's already murdered four women, you're in . . ."

"I'm in no danger," she cut me off. "I don't know that he's killed anyone. And . . . and if he has, it was only those who he thought had already murdered."

"Like Faye Zimmer," I reminded her.

"I don't condone it. Some part of me deeply believes that he didn't, couldn't have hurt those women, no matter what he suspected them to be guilty of."

"Let the police work it out," I argued.

"Atonement. We all deserve a chance for it. I will call you soon."

"Twenty-four hours. If I don't hear from you in . . ."

"I'll call you by then."

"Tell me where you are."

"In twenty-four hours."

"Okay, in twenty-four hours, I want to know where you are and that you're all right. Leave a message on my machine if I'm not here. Is that a deal?"

"Yes. I'll tell you everything then. Good-bye, Micky." The phone clicked off.

I stared for a long time at the green minutes ticking off on my clock before I finally fell asleep.

Chapter 16

I was awakened by the dissonance of the phone ringing and a cat meowing. Somehow I had slept through the alarm clock. Or woken up just enough to turn it off (always a possibility).

I jumped up and went for the phone.

"Hello?" I mumbled, too sleepy to enunciate properly.

"Do you have a pair of black fuck-me pumps?" Torbin asked.

"Me?" I started to laugh at the ludicrousness of the question.

"Then we are going shopping," Torbin sternly informed me. "How you survive without the necessities of life is beyond me."

"I am not spending my hard-earned money on torturous feminine devices."

"Just tortuous feminist devices," he shot back. "I didn't expect that you would. However, I could not forgive myself if I sent you out on a gala evening improperly dressed. My reputation is at stake."

Torbin could not be put off. We finally agreed on a meeting time and hung up.

Then I called O'Connor, but it being Saturday, he wasn't around. The person I talked to couldn't tell me much. No sign of Betty or Frankenstein. She still hadn't called me. Twenty-four hours seemed like a very long stretch of time.

I drove back out to her place. Still the same. No car, the rooms as I had spied them the day before. No one had come back here last night. I scanned the lot, no one was about. Taking one last look, I circled behind the cottage. There were two windows in back, facing into a dense tangle of trees and the remains of a dilapidated wooden fence. I pushed on both the windows, hoping that one of them might be unlocked. No such luck. I should have known Betty Peterson would have been too careful for that. The front door, of course, had a dead bolt on it. I could see that from here. I glanced again at the neat interior. Was it worth breaking a window over?

Doing nothing but waiting for her call was wearing on me. I could probably pick the lock if I went back to my car and got my lock picks. Of course, lock picking is not best practiced in broad daylight at a door visible to any car or passerby on the block. I looked back at the windows.

That she could be in danger decided me. I'd pay for the window later, when Betty was safely back home.

I took off my shoe, using it to shield my hand. Selecting a corner of the pane just under the window lock, I tapped it experimentally. Then I gave it a good solid whack, shattering half of the pane. I put my shoe back on, then carefully slid my hand through to the lock. The window easily slid open. How like Betty to keep her windows well oiled. I quickly, though gracelessly, pulled myself into her living room. It was a compact one bedroom with a kitchenette in one corner of the living room. Everything was neat and tidy, bed made, dishes done. Garbage, unfortunately, taken out. I borrowed her kitchen gloves to do a search and, also carefully wiped off the window lock. Micky Knight's fingerprints had no business being here.

The neatness carried through, her drawers carefully organized, her few magazines meticulously stacked by date, everything in her freezer labeled. Only the crumpled nurse's uniform in her laundry basket hinted that someone actually lived a daily life here.

She had an inexpensive answering machine next to her bed. There were no messages on it. I couldn't get it to run back old messages. I took the tape out to a small cassette player Betty had in her living room.

The first message was from her dentist reminding her of an appointment. The second was Millie asking about trading a Thursday evening for a Saturday morning, a hang-up, then tape hiss.

I started to rewind it, but Betty's voice came on, "Sometimes, Bill, you seem so young. The other one bothers me. He has such an odd voice. I've only spoken . . . " then her voice was recorded over by one of those annoying telephone ads. There was nothing else of interest on the tape.

If I picked up my phone while someone was leaving a message, the answering machine would record our conversation. Betty's obviously worked the same way.

I wondered who Betty had been talking to.

Bill. She had referred to the man she was with earlier as Bill. He didn't strike me as "so young." I also wondered who the 'other one' was. And if that brief snatch of conversation had anything to do with this.

I rewound the tape and put it back in her answering machine. I looked at my watch. It was time to go.

But instead of turning to leave, I picked up the Bible that she kept next to her bed.

And found it. Tucked neatly in Revelations, it was a partially filled out insurance form, the ink blotted and smeared on part of the address line. It was signed by Dr. C. James and the patient's name was Victoria Williams.

I tucked it back into its Bible home. I couldn't take it. There was no way of explaining how I got it. Particularly to O'Connor. Betty would have to turn it over to the police herself.

They had messed up one of their fake insurance forms. It troubled me that Betty didn't seem to know how damming this piece of evidence was. I wouldn't be asking questions of anyone who left this sort of evidence about.

I had promised Betty twenty-four hours. But that was all I was going to give her. If she wasn't on her way to the police at the end of those twenty-four hours, O'Connor was going to get a call from me, strongly suggesting he search Betty's cottage.

I taped old newspaper over the broken window, then exited. I peered around the cottage before heading to where my car was parked.

The old lady who had first directed me to Betty's cottage was sitting on her stoop talking to a young man. They seemed in no hurry to finish their conversation. The young man gave her a friendly wave and then started walking in my direction. I didn't think he'd seen me yet, but if he got close enough he would. I started slowly backing into the bushes. He was going to Betty's cottage, I realized. Then he got close enough for me to recognize him. He had been one of the people picketing Cordelia's clinic, the one who had asked me if I was going to get an abortion. He pulled a key out of his pocket and headed up Betty's steps.

I didn't want to be lurking in the bushes in case he noticed that broken window. I wondered if this was the boyfriend Betty had mentioned. The one she wasn't sure she even liked. I knew I didn't like him. I forced myself to bushwhack through the brush behind Betty's. I then cut across some back yards to get to a side street, then walked back to my car, approaching it from the street rather than from behind Betty's cottage.

Neither the old woman nor the young man were there when I finally got to my car.

I put a note for Betty in an envelope and left it in the mailbox for number eleven. The mail was still there. It was time to meet Torbin.

Buying shoes with Torbin is an experience to be missed. Andy had crashed his hard drive to get out of it. Or so he said.

Even though Torbin was paying, I adamantly refused spike heels. My mood wasn't helped by the salesgirl suckering up to my "boyfriend" and telling him what exquisite taste he had in women's shoes. Torbin, in and out of makeup, is a tall, gorgeous blond.

"He should, he wears them more often than I do," I retorted.

We ended up buying shoes in another store. Basic black, with a higher heel than I would have liked, but not the skyscrapers Torbin had been holding out for.

When we got back to his place, he displayed the dress he had chosen for me to wear.

"That's not a dress," I commented. "That's a fabric swatch."

"What are you? A member of the Lesbian Sexual Temperance League?"

"Torbin, I don't see how that dress can cover both my tits and my crotch."

"Trust me, it does. But who needs them both covered anyway? Besides this is an all-girl party, isn't it? What do you have that they haven't seen before?"

"Not much," I had to admit. And most of them mine specifically, I thought, since I had slept with Danny, Joanne, and, once, Cordelia.

The dress was deep scarlet, basically a simple tube, held up with spaghetti straps. It began a few bare inches above my nipples and ended at a point that left more of my thighs seen than hidden.

I hope it's red and outrageous enough for you, Alex, I thought as I drove over to her place. I patted the two bottles of quite good champagne in the passenger seat. I had certainly earned them.

Alex lived in an area on the edge of the garden district. Her apartment was easy to find. I recognized several other cars parked in front: Joanne's, of course, Danny's (presumably with Elly), Cordelia's, and others I didn't know.

Oh, great, I thought, as I got out of my car, I get to make an entrance in this dress. Hell, you can't wear a scarlet postage stamp and be demure. I rang the bell. Alex opened the door.

"Hi, Alex," I greeted. "Well, the best woman certainly won."

I handed her the champagne. Alex looked me over. I would win no decorous awards tonight.

"Micky," she said slowly, "I'm not sure whether to laugh or be offended."

"Laugh, Alex, please laugh," I replied. Oh, God, I thought, have I finally gone too far?

Then Alex burst out laughing. She put an arm around my waist and ushered me into the living room.

"Did anyone ever tell you that you're cute when you're guilty?" she said.

"No. Probably because I'm not."

Alex introduced me to the other people in the room I didn't know. Including, to my embarrassment, her parents. Joanne came out of the kitchen, took a look at me, shook her head, then went back into the kitchen. But I did catch her grinning.

"The 'in' crowd is in the kitchen," Alex pointed me in their direction, giving me the champagne to pass on to Joanne.

Danny, Elly, Cordelia, as well as Joanne were there.

"The traditional other woman gift," I said when Joanne raised her eyebrows at my bringing liquor, "via Torbin."

"Mick," Danny said, giving me a hard appraisal, "You look like you're planning to work the Quarter after the party."

"Truth in advertising, dear Danno," I replied.

Elly started asking about current movies, derailing us from my moral conduct. Or maybe by now she had heard enough of Danny's comments on my infidelity.

"Here," Joanne handed me what looked like a gin and tonic. "Club soda. Or do you object?" she added quietly.

"No. Thanks," I replied, taking a sip.

"How are you?" she asked.

"Fine."

"You sure?"

"You disappointed that I'll recover? Would you prefer I throw myself over a cliff, a la Sappho?"

"No, stay away from cliffs. I'm just doing damage control. I'm very sorry for what happened."

I shrugged it off. "Ah, hell, Joanne, it was about time I had an affair with someone I cared to be with in the morning. Part of growing up, right?"

"Probably."

"Next time I might even get entangled with someone I can't dump back with her real lover."

"I'd like to see that."

I looked at her to see if she was being sarcastic. She continued, "You think you're a hard person to love. You're not. You just need to let someone hang around long enough to prove it," she said quietly.

"Yeah . . . well," I mumbled, then, "Thanks. Thank you for that."

"Hey, what are you two being so somber about?" Danny called to us.

"Police work," Joanne lied.

Which got us started about the murders, since we all, in varying degrees, had a stake in it. I thought about mentioning Betty Peterson, but decided against it. If, as was likely, she was okay, I'd only be worrying Cordelia and Elly needlessly.

After awhile, Alex broke in and demanded we be civilized and mingle with the other guests.

Dave, Alex's brother, and I engaged in a mock battle of the sexes that ended with him mentioning how he always beat Alex in chess. Ever so innocently, I challenged him to a game. Heh-heh. And beat him in ten minutes. The next time I toyed with him and let it drag out to twenty minutes. Poor boy. He didn't have Emma Auerbach for a teacher.

During the second game, I noticed that Cordelia had pulled up a chair beside me and was watching.

"Could you teach me to play like that?" she asked after I had trounced Dave the second time.

"If you really want to learn, get Emma."

"I'd prefer you," she replied.

Danny joined us. "God, I wish I had a family like that," she said, indicating Alex's parents calmly talking to Joanne. "Whenever I mention Elly, my parents get a pained expression on their faces."

"Maybe we should introduce your parents to my parents," Elly remarked, putting her arm around Danny's waist. "They get a very similar expression whenever I talk about you."

"But worth putting up with for you," Danny replied. She kissed Elly.

"Loving couples, how disgusting," I commented.

"They're a cute loving couple," Cordelia said.

"They're an absolutely stunning loving couple, but don't tell them that," I remarked.

"You're right," she replied. Then looked at me and smiled.

I was caught for a moment, looking into her eyes, then I had to glance away. My stomach had just done a very complicated somersault and I didn't want her noticing.

"Hang around y'all," Alex said as she breezed by. "All the obligatory people are leaving." Then she headed off to say good-bye to some of the exiting guests.

"Alex does win the best family award," I said as I watched Mrs. Sayers hugging Joanne goodbye.

"Why are families so depressing?" Danny asked rhetorically.

"What's going on here?" Joanne asked as she joined us.

"We're discussing families," Elly explained.

"Whew, all gone," Alex said, having seen the last guest, save us, to the door.

"We all want to be in your family," Elly told Alex.

"Sure, no problem. Yo, Ma, five more kids," Alex called after her safely out-of-earshot mother.

"Micky, go open those champagne bottles," Danny commanded.

I saluted and headed for the kitchen. Alex joined me, finding the champagne where Joanne had put it in the refrigerator. I opened the bottle, quickly popping the cork while Alex found glasses, then followed her out to the living room.

Danny poured the champagne, handing us each a glass. I started to decline, then decided it would be easier to just park a glass in front of me than make a fuss.

"To Joanne and Alex," Cordelia said, raising her glass. They kissed as we toasted them.

"To us all," Alex said, lifting her glass. "Joanne, because I love you. C.J., you're my best friend. Danny, for your legal advice and being a devil's advocate when I need one. Elly, stitches and compassion after that oyster shell last summer. You probably saved my life. And Micky, in ways I couldn't possibly recount." She took a sip, then added, "But it might be real interesting for me to try."

After the laughter, I asked, "Joanne, how do you get her to shut up?"

"Sex," Joanne laconically replied.

"Which is why I talk so much," Alex added.

"Okay, is it late enough and are we drunk enough?" Danny asked.

"For?" Alex inquired.

"To talk about sex."

"We can't talk about families, work, politics, and religion. What else is there?" Alex said. "How did you two meet?"

"Us?" Danny asked.

"Well, I know how Joanne and I met," Alex replied.

"At a party Cordelia gave," Elly answered.

"You think Elly's shy? You should have seen her. She walked up to me, asked me if I had a lover, then got my phone number and told me she'd like to see me. I was impressed," Danny elaborated.

"I think I introduced myself first and we had talked a few times in passing. It took every ounce of courage I had to do that. But I figured you were going to be leaving any minute and if I didn't, then that was that."

"I'm very glad you did," Danny said, taking her hand.

"How'd you two meet?" I asked Alex and Joanne.

"C.J., the matchmaker," Alex answered. "I had just moved in here, having finally broken up with Louise. How did I ever get involved with a woman whose passion was watching interest accrue? Anyway, Cordelia brought some friends of hers over to help paint. I was having a painting party."

"Twenty-five words or less," I cut in.

"Actually Danny brought me," Joanne supplied.

"I was trying to fix you up with Cordelia," Danny said, "but my matchmaking went astray."

"Doesn't it always?" I commented. "I remember some of the matches you tried to make for me."

"You have no match," Danny retorted. "Fortunately."

"Now, girls," Alex refereed.

"So how'd you get her quiet long enough to get her into bed?" I asked Joanne, not taking Danny's bait.

"What a presumptuous question," Alex interjected.

"Alex told me if I wanted to shut her up, I'd have to kiss her. So I did."

"Then she picked me up, picked me up, mind you, and carried me into the bedroom. I think hunger, food, that is, finally got us out about a day later. We spent half an hour in the kitchen and went back into the bedroom. Or did we even make it back to the bedroom? Didn't we . . . ?"

"Alex," Joanne interrupted her.

"Yes, dear?"

Joanne kissed her. A long kiss. Danny started whistling, deliberately out of tune. Cordelia winked at Danny and started drumming her fingers on the table.

"I do declare," Alex said, after they finally broke off, "I totally forgot what I was talking about."

"Sex," Danny reminded her. "Tell us about your first time."

"If you insist," she agreed and looked at me. "You don't remember, do you?"

"How could I forget, Alex, dear?" I played along. "Was it Paris? Rome? Biloxi?"

"New York," Alex laughed, shaking her head. "My senior year in college. I had been curious for a while and I was in the painful position of fence-sitting. I kept getting these weird physical sensations around women and it happened often enough that I couldn't write it off to the flu.

"One evening we were making our way to ACDC—the All Campus Dining Center, not what you were thinking—and we heard rumors of tuna tetrazini. One brilliant woman said, fuck this, let's go to New York City. So, with the naiveté of youth, we galloped off to the train station and the temptations of the Big Apple.

"Once at Grand Central, division struck the troops. Three went to the Upper West Side and three to the Village (my group). Rhonda immediately headed for her NYU boyfriend, leaving Sylvia and me to our own devices. We had an Italian dinner, a tremendous improvement over re-formed tuna, then we started bar hopping. Straight bars, of course. Syl was relentlessly hetero.

"An unwound watch changed my life. Had it not been for that fickle watch, I would have left Syl to her wenching and caught the last train back to Poughkeepsie. Syl wasn't worried, she had no plans to return to her dorm room that night.

"She found a suitable male and left me defenseless with his friend. And then I did something which years of Southern female tradition should have beaten out of me: I spilled my drink on him, forcing him to the men's room while I made my escape. Out to the less-than-gentle streets of New York.

"I roamed, I wandered, I wondered what would become of me. Then I saw this very interesting group of women go into a bar. I must have walked around that block at least ten times before I summoned the courage to go in.

"It was filled with women. Only women.

"And what had seemed impossible in that het bar, to pick up some strange man and go home with him, seemed possible here. Except in straight bars, men made the advances. I stood around for about an hour, hoping someone would at least come and talk to me, but it didn't happen. And I kept giving myself all these little pep talks. Just go up and say hi. Ask for the time, my watch had stopped. I'd take a step or two, then falter. No, she's with someone. No, she's going to the bathroom. Any port in my storm. And I kept hoping some woman would come up and talk to me.

"I finally got what I wanted. A—I'm sorry, I know this is politically incorrect—bull dyke was suddenly standing less than six inches in front of me. Cigarette hanging out of her mouth, beer on her breath. My dream date. She took a step in and I took a step back until I was backed against the wall. 'Hi,' she said—I was relived to know she could talk—'wanna dance?'

"I couldn't dance with her. I'd asphyxiate on the alcohol and smoke on her breath. I do remember vaguely saying some sort of no, but she wasn't in the mood for negatives. She flung a paw around my shoulder and pulled me to the dance floor. I bumped into this tall, dark woman that I had noticed earlier, causing her to glance in my direction.

"And, being desperate, not to mention light-headed from the beer breath, I said, 'It's about time you got here.'

"She burst out laughing, then winked at me and said, 'Get your hands off my girlfriend. She dances with me or nobody.'"

Alex looked at me again. She had obviously gotten the pertinent details from Danny, who, I had to admit, was doing a very good job of keeping a poker face.

"Tall, dark, and handsome led me across the dance floor. From a nightmare to a fantasy. We danced a few times, including a slow one for appearance's sake, she told me. Slow enough to get my pants wet. Then she said, 'Let's go,' and she led me out of the bar. We were walking down the streets in the Village and I had no idea where I was. And I suddenly had these images of headlines blaring, 'Vassar Senior Strangled by Lesbian Maniac.' This woman was tall, a good eight inches over me. I didn't have much of a chance.

"Then she asked me where I lived and said she'd escort me home, making me feel a bit foolish. I explained my missed train predicament. And she very politely offered to let me crash at her place. I agreed because I'd detected a hint of a Southern accent. I knew Southern girls wouldn't be lesbian sex maniacs.

"So it was you, huh, Mick?" Danny asked as if she wasn't in on the whole thing.

"Of course," I replied. "Who else could possibly have the stamina to sleep with both you and Alex?"

"To continue," Alex continued, "we walked a bit more. She was chatting, in that Southern fashion, about this and that, pointing out where Stonewall had been. And this light bulb went on in my head. I was being taken to this gorgeous woman's apartment.

"Then she led me into the subway and I began to wonder if I'd met the first Southern lesbian maniac. At some point she noticed how nervous I was. Maybe it was my saying Hail Marys and not being Catholic that tipped her off. She said she never worried about being in the subway alone. Only if there were other people did she worry. It was only me, her, and some wino asleep on the bench in the station.

"So we were standing there waiting for the train and I found myself looking up at this woman, thinking, God, she has beautiful eyes. Then she bent down, moving slowly and I knew she was going to kiss me. And I didn't even know her name. Just as she started to kiss me, an express train roared by. I jumped back, startled by the noise and the idea of all those people on that train watching me kiss another woman in a subway station."

I sat up. A scrap of memory intruded. I had kissed a woman in the Christopher Street station and she had jumped away. I looked at Alex. Different haircut, different glasses . . . but she could have been Alex. I surreptitiously glanced around the table, but people were watching Alex as she told her story. Could I have mentioned enough of the details for Danny to have passed them on to Alex? This being true wasn't possible.

". . . and we were passing 86th street and I'm thinking, I'm going to the Bronx. After 96th, I had to ask, because I was beyond Hail Marys. She replied, 'Relax, we're going to my dorm at Barnard.' Relief. We finally left the subway."

And I remembered the woman, saying, "Hi, I'm Alex. I just thought it might be a good idea to introduce myself." Embarrassment descended with a vengeance. I *had* slept with Alex.

I glanced around the table again. Joanne was looking at me.

Then Danny caught Joanne looking and she stared at me, too, followed by Elly. I could imagine the look on my face. Alex paused, noticing that her listeners' attention had been diverted.

"Is it that dress, Mick, or are you blushing?" Danny gleefully asked. "Naw, that's not possible."

"Alex, I'm so embarrassed," I said.

"Why?" she replied. "I had a good time."

"Did you? I hope so," I answered, trying desperately to dig up a few more details from my faulty memory.

"Yeah," Alex answered again. "Didn't you?"

I couldn't remember. I tried to picture us having sex, but the images blurred.

"I'm sorry, Alex," I said very softly. "I don't . . . remember." I suddenly felt sad and empty. Why hadn't I been present then? How many other women had I taken in a drunken or drugged fog? "I'm sorry, Alex," I repeated quietly. "I should have remembered."

"What was that, Mick?" Danny inquired. "Couldn't hear you at this end of the table."

"I said, Elly, did you throw out those dental dams I left in the back seat of your car?"

"Very funny," Danny replied.

"Gosh, I hope so," Elly winked at me.

"Could we hear the end of your story, Alex?" Cordelia asked.

"Being a proper Southern girl," Alex continued, "Micky offered to let me have the bed and she would sleep on the floor. Of course, being a proper Southern lady myself, I couldn't allow it. Being a typical college cot, the sleeping space was immediately intimate. Then she . . . you started kissing me. And like a fool, I decided to be honest, so I said I'd never done anything like this before. And you rolled over and said, 'okay, we don't have to do anything.' "

"And?" Danny asked.

"Having a big mouth helps out in situations like this, because I immediately blurted out, but I want to do something. Then we did a lot of things. And I learned the virtues of keeping my mouth open and not saying anything."

"Congratulations, Alex, on a memorable first time," I said, sardonically raising my glass. I was upset.

"For at least one of you," Danny couldn't resist adding.

Damn, Danny and her needling. It suddenly occurred to me that I might find it amusing, too, if I were drunk.

"Okay, Micky, now I want to hear about your first time," Alex said.

"If she can remember," Danny interjected.

"How about a break for the bathroom?" Cordelia suggested.

"Come on, Elly," I said, standing up. "Let's get it over with. We can do it while they pee." I was trying to annoy Danny.

"No way," Danny answered for her. "Take Cordelia."

"I'm going to the bathroom," Cordelia replied.

"Hey, golden showers, Mick'll go for that," Danny said.

"Yeah, you taught me," I retorted.

"Bullshit! We never did that," Danny responded.

"Have you forgotten?" I said.

"I don't forget the things I do in bed," Danny chided.

I sat on the side of Elly's chair and put my arm around her shoulders. "You want to do some forgettable things?"

Danny shook her head and looked away, pretending to ignore us. I let my hand slide down toward Elly's breast. Danny couldn't ignore that. Elly took my hand, holding it where it was. She looked at me.

"We like you, Micky," she stated simply.

You're playing an ugly game, I thought, and not one I could continue after Elly's statement. My belligerent advance turned into a friendly hug.

"I like you, Elly," I responded. Then I got up and hugged Danny.

"You, too, Danno. I just wish you would forget a little more and I could remember more."

"Might not be a bad idea," Danny admitted, returning my hug. "But, Mick, that red dress is an awfully tempting target for us bull-headed people."

"My favorite bull . . ." I started.

Cordelia, Alex, and Joanne returned from the bathroom.

"Okay, women," Alex said, taking her seat. "Now the one we've all been waiting for. The first sexual experience of Michele Knight."

"Don't get your expectations too high," I said. "Well . . ." I began, then faltered. "Okay. My sophomore year . . ."

"I beg your pardon," Danny interrupted. "I remember women in your freshman year."

". . . in high school," I continued.

"High school?" Joanne raised an eyebrow.

"High school," I confirmed. "I had gym sixth period. A mixed class, freshmen through seniors. One of the seniors, Misty, started joking around with me. She joked with everyone actually, but I answered her back. She was the head cheerleader and very popular, and I was a gawky sophomore.

"One day after school, I was waiting for the bus, when she drove by, then stopped and asked if I wanted a ride. She drove me to the burger place where I worked. And after that she started giving me rides fairly regularly.

"Misty was dating Ned, the captain of the football team. A few weeks later, during lunch, his best friend Brian, asked me for a date. So on Saturday, Ned, Misty, and Brian picked me up after work, and we went out for a pizza.

"The next weekend it was unseasonably warm, and Misty suggested that we all go swimming. I made up some line for Aunt Greta and early Saturday morning the four of us headed off for some creek up around Bogalusa. It was in the middle of nowhere. Ned had discovered it on a scouting trip. We parked the car and hiked down to the creek.

"Ned and Brian took off downstream. Misty and I waded upstream for a bit and found a grassy place to sit down. We sat there talking for awhile. Then she asked me if I'd ever really been kissed. I hadn't. She asked me if I wanted to learn how to kiss.

"I think I said something like not yet, that I wasn't really interested in that kind of stuff. I was worried that we were out here to fool around. With the boys, I mean. I really didn't want to do that. We circled around for a while, her inquisitive, me diffident, until I finally told her I liked Brian, but I wasn't ready for sex.

"Misty told me not to worry, that Ned and Brian were absolute gentlemen and they wouldn't lay a finger on us.

"I suppose I need to mention that at this point I didn't know anything about sex. Only what I'd seen in the movies and some vague whispers in the girls' locker room." And what I'd learned from

Bayard, but I was still too ashamed to bring that out in front of everyone. "I kind of knew that if boys and girls went off together, the girl often ended up pregnant. And that wasn't good for the girl.

"Then Misty asked if I wanted to try kissing with her, just to see what it felt like.

"What harm could there be in two girls kissing, I figured. I didn't even know enough to know it might be considered perverse.

"So Misty kissed me. She told me that that was a regular kiss. Then she said 'this is a french kiss' and she started french kissing me. Then she told me to lie down and she got on top of me, still kissing the hell out of me. Then she said 'this is petting' and she put her hand on my breast, eventually working her way inside my swimsuit.

"And . . . this is embarrassing . . . some where around this point, I suddenly jumped up because I was sure I'd gotten my period. I was, well, wet between the legs. I told Misty and she said she had a tampon if I needed it. Which didn't really help because I'd never used a tampon before. Like I said, ignorant.

"I pulled off my bathing suit bottom, I didn't want to get it bloody. Misty said let me look and she pushed my legs apart and was staring at . . . well. Then she sort of chuckled and told me I didn't have my period.

"I couldn't believe I was that . . . damp down there and not have my period. So I put my finger there and came up with this clear liquid. I wondered what had gone wrong and why Misty thought it was so funny.

"Then she pushed me back down and got on top of me. She told me that it was lubrication and she would show me what it was for. She slid her fingers in and . . . well, you know.

"After it was all over — she had guided me to do her — I remember feeling stunned and vaguely ashamed. I knew it had to do with sex, we had been touching each other down there. And that it wasn't something I could talk about with anyone else. And even if I did want to talk about it, I . . . couldn't name what had happened. I'd never heard the word 'homosexual,' let alone 'lesbian' before.

"Misty and I kept seeing each other. I don't know if 'seeing' is the right word, but, anyway, she'd pick me up after work and we'd drive to some secluded spot, usually behind the garage at her parents house and we'd do it. I always felt . . . guilty about it . . . So, that's how I lost it," I ended abruptly. I noticed I had peeled and shredded the entire label off Cordelia's beer bottle.

"But what happened next? How'd you survive high school? When did you discover the 'L' word?" Alex asked.

"Actually, it was Ned who told me. Of course he and Brian were lovers. One day Ned noticed I looked bewildered. He asked me what the matter was. And I just said, 'What's going on here?' He told me, as best he could. I learned the word orgasm from him. Ned took me under his wing. Maybe he'd been as scared and confused as I was at some point."

"Did you feel like an outcast, Micky?" Alex asked.

"Actually, no. Aunt Greta had long ago convinced me that ... that I'd never qualify for polite society. And suddenly I was best friends with three of the most popular kids in high school. Sex wasn't ... that high a price to pay. The only problem was ..." I faltered.

"Was what?" Alex questioned.

"Was ... they graduated that year and went away to college. I was still in high school and ... once you let the sexual genie out of the bottle it's hard to force her back in."

"Meaning?" Joanne asked.

"I couldn't, or wouldn't, go back to being some celibate closet case, calmly dating high school boys. I ... uh ... started hanging out at gay bars. When you're as tall as I am nobody checks your ID."

"Did you just hang out?" Joanne pushed.

"Well," I said, looking down at the table, "my choice was either going home to Aunt Greta's or hanging out at the bars and maybe going home with someone else." But if I went back to that house in the suburbs ... sometimes Bayard would be there. "Time to clear up some of this mess," I said, standing up and picking up glasses and plates.

"Leave it 'til tomorrow," Alex said. "When the fairies come."

I ignored her and took my load to the kitchen. Halfway back to the living room, I met Cordelia with her own pile of glasses.

"Loving couples," she said with a nod of her head in their direction.

Danny and Elly were kissing. Joanne was touching Alex's face, then they kissed.

"We have our cats," I said and went back into the kitchen.

Cordelia and I neatened up. I rinsed plates and glasses and stacked them in the sink. Cordelia put the trash into plastic sacks.

"Help me with this," she said, indicating a trash bag.

I hefted it up and followed her outside to the garbage cans. The heat felt good after the cool of the air conditioner. Of course, I was a bit under-dressed.

"You okay?" she asked as she unloaded her bag.

"Me? I'm fine," I answered.

"Fine?"

"Well, other than being embarrassed, ashamed, and feeling like a fool, no, make that a stupid fool, yes, I'm fine."

"I think . . ." she began.

"No, I don't think I want to know what you think," I interrupted her. "It can't be . . . well of me."

"And why not?"

"After what you heard tonight?"

"Not much I didn't already know."

"Oh."

"I think . . ." she began again.

"I told you not to do that."

"Why? Don't you like thinking women?"

"I love thinking women, I mean, I occasionally think myself."

"I've noticed. I think — don't cut me off—"

I started to say something, but she put a finger against my lips, silencing me.

"I think . . . I'd like to help you take that dress off." Her hand moved to my shoulder.

"I think . . . now, I'm doing it, I probably need all the help I can get. Yours . . . would be welcome," I answered, feeling the throb of desire work its way into me. I lifted her hand off my shoulder, kissing her palm.

"This place is a dump. Let's get out of here," she said, leading me away from the garbage cans. "My place?"

"Absolutely. I doubt my air conditioner is up to . . . what I'm thinking of."

She laughed.

I'm going to sleep with Cordelia James, I thought. My stomach was doing an Olympic caliber gymnastic routine.

"Hey, did you two get lost?" Alex called out to us.

"We just thought we'd give you loving couples time for an orgasm or so," I replied

"Definitely so. But that's later."

We reentered the kitchen. Joanne and Elly were bringing in some more glasses. Danny was leaning against the counter.

"Dr. James," she asked, "How sober are you?"

"Sober enough," Cordelia replied.

"Good. Elly and I aren't. You get to drive us home."

"All right," she agreed, giving me a look and a shrug.

We got a moment alone as people were maneuvering to leave.

"Give me an extra twenty minutes or so to get home," she said.

"No problem," I answered sotto voce. "I'm going to swing by my place and get some clothes for tomorrow. I don't think I want to put this dress back on." I also wanted to check my answering machine. Twenty-four hours was almost up.

She nodded agreement.

I hugged Joanne and Alex good-bye, then followed after Danny, Elly, and Cordelia. We waved and headed for our respective cars.

I wondered if driving under the influence of extreme lust could get you a ticket. I wasn't doing a spectacular job of paying attention to where I was going, but I did make it to my place without mishap.

As I got out of my car, I noticed I was humming Tchaikovsky's Romeo and Juliet. Sappy, I thought while fumbling for my keys.

There was no sound, no warning, save for the slight shifting of shadows. The dim glow of the street light disappeared and something was clamped over my nose and mouth, a cloth wet with some powerful chemical smell. I struggled, but the man behind me was strong, his huge hand covering my face, keeping the cloth in place.

I had a horrible feeling that I had found Frankenstein.

I told my arms to pull on that suffocating hand, but I had no idea if they were responding or not. The smell seeped into my lungs. It became impossible to even issue orders for my arms to ignore. Then all I was aware of was the chemical smell and the shadows.

Then even the shadows disappeared.

Chapter 17

I woke up in what appeared to be the early morning. I was somewhat relieved since I hadn't been at all sure I was going to wake up. I was sitting, tied to a rickety wooden chair. The sounds of the city were no longer present, instead birds and the stillness of a country morning. I glanced out the windows. Trees and pale gray clouds, the soft tattoo of rain on the roof, the wet whispering of woods.

I heard slow, heavy footsteps behind me. Frankenstein walked by me toward a solid wooden table covered with arcane jugs and bottles. I tried to guess how tall he was. At least six-four, but it was hard to tell, looking up as I was. He didn't look "so young" to me. My powerlessness probably made him appear taller. His hair was a common brown, but did nothing to soften the angular juts of his cheekbones and chin. My nose and throat were raw from whatever he had covered my face with.

He turned and stared at me, aware that I was conscious. His eyes were unwavering, the glare of the righteous.

"Where's Betty?" I demanded.

"Too bad you're awake. It would be easier if you weren't."

"Where's Betty?" I demanded again, ignoring his threat.

"She asked too many questions."

"According to whom?"

He looked at me as if that was a useless idea. "Doubt. She doubted. We have no room for doubt."

"Oh, we don't, do we?" I mocked him. "What happened to her?" I asked again.

"She's safe. The safest place she can be," he replied, turning away.

"What do you want with me?" I asked.

He picked up a very nasty looking piece of medical equipment. Suddenly I didn't want to know.

"Like the others. You've murdered the innocent, the helpless. Those who could not protect themselves," he spoke in a quiet voice for a man his size. "I will protect them. 'As ye sow, so shall ye reap'."

"I've never had an abortion."

"You've never stopped one," he countered.

"No. But I'm not God to make those decisions for other people."

"I'm not God. But I read the Bible. I know what He wants."

"I've read the Bible, too. It never suggested that you brutally murder young women. What happened to 'Thou shalt not kill'?"

"Thou shalt not murder. In cold blood. Is it murder to kill a murderer?"

"Then why not let God get me? What right do you have to intervene?"

"The same right you have to intervene in the lives of unborn children. A greater right. You are not so innocent as they. You have interfered too often. You give me no choice."

"Why this way? Do you enjoy the kink of shoving things up women's cunts?"

"Huh?" he responded, then added, "That's a nasty word."

"Do you get a thrill out of killing women by faking abortions on them? It would be so much easier to just use a little more of whatever it was you clamped over my face."

"Easier, yes. But I want to stop women from killing their

children. If abortion becomes dangerous enough, they'll stop having abortions. It'll be safer for them to keep their babies."

"Only because you're murdering them. And how many women are you willing to kill to save a few fetuses?"

"As many as I have to. All of them, if that's what it takes. The Lord has given me a mission. I must fulfill it. I must stop her."

"Stop who?"

"The devil, of course," he answered as if this was an everyday topic of conversation. "I have seen her. He takes human form, you know."

"He or she?" I asked, a bit confused. I didn't think Frankenstein was implying that the devil was a transvestite.

"Satan is a he. But he's taken the form of a woman."

"How can you be sure?"

"It is God's greatest gift to me — I can always find the Prince of Darkness. He cannot hide from me. Lucifer will be mine. I will get her if it's the last thing I ever do," Frankenstein boasted.

The man was clearly playing a symphony of loony tunes is his head. "Am I the devil?" I asked, wondering if I was the "she" he was referring to.

"You? No, you're merely a sinner."

Oh, just a mere sinner. I was crushed.

He continued, "Our Lord wants you to come home."

"And you're his taxi service? No, thanks, I'll walk."

Frankenstein didn't seem to appreciate my humor. He frowned severely at me. "Pray. Pray, now. I'll pray with you."

He laid down his jolly little medical toys and crossed over to me, steepling his hand in a properly reverent pose. Standing directly in front of me, he began, "Dear Lord, I am praying for the soul of this sinner, this poor, deluded woman."

Seeing that I wasn't just brimming over with prayer, he stopped. "Join me. You must beg for mercy." He licked his lips slowly, his face flushed, sweat beading at his hairline. "Beg me," he insisted.

"You? Or God?" I retorted.

"You must beg me." He licked his lips again.

"Yeah? Did God give you that?" I demanded, staring directly at the unholy bulge in his pants.

He jerked up, raising his hand as if to strike me. But instead he hit himself in the crotch, howling, "No!" as he pounded his genitals in a frenzy. He fell to his knees, sweat pouring down his face. "Dear Lord, not now. Deliver me from this temptation. Take this cross of thorns from me . . ." his plea dissolved into incoherence, then finally a few mutters and moans as his body shook.

If this was what morality and celibacy did for you, I was glad I had done such a good job of avoiding them both.

Frankenstein let out a loud moan, then he was still. After a few moments, he calmly stood up, his frenzy over.

"You've had your chance to pray," he told me. "Now it's time to go to the devil. God doesn't want you." He returned to the less than sterile looking curette. "I must save the children."

"You're a madman," I yelled at him. "A lone psychotic. Do you really think you can change anything?"

"Yes. I'll save lives."

"You'll save lives by killing me?"

"I'm not alone," he continued, ignoring my rather important question.

"Uh-huh, I see that little green man over there."

"No, others help me. I help them. God has led us to each other."

"God? Or the devil? So you have a lunatic or two to follow you?"

"I am not a leader, only a follower. God has given us a wiser man than I to guide me."

"Who? Who are you following?" In the unlikely event that I got out of here, that would be a useful bit of information.

"A wise man given to us by the gift of God. He will lead us in our most important work. Soon, very soon."

"What is that?"

Frankenstein looked at me as if remembering who he was talking to. "You'll never know," he answered and turned his back to me.

I jerked against my bonds, more in fury, than in any real hope that they would come undone. He calmly ignored my struggling. Even if I got loose, I wasn't likely to get past him to freedom.

He moved something that looked sharp and unpleasant, then laid it down and started putting on surgical gloves. That's right, Frankie, baby, don't risk any nasty diseases while murdering us.

"I'm not pregnant," I shouted, furious at my helplessness. "The police will know I didn't need an abortion. The last girl wasn't pregnant. The fifteen-year-old."

He looked at me in surprise, then just as quickly looked away and finished putting on his gloves. There was no room for doubt in his mind.

"The back lot or the basement? Don't you think it'll raise a lot of questions when I show up conveniently dead of a botched abortion?"

"You won't be found. Not for a while," he calmly replied. "By then, who'll know?"

I jerked and pulled at the ropes holding me, unable to stay still and let the horror of my death sink in.

"You fucking butcher!" I yelled. He didn't react. I wondered where we were that he could be so calm at my noise. The windows were open. If anyone were in the area, they would have to hear. I would make sure of that. Becoming the grisly thing Victoria Williams had been terrified me. "A lot of people will know," I seized irrationally on a scrap of truth. "I don't sleep with men. A lot of people know that, and they'll know I was murdered."

He paid no more attention than he had before.

"Help! Someone help me!" I screamed. "Fire! Help, there's a fire!"

"There's no one to hear you," he said. "Scream as much as you like." He turned his back to me again.

"No!" I shouted. I threw myself at my ropes once more, jerking the chair off the floor in my frenzy. It landed back down with a hollow thud, the noise useless to save me. But still I struggled. Then I realized if I could get one of the loops holding my feet off the bottom of the chair leg, I could get my legs free. That it would be of little use against my hands and torso being tied and being in the middle of nowhere with this monster didn't stop me. Better to think of getting my feet free than of my bloated body lying in the woods. I thrust myself up again. And again, trying to lift the chair and pull down with my feet at the same time.

Frankenstein glanced over at me a few times, but my frenzy had no effect on him. He continued with his preparations for my death.

The rope finally slipped off and I kicked my feet free.

"It'll do you no good," he calmly stated. "You can't outwit God's will."

I could try. I looked around the room, searching for any possibilities. Behind and to my left was a long table covered with a sheet. I noticed an old bloodstain in one corner. I quickly glanced away.

There were four windows and a screen door leading out to a stairway landing. We were on the second floor.

Nothing could be worse than what he had planned for me. Nothing. Jumping out the window and breaking my neck would be preferable.

I watched the chill methodicalness with which he prepared to kill me, the stolid expression on his face as he adjusted the restraints. Would he really not use anesthesia?

Then I knew what I had to do. What my one chance would be. I slid off my shoes. I couldn't risk tripping on those high heels.

I wondered what Cordelia was . . . thinking. She had probably given up on me and gone to sleep. I hoped she wasn't lying awake imagining anything like what was really happening.

Frankenstein moved, again turning his back to me, making one last preparation. Then he would come for me.

I ran at him, aiming my shoulder for the small of his back.

He started to turn, but I hit him, throwing him off balance and into the screen door. It groaned and splintered under our combined weight, breaking to let us fall out onto the small landing. Frankenstein fell heavily, crashing into an overflowing rain barrel.

I deliberately spun around, hurling myself backward down the stairs. I couldn't out run him tied to the chair. My only hope was to smash it against the stairs in my very ungentle descent.

I heard the sharp crack of snapping wood, then a shot of pain in the shoulder and arm I had landed on. I slipped and tumbled down the wet stairs, landing in a heap of splintered wood and tangled rope at the bottom. I jumped up, yanking and jerking the debris of the chair away from me.

I didn't see the blue Chevy or any other car. I wondered if he had hidden it. Or did an accomplice drop him off here? Had Betty Peterson decided to play God after all? Would she have helped him to kill me?

I ran as fast as I could, flinging the last remains of the chair behind me. The rain rapidly soaked me, but I didn't care, listening instead to the cadence of my feet hitting the wet asphalt and demanding that they go faster.

I hit patches of gravel, feeling the sharp sting of the stones through my useless hose.

Be glad you're alive and able to feel pain. I couldn't slow down.

I chanced a look back. I didn't see him. But all he had to do was get a car and he could easily overtake me. The road was bordered by desolate farmland. Sugar cane on one side, cotton on the other, no place to hide.

I pounded on, letting terror drive me, forcing myself to remember the wicked looking curette. Jocasta, I thought. Run, or you'll be an unwilling Jocasta.

Then up ahead of me I saw a beat-up, old truck pulling out of a dirt driveway. I yelled and waved, but the truck didn't halt. Either the driver didn't see me, or barefoot women doing marathons in short red dresses are a common sight out here.

The truck was going slowly, loaded with chickens and hay. I sprinted, desperate to catch it before it picked up speed.

I got a hand on the tailgate just as it started to speed up. I jumped, jackknifing myself over it, annoying the chickens as I fumbled onto some of their cages. I lay on top of those squawking chickens, panting and gasping for breath, and wondered how many world records I had broken. The red dress dash.

The chickens calmed down when they realized that I was keeping the rain off them. The truck drove on, the driver oblivious to my panicked presence. I glanced at my watch. Seven-thirty on a rainy Sunday morning.

And I was still alive. I suddenly started crying, the fear I couldn't let myself feel earlier hitting me. The chickens ruffled their feathers as my tears fell on them.

The truck finally slowed as we came to an intersection. One with an honest-to-goodness stoplight. Civilization. There was a small cluster of stores, all locked up tight. But tucked in one corner of the parking lot was a pay phone, complete with Superman-type booth. Not that I had anything to change into, but I could do with getting out of the rain.

I hopped off the truck as it came to a stop.

"Thanks for the ride," I called to the driver. He didn't hear, but the chickens squawked their fond farewell.

I impatiently punched in the numbers for my phone card, then Joanne's number. Her phone rang. And rang. Finally her machine picked up. "Joanne? Joanne are you there?" I demanded. Then realized, no, of course not. She'd spent the night at Alex's.

What was Alex's number? I couldn't remember. The operator informed me that there were five 'A. Sayers' in New Orleans, none of them at her address. No Alexandra. I hung up in frustration.

I thought about O'Connor, but I didn't know his number either. Nor did I want him to catch sight of me in this dress.

I dialed Danny's number. No answer. They were either out or, more likely, had turned the phone off.

Cordelia came to mind, but I had no idea where I was, and she, unlike my law enforcement pals, had no way of finding me.

Then I knew who to call. Someone who carried a gun and was actually bigger than Frankenstein.

"Hi, Hutch," I answered to his sleepy hello. "This is Micky Knight. I'm sorry to bother you, but I've been kidnapped and someone just tried to kill me."

"Where are you?" He was awake now.

"I don't know. Somewhere. Shit, I could be anywhere. Mississippi, Arkansas, Texas even."

"Okay. Stay on the line. I'm going to get a trace."

"I'm not going anywhere. Unless . . ." A blue Chevy drives by.

"If you have to run, do it," he instructed me. "Protect yourself. But try and drop the phone."

"I will."

I waited, peering through the foggy plastic, waiting for the blue Chevy. Then Hutch was back on the line.

"I'm on my way. Have you called the local police?"

"Local? I don't have the number."

"Try 911," he suggested.

"Oh, yeah. I'm sorry, I'm really out of it," I mumbled.

"It's okay. I'm on my way," he repeated.

"Thanks, Hutch."

"Take care of yourself, Micky." He hung up.

I stood staring stupidly at the buzzing receiver for a few minutes. Wake up, Micky, I demanded. Watch for blue cars. I shook myself, then dialed 911. It took six rings before someone answered.

"Where y'all located?" a sleepy voice drawled.

"I don't know."

A silence, then the woman said, "This line is not for playin' around with. Now, do ya'll have an emergency or not?"

"Well, I'm not sure."

"Is there a fire? Or a wreck?" the woman sounded exasperated.

"No," I replied, trying to get my brain moving.

"Then why are you calling 911?"

"Someone tried to kill me. Is that an emergency?"

"Someone did, huh?" she sounded skeptical. "How did he try to kill you?"

"With a botched abortion."

Another silence.

"If y'all tell me where y'all located, I'll send a patrol car."

"I don't know where I am." Now I was exasperated.

"Then I can't send a patrol car."

"Goddamn it!" I yelled. "You live here. I don't. I don't know where I am."

The Bible belt, it turned out. After the lecture on not taking God's name in vain and the lecture on how to use 911, she finally narrowed my possible location down to three places. I almost expressed incredulity that this burg had three different clusters of stores equipped with pay phones, but decided I didn't want whatever lecture that would bring.

Hutch arrived before the local police. It had taken him less than an hour to get out here. The flashing red light stuck on the top of his car gave a clue to his speed.

I galloped across the parking lot as he got out of his car.

"Hutch!" I called, relieved to see him. Then I surprised him, not to mention myself, by throwing my arms around his neck.

"Hey, hey, Micky, it's okay," he said, enfolding me in his arms.

"Well, it's good to see someone besides murderers and chickens," I said, letting go and recovering my composure.

Hutch nodded sympathetically, then gave me a good look up and down.

"Jesus F. Christ, Micky, you look like a Quarter prostitute after a long night," he commented.

"Thanks, Hutch. I forget one of the basic rules of etiquette. Always carry a change of clothes in case some maniac decides to abduct you. You'll want to look good when the police show up."

He shook his head at my levity, then he got serious.

"What happened?" he asked.

Halfway through my story the local police arrived and I had to start all over again.

"Can you take us there?" one of them asked when I'd finished.

I agreed to try and got in Hutch's car. It was hard to reconstruct my earlier flight in reverse. I made a few wrong turns, leading us down roads that became unfamiliar and we had to backtrack several times.

But we finally came to the driveway where I had caught my ride.

"Straight on from here. It'll be on the left," I instructed Hutch.

The building was well hidden in the trees, its presence marked only by a rutted, overgrown dirt driveway.

No cars, no sign that he was still here. But no proof that he was gone either. He could be lurking anywhere in the surrounding woods.

Hutch got out. I quickly followed, unwilling to let him get very far from me.

"This ain't rightly our jurisdiction," the older of the cops said. "We prob'ly need to call in the parish folks."

At Hutch's nod, the younger cop got on the radio and called in reinforcements. But they stayed around. This was probably the most exciting thing that had happened out here in years. Probably just me and my damned red dress was pretty interesting.

"You check the first floor and I'll do the second?" Hutch suggested. "Don't want to loose him waiting for the sheriff."

They unholstered their guns, ready to do their duty.

"Why don't you stay in the car?" Hutch said to me as I started following him up the stairs.

"You have a gun, your car doesn't," I replied.

Hutch was careful entering the room, but there was no need; no one was there.

It appeared that Frankenstein had left in a hurry. All his jolly little medical toys were still scattered about. I shuddered at the sight of them, then tried to stop myself from thinking what he had planned to do to me. And had done to four other women.

The local cops came up the stairs. Downstairs was a garage and storage room. No one was there either.

Two cars pulled in, their sides reading West Felicity Parish Sheriff's Department. Introductions were made after they came upstairs. I received several rather direct stares, but I didn't care. Better they look at me alive than at me dead.

It was nice to have Hutch with his NOPD credentials to lend credence to my story. He and his fellow law officers were discussing procedure. The sheriff wondered if he should call the FBI and Hutch argued for calling the detectives assigned to solving the abortion murders.

My eyes began to glaze over as they continued discussing arcane police procedure. I was tired. My chemically induced nap had been about as restful as being knocked out for open heart surgery. Unfortunately, I had destroyed the only chair in the room.

Hutch finally talked them into calling O'Connor and his team. I looked at my watch. It was too late in the morning for me to get any pleasure out of his being summoned.

The rain had cleared, replaced by hazy sunshine. The day was becoming hot and sultry. Flies were buzzing in through the tattered remains of the screen door.

Hutch and Sheriff Whoever were making a preliminary survey, with one of the deputies taking notes on things they pointed out. Like the blood-stained sheet.

There was a large steamer trunk back in one corner. I sat down on it. They could complain about my leaving my ass print all over the place if they didn't like it.

I wanted to go home, take a shower, turn on my air conditioner as high as it would go, and crawl into bed. And call Cordelia to explain why I hadn't met her last night.

I could feel sweat forming under my armpits, the earlier rain turning into oppressive humidity. A fly started buzzing around my head. I was too hot and tired to swat at it. Several other flies joined it. Then they landed on the trunk.

"Hutch," I called, standing up.

"Yeah?" he inquired, ambling over to me.

"This trunk," I said. "This maniac's been carting bodies around."

"Good thing you're not in it," he commented.

Hutch knelt in front of it and, using a handkerchief, fumbled with the latch. It wasn't locked and opened easily. He swung the lid up.

The trunk wasn't empty.

I turned and walked away, wanting to get out of the building.

I ran when I got to the stairs, just making it to the weeds as I felt the burning in my throat. I knelt retching under the hot sun.

We'd found Betty Peterson.

"You all right, ma'am?" one of the young deputies asked. He handed me a glass of water.

I rinsed my mouth and spit out the water.

"I knew her," I said.

I rinsed my mouth again with the remaining water, then shakily stood up, assisted by the deputy. He held my elbow as I stumbled over to Hutch's car. I wasn't going back upstairs.

The deputy got me another cup of water and then went back upstairs, leaving me to sit in the car.

The shoulder that I had landed on hurt painfully. I started to rub it gingerly and noticed that there was dried blood on my back.

More cars pulled in. O'Connor was in one of them. I hastily wiped away the sweat that was dripping down my nose.

He walked over to me.

"Betty Peterson's dead," I accused him.

"I'm sorry," he replied, then he walked away.

He returned immediately and handed me a cold soda. I held it against my forehead, feeling the coolness seep into my skin.

"Let's go talk in my car," he said, opening my door.

"Why?"

"Because I'm going to squander the taxpayer's money and keep the air conditioner running."

He led the way to his car. After we got in and he had turned on the air conditioner, I told him what had happened.

"You okay?" he asked when I finished.

"Yeah, I'm okay. I'm not stuffed in any goddamn trunk," I retorted angrily.

"You want to see a doctor about that shoulder?"

"I'm okay," I replied. "You need to search Betty Peterson's place."

He grunted and got out, leaving the engine and the air conditioner running.

I sat for a while, then started to nod out, until jarred awake by the thought that I was alone down here in the parking lot. That kept my eyes open.

After about an hour or so Hutch and O'Connor appeared.

"Miss Knight, would you be willing to go with Detective Mackenzie to headquarters?" O'Connor asked.

"Must I?" I replied.

"We'd like to get a sketch," O'Connor explained. "And I have some questions."

I nodded. It made sense to me, much as my exhausted body wanted otherwise.

O'Connor turned off his engine and I got out. Hutch handed me my shoes and handbag. They had been checked for fingerprints.

"By the way," O'Connor asked, "where's Sergeant Ranson?"

"Wherever those who are smart enough not to answer their phone early Sunday morning hang out," I replied.

He grunted and headed back to the building.

"Lucky her," Hutch said as we got in his car.

"Sorry, Hutch," I apologized. "It's what you get for being a big guy with a gun."

He started the car. "S'all right, El Micko," he answered, pulling out. "The occasion warranted it."

It took a lot longer to drive back to New Orleans than it had for Hutch to get out here. Going the speed limit and late afternoon traffic were the main causes. Stopping and getting ice cream for lunch also contributed.

Hutch offered to hang around while I did the sketch, but I chased him off. This was supposed to be his day off. Millie might like his company for a few hours of it.

O'Connor showed up as I was finishing with the police artist. He motioned me to come with him.

"Just a few questions," he responded to the look I gave him. Admittedly, my looks matched my story, but so far I was the only person to have seen Frankenstein. That wasn't good enough for O'Connor.

I told him what Betty had told me. "That's why she died," I said. "She knew Cordelia never performed an abortion on Victoria Williams and that her file had no business being in that file drawer. She had to realize it was put there to frame Cordelia. And she wasn't willing to cover it up."

"So you say." O'Connor shrugged.

"I say?" I retorted. "Betty Peterson told . . ."

"The dead Betty Peterson told you, huh? How convenient that she gave you, and only you, evidence to clear the estimable Dr. James."

"Goddamn it! Would I do this to myself?" I shouted, pointing at my shoulder.

"People have done strange things," O'Connor replied.

"Fuck you! You shit, get off Cordelia being the murderer."

"I'll get off it when I got proof — courtroom-solid evidence — that says she didn't do it. Right now I don't know that you're not crazy enough to try and fake something like this to protect her."

"I fucking can't believe this . . . ."

"The more you talk like that, the more I think it's possible."

"Fuck you," I muttered, too exhausted to fight anymore.

O'Connor called out, "Shirley, can you take Miss Knight home?" Then he grunted and started to reach for the phone. I followed Shirley out to a patrol car.

"Hey, do I get a flashing light and all?" I asked as we got into the patrol car.

"If you want," Shirley answered. "How come we don't see you at Gertie's anymore?"

"Too busy tripping over dead bodies," I answered. "But tell the gang I said hi."

"Will do."

Shirley dropped me off and waited until I was safely inside before driving off.

I stumbled up the stairs; three flights never seemed so long. My phone started ringing just as I put my key in the lock. It kept ringing while I got the door open and groped for a light. My answering machine kicked in. I turned it off and picked up the receiver.

It was Joanne. "Mick, are you all right?"

"Sure, I'm fucking fine," I replied, flopping down on the couch. "Just fucking fine."

"Are you drunk?" she asked.

I realized I was so tired I was starting to slur my words.

"No, Joanne, I'm not," I answered, putting an effort into enunciation.

"Cordelia called here and said that the two of you were supposed to meet and you hadn't showed up. Where the hell have you been?"

"Joanne, I'm exhausted," I replied tersely.

"Sleep it off, Mick," she said shortly.

"I'm not drunk, goddamn it!" I shouted.

Joanne was silent.

"I'm sorry. It's really been a long day," I apologized, suddenly too tired to even be angry anymore. "Betty Peterson's dead. I almost had an abortion . . . now O'Connor suspects me . . ."

"Start from the beginning," Joanne instructed.

I did. I told Joanne the whole story. She listened without interrupting.

"Do you want me to come over?" she offered when I had finished. She also offered to come get me if I wanted to stay with them. I declined both offers.

"Call me. Anytime. Alex is A. E. Sayers," she told me. "I mean it."

"I know. I'm sorry I yelled at you. Thanks, Joanne."

"I'm sorry, too. Get some sleep."

I hung up and finally, finally, finally took off that red dress.

There were a number of messages on my machine. The first three were from Cordelia. Two asking where I was and the third to say she was going to sleep. Then Danny and Joanne looking for me and a number of hang-ups.

I had tried calling Cordelia several times. Once at the ice cream stand and twice while at the police station. Her machine had always answered and I hadn't left a message. I wasn't going to tell her about Betty Peterson via answering machine.

I dialed her number again. She was probably asleep my now, I thought, looking at my watch. Her machine picked up on the first ring.

"Hi," I said, hoping she would answer. "This is Micky." Then I blanked. I couldn't think of anything else to say. "Uh . . . I'm . . ." I stammered. "It's a long story. I'm sorry," I finished inadequately. I hung on for a moment longer, but couldn't come up with anything else and she didn't answer her phone. I put down the receiver. Danny had obviously told her that my disappearing was no cause for alarm, I had done it a number of times to her.

I forced myself to take a very quick shower and did a cursory survey of the damage. My left shoulder was badly bruised and scraped. I also had major bruises all down my arm where I'd hit the stairs. There were other bruises and scrapes on my legs. Then I looked at my face. One cheek had a black and blue thumbprint, the other four finger marks. It must have been a struggle for him to have kept that cloth over my mouth.

My shoulder stung under the hot water. When I had washed off the blood, I noticed I had splinters in it. I made a few attempts to remove them, but I don't think it's quite possible to remove a splinter from your own shoulder, at least not these. Maybe I could talk Cordelia into doing it tomorrow. If she would speak to me long enough to hear my explanation.

I fell asleep immediately, but found that any noise, the air conditioner, the cat, would wake me. I finally got up and got my gun and put it on the nightstand next to my bed.

Chapter 18

When I woke up, my shoulder was stiff and throbbing, the splinter wounds red and infected. I took another shower, not trusting the quick one last night to have done an adequate job. Not as dirty as I had gotten. Then I got dressed, gingerly putting on a shirt over my raw shoulder. Even though I knew it would hurt, I slid on my shoulder holster. I put on the lightest jacket I owned, but had to exchange if for a heavier one, since it did nothing to disguise my wearing a gun.

I drove to the clinic. Someone had to tell them that Betty Peterson was dead. But it wasn't me. I found Bernie crying on Elly's shoulder when I arrived.

"You know?" I asked somberly.

Elly nodded. Bernie lifted her head and wiped away her tears.

"Micky?" she asked, then just shook her head uncomprehendingly.

"I'm sorry, Bernie," I answered.

"Go wash your face," Elly said gently. "We'll talk later."

Bernie nodded and headed down the hallway to the bathroom.

"Danny called about ten minutes ago to tell me," Elly said. "She didn't have any details. Just another goddamned botched abortion," she added, suddenly angry. "Not Betty Peterson. It doesn't make any sense."

"No, it doesn't," I agreed. "I can tell you what happened."

"Let's go in here." She led me to an empty examining room. She sighed, then said, "I don't suppose I need to tell you that you're on Cordelia's shit list. And mine, though not so high. I did not enjoy listening to Danny spending fort-five minutes explaining to Cordelia why she shouldn't worry about your disappearing act."

"It's a long story," I replied.

"So I . . . Micky, what happened to your face?"

"Part of the long story. How are you with splinters?"

"Splinters? Where?"

"Left shoulder."

"Take your shirt off," Elly instructed.

"Don't let Danny hear you say that," I said.

She gave me a wry smile. She raised an eyebrow when she saw my gun. And more than an eyebrow when she saw my back. "You have bruises all down your spine. Lie down."

I did as I was told. The door opened. Cordelia stepped in.

"Elly, I didn't know . . ." she started, then saw me. "Micky. Nice of you to show up," she added sardonically.

She held for a second in the doorway, wavering between entering or leaving. She finally came in.

"Betty Peterson's dead," she stated.

"I know," I answered.

"I ended up calling a couple of hospitals looking for you," Cordelia said angrily.

Some perverse streak in me asserted itself. First Joanne, then Elly, and now Cordelia had jumped to the conclusion that I had been out drinking. She probably thought I had passed out on her.

"What are you doing here?" Cordelia demanded when I didn't respond immediately.

271

"Trying to seduce Elly. Now if I could just get her to take off her shirt," I retorted.

"I'm removing splinters from her shoulder," Elly explained.

"How did you get splinters in your shoulder?" Cordelia asked.

"Going down stairs," I retorted.

"You needn't be gentle," Cordelia told Elly. "She's too tough to feel much of anything."

The remark stung. It was intended to.

"Unlike your ever-so-sensitive lily white skin," I deliberately baited her. Then thought better of it.

"Damn you!" Cordelia burst out, cutting off any apology from me.

"Hey, you two," Elly cut in. "This isn't the time or the place."

"No, it's not. I'm sorry, Elly," Cordelia said. "I have patients to see. Tell me when the room is free," she added coolly.

"Fuck you," I shot at her.

She glared icily at me.

"Micky," Elly said warningly.

I jerked away from her.

"I'll take care of my own goddamned shoulder, thank you." I sat up and swung my legs off the table.

Don't. Don't do it, I told myself, suddenly realizing that Elly and Cordelia weren't the people who deserved my rage. They didn't try to kill me and they didn't shove Betty in a trunk because she asked a few questions.

"Lie down. Let me finish," Elly said calmly.

I looked at Cordelia. She was still glaring at me, her arms crossed tightly across her chest.

"I'm sorry," I said. "I'm not angry at you."

"Well, I am angry at you," she snapped. "You could have called. I was worried about you. What happened?"

"This not very nice man tried to give me an abortion, even though I told him that I had better things to do, not to mention not being pregnant. We argued about it and I had to exit rather rudely, going downstairs on my shoulders."

"Why didn't you call me?" Cordelia asked.

"I did. I kept getting your answering machine. I didn't feel like leaving a message that said, 'Hi, I've been kidnapped, almost murdered, and just found Betty Peterson's body stuffed in an old steamer trunk.' "

Cordelia and Elly just stared at me for a moment. Cordelia finally asked what had happened. I told them a more coherent version of my story.

"I'm sorry," Cordelia said when I finished. "Lie down. You need that shoulder patched."

Elly's hands guided me back down. She went to work on my splinters. Cordelia stood beside me, her hands resting on my back, carefully avoiding my bruises. When Elly finished, Cordelia didn't remove her hands, instead one massaged the back of my head and neck.

"Finger marks?" she asked, tracing a finger next to the bruises on my face.

"Yes."

There was a knock on the door and Bernie came in.

"Cordelia, I need . . . oh . . . ." Bernie said when she noticed that I was half naked and that Cordelia was closer to me than professionalism demanded. Bernie blushed, then retreated to the hall to say, "They're here, but you need to wait a minute or two."

I heard O'Connor's grunt in the background. Bernie came back in, holding out some papers for Cordelia. She moved away from me to take them.

"Thanks, Bernie," she said. "We'll be ready in a minute."

Bernie took the hint and exited.

"I'm sorry," Cordelia said. "I should have trusted you."

I shrugged, then said, "I need to prove myself trustworthy."

"To me, you always have," she said softly. "I need to stop listening to . . . others."

"Danny Clayton has to stop insisting that my behavior today is exactly the same as it was ten years ago," I said.

"Oh, no," Elly laughed, knowing she was meant to hear it. "You'll have to tell her yourself. I stay out of this one."

As soon as I was decent, Cordelia opened the door to let in O'Connor.

"Ah, Dr. James, I see Miss Knight has told you her version of events."

"Micky told me what happened," Cordelia replied.

"It seems the D.A. has gotten a lot of calls about you. It seems a number of people don't like Ignatious Holloway's granddaughter being treated like a common criminal."

"Believe it or not, I haven't pulled any strings. My grandfather may have been good at that sort of thing, but I'm not."

"No doubt. You're no longer under arrest, Dr. James. Miss Knight's story cast enough doubt that the D.A. no longer believes he has enough evidence to hold you."

"Good thing someone's got some sense," I interjected. "How convenient that Betty died before she could prove Cordelia innocent."

"How convenient, yes, but for who?" O'Connor replied.

"I want her killer found," Cordelia said.

"I'm sure you do," O'Connor returned coolly.

"I do," Cordelia answered firmly. "I'd like to put up a reward."

"How much?" O'Connor asked skeptically.

"Twenty thousand. More, if you think it would help."

O'Connor clearly hadn't expected that much, but his expression quickly returned to neutral. "A hefty sum, Dr. James."

"I want whoever killed Betty Peterson brought to justice."

"Yeah, well, I can agree to that," O'Connor replied as he turned to go.

"Did you search Betty's cottage?" I asked.

"Yes, we did. What were we supposed to find?" he asked, annoyance in his voice.

"I thought I saw some blank insurance forms there," I quickly lied.

"Through the windows?" O'Connor questioned, giving me a hard look.

"Yes, through the windows." I stared back at him, holding to my lie. I couldn't very well admit to breaking and entering.

"No, we didn't find any insurance forms in her cottage. We found a Bible, women's clothes, food, bird seed—evidently Betty Peterson liked to feed the birds—and many other things you would expect us to find. But we didn't find anything that even suggests Betty Peterson was involved in what you say she was involved in."

"Oh," I said, trying to hide my disbelief. "Just curious," I added sarcastically.

274

"I'm sure," O'Connor replied.

"One more thing, Detective O'Connor," Cordelia said. "It's too dangerous for Micky to work on this anymore."

"What?" I said, dumbfounded. "What about catching Betty's killer? What about the rest of you?" I demanded.

"Let the police handle it. It's their job," Cordelia said.

"No," I stated. "You can't just throw me off this. That monster almost killed me. He did kill Betty and four other women. I want him."

"Look, I have thought about this, but I can't allow you to . . ."

"Miss Knight," O'Connor said, "This is something Dr. James and I agree on."

"You can't stop me," I overrode them.

"I didn't think you'd like it," she sighed, "but I will not be responsible for putting your life at risk. My mind's made up."

"So's mine. I'm going to keep investigating, whether you like it or not," I replied angrily.

"Not on my property," she stated. "Stay away from this building."

I glanced at her, but there wasn't much of a reply I could make to that. Of course, I had no doubt that between Bernie, Millie, and Elly, I could get into the building. But I wasn't going to tell Cordelia that.

"Please, Micky, cooperate," she said. "Don't bang your head against the wall. Here, take your check." She held it out to me.

"Look, Miss-High-and-Mighty Cordelia James, you think your money can buy anything . . ."

"That's not what I'm trying to do," she interrupted.

"Miss Knight, stay away," O'Connor added. "Dr. James is right."

"Not me," I retorted heatedly. "You can't buy me off."

"I don't want you bought off. I want you safe. Can't you understand the difference?" Cordelia said.

"I'll be safe when that killer is in jail. Not before."

"I'm sorry, Micky, I have to ask you to leave. I haven't the time to argue with you. I'm already way behind."

I stood where I was, staring angrily at her.

"Don't make me have to have you removed."

"You can't do this . . . "

"I'll put you over my shoulder and carry you out, if I have to," she threatened.

I almost retorted 'do it,' but Cordelia was one of the few women who might actually succeed in physically throwing me out. And I doubted she'd thank me for forcing her into the undignified act of carting me bodily out of the building. Not to mention the enjoyment that O'Connor would get out of the sight.

I spun on my heel, jerked the door open and stalked out.

"Micky?" Bernie asked as I strode by. I didn't slow. "What happened?" she tagged after me.

"I've been fired."

"Why?"

"Ask your boss. Damned if I know," I answered over my shoulder, leaving her behind. I slammed out the front door.

I got in my car and punched the steering wheel, but that only made my shoulder hurt more. Damn it, I thought, now what do I do? Go home and sit around all day waiting for them to find him?

I finally started my car, realizing that sitting in the heat only made me angrier. At least the breeze of motion might cool my face, if not my temper. I drove around for a while because I needed movement. Cordelia could keep me off the property, but she couldn't keep me off the streets. I could drive by the clinic as often as I liked.

I went back to my apartment and called O'Connor. "So she bribed you, huh?" was the message I left for him. I was sure he would recognize my inimitable style.

Danny had left a message on my machine.

"I don't approve," it recorded, "but you and Cordelia are big girls. I can only hope she has enough sense to be as casual about the whole thing as I know you will."

"Eat me while I shit, Danno," I told her taped voice.

I drove to the clinic the next day and found a parking spot out on the street. A spot visible from Cordelia's window.

What point am I proving, I wondered, after sitting for over an hour in the heat. But I was too stubborn to leave. I made sure I was there when everyone left after evening hours. Millie waved and shook her head at my foolhardiness. Cordelia glanced briefly in my direction, then hastily turned away. Bernie started to make some motion, but looked at Cordelia first and kept on going. That's right,

Bern, please the person who pays you. I watched them drive away before starting my car and heading for home.

Somewhere in the middle of the next day, Elly came out to where I was parked. "Aren't you afraid of heat stroke?" she asked as she leaned against my car door.

"Me? Naw, what's a little sunshine?"

"Cordelia threatens legal action every time she looks out here and sees you."

"So? This is a public street. I'm public. What can she get me for?"

"Harassment. Loitering. Probably a few others. She and Danny have been on the phone a few times."

"Shit. In other words, rich women can make the law do whatever they want. Tell Danny that . . ."

"Nope," she cut me off. "If you want to tell Danny anything, you get to do it yourself."

"Point taken. You've warned me. Now you can go back into the air conditioning," I replied grouchily.

"What are you trying to prove? What can you do that the police can't?"

"I know what he looks like. How he walks. I can spot the color of his hair three blocks away. I might prevent something from happening, not clean up afterward."

Elly nodded slowly, then told me, "Well, I've said my piece. I don't think you need to be here, but I won't try to convince you to leave. There's a bathroom near the entrance on the second floor. You shouldn't have too much trouble sneaking in to use it." With that bit of advice, she sauntered back to the clinic.

I re-parked my car in a shady place. Where Cordelia couldn't see it.

She did see me when she left in the evening. She stopped and glared at me for a moment, took a step in my direction, then spun around and stalked off to her car. She drove by without a glance. Then Elly and Bernie appeared. Elly stopped to call out that they were all gone and that I could go home now.

I replied that things happened when people weren't around. Elly just shook her head and drove on. Bernie had the temerity to defy Cordelia and wave as she passed by.

I went to a little greasy spoon of a restaurant a few blocks away for dinner. I passed around the sketch of Frankenstein, hoping some-one might have seen him. No one had, but the food was good.

I drove back by the clinic. It was starting to rain. What am I trying to prove? If Frankenstein has any sense, he's in west Texas by now. No, he's a fanatic, I reminded myself, logic doesn't apply.

I stopped across the street from the clinic and gazed at the darkened building. The rain was getting heavier, streaking the wind-shield and blurring my vision.

Then, between the rivulets, I saw Bernie run out of the parking lot into the street. She stumbled and slipped in her haste, barely catching herself before she fell.

"Bernie!" I yelled as I started my car. "Bernie. Over here!" She veered toward me, banging into my car, then skittering around it and collapsing into the passenger seat.

"Drive. Get out of here," she gasped. "It was him. That big guy. Let's get out of here."

I looked back at the entrance to the parking lot. My first urge was to jump out and charge after him. Then I glanced at Bernie, the fear on her face. And knew I couldn't leave her alone and vulnerable. I didn't like my chances, gun or no, going after him on a dark, rainy night. I drove away.

"I was so scared," she said after we'd gone a few blocks.

"What were you doing there?" I demanded.

"I left some yarn and knitting things that I was supposed to take to my mother. Mrs. Reily dropped by with the stuff this morning. And Momma needed it for a sweater she's knitting for my sister's second kid. And I promised it'd all be there tomorrow when she returned," Bernie babbled.

I knew she was doing it out of nervousness, so I got to find out more details than I cared to about her sister's babies and her mother's knitting ability.

"Do we have to tell anyone?" she suddenly asked. "I feel so stupid."

" 'Fraid so, Bern. Starting with the police."

"The police?" she asked, looking at me.

"Yep. They have to know Frankenstein's real and still around. It'll help narrow their search. And the people in the clinic need to know how real the danger is. You learned the hard way."

I spotted a pay phone and pulled over. O'Connor was still at the station, so I told him what had happened and that we were on our way.

When we arrived, O'Connor informed me that several patrol cars were combing the neighborhood. Bernie told him what had happened. She'd seen him in the parking lot watching the building. She'd dropped the knitting stuff and ran out of the lot.

O'Connor's only comment was, "So, you saw this guy in an ill-lit parking lot during a rainstorm and you're sure it was the same man Miss Knight claims she keeps running into?"

After glaring at O'Connor, I took Bernie home, telling her not to worry about the knitting, that mom and sis would understand and the baby would never know.

Bernie was upset. Understandably. I stayed with her, just talking and letting her calm down.

After awhile Bernie started asking questions, the usual ones: How do you know? How do you meet women? How do you know if they're gay? And so forth. I gave her the best answers I could. Then came the inevitable question. "Are . . . you involved with anyone?" Bernie asked, transparently.

"Oh, Bernie," I laughed, then said, as kindly as I could, "Um . . . sort of."

She blushed and wasn't able to look at me for a few minutes after that. I offered to introduce her to some women closer to her age, (and, more importantly, but I didn't say it, her experience level). Then I promised her a list of gay groups in town where she might get more information. That cheered her up and she was able to look at me again.

I spent the night. In her mother's bed. (Mom wasn't home, being with expectant Sis.) Bernie had had a nasty scare and she didn't need to be left alone.

In the morning I drove her to the clinic where we retrieved her raincoat and soggy yarn from the parking lot.

Millie pulled in. I told her what had happened and to pass it on to the others. Then, after reassuring Bernie that I would be by in the afternoon to make sure she got safely to her car, I got back into mine. I didn't want Cordelia to catch me in her parking lot.

She caught me exiting it. She turned in just as I was pulling out.

"What are you doing here?" she called to me.

"Ask Bernie," I replied and drove on.

I went back to my place and called O'Connor. Frankenstein hadn't been found. I cursed and he promised extra passes of the clinic by patrol cars if it would make me feel better. I grunted and hung up.

I returned to the clinic in the late afternoon, driving around the neighborhood for a bit. No blue Chevy. No very tall men.

I brazenly pulled into the clinic lot and parked next to Cordelia's car. I didn't think she could pick up my car and throw it off the lot.

Bernie, Millie, Elly, and Cordelia all came out of the building together.

"Hey, Mick," Millie called. "Enjoying the steam bath?"

Elly gave my shoulder a squeeze, then said, "I hate it when you're right. Especially about killers hanging about," she added.

"Yeah, Elly, me, too."

She and Millie walked on to their cars. Then it was Bernie's turn. I handed her the lists I had promised her. And a battered copy of *Rubyfruit Jungle*.

"Lesbianism 101, Bern."

"Thanks, Micky. Thanks a lot."

"Don't let your mother see it," I cautioned.

"I won't. Thanks again," she called as she rushed off to read a real lesbian book.

Cordelia leaned into my car window.

"I suppose I should thank you for saving Bernie," she said.

"I suppose you should."

"Thank you. I appreciate what you did."

"Yeah . . . well . . . Bernie's a good kid,"

"One you're leading down the road of decadence, I noticed."

"You think being lesbian is decadent?"

"No, of course not. I was trying to be funny. She's madly in love with you."

I gave a short laugh. "Believe me, it's nothing I did. I'm the first dyke she's ever seen, that's all."

"I thought I was and she's not in love with me," she remarked easily.

"She might not know you're a lesbian."

"I guess not," Cordelia shrugged. "You're not staying here, are you?"

"For a bit. I have a gun."

"Why doesn't that make me feel secure?"

"Because it's not loaded? And even if it were, I can't shoot straight?"

"Micky," Cordelia said, then burst out laughing. "You are insane," she said, still laughing. In a more serious tone she added, "Please go home. Don't stay here. The rules that apply to us, apply to you, too."

"All right," I reluctantly agreed.

"Follow me out?"

I nodded. She got in her car and started it. I tailed her, only turning off when I had to to get to my apartment. I thought about going back to the clinic, but didn't. At least for tonight, I had agreed not to.

Chapter 19

I didn't go to the clinic in the morning. I was desperately in need of my beauty rest. I headed out in mid-afternoon, catching sight of myself in the mirror as I left. T-shirt, cut-offs, and a decent blazer doing a barely adequate job of concealing my gun. We can't all be fashion plates.

I only had to wait in the parking lot about half an hour before Elly, Millie, and Bernie appeared.

"Where's Cordelia?" I asked as they came by.

"Working late," Elly replied.

"And you let her?" I demanded.

"Only because, dear Micky," Millie said, "we knew you'd by hovering out here like some guardian angel. Why don't you go wait inside where it's cooler?"

"No, thanks," I replied. "Air conditioning rots the brain."

"Have it your way," Millie said as she headed for her car.

Elly got in my passenger side. "No one alone in the parking lot. I'll stay with you until Cordelia shows up."

"I could stay, Elly," Bernie offered.

"You go on home, Bernie. Your mother's worried enough about you as it is," Elly replied. "Besides, I want to talk to Micky."

Outmaneuvered, Bernie waved good-bye and headed for her car.

"Yes?" I said to Elly.

"She's got quite a crush on you."

"I know. What am I supposed to do?" I grumbled.

"Steer her gently in the direction of some other nineteen year olds."

"I have no intention of sleeping with her," I stated.

"I'm not accusing you."

"No, but you're insinuating that I might be. Or Danny is."

"No, Danny's not. She's not even here."

"I don't go for blushing virgins. I gave them up for Lent. I mean, what would we talk about in the morning? That's important, you know."

"Danny never mentioned much talking in the morning."

"I don't guess we did. After we started sleeping together all we did was fuck our ... uh ..." I rapidly changed the subject. "You don't have to stay. It'll be light out until around eight. I'm sure Cordelia will be out by then."

"If you wait inside, I'll go. If not, I'll stay and ask you more in-delicate questions."

"You're a hard woman, Elly Harrison."

"Maybe it's my bias, but I don't know why you did what you did to Danny. Why you wanted to hurt her like that."

"I didn't want to hurt ... I was young ... I ... anyway I guess I'll wait inside. Say hi ... to Danny for me."

I got out of the car, closing the window and locking the door. Elly did the same.

"Okay, Micky, take care," she said, seeing that I had no better answer for her.

I watched until she got into her car, then I headed for the building. The waiting room was empty and the door to Cordelia's office shut. I pulled out Dante and sat down to pass the time. The waiting room air conditioner had been turned off, but it was still significantly cooler than outside. I assumed Cordelia shut her door to keep her cool air in. Either that or she knew Elly would chase me inside the building.

After a while I heard her door open and she went down the hallway to the bathroom. She saw me when she came out.

"I had no choice," I said to forestall any comment she would have about my being in the building.

"Why don't you wait in my office, where it's cool?" she asked.

I agreed, not wanting to drip on The Divine Comedy. Cordelia sat back down and continued doing paperwork at her desk. I sat in the extra chair and went back to reading. The only sounds in the room were the hum of the air conditioner and Cordelia's pen and the soft rustling of paper. Occasionally I turned a page.

I wasn't sure what caused me to look up. Cordelia was watching me.

"You really are reading that, aren't you?" she asked.

"Don't let the cover fool you. It's really lesbian porn."

She came over to me and took the book out of my hand. After examining it a moment, she handed it back.

"Looks like Dante to me," she replied. "I don't think I've ever known a woman who's read Dante before."

"Some of them are nice people. Don't let me scare you away."

"You don't scare me. Not much anyway."

I wasn't sure what she meant, so I didn't know how to respond. She didn't move away, still looking down at me. I couldn't read her eyes. I glanced down, then away. I couldn't find a comfortable place to look. She was too close. I had to either look at her or obviously look away. Staring straight ahead put me halfway between her breasts and her crotch.

I glanced back up. Cordelia was bending toward me. Then I felt her finger under my chin lifting my head. She kissed me softly, tentatively. I didn't move for a moment, then I let Dante slip to the floor. The kiss became firm. I slowly stood up, keeping our kiss in place. I let her tongue into my mouth, savoring its explorations.

My body started responding, pressing against hers, feeling her curves and mounds against my own. I let out a gasp as her hips thrust into mine. I put my hand into the waistband of her pants, her hand traveled under my shirt.

"Can we be civilized and do this in bed?" she asked. "We'll have to stand up if we stay here."

"Civilization," I agreed. My knees were getting weak.

Cordelia hastily locked up and we headed for our cars. We agreed on her place and that I would leave my car in my neighborhood, since I didn't have a parking sticker for the Quarter. She followed me in her car, picking me up after I parked mine.

"You sure you want to do this?" she asked as I got in.

"Are you?" I asked back. She looked at me as if deciding. I continued, to cover my unease, "It's not often I get to sleep with a woman taller than I am."

"I never have," she replied.

"How about I stand on the phone book and we pretend?" I offered. "I don't think growing more is possible."

"All right," she answered, laughing. She pulled out and drove us to her apartment.

We were greeted by a yellow kitten rampaging about.

"Rook," Cordelia said as the kitten went for my sneaker laces. Rook skittered away.

We looked at each other awkwardly for a minute or two, then Cordelia said, "Would you like something to drink?"

"No, no thanks," I replied. "Well, maybe water."

She went into the kitchen and got me a glass of water. I drank half of it trying to think of something to say.

"I guess I was thirsty." I put the glass down.

Another awkward silence.

"I'm not very good at this," Cordelia said.

"No one's grading."

"I don't think I've ever really seduced a woman. I've never had a one-night stand."

"Well, first time for everything," I shrugged.

Again a pause.

"What do we do now?" she finally asked.

"Do you want me?" I countered, wondering at her reticence.

"That . . . should be obvious."

"Then take me."

I took off my jacket and gun and put them on a chair. Then I stood still, waiting for her to move. I realized I needed her to want me enough to come to me.

She came, standing very close, our bodies almost touching.

"Yes, I want you," she said.

She took my face in her hands and started kissing me. I stood where I was, not yet putting my arms around her, concentrating on feeling her without worrying about my response. Her stroking my cheek, her fingers in my hair, her lips moving against mine.

Then she hesitated, waiting for me. I led one of her hands to my breast. The other one I took and pressed it slowly down my body over a breast, across my stomach until her fingers were inside my pants. Then I put my arms around her, under her shirt, feeling the broad expanse of her back and shoulders.

I felt my nipple get hard under the motion of her hand. Her other hand dipped into my pants, playing at the fringes of my hair.

"I want to take your shirt off," she murmured.

"Please."

She slowly pulled off my shirt, kissing my breasts as they were uncovered. I took off her shirt, then unhooked her bra and took it off.

"I like your breasts," she said, her hands completely covering them.

"If you can find them."

"I like your breasts," she repeated. "A lot."

She ran her tongue around my nipples. I didn't argue with her taste in breasts anymore. She was unzipping my shorts. She didn't take them off, instead running her hand inside the zipper.

I allowed it for a moment, then I shoved my cut-offs over my hips, letting them fall to the floor. I wanted to be naked. Cordelia helped me pull off my underpants. I kicked out of my shoes.

I started undoing her pants. She put her hand between my legs, a finger spreading my lips, making it hard to concentrate on getting her pants off. I managed to get them far enough down for her to step out of them.

"You're very wet," she said as her finger found the opening of my vagina.

I wanted to spread my legs, to open myself up to her. Putting my weight on one foot, I wrapped my other leg around her.

"In me. Please."

She pleased me. I felt her finger slowly enter me until her palm was pressing against me. I shuddered as her finger started to move in and out.

Then her other arm gripped my waist firmly and she picked me up, shifting back slightly so my weight rested on her chest. I accepted the invitation and put my other leg around her waist, locking my feet against each other.

She carried me a few steps until my back was against a wall. With the aid of the wall, she easily held my weight.

This woman is strong, I marveled. Her thighs, I had noticed, were very muscled. And I wanted to explore them.

Then her finger started moving inside me again and I stopped thinking about what I was going to do to her. I became preoccupied with what she was doing to me. And doing. Her thumb, (I think, I doubt anything else was anatomically possible) began playing with the skin just underneath my clit, pulling and rubbing it.

"Oh, yes," I moaned, my breath becoming short and shallow.

"Should we go to bed?" Cordelia asked.

"No, I'm about to . . ." I trailed into inarticulateness.

The press of her body, the confinement of the wall, and the insistence of her fingers converged into one mounting pressure. I buried my head into her neck because I knew I was going to be noisy. Her fingers slipped rapidly up and back, a hot, wet press of flesh on flesh until the pressure mounted, crested and I came in a shuddering wave.

There were red finger marks on her back where I had grabbed her. I wondered how Cordelia had managed to hold me up as I convulsed. Still embracing, Cordelia walked us over to the couch. She is strong, I thought again, as she set me down, not dropping my weight as she bent over like most people would have.

She knelt on the floor in front of me, resting her head against my stomach, my arms still around her neck.

We remained like that for several minutes, while I caught my breath. I finally remembered how much I wanted to feel those thighs.

I slid off the couch, kneeling in front of her. She kissed me deeply. I responded. I wanted her. I pushed back on her shoulders, laying her down on the floor. Then I ran my hands along those wondrous thighs. Bicycle thighs. (She had one parked next to the door.)

I was on my knees, between her legs. I ran a finger through her pubic hair, then pushed on those thighs and spread her legs as wide as they would go. She was glistening and wet. I went down on her. She didn't seem like she could stand much more suspense.

Cordelia gasped as my tongue touched her, then again as my lips pressed in, encompassing her. She jerked again as my fingers entered her.

I ran my free hand down one of Cordelia's powerful thighs, entranced by their solid strength. Too heavy and muscled, perhaps to be conventionally beautiful, but I reveled in them. I put my finger in her hair, wet and slick, between my spit and her juice. When it was dry, it was the same burnt umber as the dark strands of her hair.

"Micky . . . There," she gasped.

I kept my mouth on the spot she requested, holding her thighs tightly as they shook.

Her body arched up and twisted back down. Several spasms shot through her, then quieted to tremors and finally only heavy breathing, her hands in my hair stopping my tongue and mouth. I softly kissed her, her swollen lips, the slick hair, then I lay my head gently on her, my cheek on the wet edge of her hair. I left my finger in her. Her thighs pressed against my shoulders, embracing me.

Finally I took my fingers out and slid up to lie beside her. She trembled slightly as I did and put her arms around me, hugging me tightly, then she abruptly let go.

"Your bruises," she said. "I'm sorry, I forgot."

"I forgot, too," I replied. "Don't worry about me."

"It's hard not to worry about you."

She put her arms around me, carefully avoiding my bruised shoulder. We kissed softly.

"I meant to take a shower," Cordelia said as she tasted herself on my lips.

I laughed, then replied, "You were wonderful. To me. Don't bother with decorum when I'm eating you."

"All right, I won't," she said, smiling.

I put my head on her shoulder and lay quietly in her arms, feeling the gentle rhythm of her breathing.

It was all okay, I suddenly realized. Not that the world had gone away. But here was a place where I was safe from it for a moment.

We kissed again, then she said, "I'm starving. How about you?"

I was. We agreed on pizza and she got up to phone in our order.

I stood awkwardly. I didn't want to sit down and leave wet spots on her furniture, nor did I want to go to the bathroom and wipe off the evidence of our lovemaking so quickly.

Cordelia wasn't as concerned. She flopped down on her couch, then patted the place next to her for me.

"I've got a better idea," she said as I started to sit down. She pulled me into her lap.

"I like the way you think," I commented as I put my arms around her shoulders.

It was comforting being in the circle of her arms. A lot of women didn't care to touch after sex. Consummation left no room for kindness, gentle closeness. Cordelia stroked my arm, shoulder to wrist.

Danny, of all my lovers (the ones I remembered), had most liked to touch. She would hold me after we'd made love, talking quietly, sometimes giggling and teasing, other times we just lay silently in one another's arms. It was those moments I had been most afraid of.

Cordelia kissed me on the forehead, then the cheek.

Why wasn't I afraid of her, I wondered? But, then, hadn't she said this was a one-night stand? Maybe that was the difference. And if it was just one night, I wanted to make the most of it.

I kissed her forcefully, taking her head between my hands, entwining my fingers in her hair.

"Micky . . ." she gasped, breaking off. "I have to get dressed . . . to open the door."

She slid me off her lap and got up, then changing her mind, put her knee between my legs and was on top of me, kissing me fiercely.

"Oh, hell," she said, breaking off again. "We don't have to eat it, but I do have to answer the door."

She started looking for her clothes. She had gotten her pants on and was still hunting for her shirt, when the delivery person rang.

"Where's my shirt?" she cried.

"Here, take mine." I threw her my T-shirt.

"Kitchen," she pointed, indicating that I should take my naked body in there.

I got plates and silverware while she procured our food. After the door was safely closed, I went out into the living room and put my shorts back on. I was hungry. We might as well eat while the pizza was hot. Having my shorts on would increase our chances. I couldn't put my shirt back on since Cordelia was wearing it.

Half-way through our dinner Cordelia took it off and tossed it to me.

"Here," she said. "Turn about's fair play. Now you can cover up and stare at me while I'm half naked."

"Equality," I answered, throwing the shirt over my shoulder. "Let's both be half naked."

We finished dinner that way. As I got up to clear the table, she glanced at the kitchen clock.

"How'd it get to be so late?" she asked.

"Eating took a long time."

"I have to get up early tomorrow."

"It's Saturday."

"I know. I'm taking the clinic in the morning and I'm doing rounds at the hospital before that. I have to be there at seven."

"Ouch."

"So I need to take my shower and get to bed."

"Okay. Well . . ." I said. I picked up my T-shirt from where I had thrown it, then went into the living room to find my shoes.

"What are you doing?" Cordelia asked.

"Getting dressed."

"I didn't mean you had to leave. Unless you want to," she said.

"Do you want me to stay?"

"Well . . . yes. I kind of thought you would."

I nodded and kicked my shoes back off. I wanted to stay.

"Make yourself comfortable. I have to take a shower. My co-workers may not be as understanding as you are. Watch TV if you want."

"But Cordelia," I said, following her as she headed for the bathroom. "I am the world's foremost expert on back washing. I think you should take advantage of my expertise."

She grinned at me, then motioned me to follow her. I left my shorts and shirt draped across a chair. I had no intention of putting them back on tonight.

I don't know how much back washing I did. I do know I spent a long time under the cascading water kissing her.

"You've very good at this," she commented, as I disrupted her drying off by kissing her nipples. "Experience must count for something."

"Yeah?" I replied, lifting my head. "What's your excuse? Beginner's luck? You're more than very good."

"You're kind. I don't have much of a reputation as a great lover."

"Not yet," I responded.

She gave a short laugh. "You are . . . I don't know. I've slept with five different women, including you, and three men. And I'm thirty-two years old."

"Congratulations," I said. "You've slept with more men than I have."

"Really?" She looked surprised.

"Really. I've had sex with one man in my entire life. If . . ." If I didn't count my cousin. "If . . . and he was gay. We just did it for the hell of it. Ned, my friend Ned."

She led the way to her bedroom.

"But . . ." she said, turning to look at me, "you led me to believe, that day in my office, that you had . . ."

"I . . . exaggerated," I replied, abashed at my behavior that day. "I . . . guess I wanted to shock you."

"Why?" she asked as she set her alarm clock.

"I'm not sure. I was angry. I think you hit a sore spot," I fumbled.

"Um," she nodded. "Ever been in therapy?"

"Me? No."

"Ever considered it?"

"No."

"Oh. Just a thought. Joanne's seeing a woman who's very good. You might talk to her about it."

"No, thanks, Joanne's . . . I'm not Joanne."

"What's that supposed to mean?"

"Just that . . . Joanne has reasons for seeing a therapist I don't have."

"You mean her father?"

I stared at Cordelia, "How did you . . . ?"

"Joanne, though I don't think she was aware of it, told me. I had asked her about her family, and the way she talked about her father made it obvious that there was more to it than she was telling. Joanne can be very transparent at times. And once, after I told her what had happened to me, she said, I wish I had your mother, then rapidly changed the subject."

She pulled back the covers and was getting into bed. I got in the other side, propping myself up on one elbow.

"What happened to you?" I asked.

"I had a funny uncle. A Southern one, not really related. He would corner me in the barn out at Granddad's estate and make me jerk him off. I told my mother and she was furious. I don't think I ever saw her that angry."

"At you?"

"No, of course not," Cordelia replied, looking at me. "At him. She almost brought charges, but the D. A. convinced her, that given who he was and who he knew, they would never get a conviction. Plus putting me through cross-examination. So she had to settle for making sure that every mother in his circle knew why they should keep their children out of his reach. And making sure that he was never seen with anyone in the Holloway family again. She threatened to divorce my father if he didn't cooperate completely. Once the whispers reached enough ears, he fell rather heavily from social grace and moved to some place out west, maybe Texas. When my mother knew she was right, hell couldn't stop her."

"Good for her."

"Good for me. At least I'm not in therapy to get over that."

"You see a therapist? But you're . . ."

"I'm what?"

"One of the most sane people I know."

She laughed. "Probably because of all the time I've spent in therapy."

"Oh." I lay down, fluffing the pillow under my head.

Cordelia shut off the light. "I wish I weren't so tired."

"It's been a long week. You need sleep," I answered.

"But Micky," she said, "significant parts of my body aren't interested in sleep."

She rolled over on her side and flung an arm across my stomach.

"Funny, I have a number of awake areas myself." I moved her hand up to my breasts.

"Can you still be taken?" she whispered in my ear.

"Very much so."

"Can I get on top?"

"Oh, yes," I responded, delighted at the idea of her weight pressing down on me.

"Usually it's a forgone conclusion that I'm on bottom."

"Not with me."

I moaned softly as she covered me.

"Your shoulder?"

"What shoulder? That was a clitoral message."

She laughed. Then started seriously kissing me.

Rook never once tried to get into bed with us. Some cats have a modicum of brain power. I certainly wouldn't have attempted to get into any bed with two people thrashing around as much as we did.

Cordelia finally said, "Damn, I wish I weren't so tired. I'd like to stay awake all night doing this."

"I'd like to keep you awake. But I don't think your patients would appreciate it."

She rolled back to her side of the bed, then reached out and took my hand.

We fell asleep holding hands.

The alarm clock rang at a brutally early hour. Cordelia cursed and slapped it off, then rolled over and bumped into me.

"Hey, you're here. I was afraid you were a dream."

"You might wish I was if Danny ever hears about this," I replied.

"Well, I won't tell her, if you don't," she suggested, then she half climbed on top of me.

"I won't, believe me."

"What am I doing?" Cordelia muttered as she slid off me. "I have to get up. Sorry."

Her other alarm clock went off. She slapped it off, too, then swung her legs off the bed. She shook her head for a moment or two, then got up and trudged to the bathroom.

I sat up slowly, trying to wake myself. I glanced at one of her clocks. Five-forty-five, no wonder I was so groggy. I went to bed at this hour more often than I got up at it.

Cordelia returned.

"Go back to sleep. I'll feel better if at least one of us gets enough sleep," she said as she started fishing underwear out of one of her drawers.

My response, unplanned, was to yawn.

I watched her as she gathered her clothes. She's beautiful, I suddenly thought. Certainly not conventionally beautiful. Her hair was tousled, she slumped sleepily.

"Don't watch me in the morning," she grumped. "Not before I've had coffee." She tossed her clothes over her shoulder and headed back to the bathroom.

I forced myself up and padded to the kitchen. Rook, asleep in a corner, awoke at my presence. I wasn't the right person, but that didn't stop her from rubbing against my legs in hopes of food. I made coffee first. Then, in a burst of generosity, fed her.

"Micky?" Cordelia said, stepping into the kitchen. "I thought I smelled coffee."

"Now can I look at you?" I asked as I handed her a cup. She was dressed, her hair combed neatly.

"Thanks, you didn't need to do this."

She leaned against the counter and sipped the coffee.

"Did you wash your face well?" I inquired.

"I hope so," she said with a slight smile. "Elly's going to be with me at the clinic. She can be remarkably astute about things."

"Let me check it out," I volunteered.

She raised her eyebrows questioningly. I pushed her hand with the coffee cup out of the way, then kissed her.

"Well?" she asked.

"Coffee. I think it needs a further test."

I kissed her again. Thoroughly.

"I'm late," she broke it off. "I have to go."

"I could be here when you get back."

"I don't know when I'll be back."

"How about tonight?" I pushed.

"I'm . . . having friends over for the weekend," she replied. "Do you remember Nina? I'm picking her up at the airport this afternoon."

"Oh. Okay." I turned from her and went to get Rook some fresh water.

"I'll call you sometime. I . . ."

"Yeah, do that. Say hi to Nina for me." Don't use banal clichés to get rid of me, I thought angrily.

"I will."

"Aren't you late?" I retorted.

"Yes, I am." She turned to go, then spun back. "Look, I can't just put my life on hold waiting for you to show up."

"Of course not," I replied coldly.

"Micky . . . I had a great time last night."

"So did I. I'm sure I'll remember it," I replied sardonically.

"I will call you." She started for the door.

"For at least a day or two," I called after her, then turned to scratch Rook's head.

I heard her footsteps stop, hold for a beat, then she stalked out of the apartment and slammed the door. I could hear her stomping down the stairs.

Rook looked quizzically at me.

"What did you expect? Me to believe her polite bullshit? 'I'll call you sometime.' Before hell freezes over, Rook, old buddy," I said, scratching her back. "Next time she feels so goddamned horny, she can just wait the extra day for her girlfriend to show up. Damn her. Damn her!" I hit the kitchen cabinet. Rook ran away, evidently there were people she wouldn't consort with even for food. "Goddamn her!"

I changed the sheets on Cordelia's bed, then did all the dishes. I cleaned up the living room. I even found her missing shirt and put it in the laundry.

I wrote a note,

Dear Dr. James,
You needn't be embarrassed. I've obliterated all traces of my
presence.

Then I crumpled it up and threw it in her trash can. Leaving the note would be leaving a trace.

After one last check, I left, making sure the door locked behind me.

I walked back to my apartment. The bus would probably be quicker, but I was in no mood for dealing with Saturday morning buses.

Hepplewhite meowed at my entrance.

"I have fed enough cats this morning," I snarled at her. She meowed again and I threw my jacket at her. Discretion being the better part of valor, she hid behind the refrigerator. Then I got annoyed at her for avoiding me.

Calm down, Micky, don't get angry at a cat for being a cat. In apology I gave her some of the canned food that she prefers.

Then I hit my kitchen counter. "Goddamn her!" I could still smell her on my fingers and my face. "Get out of my life."

I headed for the bathroom, throwing off my clothes as I went. I got under the shower and scrubbed myself several times, removing all traces of Cordelia.

As I stood drying myself, I realized I felt tired, but more than that, enervated and empty. Why did she have to kiss me? If that was all she wanted, a quick fuck, why take it from me?

Because that's what you have a reputation for.

I went into my bedroom, pulled back the sheet and got into bed. Sleep, Micky, maybe you'll feel better when you've had some sleep. I debated taking a few belts from the bourbon Joanne had left, but finally talked myself out of it. Fall asleep and hope you don't dream, I told myself, as I closed my eyes.

Chapter 20

Hell hadn't frozen over. Cordelia hadn't called. Not that I had expected her to. Not after my final comment.

Why the hell couldn't I have been . . . nicer? Said, yes, please call me sometime. Let's have an affair while your girlfriend is out of town. Maybe if I was nice and decorous she would dump Nina for me. Maybe if I let her fuck me a few more times she might . . . Might what? Fall in love with me? What chance did I have against Nina? The perfect all-American blond versus tall, dark, bayou trash. Who the hell did I think Cordelia was going to pick?

Saturday, I had tried to sleep after I'd gotten home from Cordelia's. But late in the afternoon, after waking from dreams I didn't want, I had driven to the old shipyard I still owned out in Bayou St. Jacks. I had inherited it from my father, and Aunt Greta was never able to make me sell it. There were some repairs I needed to do there, although the middle of summer wasn't really the best time of year to be fixing a dock. But the heat and the physical labor exhausted me and let me sleep without dreams.

I had gotten back into the city a few hours ago, hoping for some message from Cordelia. Today was Thursday. It had been five days. There were messages on my machine, but none from her. Bernie and O'Connor had called. I returned the one from O'Connor. He wasn't in. I left my name and number.

Then I sat staring at the phone, feeling betrayed by it. I looked through my mail. Bills and trash.

The electric bill demanded some compromise between my bank account and my air conditioner. My comfort, no doubt. Then I noticed a flyer with handwriting on it. It was an announcement for an oyster po-boy night every Thursday at Gertrude's Stein. A scribbled note in the corner read, "Come on by, Mick. We miss you. G." Gertie herself had signed it.

Oyster po-boys have cured many a broken heart, I told myself. And fed many a stomach, I noted, as mine growled. Tonight was the night.

The phone rang. I grabbed it, but it was only O'Connor. He wanted to look at the hate mail being sent to the clinic and asked me to bring by the ones I had. When I pressed him as to why, he admitted that some women's clinics had received bomb threats printed with a dot matrix printer and he wanted to compare the two.

At my suggestion that Frankenstein was the letter writer, O'Connor informed me that there was no evidence that the letters were linked and even if they were linked, no evidence that Frankenstein had sent any of them. And still no evidence, as far as he was concerned, that Frankenstein even existed.

I thanked him for his astute observations and said I'd be by with the letters at my earliest convenience. He grunted and hung up. My convenience would be around dinner time.

The phone spent the next half hour not ringing. I left it to its stubborn silence and headed for O'Connor's office and, more importantly, Gertie's po-boys.

O'Connor's thanks for my efforts was a nod and a grunt.

I headed for Gertie's. She had renovated since I had last been here, adding more space and a real restaurant area instead of a few tables crowded at the far end of the bar. The display of steins and exotic beers was still proudly displayed over the bar, but it was now lit properly, a gleaming collection of porcelain and pewter instead of murky shapes.

I suddenly got very thirsty for a cold beer. The heat, I told myself.

"Micky Knight, I'll be damned," Gertie greeted me.

"Hey, Gert, it looks great," I replied, bending down to kiss her cheek.

She re-aimed my face and smacked me on the lips.

"No shyness here," she explained. "What'll you have?" She wheeled herself toward the bar and I followed behind her.

"Uh . . . club soda," I replied.

"On the house," she informed me.

"Club soda," I affirmed.

She gave Lou, the bartender, my order.

"You can always come by and visit us," Gertie said. "There are no requirements here."

"I know, Gert. It was just easier . . ." I trailed off. "I'm here for oysters."

"Club soda rots the brain," Lou said with the bias of a true bartender, as she handed me mine.

"I know, but I had to do something to keep myself on the level with the rest of you."

Lou snorted, then said, "What are you doing later tonight, Mick? Carmen's out of town," she added suggestively.

"Staying out of trouble." I had, on several occasions, gone home with her. I remembered that. I waved and followed Gertie to the tables.

"Like my ramp?" she asked, as she propelled herself up it. "When you're in a wheelchair, you worry about making things accessible by wheelchair."

"I'm impressed," I said, noticing the polished wood and brass handrail.

"Here, take this table," she said, stopping.

"It's too big. Put me in a small one in back."

"Don't worry, you'll have plenty of company before long," she replied with a wink, then she headed off for the kitchen.

I sat at my assigned table, sipping my club soda and watching the women at the bar. I felt a little lonely and a little foolish sitting by myself and not drinking. Suddenly there didn't seem much point in being here. I wondered if I had the nerve to even try picking up a woman without a couple of belts of Scotch. When I got turned down before it had been easy to get another drink to ease the rejection. It all became a game. Scotch and casual sex. Ask a woman to dance, go back two spaces when she refused, get a drink, and roll the dice again. Dance a slow dance, get ten points, get another drink, and, if she goes home with you, you win the game. If not, another drink and another roll of the dice.

"Are you expecting company, or do you want to join us?"

I looked up. Danny.

"Oh, hi, Danno. You and Elly?"

"Naw, Elly's at work. She may be here later. The single lesbian lawyer's league. They meet here every week at this time."

"So, what are you doing here?" I asked as I got up.

"Honorary member. I used to be single," Danny replied, leading me back to her table.

"And you're introducing me to your single friends?"

"They're not all my friends. You know I'd prefer you to keep away from my friends." She halted just out of earshot of her table. "A few of these women even deserve you." She started again before I could reply.

"Ladies and ladies," Danny orated. "This is Michele Knight, delivered as requested."

Danny motioned me into a chair, then sat next to me, preventing any quick exits.

There were six women besides us. All lawyers, from the look of their suits and the plethora of briefcases in evidence.

"We didn't think you should be sitting all by yourself," one of them flirted.

Names were exchanged, but I didn't pay much attention. Six new names was too many to remember sober.

"Here, try this," Danny said, setting a glass of beer in front of me.

"Tastes fine to me," I said, taking a sip.

"You can have it then," she replied. "It tastes like lacquer thinner to me."

I shrugged and took a swallow. I could have said no. I could have handed it back to Danny and said I don't want it or said I don't

300

drink anymore. But had I really come here to not drink? I wanted that beer. I took another sip. A few more swallows and Marla's (as her name turned out to be) flirting became less annoying. A game even. She wasn't truly interested in me, she just wanted to sleep with someone she wouldn't run into in court.

She reached over and touched my hand.

"Next round's on me. What'll you have?" she asked.

"Scotch. On the rocks."

Marla signaled our waitress without letting go of my hand. I was glad I wasn't sitting next to her. I'd hate to think what she'd pull under the table.

I excused myself to go to the bathroom and retrieved my hand. Danny rolled her eyes at me as she got up to let me out.

"Fast work," she muttered.

"You invited me," I retorted in an undertone as I slid by her.

When I got back to the table, our food and my Scotch had arrived. I hoped eating would keep Marla's hands busy.

I was halfway through my po-boy when Elly showed up. Followed by Cordelia. Of course, they'd been at the clinic. Danny kissed Elly hello. Cordelia gave me a slight nod, but didn't say anything.

I wondered if there was a believable way to run out on a half-eaten oyster po-boy. If only it had been roast beef, I might have pulled it off.

Elly and Cordelia squeezed in next to Danny, forcing me to scoot even nearer to the dreaded Marla. The woman sandwiched between us looked ready to bolt any minute.

I found Cordelia's presence a distraction. Whenever she said anything I wanted to hear it. I looked at her as often as I could without being caught, all the while calmly trying to eat my po-boy and drink my Scotch. I got another one, hoping it would help calm my nerves.

Two of the lesbian lawyers were leaving. Fortunately, not the one barricading me from Marla. Then Danny and Elly got up to go to the bathroom. Some couples do everything together. But that meant that no one was sitting between me and Cordelia.

She looked at me with her enigmatic half-smile, then slid toward me, until we were sitting next to each other.

"Hi," I mumbled. The situation seemed to demand something.

"Hi," she replied. "How are you?"

"Pretty good. How are you?"

"Fine. Doing okay."

I took a bite of sandwich in the ensuing silence.

"How's Nina?" I blurted out after I had finished chewing, the silence being too long to bear any more.

"She's fine," Cordelia said, then obviously wanting to avoid silence as much as I did, "She flew in from Atlanta. She does business there all the time. And Robin flew in from Houston . . ."

"Who's Robin?"

"Her lover."

"But, you mean . . ."

Cordelia gave me a questioning look.

"I thought you were . . . never mind."

"You thought we were . . . lovers?"

"She is a cute blond." I shrugged nonchalantly, pretending it didn't signify.

She gave a short laugh. "Nina and I are friends, nothing else, believe me. Let me drink that first."

She took her beer bottle from me. I had been shredding off the label.

"Is that what you thought?" Cordelia asked me.

"Well, it seemed a logical assumption," I replied, fiddling with the peeled pieces of label in front of me.

"Not if you knew the two of us. Nina is . . . I'd find life with Nina boring."

"Oh, well . . ." I replied, shrugging again. I was certainly getting my nonchalant shrug practice tonight.

Danny and Elly returned. Marla started pestering me with questions, trying to get my attention again. When she discovered Cordelia was a doctor, she went in search of her attention. I was a one-night stand, but a doctor was a handy thing to have around.

At some point, I caught Danny giving me a dirty look, as if to say, keep your hands off Cordelia. I ignored her.

Cordelia signaled the waitress for another beer.

"Do you want anything?" she asked me.

Yes, you. "Scotch, on the rocks," I said.

When the waitress returned, I started to reach into my pocket for money, but Cordelia stayed my hand and stopped me. She paid for our drinks.

She could have put my hand into a socket for the jolt her touch sent through me. That one brief contact completely disconcerted me, and nothing else caught my attention until Marla loudly declared she was leaving, dropping very broad hints that I should follow. Did I need a ride home, etc.

I stayed firmly in my seat. The woman who had been between us got up and left also.

The conversation wandered. Danny and the remaining lawyers discussed an obtuse legal point while Elly and Cordelia talked about work.

Cordelia shifted and I felt her knee press against mine. I was sure she would immediately move away. But she didn't.

I didn't know what to do. I mean, I knew what to do, but not what I wanted to do. Some part of me said, pull away, just pull away, you'll only get hurt. But another part of me desperately wanted her touch.

I didn't move my knee.

Elly turned to talk to Danny.

"Well?" Cordelia asked me.

I nodded yes. It was that simple. For a brief second I wondered why I had given in so quickly. Didn't I have any pride left? But I couldn't answer that question, so I left it.

Cordelia reached down and ran her hand along my thigh and then just as casually used the same hand to pick up her beer bottle. As if nothing had happened.

The last two remaining lawyers got up to leave.

"We need to get going, too," Elly told Danny.

"Let me finish my beer," Danny bargained.

I nodded a brief farewell to the two women. While Danny and Elly were distracted with their parting, I put my hand on Cordelia's thigh. If we're going to play this game, then goddamn it, let's play it.

She gave me a sidelong glance, then looked away. Still as if nothing were happening. I kept my hand on her thigh, running my finger against the seam of her jeans, then gradually drifting higher, until my hand was almost at the V of her legs.

"I have to go to the bathroom," I heard Elly tell Danny.

"You just went," Danny said.

"But I didn't change my tampon," Elly explained.

Danny stood up to let her out, shaking her head. I watched it all in a fog of alcohol and . . . I guess lust is the only word for it.

Danny started to sit down, but looked at us. And saw clearly where my hand was. Her face hardened, she started to say something, but stopped and sat down, pointedly not looking at us.

She suddenly turned to Cordelia. "Don't you have any better sense?" Danny demanded of her, ignoring me. As if I weren't there.

"What are you talking about?" Cordelia returned.

"Perhaps it's escaped your attention," Danny said sarcastically, "but a strange woman has her hand on your thigh."

I defiantly kept my hand where it was.

"That's not a strange woman. That's Micky. And I'm aware of her hand," Cordelia replied.

Evidently I was not part of this conversation.

"Good. At least some part of your brain is working," Danny retorted.

"What's that supposed to mean?"

"Cordelia, why don't you sleep with someone who hasn't slept with every other woman in the bar?"

"Why don't you mind your own business, Danny?" I broke in angrily.

"This is my business. When I see one of my friends screwing over another one, I am going to say something," she flashed at me. "In this day and age," she continued, now to Cordelia, "you need to be a little more careful about who you allow to pick you up."

"I am careful," Cordelia interrupted her. "You're talking about one of your closest friends," she added warningly.

"And ex-lover. If you can call it that. I know what you'll get from her. She'll fuck you a couple of times. That's it," Danny replied coldly. "That's not what you want, Cordelia. You're not a person for one-night stands."

"Look, Danny," Cordelia said heatedly. "Don't tell me what I want or don't want. Maybe," she hesitated for a second, "maybe I'd just like to get my brains fucked out every once in a while."

"Bullshit!" Danny exploded. "You're making the same goddamned mistake I did. You think Micky will change for you. She won't. All she'll do is fuck you. Every way she can. Three women in one night. When we were supposedly lovers. What a joke," Danny said bitterly. "You had to tell me, didn't you?" she said to me.

"You asked," I retorted.

"I asked where you had been. How the hell could you do it with that many women?"

I knew she didn't expect an answer, but I gave her one anyway. "I faked it."

"You faked it?" Danny asked incredulously, then disgustedly, "You faked it? What kind of slut does that?"

"The kind you found attractive, evidently," I retorted icily.

"Not with me," Danny shot back. "I would have known."

"You were as easy to fool as anyone else," I told her. It was a brutal thing to say.

She flinched, then sat up very straight.

"You goddamned filthy slut! You cheap whore," Danny spat at me, furious, her face ashen and hard.

"Danny . . ." Cordelia said, "don't."

Danny got up to leave.

"Don't call me a whore," I said.

"I wouldn't if you weren't," Danny replied.

Elly returned. Danny immediately grabbed her arm and stalked away from us.

"Don't . . ." But Danny was too far away to hear me. ". . . call me a . . ."

I stared at the amber liquid in my glass, unable to look at Cordelia. She put her hand on my shoulder, but I shrugged it off, then finished my Scotch.

"Let's go," Cordelia said.

I started to take some money out of my wallet, but she threw several twenties on the table.

"Don't," she said. "It's covered."

"Don't buy me."

"I'm not. I just paid for Danny and Elly; I might as well get you, too. Let's go."

I stood up and pushed my chair away. She followed, taking my elbow as I stumbled. I wasn't drunk, I hadn't had enough to get drunk.

Cordelia steered me out of the bar.

Oh, yeah, I'm going home with her, I suddenly thought, as she led me to her car. I automatically got in. But something wasn't right. If you go home with a woman, you win the game. Why did I feel like I'd lost?

"Are you okay?" Cordelia asked me, as she put the keys in the ignition.

"Me? I'm fine."

"Sure?"

I nodded yes, drumming my fingers on my thigh.

"Danny went too far," she said.

I looked at her, then quickly glanced away. What the hell was she talking about? I was the one who had gone too far. Danny was . . . being Danny.

"Let's go," I said, suddenly not wanting to think anymore.

She started the car.

"Micky, maybe we should talk," Cordelia said, reaching over and taking my drumming hand.

"Let's not. I'm not . . . in a talkative mood."

"Are you sure? It might be . . ."

"Yes!" I snapped. Maybe I was drunk. I wasn't doing anything right.

"Okay," she answered tersely, withdrawing her hand.

I grabbed it and placed it between my legs.

Cordelia looked at me, but didn't say anything. For a moment, she didn't move, then I felt her hand pressing into me.

I didn't speak, didn't even look at her, just felt the physical presence of her hand.

She withdrew it to pull out into the street, then put it back between my legs.

"What do you want from me?" I suddenly burst out, unable to get the scene in the bar out of my head. After that, what could she want of me?

Cordelia gave me an odd look.

"I want to . . . sleep with you ," she said. "What do you think I want?"

'If you weren't, I wouldn't,' Danny's words echoed.

"Cordelia," I said, taking her hand away. "Tell Danny it's not true. Tell her . . . I never faked it with her. I never even thought of it."

"I will, if you want. But, Micky . . . what's going on here?" She stopped for a stop sign. "Do you . . . ?"

"I'm sorry," I interrupted. "I can't . . . not right now. I shouldn't have led you on."

"It's okay. I'll live," she said. "Why don't we go somewhere and talk?"

But that was the last thing I wanted to do. It would be so much easier to have sex with her. And I couldn't even do that.

I looked at her and said very carefully, "I can't not have been a whore, but I can stop being one."

Then I got out of the car.

"Micky! Wait," she called after me. "Micky!"

I kept walking. There were other cars behind her. One started honking.

I glanced back and watched her turn right. She would circle the block. I turned and headed rapidly back toward the corner, turning left when I got there, then walking down a block before making another left onto a one way street.

I entered the first bar I came to, a neighborhood dive from the looks of it. After ordering a Scotch, I sat down at a small table in a dim corner.

I hoped Cordelia didn't spent too much time looking for me. Or worrying. That hadn't been my intention. I just had to get away from her. Like I'd had to get away from Danny when she held me too closely.

I threw down my Scotch and got another one.

I had a few more drinks, giving Cordelia time to search the neighborhood, then left. The sultry air of the streets hit me. I had to stop and think for a few moments before I could remember where my car was. Sweat was running down my back when I finally got to it. My stomach was slightly uneasy. Probably the heat.

I got in my car and drove home. The light on my answering machine was on. I ran the tape back.

"I don't know what you said," it was Elly, her voice harsh, "but you either apologize and take it back or stay away, just stay away. I will not tolerate you hurting Danny any . . ."

I picked up the answering machine and threw it as hard as I could. The power cord jerked it up short and it crashed to the floor, pulling my phone with it. Then I kicked it, sending it spinning across the floor and into a wall. I had trashed my answering machine.

Why was I so angry? I wondered as I stooped to pick up the pieces.

If there had been any message other than Elly's, there was no way of telling. I dropped the pieces back on the floor. I'd clean it up later.

I went to my kitchen, for a minute prowling distractedly through cabinets. Then I went for the cabinet that had in it the bottle of bourbon Joanne had left.

I took the bourbon, a shot glass and sat at my desk. I threw back a shot in one swift gulp. Oh, yes, the liquor felt good as it burned down my throat.

After a few more shots, nothing seemed so tragic. Danny would survive. If she didn't, well, fuck her. Cordelia was a good-looking doctor; she shouldn't have any trouble getting women to sleep with her. Besides, she'd probably prefer someone . . . someone who wasn't trash that anyone could have. Elly could listen to Danny's stories of how I'd fucked her over and nod her head sympathetically and feel she'd done the right thing by yelling at me. Protecting her woman.

Joanne had Alex. I wondered if she'd meant any of the things she'd said. Maybe just taking kindness lessons from Cordelia. So I'd forgotten I'd slept with Alex. There probably wasn't much to remember.

I downed another shot.

"Cheers, girls. I had a great time. All those women. Forgotten and not. I had a fucking great time."

I laid my head on my desk. Just let me close my eyes for a bit, I thought. Close my eyes and don't think. Just me and my bottle of bourbon. Nothing else counted.

Chapter 21

I jerked awake. Early dawn light was filtering through my windows and the frosted glass on my door. I was still sitting at my desk. I had passed out. My left arm was numb. My head had been resting on it. The rest of me wished I were numb. My head was pounding and my stomach was decidedly undecided.

I looked at the bottle of bourbon. There wasn't much left.

I slowly sat up, trying not to jar my head too much. Get to bed and sleep it off. I tried to stand up, but sat down again when I realized that I was still very drunk. The bottle was almost empty.

I sat still for several minutes, breathing gently, hoping to calm my queasy stomach. I wanted to either go to sleep or throw up, but the two canceled each other out. I sat, hoping for the balance to tip one way or the other without any undue effort on my part. I glanced at my watch. A little before six in the morning.

Then I heard footsteps on the stairs. Odd, but I assumed that they were going elsewhere, until they passed the second floor and I could hear them coming up the third flight. The outline of a person appeared through the glass in my door.

What the hell? I wondered, as I shakily stood up.

The figure bent down for a second, then stood up and turned away. I heard footsteps again on the stairs.

I stumbled to my door and yanked it open, in time to catch a glimpse of whoever it was. A young man, maybe early twenties, still with the rounded cheeks of youth, perfect skin, straight brown hair. He was oddly familiar, but perhaps because he looked like the image of a perfect young man, a choirboy.

Except for what he'd left at my doorstep.

I looked at it stupidly for a few seconds, the stubby sticks of dynamite with a crude timer attached. Any second I expected the explosion, my body to be flung apart.

No! Think! I commanded. Trying to balance haste with care, I picked up the bomb. I had to get it out of the building. Nothing else would save me. Or the people living on the other floors.

I descended half a flight, then kicked out the window, thankful that I'd been too drunk to bother taking off my shoes or change my jeans to shorts. I started to pick out the glass shards still clinging to the bottom of the window.

No time, Micky. Carefully holding the bomb in one hand, I stuck my feet through the window, wiggling out on my stomach, avoiding the glass as best I could. Holding onto the sill with my free hand, I gingerly dropped onto the roof of the next building.

Then I ran, holding the dynamite at arm's length, as if the extra distance might be some protection.

I raced to the far end of the roof, then hurled the bomb, aiming for the center of an adjacent empty lot.

I watched it arc through the pale dawn, curving toward the earth. Its graceful flight ended with a jarring blast, the bright light of the explosion immediately obscured by the dusty swirl of debris. It had exploded before it hit the ground, I was sure of that.

I fell back, landing heavily on the sticky tar. It might have been the blast of the bomb that threw me back or perhaps the shock of the explosion and how little time the bomb had been out of my hands before it blew up. A second? Less? Or maybe I fell because I was drunk.

For the minute or so it had taken me to pick up the dynamite and hurl it into the morning, I had been sober. But that was gone now, drunkenness held at bay only by extreme necessity.

I slowly sat up and peered over the edge of the roof. Whoever would build on that lot had their foundation already dug.

I hauled myself to my feet and walked back across the roof. Off somewhere in the distance I could hear a siren. Even if that one wasn't headed here, others would soon arrive. Already I could hear voices in the street.

Why? Why kill me? Try to, I amended. O'Connor was wrong. Frankenstein was real and he had an accomplice.

Get back inside and get to a phone, I told myself. The broken window was a foot or two above my head.

I took a running start to be able to grab the sill.

And slammed into the wall, totally misjudging the distance. The thud I heard was my landing back on the sticky roof. I looked up at the window, disoriented and defeated by the wall.

What the fuck are you going to do? Lie here until you sober up?

I got up, but didn't try another running start. On the fourth attempt I got a decent enough handhold to haul myself up and through.

I flopped awkwardly onto the landing, hands first, some of the pieces of glass nicking at my bare arms. After brushing off the glass as best I could, I stumbled up the stairs. My momentary sobriety had deserted me with a vengeance.

It took me several minutes to find my phone, still on the floor where it had landed last night, the receiver off the hook. I had to crawl to locate it.

I tried to remember phone numbers. Only one surfaced.

"Goddamn it!" I suddenly yelled, angry at my clumsy impotence. "Damn it." Then it sunk in that someone had tried to murder me, and had come close to succeeding. Less than a second.

I punched in the one number I could remember.

"Hello?" she answered, obviously awake.

"Thanks for firing me," I yelled. "Next time tell the men trying to kill me. If you're really interested in my safety."

"Micky. Where are . . . ?"

I slammed the receiver down. My hands were shaking, from anger or drunkenness, I wasn't sure. Blood was running down one of my arms.

Think, I demanded my fogged brain, suddenly aware of my open door and how helpless I was sitting here on the floor. What if he came back?

I dialed a number that I hoped was Joanne's.

"Yeah? Hello?" Alex's sleepy voice answered.

"Joanne? I need to talk to Joanne," I told her.

"Who is this?" Alex asked, then tentatively, "Micky?"

"Yeah."

"Joanne," Alex said off somewhere. "Micky." I heard the phone being handed over.

"Micky? What is it?"

I almost started crying at the sound of her voice.

"Micky? Are you okay?" Joanne asked at my silence.

"Yeah . . . uh . . . yeah. So far. Someone . . . someone tried to blow me up."

"What?" Joanne exclaimed. "You mean a bomb?"

"Yeah. A bomb."

"Where are you?"

"My place."

"I'll be right over."

"Thanks. Joanne?"

"Yes?"

"I'm . . . drunk."

She hesitated for a second, then said. "It's okay. I'll be right there."

I sat on the floor, holding the receiver until it started bleating at me before I hung it up. I stared at the cuts on my arms, a few smears on my right arm, a steady trickle pooling at my left elbow.

Get up and close the door, at least, I told myself, but I didn't move. The door would be no protection against a bomb anyway. I thought about trying to find my gun, but did have the sense to realize I was in no condition to use it.

I vaguely wondered if I should search for O'Connor's number and call him. But it was bad enough for Joanne to see me like this.

The fewer witnesses the better. I regretted having lost my temper and calling Cordelia.

Blood was starting to drip off my arm onto the floor. I looked for something to blot it with, but all that was within reach was the telephone and my broken answering machine. A cat was peeking dubiously out from under the couch, unwilling to come closer.

"Fetch a towel, Hep," I told her. She didn't, needless to say.

Don't let Joanne find you sitting here on the floor like this. At least make it to your desk. I put the phone on the floor and slowly got up. There, that wasn't so bad.

Someone was coming up the stairs. I hoped it was Joanne.

It wasn't.

Well, that will teach me to lose my temper, I thought, as Cordelia entered.

"Micky, what . . . oh, Jesus," she said, seeing my bloody arms.

"I'm okay. Sorry, I lost my temper," I mumbled, trying not to slur my words too badly.

"You don't look okay. Do you have a first aid kit anywhere?"

"Uh . . . yeah," I tried to think where, "maybe my car?"

She went into the bathroom and came back with a hand towel. She used it to wipe away the blood on my left arm.

"A few stitches," she said, looking at the cut. "Keep this pressed tightly against it. I'm going to my car to get some things. Sit down. It'll be easier."

Yeah, it would, but my befuddled brain wasn't operating at her speed. She was heading out of the room and I still hadn't moved.

"Are you okay?" she asked, turning back.

"Me? Oh . . . yeah," I answered, still not moving. I stumbled toward the couch, but dropped the towel.

Cordelia came back and picked up the towel, then, with an arm around my shoulder, guided me to the couch.

"Sit," she ordered, firmly maneuvering me down. She wrapped the towel tightly around my arm, placing my other hand on it. "Hold it there."

"I'm okay," I retorted, angry at her patronizing me, angrier at myself for needing to be taken care of.

"No, you're not," she said matter-of-factly, as she again headed out the door.

I concentrated on holding the towel in place and cursing my stupidity. I had to reek of bourbon. I suddenly saw myself as I had to appear to others — a disgusting drunk. No wonder Danny didn't want me around her friends. Whatever respect Cordelia may have had for me was surely gone now.

She reentered, carrying a black satchel and sat beside me on the couch.

"Why don't you tell me what happened?" she asked, as she started cleaning my cut.

"I got drunk. Isn't it obvious?" I retorted.

"Who tried to kill you? The same man?" she questioned, pretending to ignore my drunkenness.

"No. But this has to be linked. Nothing else makes sense. Somewhere, I've seen him somewhere before." But I couldn't remember, couldn't even concentrate to begin to remember.

"Did he break the window?"

"No, I did."

"Why did you . . . ?"

But she was interrupted by Joanne's arrival.

I probably couldn't have told the story coherently, but Joanne led me through it question by question, her last one being, "How much have you had to drink?"

I sat, trying to remember. Joanne picked up the bourbon bottle from my desk and examined it.

"That," I said, meaning the bourbon, "and . . . some Scotch . . . beer."

"Why?" she asked.

"I don't know. I . . . just went to a bar and started drinking."

"It's probably my fault, Joanne," Cordelia said, as she finished taping gauze over my cut.

"No, it's not. I was drinking before you arrived," I countered.

Joanne paced across the room, then back, abruptly stopping in front of me.

"You just started drinking?" Then to Cordelia, "Why is it probably your fault?"

"It's not!" I burst out. "I'm a drunken fuck-up, okay? That's why I got drunk." I didn't want to go into what had happened last night and have what I'd said to Danny repeated. I could neither explain nor defend it.

"Bullshit," Joanne said. "Tell me why."

"Excuse me," I said, standing up. I staggered to the bathroom, knelt in front of the toilet and started violently retching. I tried to kick the door shut, but couldn't reach it.

Someone followed me into the bathroom. I was too busy throwing up to see who. A damp washcloth was put on the back of my neck. I fumbled for the handle to flush away my vomit.

"Here, rinse your mouth," Cordelia said.

I waved away the glass as my stomach heaved again. When I finally stopped, I closed my eyes and laid my forehead against the cool porcelain. I tried not to think of how repulsive a picture I was. Puking drunk.

I knew Cordelia wouldn't leave me alone in here, much as I disliked her seeing me like this. I flushed the toilet again, then took the cup from her and rinsed out my mouth.

"I'm okay . . . now," I rasped out, my throat ragged and sore.

Cordelia knelt beside me. I felt her brush the damp hair off my forehead, but I couldn't look at her.

"I just need . . . to sit here for a few minutes," I said, again resting my head on the porcelain.

"Okay," Cordelia answered. She gently massaged my shoulders for a minute, then got up and left.

In the silence I heard Joanne talking, evidently on the phone, arranging whatever needed to be done after a bomb blast. Probably calling O'Connor. Then she got off the phone and I heard her asking Cordelia what had happened last night. Cordelia's answer was low and indistinct, punctuated by Joanne's, "Then what?" and again Cordelia's low voice.

I wondered how long I could remain in the bathroom. A year or two minimum seemed best.

"And you let her?" Joanne's voice carried.

"What was I supposed to do?" Cordelia answered.

"Not have been polite. For once," Joanne retorted.

I couldn't catch Cordelia's reply. I didn't want to listen to them anymore. I took the washcloth off my neck and used it to wipe my face. Then I rinsed out my mouth, finally splashing cold water on my face. I flushed the toilet again to rid it of any remaining bile.

Joanne came in and knelt beside me, putting her arm across my shoulder.

"Can you sit up?" she asked.

"Yeah," I replied. "But I don't know if I want to."

"Come on," she said, helping my until I was sitting on the edge of the toilet. "Here, brush your teeth. It will help." She put toothpaste on my toothbrush.

I got up and leaned against the wall next to the sink, then took the toothbrush from Joanne.

"You going to be okay?" she asked when I finished.

"Me? Yeah . . . I've been drunk before."

Joanne took my face between her hands, forcing me to look at her.

"We all make mistakes. What you're trying to do is difficult. And you're making it twice as hard by doing it alone. If you'd let us, we'd help you."

"Help me?"

"Why haven't you told anyone you've quite drinking?"

"Well . . . it's not that big a deal," I stumbled. "And I'm not doing a very good job."

"Micky," Joanne said, "It is important and you are doing an amazing job. Considering."

"Huh?"

"What the hell do you think friends are for? Call me. Call Alex. Or Cordelia or Danny or Elly. I'm perfectly willing to talk to you or sit on you. Whatever it takes."

"Thanks," I said. I knew she meant it. "But I don't think Danny or Elly are going to talk to me anytime soon. And as for . . . I've really made a capital A ass of myself in the last twenty-four hours."

"So?"

"You didn't see me last night. I was . . . in rare form. Danny's pissed . . ."

"Danny's probably overjoyed that you finally said something tacky enough to give her an excuse to yell at you."

"Huh?" My comprehension was not at it's best.

"Danny's been pissed at you for the last eight years. Since you moved out on her. And right now, Danny's the least of your problems."

Right. Someone was trying to murder me. "Maybe I should get some coffee," I said.

"You should sleep it off. But not here. You've been attacked twice here. Unfortunately, our favorite detective is on his way. That bomb needs to be investigated."

"Yeah, you're right," I nodded my head sparingly, not wanting to wake any latent headaches. "Joanne? Thanks."

"For what?"

"For coming over. Even though I was drunk."

"Of course," she said, then put her arms around me and hugged me tightly.

At least one of my friends was still my friend. Until she found out what I had said to Danny. She kept an arm around my waist, steadying me as we went back into the living room, sitting me down gently on the couch.

"How's your head?" Cordelia asked.

"Still there. Unfortunately."

She sat down next to me.

"You had a lot to drink," she commented.

"No. Not for me," I answered.

"After four months of being sober, you had a lot," she responded. Heavy footsteps and a familiar grunt came from the stairs.

"Dr. James. Sergeant Ranson," O'Connor said, entering. "How nice of you to be here to greet me. Glad that you thought to call me, Sergeant." He glared at me.

"I couldn't find your phone number," I said. Only because I didn't look.

"With the number of attempts on your life, it might be worth your while to memorize it," he said sarcastically.

"I'll work on it."

Then, with considerable help from Joanne and Cordelia, I told him what had happened. I really just wanted to go to sleep, which made repeating my story even more difficult. I could hear sirens and voices off in the street, exploring the newly mined crater, no doubt.

O'Connor was not thrilled with my lassitude. "Wake up, Miss Knight, it's only your life we're trying to save. Why don't we go to the station and let your two guardian angels wing their way to work?" He was clearly not happy with Joanne serving as my interpreter.

"No," Cordelia answered.

"Why not, Dr. James?" O'Connor demanded.

"She's in no condition to be answering questions."

"So it appears. What are you on?" he asked me sharply.

"I'm . . ."

". . . sedated," Cordelia answered. "I gave her a sedative."

"Right," O'Connor said sarcastically. "Did she?" he demanded of Joanne.

"I believe so," Joanne answered. "I arrived after Dr. James did."

"All right, Miss Knight. When you become 'unsedated,' come by the station. Answer a few questions. Glance at a few mug shots."

"No mug shot," I muttered, "like Frankenstein. Religious nut. I saw him at Betty's." I suddenly remembered the young man who had been talking to the old woman. It was him, those innocuous looking apple cheeks.

"At Betty's, huh?" O'Connor prodded.

"Yeah, I think," I mumbled, beginning to doubt my perception without sobriety's sureness to guide me.

O'Connor grunted, "I'll expect you soon," and exited.

No one said anything until we heard the bottom door slam.

"I'll take you back to my place," Joanne offered. "You can't stay here."

"No, I'll take her," Cordelia said. "To the clinic. I'd feel better with people checking up on you through the day."

"I'm okay," I protested.

"Stop saying that," she told me. "You will be okay, but right at the moment you're cut and bruised and suffering from alcohol poisoning."

"Cordelia's right, Mick," Joanne backed her up. "Let's go."

Cordelia got her medical kit. Joanne found my keys.

"Feed the cat," I remembered.

Joanne went into the kitchen to get some cat food. Hepplewhite, at the sound of the can opener, joined her.

"Navigational aid," Cordelia said, then pulled me upright, placing my arm around her shoulder and supporting me with an arm around my waist.

"Thanks," I replied, thinking that Cordelia deserved the kindness medal of honor. I don't think I would want to be stuck with me all day. Not after the way I had acted last night.

We started down the stairs, letting Joanne lock up and wave goodbye to Hepplewhite.

"I guess I'll have to hire you back," Cordelia said as we got half-way down.

"Sure you want to?"

"Whatever keeps you safe," she responded.

Joanne caught up to us, stuffing my keys and wallet into my pocket.

"Look, I really appreciate . . ." I started.

"Don't worry about it," Joanne cut me off. "You bring excitement into our otherwise drab existence."

"Careful, Joanne," Cordelia said. "You're starting to sound like Alex. And you've only been living together two weeks."

Cordelia's car was double-parked right out front. The advantages of M.D. plates. She and Joanne loaded me into the front seat.

"I'll be by later. Get some rest," Joanne said, then she headed for her car.

I guess I nodded out. I woke up to Cordelia opening my door in the clinic parking lot. Again she put her arm around my waist and assisted me into the clinic. It was still early, a few voices from the Catholic side of the building, but none of the clinic staff were in yet.

"I'm going to park you here for the time being," she said, leading me into one of the examining rooms and letting me flop down on the table. Cordelia turned on the air conditioner, then covered me with a sheet.

"Thanks," I mumbled, my eyes already half shut.

"I've got to go on rounds at the hospital. Bernie or . . . someone usually gets here around eight to open up and turn on the air. You okay until then?"

"I'll sleep. I'll be okay," I made the effort to reassure her. I'd caught the hesitation in her voice. Bernie or Betty.

"I'll be back soon," she said, then turned out the light.

I think I mumbled some response, but I quickly nodded out.

It seemed that Cordelia had returned instantly, but I knew I'd been asleep.

"I'm moving you to the store room," she said, helping me off the examining table. "It should be cool in there by now and you won't be disturbed."

There was a cot in the storage room. I lay down and Cordelia again covered me with the sheet, tucking it under my chin. She didn't immediately stand up, looking at me for a moment. For a brief second I thought she was going to kiss me, but instead she straightened up.

"Here's a blanket, in case you get chilly," she said, putting it at the foot of the cot.

"I'll be okay. But . . . thanks."

"Get some sleep," she said, quietly closing the door as she left.

No, I wouldn't kiss a drunk I'd just watched vomit for half an hour, I thought as I fell asleep again.

I awoke sometime in the middle of the morning. Someone had been in to check up on me, because there was a glass of water on the shelf next to the cot. I was very thirsty, I realized as I drank the entire glass. Too bad they hadn't left aspirin, too, I thought as I lay back down. My head was pounding. I closed my eyes, hoping it would go away.

When I opened them again, someone was standing next to the cot. Elly. She seemed distant, guarded even.

"Hi," I said, to let her know I was awake.

She hesitated before returning my greeting. Then she asked, "Did you get my message?"

"Yeah . . . yes, I did."

She merely nodded, then turned to walk away.

"Elly," I called.

She turned to glance back at me.

"Tell Danny . . ."

"No," Elly cut me off. "You tell Danny."

Then she was gone.

I closed my eyes and drifted in and out of sleep until I heard the door open again.

"Hi, you're awake," Cordelia said, seeing me watching her.

"Yeah, more or less."

"How do you feel?"

"I'm . . . I'll be fine. This is hardly the first hangover I've had."

"You do look a little better."

"I couldn't look much worse. I hope."

She nodded distractedly, took a half-step to leave, hesitated, then finally turned back to me. "What happened? You didn't have to sleep with me. Or even talk to me. But you didn't have to worry me like that."

"I'm sorry. I guess . . . I was pretty drunk. And I . . . needed to be alone."

"You made me feel like something you had to run away from. That's not a pleasant way to spend the night."

"I . . . don't have answers. I'm sorry."

"It hurt me, Micky. I don't guess you meant to. I hope you didn't. But I still have to wonder why. If it was something I did. Something I didn't do."

"No . . . nothing."

"I guess when we're hurt we want reasons. I guess I do. If it wasn't me, what was it?"

"I didn't mean . . . to hurt . . . I don't even know."

She waited for me to continue, but there was nothing else I could say. She finally said, "Well, let me know when you figure it out," then turned to go. "If you do," she added as she shut the door.

"I'm sorry," I said uselessly.

My head was pounding. I closed my eyes again, but didn't fall back asleep. I lay still, unmoving, hoping that my headache would ease up.

The door opened and Bernie tiptoed in.

"It's okay. I'm awake," I told her.

She was bringing me some fresh water. She scurried off to do my bidding when I asked for aspirin, returning with a whole bottle.

"Thanks, Bern," I said, taking three.

"Sure, Micky. How are you feeling?" Bernie asked, pulling up a box to sit on.

"I've felt better, but I don't think I'd rather be in Biloxi."

"You got the flu?" she asked innocently.

"The flu?" I cocked an eyebrow.

"Millie said you were under the weather."

"More like three sheets to the wind." I decided to be honest, maybe un-crush her. "This is a hangover. I got very drunk last night." I gave Bernie the expurgated version.

"Wow," was Bernie's comment when I finished. She was quite impressed with my getting rid of the bomb and not at all bothered by my having been skunk drunk. Her crush continued. "I'm glad you're okay."

"So am I. Don't you need to get back to work?" Cordelia (and Elly now), might not like my hanging out with baby dykes in a dim storage room. Not to mention the handy cot. Though I suspected I had enough of a headache to keep all of New Orleans celibate.

"It's lunch time. Besides it's weird in there."

"Weird? How?"

"Well, you know we got two bomb threats last week."

"No, I didn't. What happened?" I took bombs seriously these days.

"Nothing. Just a phone call each time, but nothing happened. And then . . . well . . ."

"Yes?"

"Elly's pissed at you."

I nodded. I knew that.

". . . and she and Cordelia are barely talking," Bernie continued. "I heard them in Cordelia's office." She glanced down at the floor, blushing slightly at admitting to eavesdropping. "Elly said, 'She had no right to say it. It's ugly,' and Cordelia answered, 'Danny shouldn't have called her a whore.' And Elly said, 'Danny's got a right, don't you think?' And Cordelia said, 'No, I don't think so.' And I could tell she was mad. Cordelia doesn't get mad much. That was it. Elly walked out. Do you know who Danny is?" Bernie asked.

"Elly's boyfriend?"

My splitting headache stopped me from laughing.

"No, just a friend," I prevaricated, then changed the subject. "What about lunch? Aren't you eating?"

"I came in to see if you wanted something. I could run to the store."

"If you're going for yourself." All I wanted was something to drink. A cola to settle my stomach. I added some yogurt so it would look like I was eating something.

Bernie said she was going to the store for herself, although I was dubious.

She returned almost immediately, much too quickly to have gone out.

"Sorry, Micky, we have to leave." Her expression was somber.

"Leave?"

"Another bomb threat. A letter. Just like those other letters. And since you were really bombed . . ."

No wonder Bernie was nervous.

"Picnic time," I said, as I gingerly sat up and swung my legs off

322

the cot. Yeah, I really wanted to go sit out in the hot sun and wait for this building to blow up. Of course, I thought, as I stood up, that was probably better than sitting inside waiting for the building to blow up.

Bernie stood beside me, wanting to help, but too diffident to put her arm around my waist.

Oh, well, let the kid get her very cheap thrill of the day, I thought, draping my arm around her shoulder and letting her steady me.

"You look like death warmed over," Sister Ann observed as she joined us in the hallway and took my other arm around her shoulders. Between a nun and a nineteen year old. I hoped the bomb wouldn't go off just yet. This would be a hell of a way to die.

"The flu," Bernie lied for me.

"The Jack Daniel's strain," I corrected ruefully.

"Ah, yes, I've heard of it," Sister Ann commented.

It was bright and sunny outside. And hot. We aimed for the shade of an oak tree across the avenue. Once I was comfortably ensconced between roots, Bernie took off to fill our lunch order. Millie was talking to some of the displaced patients. I couldn't see Elly anywhere. Cordelia was down the block, using a pay phone. Sister Ann settled herself beside me.

"Do you do this often?" she asked.

"What? Wait out bomb threats?"

"No. Drink to excess?"

"Well . . . I'm trying not to."

She was quiet, waiting for me to continue.

"I . . . I know I have a problem," I finally admitted. "I've really tried to cut down in the last few months, but . . . old habits."

"How old are your habits?"

"I didn't start drinking the minute I walked into Aunt Greta's house, but . . ." I shrugged.

"But?" she questioned.

"But . . ." I shrugged again.

"Junior high?"

"High school. Sixteen," I admitted. "I . . . uh . . . hung out in bars."

"At sixteen?"

"I was tall for my age."

"How could you afford it?"

"I worked and . . ." I stopped. Was I about to admit that to a nun?

"And?" she probed.

"And I drank very slowly."

She nodded, her expression neutral.

"What was I supposed to do? Hang out at church picnics?" I demanded sarcastically.

"Well, don't you think," she said calmly, "that a church picnic might have been better than trading sexual favors for a few drinks?"

I stared at her, completely nonplused.

"I may be a nun, but I do keep my eyes open," Sister Ann added.

"A lot of drinks. I did it for a lot of drinks," I retorted, deciding on defiance. "And I slept around because I wanted to. And I despise church picnics," I added angrily. "Where's Bernie," I muttered. "I'm starving."

"I have an apple," Sister Ann offered. "But . . . I believe it's on my desk."

"Well, let me run right in and get it," I retorted sarcastically. Then by way of apology, "My head hurts. I think the heat's getting to me."

"Something is, isn't it?" Sister Ann commented.

Sometimes the best defense is to be offensive. "How do you know so much about trading sexual favors?" I asked her.

"In this neighborhood, I pass it on the street," she replied. "I'm a social worker, you know."

"A do-gooder," I snorted.

"It's endemic among nuns."

"I suppose." Then bluntly, "Are you a virgin?"

"What do you think?" was her reply.

"I think people who've never had sex shouldn't make moral judgments about those who do."

"I wasn't making a moral judgment."

"Yes, you were. Catholic picnics are better than lesbian bars. You're just so damned self-righteous you think that's a fact and not a moral judgment."

"Do you think hanging out at a bar at sixteen is better than going to a church picnic?"

"Didn't you tell me you were engaged once? What happened to him? Did you do it?

"Why do you want to know?"

"You have no right to ask me about my sex life, if you won't talk about yours."

"All right," Sister Ann replied. "No, we never did it, as you so delicately put it. I got engaged in high school. I was too young at the time. Of course, I didn't know that then. He was a very persuasive young man and a few years older than me. He joined the army and served in Korea. Once he was gone, no longer influencing me, I thought about what I wanted out of life. And it wasn't being married to him. I found God and my life's calling."

"Any regrets?"

"No, not really. I hurt Randall when I broke our engagement. He had been injured in the war and lost the use of his legs. He was very bitter about it and always believed I had left him because of it. I had hoped he would understand and we could be friends, but . . . he never believed that I could really prefer God to him."

"Ever missed love? Physical contact?"

"Of course. I'm human. But what I've gained, the spiritual life, the peace within myself, has more than compensated for what I've given up."

"So we should all bop off and be nuns?"

"No, of course not. I doubt you, for example, would be happy as a nun. I really believe it is a calling."

"I doubt I would be happy as a nun. At least we agree on something."

"Now, why don't you tell me why you preferred bars to church socials?"

"Aunt Greta would never be caught dead in a lesbian bar," I answered flippantly.

Bernie returned with lunch. Sister Ann didn't pursue her questions.

My stomach was recovering. I wolfed down my yogurt and realized I was still hungry. Bernie graciously offered me half her ham sandwich. That helped somewhat. So did half a candy bar and some of her potato chips.

"I owe you lunch, Bernie," I said. "I think I had most of yours."

Cordelia and Millie joined us.

"I just talked to the police," Cordelia said. "Five places, including ours, received threats. The bomb squad checked out our building and couldn't find anything. Should we go back in?"

We all looked at each other.

"Can you risk it?" Sister Ann asked.

"It's terrorism. The clinic can be closed with a phone call," Millie said.

"I'm willing," I stated, standing up. Everyone looked at me. "They had dogs. I trust dogs," I continued, referring to the bomb squad. Anything was better than sitting out here with Sister Ann asking questions about my sex life. "They want us scared more than they want us dead."

I started across the street.

"No," Cordelia said, grabbing my arm. "I'm going in first. I need to look around for myself."

"What do you know about finding bombs?" I questioned.

"What do you know?" she countered.

"I found one already this morning."

"Bernie," Cordelia said, "you're going home. And you're taking Micky with you."

I started to protest, but she cut me off.

"No. One bomb threat a day per person," she said, with a slight nod of her head toward Bernie.

I grumbled, but Cordelia had won her point. Giving Bernie the task of getting rid of me was a sure way of making her leave.

Cordelia assembled the troops (Elly had reappeared) and led them back into the building.

"Actually, Bern," I said, as she pulled out of the parking lot, "I need to go talk to my all time favorite detective." Bernie dropped me off at O'Connor's precinct station.

"Miss Knight. How nice of you to remember me. So glad you could come," he greeted me.

"Doing my duty," I answered.

"What were you on this morning? Just so I can have some idea how to take your story. I didn't bother with a search warrant because I'm sure the intrepid Sergeant Ranson flushed it down the toilet."

I glared at him for a minute before I answered. "I was drunk."

"Drunk?"

"Skunk-fucking drunk."

"You expect me to believe that?"

"No. When have you ever believed the truth?"

"Why don't you tell me your skunk-fucking drunk version of what happened this morning?"

I did. O'Connor wouldn't let up with questions. Every time I couldn't remember or wasn't sure, he'd say, "Too drunk, huh?"

"What the hell do you want?" I finally exploded.

"Just the facts, ma'am, just the facts," he answered. He'd probably waited his whole life to use that line.

"Fact yourself," I retorted, getting up to leave.

"So, I hear you like girls," he commented casually.

So that was it.

"You heard wrong," I answered.

"I got good sources."

"You might like girls, but I only sleep with adults," I countered.

"Are they?"

I glared at him.

"Dr. James and Sergeant Ranson?" he finished his question.

"You cheap bastard," I retorted, leaning across his desk. "You like your victories petty, don't you? You're so sure Cordelia is your murderer that it pisses you she got off. But if she's queer . . . Ranson's got you beat to hell and back as a cop, but label her a dyke and it'll make you feel better."

"Just curious," he commented blandly.

"How do you and your wife fuck? Always missionary position? Ever gone down on her? Does she give good head?"

O'Connor sat up angrily.

"Just curious, Tim, old buddy," I cut off his response, then spun away from him, stalking across the room.

"Miss Knight," he called. "Next time someone tries to kill you, call me."

I turned back to face him.

"What's one less dyke matter?" I retorted bitterly and walked out.

At the first pay phone I came to, I called Joanne.

"Don't worry about it. I'll just find excuses to talk about my ex-husband in the next few days. Where are you?"

I told her.

"I'll pick you up. I have to go to court and get a search warrant. It probably won't be ready for an hour or so. You interested in a late lunch/early dinner?"

I agreed, rationalizing that lunch with Bernie, being my first meal of the day, was actually breakfast. We hit a po-boy place near the courthouse. I settled for a plain roast beef, remembering too well the color of oysters on the upchuck.

"Sorry about O'Connor," I said, as we settled at a table in back.

"Not your fault. You did have enough sense not to say, 'Oh, Joanne, one of the hottest women I've ever slept with.' "

"I couldn't lie," I replied with exaggerated innocence.

Joanne shook her head, "I gather you've recovered from this morning?"

"Physically, at least," I replied. "Sometimes . . . I feel like such an idiot."

"You're not," Joanne told me. "Though, frankly, when I first met you, I did peg you for a fucked-up smartass."

"That's nice to know," I commented.

"You proved me wrong. Particularly in the past several months. And I hate being proven wrong, so the evidence was overwhelming."

I wasn't used to compliments, so I took a bite out of my po-boy. "What is this? Be kind to Micky Knight day?" I said between mouthfuls.

"Still a smartass," Joanne said, shaking her head. But she was smiling.

"Good. Glad to know I've still got a fault left."

"You have a number of faults. But the good outweighs the bad. And I'm glad we're friends," Joanne said seriously.

I thought to make another smart comment, but stopped myself. "So am I, Joanne," I replied. "If . . . if someone like you, whom I respect as much as I do you . . . likes me, well, maybe I'm not so bad after all."

"That's why I'm telling you. Also, it's true."

"Thanks."

"Someone did it for me once. Looked directly at me and told me I was a good person. It made . . . such a difference."

"Thanks," I said again. "It does."

She reached over and touched my hand, then said, "I have to get a warrant. I'm probably going to be working late tonight. Why don't I drop you off at my place? Alex will be home soon."

"You're leaving me alone with Alex?" I kidded.

"Sure, I trust both of you. Besides, Alex knows better than to cheat on a woman who carries a gun."

"Actually, Joanne, there's a very risky and dangerous task I need to take care of."

"Yes?" she questioned, giving me a hard look.

"Apologize to Danny."

"You should both probably apologize to each other."

"Why?"

"She called you a whore."

"After . . ."

"Not according to Cordelia," Joanne interrupted.

"I don't really remember. Besides, you don't know what I said to Danny."

"You implied you faked orgasms with her."

"Oh," was all I could think to reply, then, "Still, it wasn't a pretty thing to say."

"No, it wasn't. I never said you were perfect. But neither is Danny. Maybe the two of you should yell at each other and get it over with."

"At least let Danny yell at me."

"Should I drop you off there?" Joanne asked.

"No, I'll manage on my own. I need to figure out what I'm going to say."

"Okay. Call me if you need rescue. Should I expect you to show up later at my place?"

"Probably. I doubt Danny and Elly are going to invite me to spend the night."

"Good luck," Joanne said.

"Thanks, I'll need it." I waved as she headed up the courthouse stairs.

329

I finally found a bus that would take me within walking distance of Danny's. I still had no idea what I was going to say. And I really wanted to be comfortably chatting with Alex rather than doing what I was doing. I didn't know how Danny might react. I've done some pretty rotten things to her, maybe this was the final one.

Chapter 22

When I got to Danny's and Elly's, I went around back to the kitchen door because I knew that's where they'd probably be this time of evening. Both cars were parked in the driveway. I had been vaguely hoping they were eating out tonight, giving me a reprieve and Danny a little more time to cool down. Danny had a long fuse on her temper, but once she was angry . . . I hesitated for a moment in the driveway, wondering if it might be prudent to give her time to get over it. But I knew that was a rationalization. A week from now my apology might be meaningless, the hurt left too long to be atoned for.

Giving myself no more time to think, I knocked on the door. Beowulf barked at the sound. Elly opened the door, regarding me warily. Danny was at the stove. She didn't even turn around.

Beowulf, at least, was happy to see me, greeting me with a wagging tail and some friendly hand licking.

"I'm here to apologize," I said, taking a step into the kitchen.

Elly moved away from the door, watching me, but saying nothing. Danny had yet to glance in my direction.

"I'm very sorry for what I said last night. I didn't mean it. And it's not true."

Still Danny said nothing.

"Danny? I'm sorry. What can I say?"

"El, do we have any parsley?" Danny asked Elly, completely ignoring me.

"Danny? Can we talk? . . . at least tell me to fuck off," I finished as she remained resolutely silent.

"I think this needs more tarragon," she said to Elly.

"Danny?"

Still no response. Don't ignore me as if I'm not here, I thought angrily. I grabbed her by the shoulders and turned her around to face me. "Danny . . ."

She slapped me. Not hard, but enough to back me away from her. I tensed, ready to fight. Elly stepped forward, preparing to jump between us.

No, I told myself, you're not going to hit Danny. Turn tail out of here before you do that.

"I guess I deserved that," I said, relaxing my fists. "I'm sorry for last night."

"Don't bother," Danny replied coldly. "You think your behavior can always be excused with an apology. I should have done this a long time ago. Please leave."

"No," I said. "Let me . . ."

"What?" Danny snapped, glaring at me, her arms crossed tightly.

I looked at her. Open, honest Danny, my friend because she easily let me know her, her strengths and sorrows displayed in shadowless light. She had offered me such solid ground for friendship, and even love. I had returned smoke and mirrors.

I had to tell the truth, I realized, finally return what Danny had offered those dozen years ago when we first met. And whatever remained of our friendship would be real, because I wouldn't mislead Danny anymore.

"Look, I lied."

"I know," she said. "I knew that."

"Not just . . . last night. Everything. Between us," I stammered out, remembering how necessary I felt the lies, half-truths, I told in our early years together. Necessity had solidified into habit, a wall of lies I hadn't the courage to break. "In college. When we met. I lied . . . I told you my parents died in a car wreck. But they didn't. My mother abandoned . . . me. And I couldn't stop my father's . . . murder."

"I know that, too, remember?" Danny replied. "You're not telling me anything I don't know."

"And all the things I told you I said to my aunt? I lied about those. Maybe I thought them . . . a week later. She went after me with a belt a few times and I learned to shut up. I learned real well. I didn't rebel against her the way I said I had . . . I was afraid." How easy it had been to rewrite my history, to claim I was as I wanted to be, brave and defiant, not cowering at Aunt Greta's reprimands.

Danny stared coolly at me, no change in her expression.

"Remember me telling you how much fun I had in bars? Picking up women? How easy it was for me? I lied about that. I snuck into bars because . . . I couldn't bear to go back to that ugly house on that ugly street. And I went home with women, because, if they bought me a few drinks, I couldn't think of a way to say no. I wasn't very good at picking up women. I usually sat in a corner until someone finally approached me. Being drunk in a strange bed was better than going home sober.

"And I always snuck around so Aunt Greta wouldn't suspect. I had to get home in time to do the dishes before she woke up. If they were done, she thought I was in at night. So every night, sometimes at three or four in the morning, I would come groveling home to do the dishes. I was terrified she would find out and . . . put me away or something."

Danny hadn't moved, still standing in the middle of the kitchen with her arms crossed. Elly was distractedly stroking Beowulf. I wondered what they thought of my . . . confession, there was no other word for it.

"I put shit in Bayard's bed exactly once. I never did it again. Not after . . . after I got punished. All the tricks I told you I pulled on him? I lied about them. Not lied . . . just reversed who did what to whom." More than anything, this was the past that I wished obliterated. I had used Danny, and my lies to her, as a way to escape it, to deny that it—incest—a word I still flinched to use, had happened to me.

"And . . . and . . . " I faltered, afraid to finally let out my most humiliating secrets. I stared at the floor, unable to look at Danny any more. "I told you he got Uncle Claude's gun and demanded I give him a blow job . . . remember I said I refused, daring him to pull the trigger? I lied . . . I . . . did it. I was too chicken-shit to say no. Only once did he play with the gun . . . and it wasn't loaded. I'd said yes . . . too often to bother saying no. I just couldn't . . ."

I was still unable to look at Danny. Or Elly. I turned away, leaning onto the counter.

"So you see, Danno, I lied a lot. When you said you loved me . . . it wasn't me you loved, but the person I'd invented for you. Having sex with you was easy. I wanted . . . you to touch me. But talking to you scared me. I knew you'd start catching my lies.

"And when you caught enough of them . . . when you found out who I really was . . . you'd hate me.

"That's when I started sleeping around on you. Why I came in drunk and fucked up all the time. Why I told you . . . everything I did. That wasn't really me. And it was easier . . . easier for me, if you hated me for something I wasn't rather than something I was.

"I'm sorry, Danny." The past had come to claim me. I was who I was. What had happened had happened. There was nothing else to say. I stood for a moment, took a deep breath, then turned to go.

Danny still didn't say anything, but she put her arms around me. When I started crying, she put a hand on the back of my head and gently brought my head down to rest on her shoulder.

"Oh, shit, Danny, I'm so sorry," I said.

"Shh, honey, it's okay," she replied, stroking my hair.

"For what it's worth, Danno," I said, finally raising my head and wiping my eyes, "you couldn't have scared me so much if I didn't . . . care a lot for you."

"Mick," she said, putting a hand against my cheek, "I didn't believe half those stories you told. And the other half, I had my doubts about."

"Now you tell me," I answered, sniffling.

"Blow your nose," she said, letting go to hand me a tissue.

I noticed that Danny had wet streaks down her cheeks.

"Did I make you cry?"

"No, I've been chopping onions," she responded. "Of course you did, you goof. And," Danny took me firmly by the shoulders, "what sort of shit do you think I am, that I would . . . would want to do anything but blow that fucker's brains out?"

"I am . . . I was . . . so ashamed."

"That's how those bastards work. They dig their hooks in so deeply, twisting you with guilt and shame. Like you had a choice."

"I could've . . . told him to go ahead and shoot me. Like I said I did."

"Bullshit!" Danny exploded. "How old were you? When it started?"

"Uh . . . maybe thirteen. Just growing tits."

"Something you had a lot of choice in. How old was he?"

"Eighteen."

"So a guy five years older than you, in a household where he's God's gift to mankind and you're lower than a dog, demands a blow job, and you could have said no?"

"Well . . ."

"Tell me this, if you'd run to your aunt with his semen dripping down your shirt, what would have happened?"

I shrugged resignedly. "Nothing. He would have come up with some lie that she wanted to believe."

"Uh-huh. And you can bet he knew that. He didn't need the gun. That was just for kicks. Another penis to assault you with."

I almost started to cry again, stopped only by Danny's hand on my shoulder.

"Hell, Mick," Danny continued, "Robbery I can understand. Murder even makes sense at times. But not child abuse. Not sexually abusing a child," she added vehemently.

"I wasn't really a child. Not seven years old with a forty year old."

"I thought you had better sense than that," Danny interrupted. "Don't rank pain. It hurts. It all hurts."

"Yeah. And the worst thing is how you go on hurting other people, people you should love, because you got hurt."

"Naw, the worst thing is being used the way you were used. That's much worse than anything you did to me."

"Don't rank pain," I told her.

"Deliberate cruelty is always worse," Danny replied. "What your cousin did to you was deliberate. And cruel."

"Thank you, Danno," I answered.

Elly poked her head in the kitchen. She had discreetly disappeared into the living room.

"You two friends again?" she inquired.

"I hope so," I replied.

"Definitely," Danny added. "Now . . . oh, hell, have I burned dinner?"

"No," Elly said, "I turned the burners off."

"Good woman," Danny said, as she restarted the chicken.

I got an invitation to dinner. Followed be an invitation to stay the night. Then an invitation to go out to Bayou St. Jack's with them for the weekend.

"My parents like you," Danny explained. "Local girl and all that. If they see you talking to Elly, maybe they'll do likewise."

I agreed to not only go, but invited them to stay at the shipyard.

"Good," Elly accepted. "Danny and I can sleep in the same bed. Finally. I'm tired of the couch in her parents' living room."

Midway through dinner, Danny turned to me and said, "I guess I owe you an apology, too. I said some things I had no right to say."

"It's okay," I shrugged.

"And go ahead and sleep with Cordelia. You're both adults."

"Nice of you to notice," I replied.

"But," Danny continued, "six months, Mick. You can have an affair with Cordelia, but if you drop her in less than six months, I'm coming after you."

"Yes, ma'am," I saluted.

"I don't know . . . I just remember Cordelia right after Kathy died. She seemed . . . colorless," Danny said quietly. "I hadn't known her very long then. It's the people who don't cling to you, don't whine and plead and claim they can't bear it, that I feel for. Because they bear their own burdens so quietly. She withdrew a little piece of herself. Just wrapped it up and put it away."

"She's one of those rare people who doesn't assume that her tragedies are the worst," Elly added.

"Not to mention that her love life hasn't been . . . well, Roman candles all around," Danny said.

"Maybe she needs a cherry bomb like me," I suggested.

"Well phrased," Danny commented dryly. "So maybe I get a tiny bit overprotective of Cordelia," she admitted. "But, I mean it, Mick, six months."

"Danno? What happens if she breaks up with me?"

"It depends on whose fault it is," Danny said ominously, then in a serious tone, "Just be kind to her."

"I will," I promised. "I'll try." I wondered if I would get the chance.

"Do that," Danny admonished.

I nodded, then got up to help Elly with the dishes. After they were done, I dialed Joanne's number to tell her that I had been wrong about not getting an invitation for the night. Alex answered. Joanne wasn't home yet.

I told Alex that Danny and I were back on speaking terms again.

"Good," she answered. "And I was so worried about seating arrangements." Then she called out, "C.J., all's well that ends well. Mick and Danny can be safely invited into the same room."

"Cordelia's there?" I asked.

"Yeah, she's keeping me from biting my nails down to my shoulders waiting for Joanne. I don't think I like the idea that people might shoot at her."

"She'll be okay. Joanne's tough. And smart," I reassured Alex.

"I hope so," Alex replied. "Oh, Cordelia says to tell Danny not to let you get into any trouble."

"Me? Never."

"Stay away from strange men with bombs."

"I stay away from strange men, period," I answered. "Ask Cordelia if I'm still hired."

I heard Alex asking her and her indistinct reply in the background.

"She says," Alex came back on the line, "that you can discuss it on Monday and, in the meantime, Danny is not to let you out of her sight."

"Tell her that that presents problems with going to the bathroom, not to mention sleeping arrangements."

I heard Alex repeating my comment to Cordelia, then some banter between the two of them and Cordelia came on the line.

"Micky, I am serious. You've had two attempts on your life. Betty's dead, and so are four other women. These men play for keeps."

"Aw, maw, if I put on my galoshes and my gun, can't I go out and play?"

"Micky," she remonstrated, "I don't care to spend the whole weekend worrying,"

"Oops," I said, "then I'd better not tell you what I'm doing."

"What?" she demanded. "Don't you dare . . ."

"Trying to convince Danny's parents that Elly isn't an evil influence on their darling daughter," I interrupted. "We're spending the weekend out at Bayou St. Jack's."

"Show up at the clinic Monday morning. We'll discuss it," she replied after letting my frivolity sink in.

"Okay."

"I mean it," she said.

"Okay. Bright and early. You got it."

"Well?" Danny asked, ever the attorney, after I got off the phone.

"We'll discuss it on Monday. I think my life's improving."

"Good."

"And I've got my friends back," I told them, smiling at both Danny and Elly.

"Now all you have to do is worry about the men who are trying to kill you," Elly said.

Right. Them.

Chapter 23

If I was to be at the clinic bright and early Monday morning, I had to stop by my place even brighter and earlier. Clean underwear had become a necessity. I had borrowed some of Danny's. But the best way to become an unwelcome house guest is to use up your host's panties.

Danny insisted on accompanying me, following Cordelia's instructions to the letter. She didn't let me out of her sight, trailing me into my apartment and back out, until we had thoroughly inspected my car, in case a bomb had been planted in it.

I told her not to worry about me, that I was packing a pistol, and we waved good-bye. I drove to the clinic, shrugging my jacket back on before I got out. Pistol-packin' mamas need to be discreet.

"Micky, good to have you back," Millie greeted me as I poked my head into the office.

"Hi, Micky," Bernie chimed in.

"Any more threats, bomb or otherwise?" I asked. I was, after all, working. I hoped.

"Nope, all quiet on that front," Millie answered.

Cordelia came hurrying out of her office.

"I have to go . . . oh, hi, Micky," she said with a quick smile in my direction, then continued, "I have to go to the hospital. An hour or two, I hope. Bernie, see if you can reschedule some of my patients, so we don't get too crunched up. Millie, just carry on," she instructed.

Both Bernie and Millie nodded.

"Micky, stay out of trouble," she said as she passed me on her way out.

"I'll try," I agreed.

"Hard. Very hard," she stipulated without stopping. Then she was gone.

"Well, better tell the naked ones to get dressed," Millie said, as she went back to the examining rooms.

Bernie got busy on the phones.

I took a walk around the building, hoping not to find any more bodies.

A few more working lights had been added to the basement. The police, I wondered, or the building staff? Nothing down here but hot air and dirt.

The second floor was being worked on. A few of the rooms had been freshly painted, some with chairs and tables neatly arranged for the day's activities.

It was too hot to wander around outside, particularly wearing a jacket and leather shoulder holster. I went back downstairs to the clinic office.

"Mick, there was a phone call for you," Bernie told me. She handed me a number.

"What did they want?" I asked, looking at the number. "No name?"

"Didn't leave one. She sounded old. Something about wanting to hire you."

I nodded and headed for Cordelia's office to use her phone.

340

The number was long distance, a 601 area code, which meant my mysterious caller was in Mississippi.

I dialed the number.

"Hello?" a querulous voice answered.

I explained who I was.

"Yes," she answered. "I got your number from Sister Ann. She recommended you highly. I need a private investigator. I'm very sorry, I have to ask you to come out here. I can't explain over the phone, and I can't really get around much. I'm an invalid. It's very important that you come as soon as you can."

I tried to get some idea what she wanted me for, but she insisted, very apologetically, that she had to see me. I finally agreed and got directions to her place. A little north of Picayune, Mississippi, about an hour drive. I tried to put her off until tomorrow, but she was very insistent that she had to see me today?

"What's your name?" I finally asked.

"Oh, all my friends call me Sarry," she said.

"Okay, Sarry, I'll be there in about an hour," I told her. This had lost cat written all over it.

"See you later, Bernie," I said as I breezed past her.

"Where are you going?"

"To visit an invalid old lady," I replied and waved to her.

I glanced into Sister Ann's office, but she wasn't there. A few questions elicited the information that she had been called away by an ill client and probably wouldn't be back for a few hours. I wanted to ask her about Sarry, like how many cats she might have and if there was any way that this could be as important as she tried to make it sound. As I headed out the door it occurred to me that I wasn't really sure Sarry was a woman, the voice was a gravelly midrange. Bernie has called Sarry "her" and I had just let that guide me. Of course, it didn't really matter. Men had cats that they wanted me to find, too.

I got on I-10 and headed out of the city. Lacking an air-conditioned car, I quickly shrugged off the jacket. Then the shoulder holster, putting it under the seat. All I needed was some highly conscientious state trooper pulling me over.

A perfect day for the beach, I thought as I drove in the opposite direction, taking I-59 north, glad at least not to be driving into the glaring sun.

341

Sarry's directions took me off the main road to a well-patched country road, then to a not-so-well-patched county road, then to a not-at-all-patched country road that abruptly turned into gravel.

"And I thought my suspension was inadequate for city potholes," I muttered as I hit a spine-numbing bump.

A scrawny dog started barking, then chased my tires. But the dog worried me less than the stony and unaverted stare of his master, who looked like, if there was such a thing, a generic KKK member. I was glad to leave him and his barking dog in a cloud of yellow dust.

The gravel petered out to dirt. I finally found the turnoff for Sarry's house. Main Street, a hand-lettered sign read. I hoped it was a joke. After about a quarter of a mile, a branch that had landed in the road impeded my progress. I might have been able to squeeze my car around it, but I decided I wanted my car to get out of here alive, so I pulled onto the grass at the edge of the road. I was close, if Sarry's directions were to be believed. I locked my car, unsure of what I was protecting it from. The last house was at least a half a mile away. Deer flies are vicious out here, I rationalized, wiping sweat off my brow.

For a moment, I thought about getting my gun, but my car already seemed a shimmering mirage in the heat. I didn't need a gun to talk to an invalid old lady, anyway. I wanted to hurry up and get this interview over with and get back to the clinic. I had an uneasy feeling about being away, as if something were about to happen. But I couldn't afford to turn down any paying business.

The only signs of human habitation were a few rusty cans and the road itself. I wondered vaguely if I had been sent on a real wild goose chase, then I topped the hill and spotted a ramshackle house about fifty yards further on.

The lawn was littered with car hulks and parked out front was a wheel-less logging truck completely covered with rust. It couldn't have budged from its spot in less than a decade. Weeds poked through the assorted debris, a small pine tree growing through the steering wheel and window of an old Ford.

I wondered what this woman could possibly want to hire me for as I passed the rusty truck, weaving my way down an unmowed, but trampled path to her door.

The boards of the porch, only a foot or so above the ground, sagged and gapped. I tapped on the unpainted screen door, which had newer patches of screen woven into the older sections to keep out flies. Somewhere inside the house I heard the blare of a TV.

At least she had electricity, I thought, finding that vaguely comforting.

I knocked again, louder.

The TV switched off, then a voice called, "Come on in."

I opened the screen door and entered a dim hallway, in need of sweeping even in this light.

"This way," the voice guided me.

The hallway led to a kitchen at the back of the house.

"Are you Sarry?" I asked the figure sitting at the kitchen table.

"Yes, I am," he said.

Sarry was male. Probably late fifties to early sixties. He was in a wheel chair, his legs covered, improbably in this heat, with a knitted afghan. His hair was white, receding a bit, and his face round and pink-cheeked. A harmless old redneck, I decided.

"You're Michele Knight, the detective," he said, a statement, not a question, speaking with less of an accent than I'd expected.

"Yes, I am," I replied. "What do you want me for?"

He laughed, a high-pitched snort, then said, "I want you to die today."

I looked at this pink-faced man in a wheelchair, wondering how he was going to kill me. Then I glanced around, sure Frankenstein was going to emerge from one of the doors in the hallway.

"No one but us here," Sarry said. "My business partners," and he giggled again, "were too clumsy. Never send a boy to do a man's job. Unless the man can't go," he added angrily.

"Who are you?" I asked.

"Nobody. Just an old man."

"Why kill me?"

"Because I want to. I couldn't risk you being around the clinic today. The Bills failed. Bill and Bill, you've met them, I presume. Or at least been aware of their presence. I still don't know how you escaped that bomb."

"Frankenstein and Choirboy are the Bills?"

He chortled at my nicknames, "Oh, yes, much better than just

Bill and Bill. Less confusing. I call the tall one Will, because two Bills was driving me crazy. Sometimes two is nice, but not in names," he rambled on.

"How are you going to kill me?" I asked. I couldn't see a gun or any other weapon.

He took a small box out of his lap. It had a switch on top and two wires attached.

"Boom," he said, laughing again. Then he lifted the edge of the afghan to reveal the stack of dynamite under his wheelchair. "A big boom."

"You'll kill yourself, too."

"I'm nobody. Who cares if nobody dies?" he retorted bitterly.

"You might."

"Not anymore. Not after today," he replied triumphantly.

"What happens today?" I demanded.

"The Bills, bless their dedicated hearts, are hard at work right now. Starting at one o'clock—or is it two? I can't remember—the bombs will go off. The Bills are planting them, the two of them. Those fools."

"What do you mean?"

"The self-righteous are so gullible, don't you agree?"

"Why are you bombing abortion clinics if . . . ?" I started to ask.

"I don't give a damn about right-to-life. I never had a right-to-life," he cut me off. "No, the Bills came in handy. For a bit, like most fools. They knocked on my door one day. Trying to save my soul. I invited them in. I don't get much company out here. And those young men, with their strong legs and slow minds, gave me an idea. I talked to them for a long time that day and they came back. And I told them, that with my help, they could put their ideas into action."

"What ideas?"

"Save innocent lives. The unborn. Oh, the crocodile tears I cried for those unborn," he chortled.

"Why?" I demanded.

"I'll get there. Don't be impatient. You're not going anywhere," he said, his finger hovering over the switch. "I found her."

"Who?" I asked. "Found who?"

"Will is the more resourceful of the two," he continued, ignoring me. "He got the dynamite. He is a true believer. I made the bombs.

I turned into a regular bomb factory. Such a good boy. So helpful, got me everything I asked for."

"Your helpful boy brutally murdered five women."

"I told you he was a true believer," Sarry said callously. "Besides, it's not murder to kill a murderer. He watched and kidnapped them after they left from having their babies killed. He didn't believe those women should have abortions."

"Not all of them did," I retorted. "Betty Peterson didn't. The fifteen year old left in the lot didn't."

"We all make mistakes," Sarry said, giggling at his cleverness.

"Why, you . . ." I started angrily.

"Now, now, Miss Knight," he chided, his finger resting on the switch. "Michele. Let me call you Michele. Since we'll be spending our last few hours together, we might as well be friends."

"So you made the bombs? Where'd you learn to make bombs?"

"The Army. I served in Korea."

"Sister Ann," I said softly.

"Beatrice Jackson," he shot back. "She never would have become a nun . . . she had no right to do that. She couldn't think of any better way to get out of marriage to half a man."

"That's not true . . ."

"Don't you tell me what's true," he roared. "I was there. I saw the pitying look she gave me. Don't you repeat her lies to me."

Obviously Sarry was not going to be reasonable.

After giving him a moment to settle down, I asked, "Why kill her after all these years?"

"Why? Because I finally got the chance. After all these years. She slipped away from me. But I found her. Saw her on TV, at her wonderful community center. I wrote down the address. And I told the Bills that the clinic in the building was the worse abortion parlor of them all. They never doubted me for a minute. Gullible fools." And he laughed, harshly this time. "And Bill—Will has a score to settle with a doctor there."

"Surely they won't plant bombs intending to kill nuns? They're on the same side. More or less," I added, doubting Sister Ann would want to be lumped in the same category as the Bills. "What score does . . . ?"

"I'm to call in warnings to all the places that are to be bombed" he interrupted me.

"But you're going to 'forget' Sister Ann's building," I said angrily.

"Oh, no, I'll remember it. But my phone doesn't work anymore."

"It worked fine . . . you can't . . ." I said, as the monstrosity of his actions sank in. "How many? How many bombs?"

"Eight different places are targeted. Sister Ann's, as befits her position, will go off first."

"And the rest?" I demanded.

"Within three hours. Lots of surprises for the fine folk of New Orleans. I picked names out of the phone book. Places the Bills would be willing to bomb." He laughed again.

"My God," I yelled, "Do you realize how many people you'll kill? Hundreds will die."

"I don't care. I had my legs blown up, and they left me out here to rot. I don't care how many people die," he retorted. "Bea should have married me, should have taken care of me. I need someone to cook for me, clean for me. I can't do things like that. But she left me. Left me and no other woman would have me, damaged as I am." His pink cheeks turned red, nostrils flaring.

"Why kill me?" I asked, trying another tack. "What have I done to you?"

"You interfered. You were watching over Bea, making it hard to get to her."

"I was watching over my friends at the clinic."

"And why not kill you? You're like all the others. You'd be happy to let me rot out here."

"Call it off. I'll get you help. I'll do what I can. There are programs."

"No! I don't want those damned programs. Baby-sitting until death. You're like my brother. He visits once a month. Always brings me something, so he won't feel so guilty when he walks away. And always asks me wouldn't I be happier in a veterans home. I can't take care of myself, he says. That snot-nosed bastard."

"You just said you can't take care of yourself," I reminded him spitefully.

"Not like a woman would. Do you think I'll be better taken care of in a V.A. hospital? No. And after today he can't put me any-where!" He laughed triumphantly at the thought.

This man was crazy, I realized. There could be no reasoning or arguing with him. And I had little doubt about his intent to use the bomb under his wheelchair.

I had to get out of here. And get to a phone before one o'clock. His hand rested next to the switch.

"Turn on the TV," he ordered me.

I went and flipped on the TV. It blared forth with some stupid soap opera.

"Turn it down," he told me. "I'm only interested in the news. And there won't be any until about two or so. That's the news we want to hear."

"I don't," I said shortly.

"Go wash my dishes," he commanded.

"Why? If you're going to blow them up in a few hours?" I countered.

"I've always wanted a woman to obey me. Do it," he threatened, his finger poised over the switch.

I sat down defiantly. I didn't want to get blown up, but I did want to test his limits.

"You'll miss your newscast," I said.

"Do it and maybe I'll let you go after the first few bombs explode."

"And maybe you won't."

His jaw started working angrily. "You're a cunt, just like she is," he spat out. "You all deserve to die."

I slowly got up and started doing his dishes. I had pushed him enough. I glanced surreptitiously around the kitchen, looking for something to . . . I didn't even know. I would have to try something before one o'clock. I couldn't sit here helplessly and let Cordelia, Elly, Millie, Sister Ann, Bernie, and the others be blown to bits. If that happened, I didn't want to be around to know about it.

"Your dishes are done," I said, as I finished them. I hadn't done a very good job, but I doubted he'd notice.

"Good. What else can I make you do?"

I stiffened, wondering what he had in mind.

"Lunch," he said, "Make me lunch."

I wondered if he wasn't interested in sex, or if he'd had it blown off him.

I looked in his refrigerator. There wasn't much to make lunch with.

"You don't have much here," I said. "Why don't I run to the store and get some food?"

"I'm not that hungry," he retorted.

"How about a beer?" I suggested. There were a few in the refrigerator. Maybe I could get him drunk, although what good that would do I wasn't sure.

"No, no beer. Make me coffee. Real coffee Not instant."

"It's too hot for coffee."

"Make it," he ordered.

He had an old drip coffee pot. I hoped I was doing it right. After what seemed a reasonable amount of time, I poured some into a cup and brought it to him.

"You taste it first," he demanded.

I took a sip.

He chuckled and took the cup from me.

"Did you write the letters?" I asked.

"Yes, of course. My brother brought me a little computer. I really just wanted to write Bea, but she would have known. By writing the others first, it made hers seem like just one of many. Misdirection can be very useful," he added bitterly. "Yes, I like misdirection."

"How did you get the information?"

"Bill told me those things. Some young girl worked there and he knew her."

"Betty Peterson?"

"Who? I guess," he answered offhandedly.

"Will murdered her," I said heatedly. "She didn't do anything . . ."

"She's not important," he cut me off, dismissing Betty.

I started to make an angry reply, but stopped myself.

"More," he demanded, pointing to his coffee cup.

I picked up the pot and refilled his mug. His hand never moved away from the switch. I set the coffee pot back on the stove, turning the burner on low to keep it warm.

"Don't you want to ask me how I got the dynamite?" he gloated.

"No," I replied.

"It took awhile. I wanted to start bombing much sooner, but Rome wasn't built in a day, they say," he chuckled at his witticism. "So I had to content myself with letters. Did you like yours?"

"Oh, yeah, a brilliant epistle," I retorted.

"Love letters from an old beau."

"An old bastard," I amended.

"Don't try my patience," he chided me, then continued, "If you'd learn to shut up, you'd make some man a good wife. Coffee, dishes, all the domestic chores. Too bad you'll never get a chance."

"You could let me go."

"No, I think not." Then he looked me over appraisingly. I didn't like the glint that came into his eyes. "Too dark, too tall, but you might do," he finally told me after having thoroughly raked me over with his eyes.

I said nothing. His game was power, humiliation. The best response was none. He wanted my anger and rage.

"Take off your clothes," he ordered me.

"No."

"I'm still a man, you know. I should have had a wife. Instead of looking at girlie magazines. Just take off your clothes. Let me look at you. Fifteen years ago my brother brought a whore out here for my birthday. That was the last time I saw a real woman."

"No."

"You don't have to do anything," he cajoled.

"No."

"You think I'm disgusting, like Bea, don't you," he spat out bitterly. "An ugly cripple."

"I think you're disgusting because you're about to murder hundreds of people. I don't give a damn about your legs."

I turned my back to him, to make my refusal more adamant.

And then I wondered if I had done the right thing. Offer him sex, a hand job. Get his fingers away from that switch. I shuddered at the thought. He didn't look like he'd had a bath recently, an odor of decrepitude hung about him. I glanced at my watch. A little past eleven-thirty. I didn't need to get back to the city, just the nearest phone. Not yet, I told myself. A few minutes before I do that to myself. He and his prick aren't going anywhere.

"More," he commanded.

I glanced back at him. He was pointing to his coffee cup, retreating to something he could order me to do.

I got the coffee pot off the stove.

"Fill 'er up, honey," he told me, as I reluctantly made my way over him. "See, you can be made to do things."

349

Then it happened, the half second I needed.

One hand was curled around the coffee mug, the other, the hand next to the bomb switch, moved, absentmindedly to wipe sweat off his brow.

It was the only opening I would get.

I threw the coffee grounds into his face, letting the coffee spill into his lap. At the same instant, I pushed against the table, not sharply enough to jerk the wires, but enough to make sure he would have to grope to find the switch.

Then I ran. I could hear his furious screaming, as I crashed into the screen door, throwing it open. I hurdled off the porch and over the debris in the yard, trying not to wonder how far the explosion would carry, how far away I had to be.

The truck. Get to the far side of the truck, I thought as I reached the dirt road. I ducked behind it, crouching on the running board next to the cab door. For a second I debated moving on, trying to run to my car.

My decision was made by the roar of the explosion, the torn timbers of the house booming hollowly against the other side of the truck, rocking it. Debris flew over my head, landing in the road and beyond to the woods. Part of a cheap printer bounced off the hood of the truck and into the ditch. I clung to my perch, wondering how long the deadly hail could last.

Then there was an eerie silence, the cacophony from the explosion suddenly ended. No birds, no breeze, just an empty stillness. I didn't move for another minute, to be sure. More lives than just mine were at stake now.

Then I hit the road running, not looking back. I didn't want to see the destroyed remains of the house. And perhaps bits and pieces of a body belonging to an ugly, bitter man.

By the time I got to my car, I was drenched in sweat, the humid air a heavy weight in my lungs. I quickly started it and pulled out, ignoring the bumps and jars from the road.

No one was home at the first two houses I came to.

Get to a phone. There was a little grocery back at the not-too-well patched road. The people out here might shoot me on sight.

I drove, going as fast as I sanely could, until I got to the store. I glanced at my watch. A little past noon. I hoped he hadn't been lying about the timing for the bombs.

I called the clinic first. Bernie answered the phone.

"Clear the building," I said before she had even finished her hello. "There's a bomb set to go off at one o'clock."

"Micky, where are you?" she asked, her voice scared and confused.

"Never mind. I'm on my way. Get everybody out."

"Okay," she agreed and hung up.

Then I dialed O'Connor's number.

I told him that there were bombs set to go off at eight different clinics starting at one p.m.

"Which ones?" he asked.

"Cordelia's. I don't know the rest," I replied.

Then, maddeningly, "Are you sure?"

I gave him the abbreviated version of my morning, finishing, "So, I'm being a good girl. Someone tried to kill me and I'm calling you."

I didn't get a gold star, but I didn't expect one.

I got back in my car and drove, basically on the wrong side of the speed limit, back to the city. I wanted to get to the clinic before one o'clock.

Chapter 24

I arrived a little after twelve-thirty, parking my car a few blocks away. A crowd was gathered across the main street from the clinic, along with several police cars. And the ubiquitous camera crew.

"Hi, Micky," Bernie called out as I approached them.

I had to stifle a sudden urge to run to her and hug her, glad that she was alive and well. I liked Bernie. I wanted her to have the chance that Betty had had taken from her. To grope and fumble for her own answers until she found them.

"Hey, Bern, what's up?" I said, settling for giving her shoulder a squeeze.

"Just waiting," she answered. "And worrying."

I nodded agreement. I spotted O'Connor and headed for him, giving Bernie's shoulder a parting pat.

"Miss Knight, back so soon?" he commented. "You must have driven over the speed limit to get here so quickly."

"Naw," I replied. "It was down hill most of the way. Have you found the bomb yet?" I asked, to forestall him giving me a speeding ticket on the basis of probability.

"No, not yet. Most of the bomb squad is occupied trying to find your supposed eight other targeted places."

"Supposed?" I retorted irately. "I wasn't making it up."

"Probably not," O'Connor agreed annoyingly, "but all you've given me is the ravings of a mad man."

"With two mad men helping him, who've already murdered a number of people."

"Perhaps. Again his words. Too bad we can't question him."

"So what are you going to do?" I demanded. "Wait until a few buildings blow up and then decide I was right."

"We're doing what we can. A lot of cops are searching for those bombs. We've called every clinic and hospital in the city and warned them."

"Warned them? Is that all?" I questioned. "Haven't you evacuated them?"

"Not yet. We're looking for bombs. Also, we're waiting to see what happens here."

"What if I'm wrong? What if some of the other bombs go off first?"

"I just can't call up every place in this city that might do abortions and order them out of their buildings," he argued heatedly.

"Why not? Do you have to be a Detective Sergeant to do that?" I retorted.

He glared at me. "Don't push your luck, Miss Knight," he finally said, then he turned away, shaking his head. "No wonder you have so many people trying to kill you."

"Go f . . ." I started to say, then realized I was two feet away from a nun. ". . . find the bomb," I finished lamely, my Catholic training kicking is. "Hi, Sister," I said politely. It was Sister Fatima.

"Oh, hello," she peered at me, trying to place me, it seemed. "Michele, isn't it?"

"Yes, sister. Pretty hot out here," I replied, scanning the crowd for Cordelia.

"Yes, terribly," she answered. "I think I need to find some shade to sit down," she continued, her voice fading. "I'm not as young as I used to be."

"Here, let me help you," I said, offering her my arm. I led her to the steps of a close building that was shaded by a nearby tree. Then I went inside and got her a glass of water.

"Thank you so much," she said after I handed her the water. "You're a very nice person, very helpful."

Good thing she didn't know my underwear had, "Sappho's Diner. Eat out or Come on in," printed on the crotch.

After making sure Sister Fatima was comfortably settled, I headed off to find Cordelia. Tall women are easy to spot. At least when they're standing up.

"Micky," Cordelia said as I approached. "Where have you been? Bernie said you called with a warning before the police did?"

I wasn't thrilled at the prospect of telling her about my morning's adventures. I didn't think she'd be happy to hear how close I came to getting killed. Again.

"Well, it's like this . . ." I started.

But I was interrupted by an explosion. Well, sort of, really a loud bang from the basement. One window broke. That was it.

Cordelia and I looked at each other for a moment, then she started laughing.

"I've been standing out here in the heat, waiting for my building to blow up," she explained. "Not a cherry bomb."

I glanced at my watch. One o'clock. Something was wrong, I puzzled. Maybe me. Maybe Sarry wasn't the master bomb builder he had led me to believe.

"Well, Miss Knight?" O'Connor inquired, standing at my elbow.

I shrugged. I couldn't think of anything to say.

"How soon can we go back in?" Cordelia asked him.

"Soon," he answered. "Let my men check it out." Then he walked away.

Elly and Millie joined us.

I didn't follow their conversation. I was wondering what had gone wrong. I couldn't believe this minor hiccup was the blast Sarry had intended. The bomb this morning had been real enough. So had the one left outside my door. Revenge on Sister Ann was his raison d'être. It didn't make sense that he would blow it (so to speak) so

354

carelessly. The two Bills? Had they tampered with the bombs? After his brutal murder of five women (and perhaps others not found, I shuddered), I had no faith in Frankenstein's reverence for any life other than the unborn. That left Choirboy. Hard to believe that innocent face could do anything other than sing "Nearer My God to Thee." But he had no problem leaving a bomb on my doorstep. That left me with a lot of unanswered questions and a vague sense of uneasiness.

It's just that after everything, particularly this morning, this burp of a bomb was anti-climatic, I told myself. Be glad your sense of drama wasn't appeased.

"Okay, ladies," O'Connor said, rejoining us after leaving us sitting in the sun long enough to get close to heat stroke. "It looks like his intent is disruption, not destruction. There's nothing else in the basement. We've checked it thoroughly."

"What about the rest of the building?" I asked.

"We checked that earlier," he answered.

"Can we go back in?" Millie asked.

"Sure. I think we've had all the excitement we're going to have today," O'Connor answered, with a pointed look at me.

"Okay, back to the salt mines," Cordelia said, waving Bernie to join us.

They started across the street back to the building. I stood where I was, mistrustful of our good fortune.

"Something the matter?" Elly asked, hanging back.

I shook my head. "Half an hour ago, nothing could have convinced me that this building wasn't destined to be a pile of dust right now."

"Let's not look too askance at our good luck," she answered. "You coming in?"

"No, I'm going to stew out here for a while longer," I said.

"Call us when you sense heat stroke approaching." She followed the others across the street and into the building.

I noticed Sister Ann leading Sister Fatima back into the building, cars stopping reverently for the two nuns, as I plopped myself down on a curb.

I looked across the street at the building, sturdy and sound in the glaring afternoon sunshine. I felt a bit foolish, happy to be wrong in every way, except for my ego. Go into the air conditioning and chill out. Maybe work up my nerve and ask Cordelia to dinner. Probably Dutch treat, I thought, pulling out my wallet to confirm my suspicions. Only two dollars. Scratch dinner, I decided, starring forlornly at my two lone bills.

Something nagged at me. I looked at my watch. Ten minutes to two.

Go inside. Maybe a cool brain can think better. I got up, crossed the street and entered the building. I ran into Sister Ann leaving her office carrying a large basket of flowers.

"Am I getting older, or are flowers getting heavier?" she asked, smiling at me.

"Nice bunch of posies," I commented. I decided not to mention Sarry just yet. Sister Ann looked busy and happy.

"Yes, they add such a pleasant touch. I'm taking them upstairs for my evening group."

I noticed another bunch of flowers on her desk.

"Who sent them?" I asked.

"Emma Auerbach. I believe you know her. It was very kind of her to mend fences this way."

"Mend fences?"

"Between us and the clinic. Though I must say I wish she had sent a donation instead of half a dozen flower baskets," she answered as she continued toward the stairs.

"Sister, can I use your phone?" I called after her.

"Certainly," she replied from the stairs.

I dialed Emma's number. No answer. Then I dialed Rachel's separate number, hoping to catch her.

"Hello," she answered.

"Hi, Rach, it's Micky. Would you know if Emma sent flowers to anyone today?"

"The only flowers I don't know about are the ones she sends me," Rachel answered. "Why? Did you get some mysterious flowers?"

"Not me. The Catholic side of Cordelia's building."

"Nope. She'd send them to Cordelia first. And she hasn't done that."

"Thanks, Rach. I have to go. I'll talk to you soon," I said, quickly hanging up.

It doesn't prove anything. Emma might have sent the flowers and forgot to mention it to Rachel. I glanced at my watch, as if expecting it to tell me something. All it said was five minutes to two.

To two. Two bombs. At two.

Horror slammed into me. I looked at the innocuous basket of flowers on Sister Ann's desk and remembered Sarry's ravings about misdirection and twos.

"My present to you for all you've done," the card said.

I pushed aside the flowers. They were stuck in Styrofoam. I carefully probed under it with my hand. Water. Then plastic wrapped around a hard object. I didn't risk pulling apart the basket for fear it would set off the bomb. Half a dozen, she had said.

"Clear the building," I ran into the hall yelling. "Everybody out! Now! There's a real bomb this time!"

I raced into the clinic, literally grabbing Bernie by the shoulders and pulling her out of her seat.

"Get out! Everybody out of the building," I yelled into the waiting room. "Hurry!" I screamed at the bewildered looks I was getting. I shoved Bernie toward the door. "Follow Bernie. She'll lead the way," I instructed. "Go," I said as she glanced back at me. "Now!"

Bernie exited, followed by the people in the waiting room.

"Micky?" Millie asked, coming out of an examining room.

"Get everyone out of here," I said. "There's another bomb."

"What?" she said. "But the police . . ."

"Hidden in flowers. Get people out now. We only have a few minutes, at best."

Cordelia came out of her office.

"What's going on?"

"Another bomb," Millie said, then told the people in her examining room to get dressed and out.

"Are you sure?" Cordelia asked, a look of bewilderment, then anxiety on her face.

"Yes. Too damn sure."

"But how do you . . . ?"

"I'll explain later," I cut her off. "Just get out. You have a minute or two."

"Of course," she replied, the uncertainty gone. "Everybody out now!"

I left the clinic. Cordelia and Millie would take care of it. I hurriedly stuck my head in the doors on the other side of the hallway, making sure they were clear.

Sister Ann, I thought, as I told the daycare workers to leave. There weren't many kids, fortunately.

I ran back up the hall, heading for the stairs I had watched Sister Ann climb.

"Micky?" Cordelia called as I shot past her. She was the last one out of the clinic.

"Go," I told her. "I'll be right behind you."

Halfway up the stairs, I glanced back, catching sight of her going through the door. The hallway was empty.

"Sister. Sister Ann," I called as I reached the top of the stairs.

"Yes?" her voice answered from one of the classrooms.

I ran into it. She was arranging the flowers.

"What's the commotion downstairs?" she asked.

"We've got to get out. There's another bomb," I hastily explained. "In the flowers."

She looked at the iris in her hand as if it had turned into a spider.

"No, that can't . . ." she said, like the others, denial her first reaction. Then she pulled the flowers out.

"Careful, you might . . ." I started.

"Oh, dear Lord," she said.

I looked into the basket at what she had uncovered. It sat there, an obscenity wrapped in plastic to keep it dry, a small timer ticking softly through its wrapping. A quick glance at the dial confirmed my fears. It was almost two o'clock. And that bomb was about to go off.

"The back door's chained," Sister Ann said, realizing, like I had, that we could never run downstairs and to the front door in the few remaining seconds.

"Out!" I shouted, shoving open a window wide enough for us to get through. I pushed Sister Ann over the sill, guiding her hands to the drain pipe next to the window. I was right behind her, my arms around her to grasp the pipe. We slid a few feet in tandem, before the rusty tin pipe gave way under our combined weight, peeling off the building.

"It's faster," I said, as the collapsing pipe hurled us toward the ground.

I heard Sister Ann's groan as we landed. I jumped up, pulling her with me. My shoulder was throbbing, but there was no time for that.

"My ankle . . ." Sister Ann said, as she started to fall.

I wrapped an arm around her waist, dragging her with me as I raced across the lawn for the stone part of the fence. Without its protection we didn't have a chance. Even with it . . . I wouldn't think about that.

"Leave me," Sister Ann told me.

"No!" I cried, carrying her along. We were almost to the end of the ragged row of cast iron spears. I grabbed the shaft of one and flung us around it to the far side of the fence and on the sidewalk.

"Get down," I ordered, as I pushed her roughly against the stone section of the wall. If we survived, I would apologize later.

Sister Ann was on the sidewalk, huddled against the wall. I was on top of her, no time to find separate places. I covered my head with my hands, feeling the hot sidewalk against my cheek. Sister Ann's head was under my stomach. I hoped it did some good.

"Sister, we've got to stop meeting like . . ."

There was an explosion. A series of explosions thundering through the hot summer air, like a huge cloudburst opening up with a vengeance. But this rain was a deadly shower of bricks and boards, debris from a dying building.

The cacophony of destruction seemed interminable. Something hit me in the back, guaranteeing matching bruises on both my shoulders. I grunted at its impact, flattening my head further against the sidewalk.

Then there was a sickening groan as some huge timber slammed into the wrought iron spears, bending them to the breaking point. They collapsed over us, forming a tent where we were. But a few scant yards away, the weight had bent and mangled the shafts, forcing the raw edges into the sidewalk, scraping, like fingernails against a blackboard, into our protective wall, gouging wounds into the stone.

The initial explosions were followed by the hollow boom of walls and floors collapsing, bricks and timbers sliding and shifting as one fell into another.

The day slipped into shadow, the sun hidden from us by the dust and dirt of the blast.

"Are you all right?" I asked, when it appeared the explosions were over. I had counted four, but they had overlapped.

"Yes, I think so," Sister Ann replied from somewhere underneath me. "Are you?"

"Yeah, I hope so," I answered, spitting out dirt.

There was another loud rumble as some part of the building collapsed, but it was the sound of brick on brick, not the roar of dynamite.

"What kind of evil would do this?" Sister Ann asked.

"Does the name Sarry mean anything to you?"

She didn't reply.

"Sister?" I prompted, suddenly worried.

"Randall Sarafin," she answered softly. "Oh, dear God, could he hate me so much?"

"Yes, I'm sorry, he could."

"Have mercy on him, Lord. He cannot know what he has done," she said very quietly, not to me at all.

"I'm going to try to get out of here," I told her.

I had to crawl slowly backwards, gingerly pushing past Sister Ann. She had to have a painful array of bruises by now. I didn't want to add to them. I was afraid of dislodging our fragile spear lean to. Its weight would be deadly. The open end was blocked by timber and debris. I had to kick it away, finally opening a hole large enough for me to slip out of.

"Okay, I'm out. Your turn," I told Sister Ann.

She didn't say anything, but started crawling back to me, groaning when she was forced to use her hurt ankle.

"Almost out," I encouraged as her feet stuck out of the opening, then slowly her calves and thighs. I reached in and put my arms around her waist, lifting and pulling her as gently as I could out from under the listing wrought iron. I was still worried it might cave in.

We rolled a few feet away and collapsed against a heavy timber angling across the sidewalk.

"Well, Sister," I finally said, after we spent a few moments catching our breath, "you're the first woman I've ever really felt the earth move with."

"And hopefully the last," she replied. "At least this way."

She sat up very slowly and carefully, as if everything hurt. It probably did, I realized as I shifted.

"You're bleeding," I said, noticing a cut on her forehead.

She wiped at the place where I pointed. "Yes, well, I've always been told I have a thick skull." Then she looked toward the building, through the slowly settling dust. "It's not there. It's just not there," she whispered.

All that remained of the building was a few jagged walls and a pile of bricks and boards.

"No, it's not," I said as I stood up. "But we are."

I extended a hand to help her up.

"Yes, we are. The others?"

"Everyone got out. You were the last."

"And you came back for me," she said, taking my hand.

"I was in the neighborhood," I remarked offhandedly.

Sister Ann slowly got up, with my help. She put an arm around my waist, leaning heavily on me for support.

"Not that I'm ungrateful, but it was a foolish thing to do."

"I won't ever do it again," I promised.

We started carefully making our way through the scattered building pieces littering the side street.

"Why?" she asked. "Why come back for me?"

"To prove Aunt Greta wrong," I said, not even knowing I was going to say it until I did. "Besides," I hastily covered, "us promiscuous dykes need all the help we can, to get into heaven."

"But you have, you know. At least on the outside."

I didn't think she was talking about getting to heaven.

We slowly picked a path down the far sidewalk, covered and cracked as it was with the detritus of the building.

"The outside?"

"Outside yourself. I think you're the only person left to convince," she answered.

"Except for Aunt Greta, Bayard ..."

"The only one that matters," Sister Ann said quietly.

I didn't reply, just a bare nod of my head.

The main avenue was crowded, people jockeying for the best

view of the destruction. I heard sirens in the distance. The TV cameras were madly filming away. One lone policeman was trying to string up a barricade between the crowd and the remains of the building. I couldn't spot anyone from the clinic. For a moment I panicked, afraid they hadn't made it. They're okay. You saw them leave, I told myself.

I could see a group of nuns through the crowd, their blue habits singling them out. I pushed through the onlookers, taking Sister Ann to them.

"Sister!" one of them exclaimed and about three or four nuns relieved me of Sister Ann.

"I'll talk to you later," were her parting words.

I nodded and went in search of my friends.

The crowd shifted and I spotted Cordelia, surrounded by Elly and Millie. She was back on the building side of the avenue.

As I got closer, I realized that Millie and Elly were holding Cordelia, almost as if struggling with her.

"There's nothing you can do," I heard Elly said.

"Except get yourself killed, too," Millie added.

Bernie? I thought wildly, then I noticed her down the road, leaning into an oak tree and crying.

What the hell? Who?

Millie saw me. And looked like she had seen a ghost.

Me?

"Micky!" she screamed. "She's alive!"

"Hi, ladies," I said nonchalantly.

"Micky," Cordelia said, wheeling around to look at me.

Then her arms were around me, holding me very tightly, picking me up off the ground.

"Thank God you're alive," she whispered in my ear.

"Hey, Bernie," I heard Elly call. "Micky's okay."

"Sorry about your building," I told Cordelia.

"The hell with my building. I'm so glad you're all right," she replied, putting me down, but still holding me tightly. "You have blood on your back," she said suddenly, letting go of me and gently turning me around to look at me back.

"Matching shoulder wounds," I said as she pulled up my jacket and T-shirt to examine my cut. "Careful, I'm not wearing a bra."

Elly put her arms around me, low enough to keep out of Cordelia's way.

"I hate it when you're right. About bombs," she said.

"Yeah, me too," I agreed.

Millie squeezed my hand and brushed some of the dust out of my hair.

"You'll live," Cordelia said, finishing her examination of my back. Her voice broke.

I started to turn to her, but Bernie edged between Elly and Millie.

"Hi, Bern," I said, picking her up and hugging her. "Hug back, but either low on the waist or high on the neck," I cautioned.

She threw her arms around my neck.

"Micky," she sniffed. "We thought you were dead."

"Me? No way." I gave her an extra squeeze, then set her back down. "Us tomcats have nine lives."

Then I turned to Cordelia. Her eyes were red. Had she been crying for me?

"Everyone okay?" I asked.

"Yes. Now," she replied.

She took my face between her hands, gently brushing dirt off my cheek. I tentatively put my hands on her waist, wanting to pull her to me, but shy in front of the too numerous onlookers, from camera crews to nuns to nineteen year olds.

Cordelia leaned toward me, as if she was going to kiss me anyway. And for that split second, nothing hurt.

But one of the nuns rushed up to us, asking worriedly, "Has anyone see Sister Fatima?"

Cordelia and I broke off, backing away.

"No," I said. "Not since before the bomb."

And no one else had seen her after the explosion.

The look on the nun's face told us that we were their last hope, the last unchecked group.

"She was a little hard of hearing," the nun said slowly, turning from us.

"Oh, no," Millie said for us. "I thought we had all . . ."

"I had hoped," Cordelia added, her expression drawn and tight.

"She was so nice," Bernie said helplessly. "Why?"

Elly put her arms around Bernie, the only possible answer.

"You might go look at Sister Ann," I told Cordelia, to give her something useful to do. "She hurt her ankle rather badly."

"Yeah, let me go do that," she said grimly, "although . . ." with a look back at the ruins of her clinic, "I haven't much to work with."

She walked over to the nuns.

"Damn whoever did this," Millie cursed. "Damn them." Then she followed Cordelia.

The one lone cop had gotten reinforcements and they were hustling us back to the far side of the street. Elly kept a protective arm around Bernie.

I started looking for O'Connor, to scream and curse at him, but he wasn't here. Then I saw another face in the crowd. Odd that he should be here. I kept expecting Frankenstein to show up. It appeared that he had decided to run away and fight the devil another day.

"I'll be back," I told Elly, as I started threading my way through the throng.

He was at the far edge of the onlookers, by himself. I stalked him slowly, not wanting him to see the intensity of my hunt. For a moment, I placed a tree between us, hastily brushing myself off, trying to make it look like I was just some curious bystander. I patted my gun, reassured irrationally by its warm metallic presence.

I circled the tree. He was still where he had been. I slowly ambled up to him. It was him, I made sure as I got close, the same scrubbed innocent face I had glimpsed running down my stairs and at Betty's cottage. Had he helped Frankenstein murder her? But this time Choirboy wasn't in a hurry. He stood, rocking slightly back on his heels, trying not to smile, but he couldn't really prevent the corners of his mouth from twitching in satisfaction.

"Howdy," he said to me, not recognizing me.

Always learn the face of your murder victims, so they can't sneak up on you if you miss.

"Hi," I replied as calmly as I could. "What happened here?"

"An abortion clinic got what it deserved," he said smugly.

"Oh? I thought that was a neighborhood clinic and a Catholic community center," I answered.

"No. No, it was an abortion house," he corrected me. "A beautiful sight going up."

"I think we've met before," I said. "Isn't your name Bill?"

"Yes, yes, it is," he smiled, trying to place me.

I reached out to shake his hand.

"Bill?" I asked as he took my hand.

"Bill Dolton."

I tightened my grasp on his hand.

"Micky Knight. You left a bomb at my door."

His expression started to change from smug gleefulness to worry and perhaps even fear, but he didn't have time. I punched him in the nose. He went down, blood streaming onto his lower lip.

"And congratulations, Bill," I remarked acidly. "You've just murdered a seventy-year-old nun. She was hard of hearing and didn't get out of the building in time."

He started to get up, but I put a foot on his shoulder and pushed him back down.

"Wha . . . ?" he started in disbelief.

"Your friend Sarry had other plans," I told him, grabbing him by the shirt. "He never made any of the warning calls. He wanted to murder the people in that building, and he lied to you. It wasn't an abortion clinic."

"No, you're lying," he sniffed.

"Where's Will?" I demanded. I didn't ever want to be surprised by him again.

"Will?" Choirboy echoed stupidly.

"Yeah, Will. The big, tall, ugly guy who jerks-off with prayer. You know who I'm talking about."

"I don't know. I mean, I don't know where he is," he answered hastily, seeing that I had little patience. "I was supposed to meet him here."

"When?"

"Uh . . . now, I guess. He was supposed to be here," Choirboy replied, looking around, obviously hoping for and ally.

Keeping a tight grip on him, I scanned the crowd. I couldn't see Frankenstein anywhere. Choirboy would have to do.

"He said he'd be here," Choirboy sniveled.

"Where are the rest of the bombs?" I demanded, shaking him.

"I don't have to tell you," he said, like a petulant child.

"No, you don't. But I don't have to stop hitting you, either," I informed him.

He looked scared. No one had ever really hit him before. That was obvious. He lived in a world where God was on his side and being wrong and being hurt weren't possibilities for him. I gave him a quick kick in the groin to prove my point.

"And that was gentle," I said as he sputtered a protest. It was, compared to how hard I wanted to hit him.

"Police brutality," he finally spit out through the blood on his lips.

"I'm not the police. And this isn't brutal. Not compared to the ton of brick and board that you let crush the life out of Sister Fatima. Did you kill Betty Peterson?"

"No, I swear. I had nothing to do with that. She was my girlfriend."

I stared at him. He could have said, 'She was my second grade guppy,' for all the remorse in his voice. "Your girlfriend?" I shot back incredulously. "Did you plant her in the clinic?"

"No, she worked there all on her own. She wanted to be that kind of nurse. I just asked her to do me a few favors."

"Did you get the women's names from her?"

"What names?"

"Beverly Morris. Alice Tresoe. Faye Zimmer." I wondered if I would ever stop remembering their names.

"Yeah, I guess. We were just supposed to send them stuff. To keep them from killing their kids. She got their names off some list, women who were going to have abortions."

"Faye Zimmer wasn't going to have an abortion. She was fifteen years old," I hissed at him.

"Oh," he said. "I guess that was a mistake. I must have read the codes wrong," he muttered.

"You read the codes?"

"It was an accident. I was picking up Betty one day and I just happened to see that secret file. Faye Zimmer had an A by her name. A for abortion."

"How about A for adolescent?"

"I didn't think of that," he replied slowly.

"You stupid shit. You didn't think."

"Betty wouldn't give me any more names. I thought she was on our side. I don't know what went wrong," he complained.

I roughly pulled him up. "I'll tell you what went wrong. Betty really was pro-life. She started asking questions. And she realized your answers weren't her answers."

"She just didn't understand." It was almost a whine.

"And you murdered her," I spat at him.

"No, no I didn't. All I did was tell Will what she was going to do. He said he wanted to talk to her. I didn't think he would ... "

You unctuous little shit, I thought as I stared at him, you didn't think. Betty was a problem and you handed her over to Will to solve. Will, who got his jollies out of ramming sharp, unsterile things up women's vaginas and probing around until he found a major artery. You didn't think because if you had thought for half a second you would have known you were handing Betty off to her death. How damned convenient to never let a thought enter your head.

"Like Pontius Pilate, you washed your hands of her and let someone else do your dirty work," I hissed at him. Then I hit him as hard as I could, in a very soft place. He gave a strangled groan and crumpled to his knees.

But hitting him wouldn't bring Betty back. And there were other lives to save now. I had to get the location of the bombs out of him, not beat him senseless.

We were starting to get attention, a crowd forming. I wanted them on my side.

"Where did you plant the other bombs? How many more people are you going to murder?" I yelled at him. "I'll beat it out of you if I have to." I jerked him up to half standing.

"I want to see my lawyer," he cried. "You can't just hit me. It's not legal."

One of those white boys the world has always been fair to, I thought. He can blow up people's dreams, but we can't hit him. Where were his legal protests when Betty Peterson was being murdered? I lost my temper again and jerked him fully upright, then punched him in the stomach. He staggered back, but was caught and held by someone in the crowd.

"Where are those bombs?" I screamed at him, grabbing his shirt and cocking my fist to hit him again.

"No," he cried, putting his hands up to protect his face. "I'll tell."

"Where? The next one?" I demanded.

"Uh ... that AIDS place on Decatur. At two-thirty."

I heard O'Connor's voice behind me say, "Radio that in. Hurry."

I didn't give a damn. Let him arrest me. I didn't let go of Choirboy.

"Next?" I demanded. "Next?"

"She's beating me," he whined to the police officers who where behind me. The only white male faces in the crowd.

"Next?" O'Connor echoed me.

Choirboy got a lesson in fairness. He mumbled out the entire list. O'Connor made no move to take him until he had gotten every scrap of information out of him. Only then did he motion two uniformed officers to take Choirboy from us, handcuffing him and dragging him off. He looked like a little boy, with his bloody nose and eyes red from crying. I had no sympathy for him.

"Well?" I demanded of O'Connor.

He cocked an eyebrow at me.

"Aren't you going to arrest me?" I asked.

He grunted, then said, "No one's pressed charges. Besides, it looked like self-defense to me." He shrugged and started to walk away, but stopped for a second and threw over his shoulder, "You know, Miss Knight, I like your style."

Then he sauntered into the crowd.

It's over, I thought. Sarry dead, Choirboy in custody, Frankenstein . . . I looked over the crowd again, still half-expecting to see him. Logic said he was probably on his way to west Texas by now. But it was hard to find anything logical in him.

I stopped at the store and got some juice. It's thirsty work beating up guilty choirboys.

Sister Ann was propped under the oak tree, with her ankle bandaged and gauze on her forehead. I offered her some of my juice. She looked hot and tired.

"Thank you," she said, taking the bottle from me. She took a long swallow. "Here, take it back before I finish it."

"Go ahead," I offered.

"Sit beside me and we'll share," she compromised.

"Naw, finish it," I said, there wasn't much left. But I sat beside her anyway.

"What happened?" Sister Ann asked. "I haven't seen him in—it must be thirty years."

"He was crazy. It's not your fault," I said.

"I know. I do realize that. Still it is sobering to be somehow connected with . . . this." She gestured to indicate the destroyed building.

I gave her an as-delicate-as-possible version of my meeting with Randall Sarafin.

She said nothing for several minutes after I had finished. "What changes a man? What makes him capable of this?" she finally asked softly.

"I don't know," I replied. "Maybe he had nothing else to do. Nothing to take him away from that moment when he saw you abandoning him."

"Perhaps you're right," Sister Ann answered. "All those years of hatred. The only way he could ever touch me again was to hurt me."

"I guess we all need some semblance of control — power — somewhere in our lives."

"Yes, we do. It's a pity when it's only the power to destroy," she replied.

"Hi, Mick," Bernie joined us. Then seeing the almost empty juice bottle being passed back and forth, "Do you want more? I'll go get some," she offered. "I'm going myself."

"Sure," I accepted, reaching for my wallet. "Whatever two dollars will buy."

"It's okay. I've got money." She took our order and trotted off to the store.

"Ah, youth," Sister Ann commented. "I think she has . . ."

"Don't tell me she has a crush on me," I said.

"She does, though she's a little old for female crushes."

"Unless it's a lifelong occupation," I amended.

"Is she?" Sister Ann asked, catching my implication.

"Heading that way, I suspect. Don't tell her mother," I replied. "I don't recruit."

"Of course, I never doubted that. Will she be happy, do you think?"

"Yes, I think so," I answered.

"Are you?" Sister Ann probed.

"Me? Sure," I replied offhandedly. "Or, if I'm not happy, it has nothing to do with being a lesbian."

"If you say so," she answered noncommittally.

"Do you blame every problem you have on being a nun," I

defended, "or do you think they have something to do with life just being difficult, period?"

"Point taken. Believe it or not, I'm not arguing with you. Not only is it too hot to argue, but you and I really have no argument."

"We don't?"

"No. If you have no problem with being a lesbian, then I don't have any problem with it."

"Oh," I said. "Well, I don't. I think . . . it's one of the better things that's happened to me. Or that I chose."

"Good. I'm glad to hear that."

I looked at her. Nuns weren't supposed to approve of lesbians.

"Now, why don't you tell me what happened on that church picnic," she continued.

"What does that have to do with my being a lesbian?" I asked defensively.

"Nothing," Sister Ann replied. "But since you don't have a problem with that I thought we'd talk about something you do have a problem with."

"I don't have a problem with church picnics," I said shortly.

"Then you can have no objection to telling me what happened. You see, I remember looking for you. I was always curious why you hid. And what happened to your shoe?"

"What do you think happened?" I retorted.

"At the time, I'm afraid I took your aunt's explanation at face value. That you were a difficult, disobedient child, getting into trouble for no reason."

"I probably was."

"Not for no reason."

I shrugged. It was too hot to get into all this.

"You do have a problem," she pressed.

"No, I don't," I returned sharply, starting to lose my temper, then backing off as I realized it wasn't her I was angry at. "Oh, hell, isn't it obvious? A fourteen-year-old girl goes for a walk in the woods. Her . . . nineteen-year-old cousin and some of his friends follow her. What do you think happened?" I stared at the ground, not looking at Sister Ann.

"They made you do something you didn't want to do."

"Yeah," I nodded, shredding the label off the apple juice bottle.

"Sexual?"

"What do you think?"

"Something sexual, that even fifteen years later, you're too ashamed to mention," she said.

"Do you know what a blow job is, Sister?" I retorted sarcastically.

"Celibacy isn't ignorance," she replied. "Is that what they made you do?"

"Yeah, that's what they made me do."

Bernie returned with our drinks.

"Made you do what?" she asked innocuously.

"Made me . . ." I started to make up some lie, not to seem tainted in front of Bernie, then I stopped. Silence was the trap. What if, when I was nineteen, someone I admired had admitted in front of me, that she was molested? "When I was fourteen, I went on a church picnic, some place up north. I hadn't been out of the city since I was ten, and, anyway, I went off, wandering by myself in the woods. My despised cousin Bayard, who was nineteen, and some of his friends . . . I don't know if they followed me or just ran into me by chance. They . . . cornered me out in the woods away from the others." I was shredding the label off one of the new apple juice bottles, I realized. "They made me . . . one did . . . a blow job. The next one . . . I started gagging. I got sick . . . started throwing up. Some of it landed on Bayard's shoes. So he got angry. I had embarrassed him in front of his friends. I was supposed to 'behave' and do them all, not vomit on his shoes. They laughed at him, at his messed up shoes.

"I don't know what he would have done if one of the other guys hadn't stopped him. I guess I lost my shoe somewhere in the fight. He kept punching me in the stomach and . . . between my legs. Calling me ugly names.

"The other guys finally stopped him. And they just left me there. I didn't want to come out of the woods. I figured I had a better chance there than . . . Bayard had promised I would pay for it."

I stopped, taking a drink of the unlabeled juice.

"Did you?" Sister Ann asked.

"Yeah. Yes, I did. I . . . made up for everything I got out of that day," I replied bitterly. I had lied to Joanne, maybe just couldn't tell her the truth, when I had said it hadn't happened that often. "What a good Catholic boy he was."

"Not by my standards." She took my hand and held it. "I am so sorry. I should have seen it. And done something."

"What? It would have been my word against his. Aunt Greta would never believe him over me. You know that."

"Yes, I do," she replied. "And it's too late for regrets over what I should have done."

"It's okay. I survived."

"Yes, you have. Without becoming like them."

Something across the street caught my attention. The workers, police, and firemen digging through the rubble had stopped. Then they started again, slowly and carefully, gently even. They had found Sister Fatima.

Sister Ann bowed her head.

I wanted to turn away, not to have a memory of her battered body, but I couldn't, transfixed as I was by the reverent movements of the workers. I guess they felt that they were uncovering a true victim, one of unimpeachable innocence. We were spared the sight of her, instead seeing only the vaguely human shape in a black body bag.

"I guess it's time to make funeral arrangements," Sister Ann said wearily as some of the other nuns joined us. Two of them extended hands to help her up. "You will come by and talk to me, won't you?" she asked me. "When I have some place to come to?"

"Sure, Sister," I agreed.

"I think once a week will do," she said as she hobbled off. "I'll call you."

I started to protest, but she was too far away. Oh, well, I shrugged, then thought indelicately, wait until we start getting into my sex life. It would be interesting to see how far her liberalness went.

I glanced at Bernie, wondering what she thought of my revelations. Suddenly my bravado was gone, the empty feeling of 'if only they knew' was back. And she knew.

"Bet you thought I was a tough guy," I said.

"But, Mick," Bernie answered, "isn't it the tough guys who survive?"

I looked at her, embarrassed that it took someone I'd thought of as young and naive to point out the obvious to me.

"Yeah, you're right, Bern, it is the tough ones who make it. And, goddamn it, I made it." I ruffled Bernie's hair in thanks.

"I hate insurance agents," Cordelia fumed, as she joined us. She reached down and took the apple juice out of my hand. "Thanks," she said, taking a swig, then handing it back to me. "Label shredding again, I see," she said.

"Insurance on the building?" I asked.

"Yeah," she replied, sitting down next to me. "And my car. I parked it in the shade, next to the building."

"Oh, my car," Bernie suddenly said. "I'd better check it out."

"Be careful," Cordelia cautioned. "I think they're going to pull down the remaining walls."

Bernie got up, dusting herself off and headed across the street.

"What are you looking so serious about?" Cordelia asked me. "Sister Ann playing social worker?"

"I don't think she was playing," I commented ruefully. "Just childhood memories."

"Unpleasant ones, I gather," she said, pointing to my shredded labels. "Two bottles worth."

"Yeah, fond memories of life with Aunt Greta and . . . my cousin Bayard."

"I can imagine."

"I hope you can't. I hope . . ." I trailed off.

"I can guess. Believe it or not, you're no less transparent than Joanne. Probably more so, since you're more . . . expressive," she finished politely.

"Oh . . . you're not . . ."

"Surprised?"

"Upset?"

"Yes, of course I am. I hate seeing my friends hurt like that."

I had meant upset with me. At my . . . weakness, defilement, all the ugly things I still carried.

"Hi, girls," Millie said, taking Bernie's spot in the shade. "Great way to spend a summer afternoon, huh? I finally got through to Hutch. He can pick me up after work."

"Your car, too?" Cordelia asked sympathetically.

"Yeah, same shade, same damage," Millie answered. "Hey, where's your car?" she asked me.

I pointed down the street. "If any car deserved to be put out of its misery, it's mine."

"Let's find an air-conditioned bar," Millie suggested.

"I'm waiting for insurance agents," Cordelia said.

"I'm no longer a bar girl," I admitted.

Bernie returned. "I've been wanting a new car," she said with a grimace.

"This has been a hell of a day," Cordelia remarked.

No one disagreed.

Chapter 25

Hutch arrived a little after six. Joanne was with him.

"Geez," he said at seeing the destruction.

Joanne stood silently looking at the rubble, her features set in a hard line. Brusquely, she turned away from it.

"Good to see you're in one piece," she said to me. "Two bombs in one day is probably some sort of record."

"Two?" demanded Cordelia.

"Two?" Elly echoed.

I had, in all the excitement, forgot to mention my morning's jaunt. So I regaled them with tales of bomb number one. It took a while, with both Joanne and Hutch asking pesky police-type questions, but I finally got through it.

"That's it?" Millie said when I'd finished. "Some jilted suitor?"

"No, the conjunction of three mad men, with just enough

knowledge and fanaticism between them to do what they did," I replied.

"It's a miracle only one person was killed," Hutch said, "with the number of bombs they had."

Danny arrived, restoring my confidence in the law enforcement grape vine.

"Holy shit!" was her comment on seeing the ruins.

She, Joanne, and Hutch, new on the scene as they were, had to walk around for a bit, viewing the rubble in all its glory. I flopped down at the foot of my favorite oak tree. It would be dark soon. Hopefully the retreating sun would take some of the heat with it.

Our latecomers returned from their amble around the ruins.

"I'm ready to get out of here," Danny said, still shaking her head at the destruction.

Everyone agreed, but no one wanted to just go home. We decided on dinner together. Danny offered hamburgers in her backyard, while Millie was more in an air-conditioned restaurant with tall, icy drinks mood.

Influenced by my wallet, I sided with Danny.

It's amazing how long it takes to make a simple decision when people's taste buds are the deciding factor.

"A pitcher of margaritas," Millie opined.

"Beer, in a cooler submerged in ice," Danny countered.

"Both," Joanne said decisively. "We'll have dinner in some freezing restaurant, then to your place. Somehow I think we're going to be talking for a while tonight."

The sun had set, turning the building's ruins into vague, ominous shapes. The corner street light still hadn't been fixed, or was re-broken, and, without the security lights from the clinic, the street was very dark indeed.

After deciding on which freezing restaurant, Hutch and Millie got into his car.

"You coming with us?" Danny asked Cordelia as she, Elly, and Joanne headed for their cars.

"No, I'll go with Micky," she replied. "If it's all right?" she asked me.

"Be forewarned, it's a black interior."

"I'll manage."

I waved Bernie along with us, clearly where she wanted to be. We walked toward my car.

"Can you wait a minute?" Cordelia suddenly asked. "I'd like to get some things out of my trunk."

"Sure," I agreed, opening my car to air it out.

She crossed the street. Then it occurred to me that she might need some help moving sticks and stones. Perhaps a flashlight. I grabbed mine from under the seat.

"Back in a minute," I informed Bernie.

I followed Cordelia. I could barely see her, a vague outline at the far end of the lot. I turned on my flashlight to pick my way over the rubble. Too bad the batteries were dead. I clicked it back off. Almost prepared. Good thing she's wearing a light shirt or I'd never find her, I thought as I again picked up Cordelia's shape at what I guessed had to be her car.

Then the darkness behind her shifted, coalescing into a tall shadow. It moved toward her.

Why the fuck aren't you in west Texas, I thought wildly.

"Cordelia!" I shouted as I ran. "Look out!"

My warning saved the blow from landing, the timber he wielded instead ringing hollowly against her car.

I found a use for the flashlight. I threw it at him, hitting him in the shoulder. He ignored it, raising his club to strike again.

I jumped at him, managing to get a hand on his arm, forcing the blow astray.

He threw me off. I landed painfully on the littered asphalt.

"No!" I heard Cordelia scream as she grappled with him. The club was now aimed at me. I forced myself up, grabbing the end of it, trying to pry it from his grasp.

He suddenly let go, throwing me off balance. I stumbled back, landing against a car, the timber swinging into me.

He struck Cordelia with his fist, hitting her squarely in the stomach. She doubled over.

I came at him with the timber, but it was too heavy for me to raise over my head. The best I could do was slam it into his knees, a blow he was able to ignore. He hit Cordelia again, throwing her off into the blackness. I heard her land, then nothing.

I kicked him as hard as I could in the groin.

He grunted. It should have laid him out, but he was still coming for me.

"Help! Joanne, Danny!" I yelled as loudly as I could, hoping that they hadn't left yet. "Help . . ."

Suddenly his hands were wrapped around my neck. "You can't save the devil," he bellowed. "I'll send you to hell with her."

I couldn't yell anymore. I couldn't even breath. I grabbed at his fingers, attempting to pry them loose, backing away, until I could go no further, caught between him and one of the wrecked cars, bent back across the hood while he loomed above me. For a second, I had the pressure off, but it was a losing battle. He was much stronger than I was. I swung wildly at his face, trying to scratch his eyes, but his long arms kept him well out of my reach.

Three strikes and you're out, I thought as I started to become light-headed.

Then Cordelia was pulling at his arm, trying to get his hands off my throat.

He made a deep, angry, animal sound as he struggled with her. One hand released. He struck her with it, knocking her back down. But it allowed me to take a breath.

My gun.

His hands were back around my throat.

He'll break your neck if you let go with even one hand, I thought. He'll choke me even if I don't.

I fumbled in my jacket for the gun, his hands a circle of intense pain around my throat. I finally managed to get a grip on it, pulling it out of its holster and clicking off the safety.

Dizziness was coming back. I aimed at his thigh and pulled the trigger. The gun roared into the hot summer night. It was hard to hold steady with one hand; I almost lost my grip as it kicked.

Frankenstein bellowed in rage, the bullet doing damage.

But he didn't let go of me.

Fire again, I told myself, but fog was creeping in. I was only vaguely aware of the metal shape in my hand. I couldn't be sure where the barrel was pointing. At him? Or out somewhere in the night where Cordelia lay?

The world dimmed to a tiny point of light, only his twisted face at the end of the tunnel.

I thought I was lifting my hand with the gun. I thought I could feel the trigger under my finger, its resistance an almost impossible obstacle.

I wouldn't have known I'd even pulled the trigger without the sound, the crack ringing in my ears. Then another and another, echoing in my head.

He jerked back, his hands still wrapped around my neck. He twisted again, thumbs digging deeper.

Some hot liquid spurted against my face and throat. His hands seemed to slip in it. Then they loosened. Or I couldn't feel anymore.

Another convulsion shook him. And another person's hands were at my throat, prying his away. I couldn't see who, sinking, as I was, into oblivion.

"Breathe, dammit," a voice from very far away said.

Cordelia?

I wanted to ask if she was all right, but I couldn't.

The same hands were at my face, then a touch, and air was forced into my closed throat. I gasped and shuddered, drawing in breath after painful breath, rolling to my side to spit.

It was Cordelia. Air had restored my vision. I glanced at her between breathing and spitting. There was blood on her chin. I tried again to say something, but nothing came out.

"Is she all right?" Joanne asked.

"I think so," Cordelia responded.

"Are you okay?"

"A few bruises. A split lip. I'll be fine," Cordelia answered.

"I hate to ask this," Joanne continued, "but could you look at him?"

For a moment there was silence. "Stay with her," was Cordelia's only reply.

I felt Joanne's arm lightly around my shoulders while I continued my alternate gasping and spitting up.

"Take it easy," she said, as I attempted to get up. I made it to my hands and knees.

Frankenstein was sprawled out, his limbs at the impossible angles of the dead or dying. He was illuminated by the harsh beam of a flashlight. Pools of red in its circle of light flowed into dark liquid puddles beyond it.

Cordelia was kneeling beside him, O'Connor holding the flashlight, his gun still in his other hand.

"He says he wants a priest," Cordelia said, standing up.

"Go to hell," O'Connor savagely replied, then to Cordelia, "An ambulance is on its way."

She slowly shook her head.

Then the night was quiet, broken only by my gasps and his heavy, bloody breathing.

I struggled to sit up, unwilling to listen to him die. Joanne helped me until I was sitting propped against the tire of Cordelia's car.

"Careful," Joanne told me. "You're not as tough as you think."

I tried to tell her I was okay, just a minor sore throat, but it only came out as a wheeze. I had to settle for a half smile and a bare wave of my hand.

Somewhat reassured, Joanne stood up and moved back to Cordelia.

"How many shots did you fire?" O'Connor asked.

"Until he let go," she replied. "You?"

"Six," O'Connor replied. "Not enough, not nearly enough," he added softly.

And again the silence of the night, this time broken only by my rasping breath.

"He's dead," Cordelia said.

"I'm not sorry," O'Connor muttered. "He got an easier death than the women he murdered."

"Come on, Cordelia," Joanne said. "It's over."

"Yeah, for you, Dr. James, it's finally over," O'Connor added.

Using the car for support, I slowly stood up. I was okay, I told myself. No sense having people worry about me for no reason.

"How are you?" Cordelia asked, returning to me.

I tried to reply, but my larynx rebelled. I let go of the car to show I was fine and could stand by myself. Too bad I was wrong. I pitched forward and would have hit the ground if Cordelia hadn't caught me.

She wasn't content to merely catch me, instead, putting one arm around my back and the other one under my knees, she picked me up.

I tried to tell her I was all right and this fuss wasn't necessary, but my vocal cords weren't at home.

"I'm taking her to the emergency room," Cordelia informed

Joanne and O'Connor. She proceeded to carry me across the parking lot. "Put your arm around my shoulders. It'll make it easier to carry you."

It's hard to argue when you can't talk. I did as I was told.

The gunshots had evidently drawn a crowd. Danny was keeping people out of the parking lot. Elly was off to one side, doing her best to reassure Bernie.

"Micky!" Danny called, running over to us.

I waved to show her I was okay. It was a half-hearted effort because I was very tired, I suddenly realized. Maybe the fight took more out of me than I thought.

"She'll be okay, I think," Cordelia said. "But a trip to the hospital won't hurt."

Bernie and Elly arrived in time to hear this.

"What happened?" Bernie asked, her voice wavering.

"Joanne will tell you," Cordelia replied as she crossed the street to my car.

"You want me to drive?" asked Danny, who was trailing us.

"Could you open the door?"

Danny did and the two of them situated me in the passenger seat of my car. Cordelia got in the driver's side.

"You got some bruises, too, lady," Danny told Cordelia.

"I'll be okay," she shrugged. "I'll call you later."

"I'll see you there," Danny said, "as soon as I'm through here."

"Okay," Cordelia nodded.

She fished the car keys out of my pocket, started the car, and pulled away.

At the hospital, I tried to get out of the car and stand up to prevent the me–Jane approach to transportation.

Cordelia was still in Tarzan mode, however, and picked me up, saying, "You'll get more attention this way."

She carried me into the emergency room.

I don't know whether it was her carrying me or that I was still splattered with Frankenstein's blood or the familiarity with which she said, "Hi, Albert, I've got a strangulation victim here," to the man behind the desk, but we got attention. First from a nervous intern who, after a few pointed questions from Cordelia, gave way to the head of the emergency room.

After a painful exam (I guess I reacted to the pain in a lively enough manner that they were assured I wouldn't die) I was taken to a room. I gathered that I was not to be released tonight. Cordelia was with me most of the time, only disappearing briefly to wash the blood off her face.

She would behave the same way if it were Danny or Joanne, I told myself. Don't let her concern get your hopes up too high. But, of course, I did.

She sat on the side of my bed, absentmindedly drying her face with a paper towel.

"Excuse me, it's after visiting hours," an official voice said from out in the hallway. "Are you related?"

"Yes, I am. That's my sister in there," came the reply.

Danny entered. I think the hallway monitor was more impressed by the D.A.'s office identification she was putting away, than her claim to be my sister.

"Elly's taking Bernie home," Danny explained. "Ms. Knight, I must say, you've had a busy day." She sat on the other side of the bed. "How are you feeling?"

"Not very talkative," Cordelia answered.

"No? I still want to hear about this morning." When I didn't reply, Danny caught on. "You mean she can't talk?"

Cordelia nodded.

"Any chance it's permanent?" Danny asked, a slow smile spreading over her face.

Cordelia started giving her the technical answer, until she noticed Danny's glee.

"This is definitely the most novel position I've ever found Mick in," Danny said cheerfully. "Silent and in bed all by herself."

Fortunately there are other means of communication besides verbal. I made the appropriate hand gesture.

Danny was still chortling much too happily when the official voice again inquired, "Are you related?"

"Of course I am. That's my dear, sainted mother in there," followed by a familiar grunt. O'Connor entered.

"I have a few questions," he said.

"She can't talk," Cordelia told him.

"Yes or no will do," he replied. "Was the man who attacked you in the parking lot the same one who abducted you earlier?"

I nodded yes.

He handed me a picture. "Is this the man who tried to blow you up this morning?"

Again I nodded yes.

"Bill Dolton, Choirboy to you, has confessed. I guess God finally got to him. He helped Frankenstein kidnap the women, though he claims he didn't know they were to be murdered until too late."

"Too late for whom?" Danny interjected. "To save any of the women or avoid a murder rap?"

O'Connor gave a tired shrug. "Frankenstein, Bill Mahoney, worked as an orderly in some hospital, wanted to be a doctor, but couldn't even keep his orderly job. I just finished searching his apartment. He had a couple of medical textbooks on abortion. With what to avoid marked in yellow highlighter. He learned enough about abortions to botch them," O'Connor paused for a moment, taking a deep breath, then continued, "Choirboy claims Frankenstein got the dynamite for Sarafin. He just put the bombs where they told him to. Empty buildings, he thought."

I made an angry gesture.

"Which we know is bullshit," O'Connor said. "His two partners are dead. Why not put as much blame on them as possible?" He continued, "I would like to get a statement from you, Dr. James. I know you've had a long day, but if you don't mind?"

"It's okay. Can we do it somewhere else? Micky should get some rest. She'll just want to ask questions if we hang about."

"I won't stay very long," Danny assured her.

"I'm borrowing your car. You won't need it for a while," were Cordelia's parting words for me. She followed O'Connor out.

"You are going to have one hell of a bruise," Danny observed, looking at my throat.

I nodded.

"Anything I can do?"

Ice cream came to mind, but I stoically shook my head no.

"Good. Then let me start on the list of all the things I wanted to say but didn't, because I knew that smart mouth of yours would make me regret it."

I reached out and took Danny's hand, kissing it softly on the palm.

"Damn," she said, blinking. "I can't think of a thing. Except I am so glad you pulled out of this one."

"Are you related?" emanated from the hall.

"No. Fortunately," came the reply.

Joanne came in, followed by Alex.

"Hail the conquering hero," Alex said. "Hi, Danny."

"She can't talk," Danny cheerfully informed them.

"Yeah?" Joanne asked, returning Danny's grin. "I'll be damned, a silent Micky Knight."

"But I wanted to hear your adventures," Alex lamented. "Where's C.J.?"

"With O'Connor. Doing her civic duty," Danny said.

Joanne and Danny did their best to fill Alex in on the day's numerous events. I tried to pay attention, but my throat was a pain in the neck. I was also starting to nod out.

Elly arrived to retrieve Danny. And, nurse that she was, she shoo-ed everyone out, telling them to let me get my rest.

The minute they were gone, I missed them. Particularly since I know they were probably going to convene at Danny's and Elly's to talk, party, and . . . eat ice cream.

It's over, I thought as I dozed off, relieved that no more bombs would be exploding, no more women cast as unwilling Jocastas. Then I realized it was all over. No excuses to go back to the clinic to see Cordelia. No clinic. Well, she'll have to give my car back, I consoled myself. Unless she leaves it with Danny.

I counted ice cream flavors and fell asleep.

Chapter 26

The next day, a little after lunch (applesauce), Emma and Rachel came by to pick me up.

"You're going to spend a week or so out in the country," Emma informed me, handing me some clean clothes. "Your friend Danny helped us get the things you'll need from your place."

I winced at the thought of Emma prowling through my drawers. Hell, just my apartment.

"You are bruised all over, Micky, girl," Rachel said as I shrugged off my hospital gown.

I quickly dressed, embarrassed by both my bruises and nakedness under Rachel's and Emma's scrutiny.

We checked out of the hospital.

After making sure I was comfortably positioned in the back seat, we drove out of the city, heading across Lake Pontchartrain.

Listening to Emma and Rachel talking in the front seat, I suddenly realized: they're lovers. It wasn't what they said, but the tone of voice, perhaps body position as they conversed, that bespoke intimacy.

I'm an idiot, I thought, for not having noticed before. Separate rooms were only a token nod to decorum, to circumvent the racial and sexual rules of the South. Or perhaps a harsh necessity. What had it been like, thirty years ago? Before Stonewall? Before even Rosa Parks?

I had first met Emma when I was just seventeen. She was Miss Auerbach to me and I didn't know enough or dare enough to look under the surfaces I was shown. She and Rachel were both in their late forties then. Afraid as I was that Emma wanted something sexual from me, I was more than willing to see only the scholarly, asexual spinster front she presented. In some way, I realized, I had demanded the distance, building a wall of reserve between us to protect myself. Emma had always respected that distance.

I recalled that horrible last year of high school. I was aloof and a loner there, despising that ugly house in Metairie that I had to return to. I didn't have many friends. I couldn't risk it. I knew what I was. Queer. A pervert. I was haunted by a constant refrain of "if only they knew . . . " Every time a teacher wrote "good" on a paper, every time someone said 'hello' in the hallway.

From school I went to work, a local burger place that left me with the smell of day old cooking oil and greasy ground beef, even after a long scrubbing shower. Then I went to Aunt Greta's house, where I lived. It wasn't home, I couldn't call it that.

Bayard was there on weekends. He was still taking courses at LSU to graduate in December. He came home on Fridays and left on Mondays. I did the best I could to avoid him on those weekends, taking extra shifts at the burger joint, barricading myself with Uncle Claude and feigning interest in whatever TV show he was watching. But after Christmas, Bayard would be living at home. And I would be like a caged animal with only a small area in which to run from him. I dreaded the thought of December.

Late in November, one of my teachers, Miss Silver—I later found out she was a lesbian—was handing back papers and mine "just happened" to be on the bottom, making me the last student there. She gave me my paper and a business card, saying, "Call her, I think you need to talk to someone." That was all. The card was for Rene Harper, a social worker at the local health clinic. And, I suspected, Miss Silver's lover at the time, but I never did find out.

I did need to talk. I told her everything. Almost everything, I was still too ashamed to mention incest. I told her that I preferred women, though it took a few sessions for me to admit that I was sexually active.

One day, she asked if I would be interested in earning money helping organize and catalogue a private library. It was Emma's, of course. I was so nervous on that interview, feeling very out of place in her Garden District home. I was sure that she would spot me as perverted bayou trash. But at the end of the interview she asked me when I could start.

Several weeks later, Emma offhandedly inquired where I was going to college. The question caught me off guard because I had never thought about going to college. I didn't have an answer.

A few days later, Emma handed me a sheaf of college applications and told me that my job that week was to fill them out. I did as I was told, but I knew it was impossible. Aunt Greta wouldn't let me go part-time to UNO, let alone the places Emma was having me apply to. I remembered resenting Emma for making me want something I couldn't have.

The holidays came and went. Bayard was home, in no hurry to get a job. I stayed out late, changed my hours, snuck around, but I didn't always get by him.

My eighteenth birthday was on the last day of February. I decided that on that day I was going to leave Aunt Greta's house. I realized that I would have to drop out of school. But I couldn't stay there any longer.

I didn't tell anyone. I knew they wouldn't understand or approve.

Until, one day in early February, Emma came into the library to talk to me about college, telling me she had spoken to some people who were quite impressed with me and thought I had a good chance at . . .

Something in me broke, the control I thought I had. I couldn't bear Emma's animated face telling me what I knew to be impossible.

"I'm not going to college," I burst out. "I can't. I can't live in that house anymore." Then I cried, I just sat down and cried, unable to hold back my despair anymore.

Emma put her hand on my shoulder, but I shook it off, humiliated at breaking down and sobbing in front of her. A few minutes later, Rachel came in, wrapped her arms around me and led me to the office she had near the kitchen. She held me until I cried myself out. I told her about dropping out of school and leaving on my eighteenth birthday, that I couldn't stand to live with Aunt Greta a day beyond that.

The next day Emma was waiting for me when I came to work. She told me that it was all arranged, she had talked to her lawyers. On my eighteenth birthday, I would come and stay with her, finish high school, and go to college.

She brushed off my attempt to thank her by saying she had plenty of room and, besides, I was such a hard worker she didn't want to lose me.

Emma kept her word. At midnight on February 28th, she drove out to that ugly Metairie house and got me and my few belongings.

I lived with Rachel and Emma until I went off to college in the fall. I became one of Emma's "girls," women who received money from the scholarship fund she had established.

I had, in some way, been closer to Rachel, spending more time with her. I sensed some equality between them, knew that Rachel wasn't just a servant, but she and Emma kept their sexuality carefully hidden from view, mine included. (I don't guess they knew I was a lesbian for sure until I was twenty-one and Rachel caught me with another woman in a very compromising position on her kitchen table.)

I'm ashamed to say that the idea that these two women could be lovers wasn't a possibility to the eighteen-year-old that I was. Partly it was race, class, those ugly things I was only beginning to see beyond, but also my own conflicted views about sex and love. It was easier and safer for me to believe completely in their asexual front. If Emma was a sexless spinster, she wouldn't want from me what Bayard said she would want.

I cursed my closed throat, wanting to apologize for my blindness and to congratulate them. For the years they had endured together and the courage to break every so-called rule for love.

Maybe I should break a few rules. Like the one I had imposed on myself about rich doctors and bayou trash.

"Are you doing okay?" Rachel leaned over the front seat to ask.

Oh, hell, I realized, that means everything I've told Rachel, Emma probably knows. And I'd told Rachel a fair bit, since she had a recipe that could cure everything from a hangover to a broken heart.

I nodded, trying to speak.

Rachel cut off my feeble attempt with, "Not a word out of you for the next week."

I nodded again, not sure I could violate her dictate if I wanted to.

After we arrived, Emma insisted on carrying my suitcase up to my room and told me to take a nap if I wanted to. I demurred, intent on getting ice cream on the grocery list. I headed for the kitchen to find Rachel. Since ice cream was already on the grocery list, I underlined it three times so she would understand the importance of this particular item.

Rachel laughed, promising not only the store-bought kind, but her special homemade brand, a treat worth getting strangled for. Well, almost.

Time passed, lazy summer days of sleeping late, eating too much ice cream (is there such a thing?), and swimming contentedly in the pond. At night, Emma and I played chess. I even won a few games after spending a day or so reading and memorizing strategy books. Sometimes I listened to her practice on the piano or harpsichord. Rachel usually joined us during these private concerts. She claimed she preferred more tangible pursuits, like gardening and cooking. Once, when I asked via notepad, why she liked being in the kitchen, she said, "No chicken ever called me nigger. Besides, I like to cook," she added. "Truth be told," she said and winked, "it's a real hard choice between good oyster dressing (the only kind I make) and sex. Good thing I don't have to choose."

I nodded agreement. I could think of several encounters I would have enjoyed more had I been eating oyster dressing instead of a woman.

No less than one friend a day called. And talked to either Rachel or Emma.

Torbin left a message that he hoped I got well soon and to be sure to let me know that he never did approve of my being sick in bed. Pun intended, no doubt.

Danny called to let us know that they were throwing the book at Choirboy—Murder One. "But he's so damned innocent-looking, he'll probably only get manslaughter," Rachel repeated to me. Danny also said that, whenever I got back to the city, the first thing I was to do was to come over for dinner. By the end of the week, Rachel and Emma were included in the invitation and Danny and Rachel would spend half an hour discussing recipes and the latest in green growing things.

Joanne and Alex both called. Alex to say hi and that she hoped I could talk soon. Joanne the same and also to tell us that the search of Frankenstein's apartment turned up evidence to link Frankenstein to all the murdered women, including Vicky Williams, the murdered woman left out in the woods. She had been his first victim. He had waited outside a clinic that specialized in abortions and, finding her an easy victim, kidnapped and murdered her. He kept a journal describing his actions. From Betty he had gotten a list of board members of the clinic, which gave him Emma's address in the country. After hearing about the party and that Cordelia was going, he had decided to dump the body there. When he wasn't caught, he took that as a sign to continue.

They had also found out why Frankenstein was so obsessed with Cordelia. When she was a resident, she had reported that a patient, who had just had an abortion for an ectopic pregnancy, was disturbed by an orderly telling her that she was going to hell because she killed her baby. The woman was quite upset, borderline hysterical. The patient subsequently identified the orderly, a B. Mahoney and he was fired. When Sarry suggested Cordelia's clinic as a target and Frankenstein realized it was the same Dr. C. James who had gotten him fired, he found a way to get back at her and "save innocent lives."

The first three women, Victoria Williams, Beverly Morris, and Alice Tresoe, all really had abortions before Frankenstein gave them his butchered version. The autopsies didn't reveal that two separate abortions had been performed in one day. Then he made his first mistake. He killed Faye Zimmer and she wasn't pregnant. His next mistake was putting a file for Victoria Williams in Cordelia's clinic.

But he thought God was on his side and he could get away with anything.

It was, Joanne said, an ugly conjunction of hatreds.

Emma confided to me after talking to Joanne, "I'm against capital punishment, but I can't regret the death of that energumen." Religious fanatic. I had to look it up in the dictionary.

Cordelia called several times, mostly, I suspected, to talk to Emma about the clinic and what would happen now, since Emma was a board member. Emma did pass on that Cordelia asked how I was doing.

"Of course, we're going to rebuild," Emma informed us after one of the calls. "The main problem is what to do in the meantime. We're looking for a suitable building in the area to rent, but that's proving difficult."

I got cards from Bernie, Sister Ann, Hutch and Millie, and even one from O'Connor that said, "Get well soon. I need you to testify."

After about a week, Emma and Rachel went back to the city for a few days, promising to return by the weekend. Though I sounded like a drunk, chain-smoking bullfrog, I could, if need be, talk long enough to call the fire department if the house burned down, making it safe to leave me by myself. Rachel left me with two gallons of homemade ice cream. I wondered if it would be enough.

I was sitting in the kitchen finishing the rest of the ice cream when they returned.

"Welcome back," I greeted them, showing off my new-found voice.

"I see you've moved from bass to baritone," Rachel kidded.

"I thought to call you, but didn't want you talking on the telephone," Emma said. "But since my last party out here was so rudely interrupted, we're having another one this weekend. Not very elaborate, just a few close friends."

"And since your friends have been calling, we couldn't leave them out," Rachel added.

"When are they arriving?" I croaked.

"Sometime this afternoon or evening," Emma informed me.

"So, if you're recovered enough, there's a load of groceries in the car you can help with," Rachel said.

I did, hanging around the kitchen doing all the available peon chores until the master chef chased me out, preferring to create in peace.

I ended up on the front porch, sipping lemonade, watching for arrivals, directing Emma's friends to the music room and Rachel's to the kitchen. It was too early for either Joanne or Danny (and by default, Elly and Alex) to get off work and get out here. Theirs weren't the kind of jobs you could slip away from early on Friday afternoon, even in the dog days of summer.

Of course, that left me wondering if Cordelia was coming, and, if she did, what I would say to her.

After pointing Julia and Herbert in the direction of the music room, I sat back down. And watched my car drive in. My first thought was to hightail it off the porch and hide until I could think of something profound to say, something witty and passionate, but self-contained and honest (yet without risk) not to mention explanatory without being self-serving. Nothing came to mind.

Get up and go over to meet her, I told myself. You'll think of something to say. Highly inappropriate, I'm sure, I added as I put down my glass and started walking across the lawn.

Cordelia got out. She waved at me, giving me no choice but to continue walking toward her.

"Hi," I rasped out. So far, so good.

"Hi. How are you?" she asked, smiling at me.

"Much better. How are you?"

"I'm fine." Then she frowned, which took me aback until I realized it was at the still discolored marks on my neck. "Bruise yellow. My least favorite color," she commented.

Then we both didn't say anything. She turned and opened the trunk.

"I guess I owe you an explanation," I finally said. We both knew for what. The night I had walked away from her.

"Yes, you do."

"Too bad I don't have one," I said, which was partly true. The only explanation I did have was "I love you and I couldn't just use you for sex. It would have hurt too much to leave in the morning." But I was afraid to say that.

She shrugged, turning back to the trunk and taking out her overnight bag slowly.

392

"It's not a good one, I mean," I fumbled. "I couldn't just sleep with you . . ."

"Understandable," Cordelia answered quietly.

"Oh, hell," I blurted out, my voice cracking, "I'm fucking this up, aren't I?"

"No, I think you're doing what you have to," she said, her back still to me.

"No, I'm not. I'm making myself . . . I'm not very good at this."

She turned to face me, waiting for me to continue.

"I got out of your car because . . . I respect you too much."

"You respect me too much to sleep with me?"

"Yes . . . No, I . . . Hell. I use sex, at least I have, to avoid . . . love. And . . . not with you. I didn't want to do that. I was pretty drunk by the time we left the bar. I'm sorry if I . . . led you on. Danny got me angry. It was better for me to be by myself," I finished lamely.

"Waiting for bombs on your doorstep?"

"Well . . ." I shrugged.

"Micky, it's okay. We can be just friends, if you want."

"No," I blurted.

"No?" she answered, surprised.

"No, I . . . yes, let's be friends, but . . . I would like to see you." I leaned against my car.

"Aren't you at the moment?" she asked, with her half-smile.

"I mean . . . go out. Maybe the zoo or something. I can be a reasonable human being when people aren't trying to kill me. We don't even have to hold hands. Just . . . give me a chance."

"No," she said.

"Oh," I said, staring at our feet. Mine were ready to run across the yard. Hers were calmly crossed at the ankle.

"No," she repeated. "If you want to see me, you'll have to at least hold my hand. Actually," she continued, "even that won't do. My minimum in a protracted good night kiss. But," she put her hand on my shoulder, "I'd prefer to do it in the street and scare the horses. Think of my reputation."

"Your reputation?" I stopped looking at my feet.

"Yeah," she answered. "What would people say if they knew we were seeing one another and not even holding hands?" She was facing me now, her forearms resting lightly on my shoulders. "Alex once said I was the only real lesbian nun she knew. You have no idea how out of character it was for me to put my hand on your thigh. Let alone kiss you that evening in my office."

"Why did you?"

"I . . . I'm very attracted to you. I couldn't . . . stop myself," Cordelia replied, half-sheepishly.

"Well, I have to admit my offer not to hold hands has a few practical problems. Like I would only be able to manage it if Sister Ann and five other nuns were always in attendance."

I put my arms around her waist. Her elbows were now resting on my shoulders.

"Really?" Cordelia queried, a smile slowly spreading from her eyes to her lips.

"Really." I heard a car drive in. "Danny's probably going to show up any minute now."

"Good. Let her," Cordelia answered. "I think you owe me a ruined reputation."

Never refuse a lady a reasonable request.

I kissed her. And kissed her.

For a very long time, we stood in the yard kissing each other. I was vaguely aware of more arrivals, but they were a very minor distraction. "I think my knees are getting weak," I finally said.

"Let's go," Cordelia suggested, picking up her bag, one arm still around my shoulder.

"No," I said, seeing which direction she was leading me. "Not the blue cabin."

"That's where I'm staying."

"No, you're not. You're staying with me. In my room." I pulled her toward the house.

"Don't you want to be with the gang?"

"No, I don't think so."

"Why not?"

"Because, I've . . . slept with most of them."

"So?" Cordelia replied.

"But they'll be so embarrassed when they hear us and wonder why I never made that much noise when I was with them."

Cordelia burst into laughter. "You are crazy," she told me.

"No," I replied. "I'm . . . in love." There, I said it, I thought, caught between panic and pride.

Cordelia stopped, forcing me to face her.

"So am I," she said, looking directly at me.

We started for my room.

"Well, I won that bet," Cordelia continued. "Danny said you'd never say it."

"Damn Danny and her interference," I said, not really too upset at Danny. "She made me . . ."

"Yes?"

"Promise I would stay with you at least six months," I admitted, as we climbed the steps to the front porch.

"You got off easy. Joanne made me promise at least a year," Cordelia said amiably.

I just shook my head at the presumption of our friends. We entered the house and headed up the stairs.

What's Emma going to think, I suddenly wondered. Getting a bit above yourself, aren't you, Micky? But it wasn't her voice saying it. It sounded like Aunt Greta's. And I didn't give a damn about what she thought.

I let Cordelia into my room.

"You might not believe this," I said, as she put her arms around me and started kissing my cheek, "but you're the first woman I've ever slept with in this bed."

"Really?" she asked, looking up.

"Yes, really," I answered. "I mean, I've fooled around out here. A couple hundred acres is very inviting, but . . . somehow I couldn't, not with Emma right across the hall."

"I feel privileged," Cordelia replied. "But promise me one thing?"

"Uh?" I grunted, somewhat distracted by the movement of her hands.

"That sometime over this weekend, we'll make love in the woods."

"Anywhere you want," I agreed.

Cordelia led me to the bed.

"Are you okay?" she asked.

"Yes," I said. "Believe it or not, I'm shy."

"I know," she replied. "I finally figured it out. Underneath that brazen smart mouth lurks a shy woman. It took a while, although it should have been easy."

"Why?" I asked, lying back under the gentle pressure of her hands.

"Believe it or not, I'm shy, too." She got on top of me.

"You are?"

"Haven't you noticed?"

"No. I've always seen a competent, strong-willed woman."

"You must be in love."

"I am," I told her. "Did I mention strikingly beautiful?"

"Uh-huh," she murmured skeptically, wrapping her tongue around my nipple, one hand delving under the waistband of my pants.

"You don't seem shy," I commented, as her hand continued to move.

"No point in being reserved with you," she said softly.

"Oh. I do have a bit of a past, don't I?"

"That's not what I meant," she said, ceasing her explorations for the moment. "I always figured that some day I'd end up with someone . . . I could settle for. I never thought I'd get the one that I really wanted."

"Me? You mean me?"

"Micky, you idiot," Cordelia said. "Danny has carried a torch for you for years. I don't think even Elly's extinguished it completely. And Joanne? I always figured I was at the end of a very long line."

I shook my head, disbelieving.

"When you walked into my life, what was it, six months ago?" she continued, "you just . . . after you arrived, I didn't know where I was, but I wasn't in Kansas anymore. Life with you won't be boring."

"No, it won't," I agreed with that.

She kissed me, then paused to say, "Getting you has done wonders for my ego. I feel like I've just been sent to the head of the class. Alex can't make any more tacky comments about my love life. And Danny will have to stop trying to fix me up with other women."

Then our kiss continued. My shyness vanished.

I don't know when she stopped kissing me. I don't know if she ever really did. All I know is that some time later, with the last faint glow of a summer sunset slanting through my window, I was lying in her arms, some deep part of me at rest, finally comforted and stroked to surfeit.

"I bet the gang is here by now," Cordelia said, gently rubbing the back of my neck, "and wondering where we are. You need to make an appearance to convince them you're alive and well."

"I suppose," I answered.

There was a knock on the door.

"Micky?" Emma's voice called.

I jumped out of bed, not that I had any place to go. "Just a . . ."

Emma opened the door. I dived back toward the bed, figuring my back was less revealing than my front.

"Well," Emma said, chuckling softly. "I've been looking for both of you, but I didn't think it likely to find you in the same location."

"Hello, Emma," Cordelia said easily. "I suppose we're an odd sort of couple."

"Not in the least. I've always thought the two of you would make a wonderful pair. I just didn't think it possible that both of you would have the good sense to realize it."

Cordelia laughed. I was still fumbling with the sheets, trying to make them cover at least some portion of my body.

"I'll tell your friends not to expect you for dinner. And possibly not breakfast either," Emma said, and then her exit line, "And not only to have the good sense, but both of you at the same time. Wondrous strange, indeed."

She closed the door.

I jumped back out of bed.

"Watch," I said to Cordelia, running after Emma.

I yanked open the door, calling after her in the hallway. "We fooled you, didn't we?"

She stared at me, standing naked in the hall.

Then I caught her and threw my arms around her, hugging her and picking her up.

For once, I confounded Emma Auerbach.

Cordelia was standing in the doorway, a big grin on her face when I set Emma down.

"Well . . ." she said.

"We'll see you sometime, Emma," Cordelia said, extending her hand to me.

"We might be down for supper," I hedged.

"Ah, youth," I heard Emma finally say as we closed the door, remembering to latch it this time.

"No, life with you won't be boring," Cordelia said as we lay back down. "I keep thinking that there's nothing you can do that will surprise me. And yet, you keep surprising me."

"Don't feel too bad. I still surprise myself."

"Good," she replied, putting her arms around me. "That means we're really in this together."

Then she kissed me. I lied about dinner. We never made it.

About the Author

J.M. Redmann grew up in Ocean Springs, Mississippi, a small town on the Gulf of Mexico. At eighteen, to escape the South, she headed north to attend Vassar College in Poughkeepsie, New York.

The day after receiving her degree in drama, Redmann boarded a train for New York City. Determined not to become just another rich yuppie, she embarked on a career in theatrical lighting. Riches never once threatened her doorstep. To this day, they remain far afield. Her theatrical work even included a stint as lighting director of the New York Playboy Club. (No, she never wore a bunny costume.) In 1988, while living in New York City, she began writing the book that became *Death by the Riverside*.

Due to circumstances beyond her control (following a partner who had decided to go to law school) Redmann moved to the City That Care Forgot — New Orleans. She is the first to admit that this isn't exactly what she had planned. When pressed, she will admit that few things are as she had planned.

Redmann currently works as Director of Education at NO/AIDS Task Force, the largest AIDS service organization in Louisiana. She also presents workshops on Safer Sex, which gives her a great excuse to watch dirty videos, talk about sex, and ask questions such as, "What do you do with that pink thing?" during a normal work day.

The author's most recent Micky Knight adventure, *Lost Daughters,* was published by W.W. Norton in 1999. Other books include *The Intersection of Law and Desire,* which won a 1995 Lambda Literary Award, *Death by the Riverside,* and *Deaths of Jocasta.*

Presently, J.M. Redmann lives, works, and frolics in that city built on a swamp — New Orleans.

DEATHS OF JOCASTA: The Second Micky Night Mystery by J.M. Redmann. 408 pp. Sexy and intriguing Lambda Literary Award nominated mystery   ISBN 1-931513-10-4 $12.95

LOVE IN THE BALANCE by Marianne K. Martin. 256 pp. The classic lesbian love story, back in print!
ISBN 1-931513-08-2 $12.95

THE COMFORT OF STRANGERS by Peggy J. Herring. 272 pp. Lela's work was her passion . . . until now.
ISBN 1-931513-09-0 $12.95

CHICKEN by Paula Martinac. 208 pp. Lynn finds that the only thing harder than being in a lesbian relationship is ending one.   ISBN 1-931513-07-4 $11.95

TAMARACK CREEK by Jackie Calhoun. 208 pp. An intriguing story of love and danger.   ISBN 1-931513-06-6 $11.95

DEATH BY THE RIVERSIDE: The First Micky Knight Mystery by J.M. Redmann. 320 pp. Finally back in print, the book that launched the Lambda Literary Award winning Micky Knight mystery series.   ISBN 1-931513-05-8 $11.95

EIGHTH DAY: A Cassidy James Mystery by Kate Calloway. 272 pp. In the eighth installment of the Cassidy James mystery series, Cassidy goes undercover at a camp for troubled teens.   ISBN 1-931513-04-X $11.95

MIRRORS by Marianne K. Martin. 208 pp. Jean Carson and Shayna Bradley fight for a future together.
ISBN 1-931513-02-3 $11.95

THE ULTIMATE EXIT STRATEGY: A Virginia Kelly Mystery by Nikki Baker. 240 pp. The long-awaited return of the wickedly observant Virginia Kelly.   ISBN 1-931513-03-1 $11.95

FOREVER AND THE NIGHT by Laura DeHart Young. 224 pp. Desire and passion ignite the frozen Arctic in this exciting sequel to the classic romantic adventure *Love on the Line*.   ISBN 0-931513-00-7 $11.95

WINGED ISIS by Jean Stewart. 240 pp. The long-awaited sequel to *Warriors of Isis* and the fourth in the exciting Isis series.   ISBN 1-931513-01-5 $11.95

ROOM FOR LOVE by Frankie J. Jones. 192 pp. Jo and Beth must overcome the past in order to have a future together.   ISBN 0-9677753-9-6 $11.95

THE QUESTION OF SABOTAGE by Bonnie J. Morris. 144 pp. A charming, sexy tale of romance, intrigue, and coming of age.   ISBN 0-9677753-8-8 $11.95

SLEIGHT OF HAND by Karin Kallmaker writing as Laura Adams. 256 pp. A journey of passion, heartbreak and triumph that reunites two women for a final chance at their destiny.   ISBN 0-9677753-7-X $11.95

MOVING TARGETS: A Helen Black Mystery by Pat Welch. 240 pp. Helen must decide if getting to the bottom of a mystery is worth hitting bottom.   ISBN 0-9677753-6-1 $11.95

CALM BEFORE THE STORM by Peggy J. Herring. 208 pp. Colonel Robicheaux retires from the military and comes out of the closet.   ISBN 0-9677753-1-0 $12.95

OFF SEASON by Jackie Calhoun. 208 pp. Pam threatens Jenny and Rita's fledgling relationship. ISBN 0-9677753-0-2 $11.95

WHEN EVIL CHANGES FACE: A Motor City Thriller by Therese Szymanski. 240 pp. Brett Higgins is back in another heart-pounding thriller.   ISBN 0-9677753-3-7 $11.95

BOLD COAST LOVE by Diana Tremain Braund. 208 pp. Jackie Claymont fights for her reputation and the right to love the woman she chooses.   ISBN 0-9677753-2-9 $11.95

THE WILD ONE by Lyn Denison. 176 pp. Rachel never expected that Quinn's wild yearnings would change her life forever.   ISBN 0-9677753-4-5 $12.95

SWEET FIRE by Saxon Bennett. 224 pp. Welcome to Heroy — the town with the most lesbians per capita than any other place on the planet!   ISBN 0-9677753-5-3 $11.95

Visit
Bella Books
at

www.bellabooks.com